25/4/15.

Please return/renew this item by the last date shown

Beverly Connor is the author of the Diane Fallon Forensic Investigation series. She holds undergraduate and graduate degrees in archaeology, anthropology, sociology, and geology. Before she began her writing career, Beverly worked as an archaeologist in the south-eastern United States, specialising in bone identification and analysis of stone tool debitage. Originally from Oak Ridge, Tennessee, she weaves her professional experiences from archaeology and her knowledge of the South into interlinked stories of the past and present. Beverly's books have been translated into German, Dutch, and Czech, and are available in standard and large print in the UK.

For more information about Beverly Connor visit her website: www.beverlyconnor.net

Also in Beverly Connor's
Diane Fallon Forensic Investigation series:

Beverly
CONNOR

ONE GRAVE LESS

A DIANE FALLON FORENSIC INVESTIGATION

piatkus

PIATKUS

First published in the US in 2010 by Obsidian, an imprint of
New American Library,
a division of Penguin Group (USA) Inc., New York
First published in Great Britain in 2010 by Piatkus

A CIP catalogue record for this book
is available from the British Library.

ISBN 978-0-7499-5477-2

Printed and bound in Great Britain by
MPG Books, Bodmin, Cornwall PL31 1EB

Papers used by Piatkus are natural, renewable and recyclable
products sourced from well-managed forests and certified
in accordance with the rules of the Forest Stewardship Council.

 Mixed Sources
Product group from well-managed
forests and other controlled sources
FSC   www.fsc.org Cert no. SGS-COC-004081
© 1996 Forest Stewardship Council

Piatkus
An imprint of
Little, Brown Book Group
100 Victoria Embankment
London EC4Y 0DY

An Hachette UK Company
www.hachette.co.uk

www.piatkus.co.uk

This is to Charles Connor for all his love and support

ACKNOWLEDGMENTS

A very special thanks to my editor, Brent Howard.

Chapter 1

Somewhere in the Amazon

The woman sat on the bare floor of the wooden cage hugging her legs to her chest. Her forehead rested on her knees. Her long chestnut brown hair, dirty and tangled, covered her shoulders like a tattered blanket. She kept her sobs silent and tried to swallow her fear and pain. She lifted her head furtively for quick looks around her, taking in her surroundings. Her cage had hardwood saplings for bars, a thatched roof, and a rough-hewn floor of similar saplings. It sat on stilts three feet off the ground near the tree line in a village clearing, one of a cluster of clearings dotted with grass-covered huts on stilts. On all sides of the village clearings was the dense, almost impenetrable, endless jungle.

The captive was alone. She was hurt and in pain, and she couldn't talk. Her abductors had bruised—almost crushed—her windpipe when they snatched her. She didn't know where she was. She couldn't even identify the tribe of the villagers. They looked to be a blend of groups. Dress was a mixture of traditional sarongs and ragged Western clothes. Most were barefoot. There were no clear identifying marks to tell her who they were.

But they were not her captors. That distinction was held by the ragged band of "soldiers" among them who had attacked her Jeep as she drove on her way to Cuzco.

She wondered whether there was an ally among the tribespeople. Surely there was someone who didn't like the guerrillas holed up in their village. She searched their faces. None looked in her direction. She put her head back down on her knees, trying to wish her predicament away, trying to force herself to keep calm, trying to think of some plan of escape. There must be a way.

There was a crunch of the vegetation, the sound of some-one walking toward her. She lifted her head again. It was a man she hadn't seen before, an older man, perhaps in his forties. His appearance suggested he was one of the crimi-nals who held her. His worn khakis and green camouflage looked vaguely military. He grinned as he approached and swiped his dark black hair from his eyes. He gave his beard a cursory scratch. With him was a woman in jeans and a T-shirt. Her face was familiar. Her name was Patia—one of the workers at the Incan dig site. She was involved in this?

The two adults were followed by a small barefoot child in a tattered dress, holding a bowl.

The man squatted in front of the cage.

"Doc-tor Fallon," he said in English washed in a heavy Spanish accent, "I hope you feel comfort. You are going to do me a lot of money, so I want you well."

Doctor Fallon? So that was it. It was some kind of hor-rible case of mistaken identity. He had the wrong woman. She weighed the advisability of somehow conveying to her kidnapper that he had made a mistake—that he had the wrong person. He would not believe her. Even if he did, he was unlikely to say "oops" and simply let her go. It was more likely he would kill her right then to cut his losses. Perhaps she should keep it to herself for now.

"You say nothing?" he said with no irritation.

She stretched her neck and pulled back the collar of her shirt, revealing dark bruising. She attempted a whisper, but nothing came out.

"Oh." He put a hand over his heart. "It hurts me to see violence on woman. Some of my men, they are brutes. I speak to them."

Patia, the black-haired woman standing behind him, grinned as if she thought the injuries were funny.

"Please accept my sorrow and take soup." He gestured to the child and said something in Spanish to her.

The little girl approached and stuck out her hands, hold-ing the soup bowl. Her face had no expression, but she made eye contact. The woman was surprised at how that one gesture lifted her spirits. She reached for the bowl. The man put a hand on the little girl's arm, holding her back.

"You must be good." He stared at his prisoner with a hard black gaze. "Make trouble for me, I make trouble for you. Understand?"

She nodded. He released the child and she took the bowl of soup from the little girl's hands.

"Good." He grinned broadly. "See, we friends."

He lifted a satellite phone from a hook on his belt and made a call. It took a while to go through. The prisoner sipped the soup from the bowl. It was surprisingly good. The man moved away and spoke into the phone—Spanish, at first—something about May 3. The prisoner's Spanish was almost nonexistent. He changed to English. She strained to listen with her head down, as if interested only in her soup.

"*Sí*, I have her. I am looking at her now. *Sí*, forensic anthro-pol-ogist from Georgia, U.S.A.," he said. "She ask many questions about the bird feathers. She wanted to know everything about them."

Patia nodded, as if verifying what he was telling the person at the other end. Patia's eyes gleamed brightly as she looked at the captive, who, for her part, was feeling a great deal of confusion.

When he finished his conversation, he said, "Everything is okay. You be good."

He rose and walked away with Patia. The child tagged along. Of the three, only Patia looked back. Her face wore a sly grin of triumph.

At nightfall the prisoner was curled into a ball in the center of her cage, trying to hide her exposed skin from mosquitoes. She opened her eyes at the sound of someone approaching from the jungle side of her cage. Whoever was advancing was quiet. She barely heard the sound. But it was there. She froze, holding herself rigid, mentally preparing for a fight, an attempt at escape.

"Miss." It was a delicate whisper.

In the deep jungle shadow illuminated only by slivers of moonlight was the child who had given her the soup.

"Be still, please. They should not see us," she said.

Her English was surprisingly good.

The prisoner nodded.

"I will help you to get free if you will take me to my mother," the girl said.

"Who are you?" the captive whispered.

"My name is Ariel Fallon. Diane Fallon is my mother. Do you know her?"

The impossibly steep steps of Chichén Itzá's Kukulkan pyramid rose in front of Diane Fallon.

Remarkable, she thought. *It looks so real.*

The brown-gray-white-green fake stone had the same mottled appearance as the original.

Visitors will love it.

But Diane found it frightening. It brought horrible images up from her memory. She closed her eyes, took a breath, and put a hand on her chest, as if that would slow down her pounding heart.

She'd seen the display many times as it was being built, approving the plans along the way, feeling no apprehension, believing that the step-by-step process was desensitizing her to its effect on her emotions as the rising structure gradually took shape. But here, alone before the finished monument, the large presence filled her with dread and sorrow.

The pyramid was a facade. It was the entrance to the new Mayan special exhibit scheduled to open in just two weeks at the RiverTrail Museum of Natural History where Diane was director. The entry into the exhibit hall was via a passageway through the lower steps of the pyramid. The artifacts on display in the exhibit were on loan from Mexico's National Museum of Anthropology.

As she looked into the dimly lit passageway under the pyramid, the quickening of her pulse and her sense of dread accelerated. The Mayan ruins looked too much like the ruins where Diane had hopelessly searched for her daughter after the massacre in South America.

Diane had worked for the human rights organization World Accord International, collecting evidence of crimes against humanity. She and her team excavated mass graves, interviewed frightened witnesses, and exposed secret torture rooms, accumulating a mountain of evidence of the atrocities committed by dictator Ivan Santos. During his rule he'd massacred thousands of the native population, along with anyone who either disagreed with him or got in his way. He was deposed eventually, but he and his illegal

army continued a reign of killings and intimidation against
his enemies. Even out of official power he was still a dangerous man, and he was out there somewhere.

During her work in the area, Diane and her crew often
stayed at a mission just across the border in Brazil. Her
team shared food, blankets, and medicine with the sisters
running the mission in exchange for their hospitality and a
safe haven. Over the years the mission had taken in count-
less refugees running from cruel regimes.

One day, outside the mission compound, a tiny girl who
couldn't have been three years old emerged at the edge of
the forest. She appeared, as if just birthed by the jungle.
She was defenseless and alone. It was a miracle she had
survived to find her way to them.

She was dirty and crying, which wasn't an unusual
occurrence—there were many orphans. But this little girl
was different. Diane remembered that as soon as the little girl looked at her, she smiled through her tears. Diane
picked her up and carried her into the mission and took
care of her for the next two and a half years. The sisters
who ran the mission tried to find the little girl's parents or
relatives, but no one came forward. Diane spent all her free
time with her and, as time passed and still no relatives were
found, decided to adopt her. She gave her the name Ariel
Fallon. Then the massacre occurred.

Tears welled up in Diane's eyes and spilled onto her
cheeks as she remembered Ariel's raven hair and velvet
dark brown eyes. She couldn't count the number of times
she cursed herself for not just taking Ariel out of there to
a safe place, even if it meant smuggling her into the United
States or . . . or just someplace that was safe. Diane had
the connections to do it. But she wanted to do everything
legally. That was what she and her team always did—they
followed the rule of law. If she had been a good mother, she
told herself over and over, she'd have taken her daughter
to safety.

Diane sat down on the bench near the wall and put her
head in her hands, regretting all the death that had come
from revealing the dictator's atrocities. She shivered as the
memories swept through her mind—Ariel's bloody little
shoes, her CD player that Santos left in the compound
playing the child's favorite songs. So much blood every-

where ... but few bodies. He had carried most of the bodies away, probably to one of many hidden mass graves.

She hoped that somehow Ariel had managed to slip away and hide in the Incan ruins or in the jungle. Diane had run through the bush yelling for Ariel, searching deep within the ruins, heedless of the dangers, until her friends had dragged her away.

Diane lifted her face from her hands, wiping the tears off her cheeks. She looked back up at the facade. *This is absurd*, she thought. *I've replayed the horror in my mind a thousand times. I've been over it and over it. Why again now? What the hell's wrong with me?* But she knew. It was her engagement to Frank. She was feeling guilty about her upcoming marriage ... about her happiness. Deep inside her a little demon said she didn't deserve to be happy, because Ariel was not there to share it with her. Diane stood and took a breath. *I have to keep moving forward with my life*, she said to herself.

The daytime lighting switched to night, startling her out of her thoughts. With only floor lights providing illumination, the facade was now bathed in long shadows, adding stark drama to the fake edifice. Diane shivered again.

When she first heard the moan she thought it was her imagination, or maybe her own tortured voice escaping her in the dark. She stopped a moment and listened. There it was again ... a soft moan, a whisper, a wheeze ... a person.

Diane called security on her cell and asked for the daytime lighting to be turned on again and for an officer to bring a first-aid kit to the Mayan exhibit, just in case. She listened as she walked through the short fake-stone-lined tunnel to the room beyond.

The room was like a cave—dark, rocky-looking. The false rock and empty glass pedestals that would hold the artifacts stood like shadowy stalagmites. Suddenly the room lit up as the lights came back on, and the analogy was gone. Diane was standing, from all appearances, in a Mayan ruin. The exhibit designers had done an outstanding job.

The thought popped into her head that the sounds might be of an amorous nature. If that were the case, there was going to be some embarrassment. Diane stood in the entryway looking and listening.

"Is someone in here?" she called out.

Quiet. No shuffling sounds of people scrambling for their clothes. Diane walked in, listening, looking behind the soon-to-be-filled pedestals. Maybe she had imagined it.

But she heard it again—a soft plosive sound that she might not have heard if she had not been listening so intently. She followed the sound to the back of the exhibit room.

"Is anyone there?" she asked again.

A groan. Louder this time. Behind a display case. Diane hurried to the point of origin and peered behind the case.

No lovers caught in flagrante delicto. A man was lying on his back on the floor. The entire front of his shirt was soaked in blood. There was blood splattered and smeared over much of his face. He was breathing through his mouth in short explosive puffs.

Chapter 2

Diane knelt beside the man just as she heard the sound of footfalls coming into the room. She stretched her neck to look through the glass of the display case and saw two museum security guards.

"Over here," she called out. "I need an ambulance."

While one guard called for paramedics, the other knelt beside Diane with the first-aid kit. He was Rufus Diggs, a ruddy-faced, brown-haired man newly hired. Diane had liked his résumé because of his extensive paramedical training.

He opened the first-aid kit and quickly slipped on gloves, tossed a pair to Diane, and began to examine the man on the floor. The blood appeared to be coming from a wound in his abdomen. It soaked his shirt and was spreading in an ever-widening pool on the floor. Diane tried to avoid it, but it was nearly impossible if the man was to be attended to.

Security officer Diggs worked quickly cutting open the shirt and examined the gash in the man's stomach.

"Knife wound," he said.

Diane nodded in agreement.

"Losing a lot of blood. Hold this firmly in place," he said, indicating a large square of gauze he was placing over the bleeding wound. "I need to check his back."

Diane placed both hands on the gauze and held it compressed over the source of the bleeding. It quickly soaked with blood and she put another on top of it as Diggs carefully rolled the unconscious man to his side and checked him for more injuries. There did not appear to be any visible injury to his back.

The man's cheek was bruised and his features were distorted from the smeared blood. Diane didn't recognize him. He was young, in his thirties perhaps. It was hard to tell.

How the hell did he get in here? she wondered.

"An ambulance is on the way," said the other security guard.

Diane glanced his way and nodded. He was another of the new security personnel. One she hadn't met. He was young. Diane thought he might be a student at Bartrum, the local university. His physique looked like he lifted weights in all his spare time. His gaze was traveling aimlessly around the room.

"Wait outside for the ambulance," she said. "Don't touch anything. This room's a crime scene now."

He glanced at her for a moment as if he hadn't understood. "Oh, uh, yes, ma'am," he said finally and went out the door.

"New guy," said Diggs. "Real nervous on the way over here. Hadn't expected anything like this, I'm sure. I think he's seen *Night at the Museum* too many times."

Diane pressed on the bandage. Blood was still squeezing up between her fingers. She put another layer of gauze on the wound and continued the pressure. Her gaze drifted around the room. She was mentally searching the crime scene. She noticed more blood on the floor several feet away, near the door to an adjoining lab and storage rooms.

It was hard to see on the dark floor, but she thought there was a trail of drops leading to where the injured man lay collapsed. Was he coming from the adjoining rooms when he fell here? If so, then, the way he was hemorrhaging, why wasn't there more blood along his path? There were only drops.

Diane squinted her eyes as she examined the drops on the floor. It was all in the shape. The tails of the elongated drops pointed in the direction of travel. And they pointed toward the door, not away from it.

"Hell," said Diane.

"What?" said Diggs.

"We may have another victim in the lab through that door. Take over for me, can you?"

Diggs nodded, momentarily taking his eyes off the patient, glancing at the door, then pressed his hands on the bandage as Diane took her hands away.

She slipped off the gloves, grabbed a new pair, and slipped them on. She still wore her running shoes from her earlier jog around the museum's nature trails. She slipped them off, put them on top of the glass display case and carefully walked toward the lab, watching the floor to avoid the drops of blood. She slowly opened the lab door. It was dark inside. She flipped on the light, hoping she was not making herself a target for some maniac. She should have called security for more help.

Nothing happened. No gunfire. No knives hurled at her.

The room showed signs of a struggle. Things were in disarray. A chair lay overturned. Several boxes of supplies had been knocked about.

It was there that Diane saw a shoe attached to a foot sticking out from behind the boxes. She hurried over. A woman in khaki slacks and a yellow shirt lay on the floor, her face turned away from Diane, one arm across her abdomen. Her other arm was to her side. She had short dark blond hair.

Diane knelt beside her and felt for the pulse in her neck. It was faint, but she was still alive. She slid the boxes away from the woman and moved around to look at her face. Diane was startled. She knew her—Simone Brooks—one of the team who worked with her in South America at World Accord International.

Simone had been an interviewer, a very good one. She met her fiancé, Oliver, in WAI. He was killed in the massacre along with Diane's daughter, Ariel, and many of their friends. His was one of the few bodies that was found.

They told Diane afterward that when Simone found Oliver—clearly dead, clearly slaughtered—she held on to him and refused to let go of him. They had to drag her away. Diane had been barely aware of it. She had her own devastating grief to deal with. She also had to be dragged away from her search for Ariel, dragged away from her hopes that Ariel was still alive and that the bloody little shoes didn't mean she was dead.

Diane had heard that Simone eventually went to work for a detective agency somewhere. What was she doing here?

"Simone?" said Diane. "Can you hear me?"

Simone groaned and turned her head. After a moment she opened her eyes and closed them again.

There was a little blood, but without a closer look Diane couldn't determine where it had come from. She hurriedly examined Simone for wounds and discovered that her hand was cut severely across the palm. Diane had seen that type of wound many times. It happens when you stab someone and your hand slips from the handle onto the blade.

"What the hell?" Diane whispered. Had Simone stabbed the victim in the other room?

Simone groaned again, opened her eyes, and fixed them on Diane's face. She appeared sluggish.

The cut was the only open wound Diane could find. She gently felt Simone's scalp. On her right parietal was a knot. The skin wasn't broken, but Simone flinched when Diane touched it. The knot and her lethargic manner suggested she was suffering from a concussion.

"It's me, Diane, Simone. Lie still. Help is coming."

Simone looked confused and tried to speak. Nothing came out.

"Just lie still," said Diane.

Diane reached for her phone to call for help. Suddenly, Simone's bloody hand was on Diane's arm.

"Us . . . ," Simone whispered.

"What?" said Diane, leaning closer, trying to hear what she said.

"One of us . . . It was one of us . . . ," she whispered.

"What was one of us?" Diane said. But Simone had lapsed back into unconsciousness.

Diane punched in 911 on her cell phone and announced who and where she was. As she spoke she heard the EMT paramedics who had been called arriving next door in the exhibit room.

"I need another ambulance," she said into the phone. "We have another victim."

"Another ambulance? This is the first call we've received from the museum," said the calm female voice. "You have two people injured and need help. Is that correct?"

Diane was silent for a moment, confused.

"Yes, that is correct, but my security people also called about ten minutes ago."

"We have no record of another call. No ambulance has been dispatched to your location."

"But the paramedics are here," Diane said.

Just as she spoke she heard a commotion in the other room. By the time she stood up and started in that direction, she smelled something burning and saw smoke coming under the door.

Chapter 3

Ariel Fallon. Diane Fallon's adopted daughter. The prisoner knew Diane Fallon in passing. They had presented papers at the same professional conferences in forensic anthropology. She had heard about Fallon's terrible loss, but not all the details. She knew of the daughter murdered by renegades. Everyone in the small community of forensic anthropologists had heard some version of the story. If the two of them could get out of this jungle alive, Diane Fallon was in for one of the greatest shocks—and joys—of her life.

So this was Ariel Fallon, in the flesh. Ariel wore different clothes from earlier in the day—long pants, long shirt, and the little boots that still looked too big for her. She was a pretty little thing even in the dark and covered by dirt and grime. But the most notable thing about her was her intelligent eyes. They weren't little girl eyes. They were eyes that had probably seen too much of the worst in humanity. And there was desperation in them.

The prisoner didn't hesitate to accept Ariel's offer, as strange as it was, coming from a child less than four feet tall. The kid had come prepared. She took a key she had secreted in the pocket of her pants and worked it into the large rusty lock on the chain holding the door to the cage closed.

The cage itself was about six by six feet and provided a full 360-degree view around the compound and into the jungle. A small hole cut in the sapling floor was the bathroom. The prisoner had used it only at night to avoid being seen exposed, which would result, she feared, in a host of other dreadful problems. She was almost faint with relief at the prospect of leaving, and her heart beat loud enough to wake the village. But her relief was companioned by terror. If they were caught, what would happen to them? What would happen to this little girl?

Don't think about that.

The two of them quietly pushed and pulled the door open. The prisoner jumped out onto the ground and Ariel picked up a bundle of rags she had brought and tossed them inside in a heap, closed the door, and locked the chain back in place. At a distance and without close examination, it appeared that the prisoner was curled up asleep on the floor of the cage.

Off to one side sat a ragged backpack. Ariel picked it up in one hand and grabbed the woman's arm with the other and pulled at her. As the woman turned her back to her prison, she grabbed a large bat-sized stick that she'd been eyeing from her cage—the only part of an escape plan she had come up with . . . If she got out, grab that stick as a weapon.

Ariel walked quietly and quickly ahead of her and tugged at her until they were out of the moonlight of the village clearing and covered with the darkness of jungle. Very little moonlight filtered through the thick canopy. In the dark the dense foliage had a bluish black cast. Already the woman was lost. She was good at woodcraft, but in the kind of woods that grew in Kentucky and Georgia. Not here. Here all the signposts were different.

The sounds were muted at night in comparison to the daytime—sounds of night birds, insects, frogs, occasionally the call of a higher food chain creature. The sounds would be appealing were she not at the mercy of the creatures that made them—and at the bottom of that food chain. It was terrifying, but did not trump the fear produced by the men who had kidnapped her.

Ariel grabbed her hand and whispered, "This way." She pulled her along until they were out of sight of that part of the village. Ariel seemed to know the path by heart . . . or she had incredible night vision. She stopped abruptly. She looked like a shadow amid the dark foliage.

"We have to be careful. Not just of the men, but of the jungle."

The woman nodded and tried to whisper. "Ariel, my name is . . ."

"Maria," Ariel said quickly. "And mine is Rosetta. You are my mother. We must have a story until we get to a place where you can contact people you know who can get us to America. Until then, it's best if people don't know who we really are. Julio has many friends around here for a long way. Remember that. You are Maria."

The woman had the impression that Ariel feared she was an idiot. She supposed she looked like one. She had never been filthier in her entire life. *Okay*, she thought. *Maria it is. I am Maria, Maria, Maria. I am the girl named Maria.*

"That's a big pack you have. Let me carry it," the newly christened Maria said.

Ariel—or rather, Rosetta—reluctantly relinquished the bag, and Maria shouldered it.

They stepped quickly down a path, trying to avoid protruding roots, logs, or any one of other abundant hazards. Walking through the jungle at night was dangerous, but both were far more frightened of her captors.

Rosetta stopped just before the thick jungle flora met the openness of the giant kapok trees, the tall signature rain-forest trees that supported an entire ecosystem in their canopy. They would be leaving the overgrown part of the forest. That in itself was a relief. The jungle was thicker near the river where they had been and their proximity to the village still was not safe. The woman, Maria, shivered thinking of the dangers.

The human smells of the village—and the cage—had disappeared behind them. Now there was only the fresher scent of the jungle. Maria took a deep breath.

"We need to talk about your plan, Ariel—I mean Rosetta."

"First, we must get out of this territory of Julio—he's the man who kidnapped you, the one who came with his girlfriend yesterday to talk to you."

"They think I'm Diane Fallon?"

"Yes. Patia doesn't speak good English. She heard them talking and she knew that you are a forensic anthropologist and are from Georgia."

"She understood the words *forensic anthropologist*?"

"Julio was told to look for a woman named Diane Fallon, a forensic anthropologist from Georgia looking for"—she shrugged—"bones or skins or feathers. I don't know why. Julio calls himself *alambre de atropellada*."

"What does that mean?"

She shrugged again. "It doesn't make sense. It's a wire you run over."

Maria wrinkled her forehead. "Trip wire," she said. "His job was to look out for someone investigating something specific. But don't they know you are Diane's daughter? Wouldn't they try to use that?"

She shook her head. "I'm Rosetta, as far as they know. It's a long story. Too long for now. We must go."

"Where are we going?"

"I told you—out of this territory."

"What's in your backpack?"

"Supplies. Some food. Clothes. A map. Can you read a map?"

"Yes, I can. How old are you?"

"Almost nine."

Eight years old, the woman thought. Growing up too fast.

"Is there a place we can stop and take stock of our situation?"

They first heard a crack and a rustle.

"*¿Qué tenemos aquí?* Two little fishes out for a walk, eh? Who let you out, woman? Not the little one here?"

Both were startled. Ariel stood still. The two of them watched a man approach. The woman didn't recognize him, but he wore the ragged pseudo-uniform of Julio and his men and he knew she was a captive.

"Looks like you need the protection of a man, out here alone."

He walked toward them, grinning, cupping his crotch and flourishing a large knife that he pulled from his belt.

"Eh, woman. You like what you see? You nice, maybe I don't cut—"

Whack!

Ariel jumped.

The man fell to the ground, blood running from the side of his head.

The woman approached him with the bloody stick in her hand. She knew it had been a good plan to take it.

"*When you have to shoot, shoot—don't talk*," she said. The first words she had said in more than two days, the first words her damaged throat and vocal cords could manage. The voice did not sound like her own. It was hoarse and scratchy. It was a voice that might have come from a hard life, cigarettes, and whiskey. But it wasn't. It was a voice shaped by an unprovoked vicious attack against her that had left her injured and angry.

"Maria . . . ," whispered Ariel.

The woman looked back at her and said, "That wasn't Maria. That was Lindsay."

Chapter 4

Diane ran across the room, sliding to a stop in her sock-clad feet when she reached the closed door. She reached for the doorknob and stopped.

What's the rule about fires and closed doors?

She couldn't remember. *Something about oxygen and blowback. Or was it* blowup?

She had to do something. She touched her finger gently to the doorknob. It was not hot. She turned the knob and opened the door just a crack to see what would happen.

No explosion, no burst of flame, just a billow of smoke and a shower of soot from above. She opened the door and stepped into the Maya display room. She could see some kind of liquid flowing across the floor in her direction. Above the moving liquid and advancing toward her was a burning layer of gases and flame. The alarm was blaring its warning and the sprinkler system was spraying a rain of water, making the smoke and soot worse, but the fire was continuing to burn. The smell of kerosene filled her nostrils.

Water on a kerosene fire, she thought. Not the best solution, but the only one available until help could arrive.

She retreated back into the lab, wet a paper towel at the sink and put it over her mouth, and went back into the exhibit room, skirting the edge of the fire. The injured man who had been on the floor was gone and she couldn't see Rufus Diggs.

The fire alarm rang loud in her ears as the fire continued to burn. That and the sound of the water from the sprinklers on the fire, and the smoke, added to Diane's increasing anxiety and an increasing disorientation. Her gaze searched the room for Rufus. She heard him groan at the far side of the room. She saw him rolling. His clothes were smoking.

Dear God.

She rushed over to him, taking short breaths through the wet paper towel.

"I'm all right. I'm all right," he said, coughing, trying to sit up.

Diane assisted him to a sitting position.

Patches on his hands and face were red. Half his beard was singed, as was his hair.

"I'm all right," he said again, struggling to rise to his feet with Diane's help.

"If you're able, I need to get you out of here so you can direct the paramedics to the lab when they come," said Diane.

"I hope they're friendlier than the last ones," said Rufus, gritting his teeth and standing.

She led him toward the exhibit entrance.

"We got someone else hurt in the lab?" he asked between gasps for air as Diane urged him toward the door.

"Yes."

"Then I need to see to them. I'm fine. Just a little singed around the edges. Strained my leg a little falling. Bad knees."

Diane could see he wasn't going to be dissuaded, short of her ordering him out. Recognizing his need to help, she led the way as he limped into the lab.

Simone was still lying amid the overturned boxes.

"My bag was in the fire," he said.

"We have gloves here in the lab—and a first-aid kit. Not as good as yours . . . ," said Diane.

She hurriedly retrieved the gloves and kit from a cabinet and took them to Rufus. He was looking at Simone's eyes when Diane returned.

"Her pupils are slow to respond," he said, speaking rapidly.

"What was the other guard's name?" she asked Rufus. "The one who came with you."

Rufus paused a moment. "He had to be in on this. He didn't call the ambulance, did he? He called someone else. Of course," he said, as if just realizing. "V. Jones. It was on his shirt." Rufus pointed to the pocket of his own shirt.

"That wasn't Vic Jones," said Diane. "Vic Jones is on vacation. I don't understand why this guy wasn't discovered in the security office."

"He met me on the way," said Rufus. "Said he'd been called. I just assumed . . ."

"I would have assumed too," said Diane.

But she should have realized something was amiss when she didn't recognize him. It was her standing practice to meet every employee who was hired at the museum. She had reviewed all the applications, but she still hadn't met with all of them. She had assumed that he was someone she had approved on paper, and Chanell, head of security, had hired him.

Noise in the exhibit room brought their attention to the door. They glanced at each other, apprehension in their gazes.

"Stay here with the woman," she said, and made her way to the door.

It opened almost in her face. It was the paramedics—and they were people she knew. She sighed with relief.

"Over here."

She led them to Simone and Rufus, with instructions to check Rufus out also.

On the heels of the paramedics were the firemen, checking out the exhibit room, spraying fire-suppressing foam in spots where the sprinklers had not put out the fire completely. Fortunately, there were no flammables in the room—other than the kerosene that had been poured on the floor—mostly stuff that wouldn't burn. But there was still smoke and soot damage aplenty. Diane pushed that problem into the back of her mind.

The fire chief instructed Diane to leave the area. Her own security staff had stationed themselves outside the door, keeping out any stray visitors who might wander from the various courses the museum offered in the evening.

The fresher air was a relief. Diane sat down on the bench outside the exhibit room and looked at the pyramid facade. A wisp of smoke found its way out the door and was rising to the ceiling, making it look as if the Mayans were under attack.

Douglas Garnett came over and sat down with Diane. He was the chief of detectives in Rosewood. Chief Garnett was a tall, lanky man in his mid-to-late forties. He had a full head of well-styled salt-and-pepper hair. This evening he was well dressed, as usual, in a brown herringbone suit and brown Italian shoes.

The museum housed a crime lab headed by Diane. The lab was under the authority of the City of Rosewood. Even though Diane was director of both the museum and the crime lab, the two units had an often tenuous relationship with each other. Garnett knew that if the museum were ever in any danger from the crime lab, the lab would have to go. So he made it a priority to protect the museum and the relationship. He did his best to make sure, when he could, the museum didn't get any bad press. There was a standing order to the police dispatcher to contact his office by phone rather than the radio, which could be picked up by reporters, if there were any calls from the museum. But there would be little chance for damage control this time.

Diane realized she didn't know exactly what had happened in the exhibit room when the fake medical personnel came in and wrecked the place. She hadn't seen it. She had been in the lab inspecting Simone.

"What happened?" Garnett asked, unnecessarily smoothing a side of his styled graying hair with his hand.

"I'm not entirely sure," said Diane. She described the sequence of events, and a quick rundown of what she was sure of—including the name of the female victim.

As he listened, the crease between Garnett's eyebrows seemed to grow deeper.

"This Simone Brooks, she was someone from your past work in South America?"

Diane nodded. "Yes. The main work she did with me was to conduct interviews of witnesses. She was very good at putting people at ease."

"What was she doing here?" he asked.

"I have no idea," said Diane.

The paramedics came by with Simone on a stretcher. Rufus walked over to where Garnett and Diane sat and stopped. They stood up and motioned for him to sit. He shook his head.

"I guess you'll be wanting a statement from me," he said to Garnett. He had ointment on his face and neck as well as his hands. He was wearing a white T-shirt. He had taken his outer shirt off and was holding it in one hand. Diane could tell from his face that he was very uncomfortable.

She gave him a quick smile. "Anything to get out of going to the hospital?" she said.

He shrugged. "I'm fine. I just need some ointment—and some painkiller. The burns hurt like hell. But that's good. I have nothing more than first-degree burns, really."

Diane raised her brows at him and he shrugged.

"I have a very mild second-degree burn on the top of my hand. It might not even blister very much." He raised the hand with the shirt. "Thanks to my fire-retardant uniform."

"Can you give me a brief statement of what happened?" said Garnett. "I can get something more detailed from you tomorrow."

Rufus nodded. "I was tending to the first victim—the guy who seems to have disappeared—when three paramedics came in with a stretcher. I turned to say something to them when one of them hit me, knocking me into the display case. Before I could recover myself, two of them hauled the victim onto the stretcher. The third one started spreading kerosene and struck a match to it." He took a deep breath and his face screwed up with emotion. "What kind of person would do that, try to set someone on fire? He didn't give a damn that I was there."

"A very reckless, wicked person," said Diane. "Certainly someone desperate to hide something. If Chief Garnett is finished for now, why don't you go home and take it easy? You don't need to come in tomorrow. Wait until you heal some."

"I'm fine," he said again.

"If you wouldn't mind," said Diane, "change clothes and leave what you were wearing with security."

He nodded. "Oh, sure thing. I'll do that." As he left them he was muttering, "Who would do that to a person?"

"You have any ideas?" asked Garnett. "It obviously had something to do with this Simone Brooks."

"I have no idea whatsoever. Simone said 'It was one of us.' I don't know what she meant."

Garnett nodded. "I'll need to see your security tapes," he said.

"Sure," she said.

"Do you think they destroyed all the evidence? That was what they were trying to do with the fire, I imagine."

"Yes, I'm sure that was their intent. Kerosene is good for getting rid of blood evidence. The fire just helps make sure. But apparently they didn't think about transfer."

"Transfer?"

"Mine and Rufus' clothes. My shoes are on top of the case in the exhibit room. We still have samples of the victim's blood on their soles. If that's what they were trying to get rid of, it was a wasted effort."

Diane retraced her steps back into the exhibit room to retrieve her shoes. On her way out she saw a telltale piece of something sticking out from under one of the cases at the far end of the room. She went over to have a look. Probably building waste that hadn't been picked up. She took hold of it and tugged. It was a strap attached to a backpack. The pack was half open and Diane could see a bone sticking out—a human bone.

Chapter 5

The two of them, Maria and Rosetta, the tiny ad-hoc family, stood still in the dark, gazing at the man on the ground illuminated by the flashlight. He wasn't dead, but he wouldn't be getting up for a while either—maybe never.

Finally little Rosetta spoke. Her voice shook.

"He will have things on him that we need."

"Yes," said Maria. "I'll search him." She squatted down beside him.

"I'll help."

Maria shook her head. "I need you to stand watch. He may not be alone. We don't want to be sneaked up on again. We have to be more alert."

Rosetta nodded and took up a post a few feet from Maria and began watching the jungle around them.

Maria took his knife first, carefully removing it from his hand. Then she unbuckled the holster and gun strapped to his torso. She swallowed any squeamishness she had and began going through his pockets. The back of her fingers and hands brushed against his body. He was warm. She expected him to grab her arm at any moment. Her hands shook. She glanced at the wound on his head. He wouldn't be grabbing her. A pang of guilt rushed through her. She parried the feeling by thinking about what he had intended to do to them.

Deep in his front pants pocket she found a billfold that looked like crocodile skin. She opened it.

"This is going to be helpful," she said out loud.

"What?" Rosetta peeked over her shoulder. "Is that real?"

"Let's hope. We're going to need to spend it to get home."

The man, Luis Portman, according to the information in his wallet, was carrying about three hundred U.S. dollars in mostly twenties and tens. Maria put his wallet back in his pants and stuffed the money into her pocket. When they had a chance she would secret it in a better place.

Maria continued searching. She discovered another knife and another small gun in his boot and, in another pants pocket, what appeared to be good luck charms made from animal paws. She also found a slider heart on a chain. It was hers, given to her by John, her boyfriend. So this man probably was one of the gang who pulled her from the Jeep. She remembered the necklace being jerked from her throat and the rage she felt at the theft. The memories hardened her heart against errant feelings of guilt at what she was doing, at what she intended to do, which was to leave him on the ground in the jungle, wounded. Probably a death sentence. She continued her search of his many pockets.

His clothes were frayed along the edges of the collar and cuffs, and there were holes and tears, but the material was good. They had been expensive clothes.

In the inside pocket of his khaki vest Maria came across a set of car keys.

"He has a vehicle somewhere," said Maria, looking at her young liberator. Of course he would have. He didn't seem like the kind of character who would be out walking alone in the jungle. Alone. That bothered her too. There was a very good chance he wasn't alone.

Rosetta's eyes grew big looking at the keys. "That would be good. We could drive all the way to America."

"Part of the way anyhow, but there are hazards," said Maria. "Like, what if we run across someone who recognizes the vehicle and knows who's supposed to be driving it?"

"It will be good to sleep in," said Rosetta. "Keep out bugs and snakes."

"That certainly has its appeal. But we'll have to find it first."

Maria stood and began stuffing her finds into the knapsack. She kept the guns with her. One was a semiautomatic. The other was something smaller. Maria didn't know guns. She had serious doubts she could figure out how to fire the automatic. She did look for a safety to turn before she put the gun back in the holster.

"Now let's look for the vehicle," she said.

She examined the key. It was a modern key with a plastic bow and metal two-way shank. There was no remote on it, only a monkey's paw that Maria removed.

She took the map out of the backpack. If she could find a road nearby, she could probably find the vehicle. It wasn't easy examining the map with the flashlight, standing in the jungle. She noticed she was shaking slightly. She gripped both the map and the light harder. It made her nervous not being on the move. She stopped her study of the map several times and listened. Nothing but night jungle noises.

"They will not come after us quickly," said Rosetta, watching Maria closely, as if detecting her unease.

"Why?"

"I drugged them," said Rosetta.

"You drugged them?" Maria stared at the shadowy little girl.

"It won't hurt them, just make them sleep," she said.

There were so many questions Maria wanted to ask the girl, but they would have to wait. Drugged or not, the thugs would wake up sooner or later and find that their valuable captive had escaped. She turned her attention back to the map.

It was crude—a basic map with roads and villages— places that hadn't made the original map—drawn in. Most roads in the area were mere dirt paths barely wide enough for a vehicle, and the villages were tiny. She looked at the villages that had been marked on the map. One was circled several times.

"Lugar del Río." Maria said it aloud. "Is that where we were?" she asked Rosetta.

"Yes, that is its name." She didn't take her eyes off the jungle.

Maria was beginning to wonder if Rosetta heard or sensed something.

"Do you know where he might have been coming from—or going?" she asked.

"They go to Alta for supplies. They know people there. We must stay away from there. Sao Rosa, that is a place they don't go," she said.

No road to Sao Rosa was drawn, but there were initials SR by one of the creeks marked on the map. It wasn't far.

They could get there. But the thing drawn on the original map that most interested Maria was railroad tracks. If they could catch a train, that would take them a long way. The rail line was to the east of them and they wanted to go north. But the extra trek would be worth it. On the other hand, they could connect up with the railroad farther north. They might make it in a vehicle fairly quickly.

"Do you think we can find a place to clean up in Sao Rosa?" said Maria.

"Maybe. I've never been there. I just know that Luis and his men never go there," said Rosetta.

"That may mean that there's a rival gang there," said Maria. "That would not be good. But before we decide where to go, let's see if there is a vehicle. The road to Alta is here." She pointed at the map. "I think we are here."

They collected the spoils of their victory over the man and Maria glanced at him once more before they set off. Already ants had found him. She felt another pang of guilt.

Maria concentrated hard on making a minimum of noise as she moved. Rosetta seemed to be a natural. They had walked about five minutes when they saw the vehicle—a beat-up four-wheel-drive pickup. There was a man sleeping in the driver's seat.

Chapter 6

"Is it some kind of voodoo paraphernalia?" asked Garnett.

"Looks more like a Native American medicine bundle," said Jin.

"Just looks spooky," said Izzy.

Diane, freshly attired in jeans and a T-shirt, having surrendered her clothes to Neva to process for blood and any other evidence, looked at the large high-definition TV screen on the wall near the shiny, round stainless-steel conference table in the crime lab. The screen image showed the contents of the knapsack laid out on white butcher paper in one of the evidence rooms. Diane had installed the cam system so people like Chief Garnett could have a look at the evidence before it was processed without worrying about contaminating it with any of their own trace. She and several members of her crime lab crew stood around the conference table looking at the items on the screen.

There were several brightly colored feathers of blue, red, green, and yellow; two dried monkey paws; a large orange beak; numerous sharp teeth; several talons; and a long bone. All had been stuffed in a long woven black textile bag embroidered with sunbursts and what appeared to be stylized leaves.

"What does all this mean?" asked Garnett, looking at Diane as if she should know.

"I don't know, but the bone is a humerus from a human," she said.

"Who had this? Did your friend hide it?" asked Garnett.

"I don't know," Diane answered.

"I think the chief's right," said Izzy. "Looks like voodoo to me."

"I don't know what it is," she repeated.

She stared at the bone. The epiphyses—ends of the long bones and the place of growth—were missing. They had become detached because they hadn't yet fused.

"The bone is from a child. A young child."

Each of them sat down around the table and stared, as if getting off their feet would give them more energy to figure out what the collection meant. They studied the items without speaking. The various machines in the glassed-in cubicles of the crime lab gave off a soft, quiet background hum. The jarring sound of the opening of the elevator doors startled them.

There were two main entrances to the crime lab—one on the museum side and one from an elevator that went up the outside of the west wing of the building. The entrances could be accessed only by members of the crime lab, so none were surprised when David stepped out of the elevator into the room. He made his way through the warren of glass cubicles to the stainless-steel table.

"You weren't going to call me on something like this?" he said. He looked at Diane as he pulled up another chair and sat down.

David Goldstein was a friend from World Accord International. He knew Simone. Like all the members of the WAI team, he suffered from the loss of their friends. After drifting around the country and after the breakup of his marriage, he had come to Diane for a job. She was glad to have him. He was one of the best forensic investigators.

"We figured that since you were out doing something normal for a change, we wouldn't bother you," said Jin.

David made an exasperated face at Jin. He rubbed the dark fringe of hair around his balding head as his attention focused on the contents of the bag.

David had been out on a date. One of the rare times he ventured away from work to do something simply for the fun of it. Diane had been reluctant to disturb him.

"How did you find out?" asked Diane.

"I have my sources," he said.

"David, you're going to have to learn to unplug yourself sometime," said Diane.

He gave her a half smile. "Like you do? What are you doing here this late? Why aren't you getting fitted for a wedding dress or something? What actually happened here anyway, and what is this stuff?" He gestured to the screen. Then paused. "Was it really Simone?"

Diane nodded. "Yes. I don't know what she was doing here. And I'm not sure what all these items mean. Have you heard from Simone anytime recently?"

David shook his head. "She flew home to her family shortly after . . . after we all came home. I haven't heard from her since. But I'm not the best at keeping in touch."

"Nor am I," said Diane.

"But she said something," said David.

"She said, 'It was one of us.' That was all," said Diane. "I don't know what *it* refers to, or who exactly *us* includes."

"I'll contact her employers and her family tomorrow," said Garnett. "Perhaps they can shed some light on what she was doing here, and whether she was carrying around this bag of voodoo trinkets. I know you don't know what this collection of things means, but can you identify the individual items?"

"The feathers, I believe, are from a macaw," said Diane. "The beak is from a toucan. I don't know what kind of monkey is represented by the paws. The teeth are canines from a predator, but I don't know the species. I don't know what animals the talons were taken from. But we will know tomorrow after we process."

"What about the bag?" said Garnett. "Looks kind of nativelike."

"I'm not familiar with the design," said Diane. "But we can identify it."

Garnett rose. "I'll talk with you tomorrow, then," he said. "I think it would be a good idea if, officially, you let Neva, Izzy, or Jin work on the evidence, since you and David know this Simone woman."

"Please let us know what you find out about her," said Diane. "She was a friend and she came here for a reason."

A growing unease that started with a chill in her spine was now resting in the pit of Diane's stomach.

"I'll keep in touch," he said.

It sounded noncommittal, but Diane knew he would keep her in the loop.

"Right now, I'm treating this like a theft gone wrong," he said. "That's what it looks like."

Diane knew that Garnett sensed there was something more to this. But he was going to take the easy way with the press. Not let them speculate. In a way, that was good. The idea that it was an attempted theft was not good. But she couldn't think of a better story. Garnett left, probably to go home.

Diane was far from that pleasure yet. She had to tell Vanessa Van Ross about the damage to the new special exhibit; that it probably would not be ready to receive the artifacts from Mexico on schedule; and that the Mexican officials were going to worry about the safety of their cultural treasures when they heard what had happened.

Vanessa Van Ross was a tall, elderly woman who was the real power behind the museum. People called Diane the queen because of the extraordinary powers the museum covenant granted her as director. But she liked to tell them she was only the viceroy. Vanessa was the queen. And now she had to tell the queen that something bad had happened in the kingdom.

"We'll meet tomorrow," Diane told her crime scene team. "Neva, would you put the evidence in the vault?"

Neva nodded. "This is all very strange."

"Yes," agreed Diane. "I'd like to find out what it's about as soon as we can."

She left them talking amongst themselves and went to her osteology office. David followed her.

"There is only one *it* we all have in common," he said.

Diane glanced at the lone-wolf watercolor hanging on the wall in her mostly bare osteology office.

"Yes," she said.

She knew what she had in common with Simone: the massacre. They each lost someone close to their hearts in the massacre.

"But the sentence didn't make sense, did it? *It was one of us.* That doesn't make sense."

"If she was referring to the massacre, we know it was Ivan Santos who carried it out. But she meant something," said David. He rubbed his hands over his face. "She meant something."

"And who was the *us* she was talking about?" said

Diane. "Simone and me? The three of us? The three of us and someone else? Who? She was in very serious condition from a head injury. She probably didn't know what she was saying. It might be nonsense."

"Maybe. But we need to investigate this. Garnett doesn't know the people we know. He doesn't know Gregory. We need to call him."

"Maybe. Let's see how Simone is doing tomorrow. Perhaps she'll straighten it out. If not, I'll call Gregory tomorrow evening, or whatever time corresponds to a decent hour in England. Now I have to tell Vanessa I allowed the special exhibit to get torched."

Chapter 7

Telling Vanessa about the fire at the museum had gone better than Diane expected—mainly because of the long silences on Vanessa's end of the phone line. Diane told Vanessa she was calling a meeting of the board for the next day to tell them the news and to tell them to refer any reporters to her. Vanessa agreed but suggested that Diane leave out certain information. Diane agreed. Until she knew why Simone Brooks was in the museum, it would do no good to tell the board about her and her connection to Diane. Some members of the board had great temptation to gossip.

So here she stood in front of them in the boardroom on the third floor of the museum. Diane hated meetings in the best of times. She wasn't looking forward to this one. She had dressed in what Andie Layne, her assistant, said was her power outfit. Diane wasn't sure why the suit had power, but she bowed to Andie's superior knowledge of clothes. The linen navy pantsuit with its long fitted blazer looked good with the blue silk blouse she usually paired with it, and it was comfortable. She stood at the head of the long mahogany table and finished giving the board members a brief description of the events of the previous evening, hoping Andie was right about the power thing.

"Do you have an estimate on the damage from the fire?" asked Harvey Phelps.

Harvey was usually Diane's ally, but he was clearly disturbed by this turn of events. Diane didn't blame him. He had gone to Mexico with Kendel to work out the details for the loan of the artifacts. Now the Mexican treasure's temporary home had been firebombed.

"The exhibit designers are working on that right now.

They and Korey from Conservation are looking at how much can be restored and how much must be rebuilt. There's not much fire damage and the water damage is minimal. The smoke left stains that will require some repainting, refinishing, and cleaning. The real damage is to the partnership with the museum in Mexico. They will need to be convinced that their artifacts will be safe here."

"Do we have to tell them?" said Madge Stewart.

"Of course we have to tell them," said Diane.

She tried to keep her face straight and not show annoyance at Madge, who often seemed clueless about ordinary protocol and had a child's view of candor in the face of calamity.

Thomas Barclay, the banker member of the board, was usually at odds with everything Diane did, but only because he didn't like anyone but himself to be in charge. The governance of the museum was set up so the board was only advisory and the director held all the power. Only in the most extraordinary conditions could her decisions be overridden, and that rankled his sense of self-importance. Barclay had been silent. Diane could see he was building up for something. But when he spoke it was a simple question.

"What do the police think happened?" he asked.

"That it was an attempted theft that went wrong," said Diane.

"And you're saying they just waltzed in and took over," said Barclay with a flourish of his hand. "What do we have security for if they can't keep track of their own?"

The dam that kept Barclay's temper in check was developing a crack. It was Diane's policy in these situations to encourage the dam to break. Laura Hillard, another board member who was a good friend of Diane's from childhood—and a psychiatrist—had the opposite viewpoint. Whereas Laura liked to smooth over ruffled feathers, Diane liked to make them fly.

"If they had been waltzing when they entered they would no doubt have attracted attention. As I briefed all of you earlier, the perpetrator who joined Diggs in responding to my call for security wore a uniform virtually identical to those our security people wear. Diggs is new on the job and didn't realize the man with him wasn't Vic Jones. The impostor never went near the security office, where he would have been outed. It appears he was secreted some-where in the museum. We are still investigating."

"I think Thomas just wants to understand why security didn't catch this person earlier—where he was hiding out," said Laura, smiling sweetly at Diane.

Diane gave her an amused half smile before she turned to Thomas Barclay. "Was that what you were asking?" she said.

Barclay gave Diane a curt nod.

"He could have worn a jacket or coat over the uniform and blended himself among participants in a class. We have several classes in session every evening. That is one of the challenges for our security people—guarding a place where the public is invited."

"Perhaps we should close down the classes," Barclay said.

"This is a museum, not a bank," said board member Anne Pascal.

Anne's hands were flat on the table in front of her. Diane got the impression that she wanted to pound them on the wood surface. Anne was one of the newer members of the board and a schoolteacher. Diane liked her for many reasons, but she especially liked her for frequently being at odds with Barclay.

"The classes are of value to the community and they are good for the museum," said Anne.

Barclay brought his gray bushy eyebrows together as if he were about to turn Anne down for a loan. "But if they pose a problem for security . . . ," he began.

"I didn't say they pose a problem for security," said Diane. "I said they pose a challenge."

"Same thing," he said.

"You think so?" said Diane.

That explains so much, she thought. She didn't speak it. Laura gave her a brief warning glare. Laura probably knew what Diane was thinking. Her face was easy to read.

"We work from a different dictionary," Diane said.

Barclay huffed. "You know, you haven't told us much of anything. Are you withholding information?"

"Of course," said Diane. "However, I've told you as much as the police will allow. They are very concerned about in-formation leaks that would give the thieves an advantage."

"I'm sure they didn't mean the board," he said, taking in the whole group with a nod.

"I'm sure they did," said Diane. "Let's face it—in the past the board has been a sieve."

Out of the corner of her eye Diane saw Madge shift uncomfortably when several members glanced her way. More than once, Madge's loose tongue with the press had caused Diane problems. Laura, she saw, was about to throw up her hands and give up trying to rein Diane in. Diane didn't mind making board members uncomfortable—at least, the ones who didn't contribute anything helpful to the conversation.

Kenneth Meyerson, computer company owner and another member friendly to Diane, cleared his throat. The board members looked over at him, it seemed to Diane, hopefully.

"If I've understood everything correctly, the thieves knew the name of a security guard who was on vacation. They knew how to hide in the museum. They had people and tools on hand in case anything went south. And they carried out the rescue—if that's what it was—quickly, with a fair amount of precision. They sound like professionals, yet they didn't know the special exhibit didn't have anything in it." Kenneth paused and took a sip of the orange juice he had in front of him. "Two things come to mind. Have they hacked into our computer system to discover schedules? And could they have been after something other than the Mayan artifacts, and simply used the special exhibit room as some kind of staging area because they thought it would be empty at night?"

"I've asked the curators to inventory their items," said Diane.

Kenneth nodded. "What is the most valuable thing we have?"

"Other than the dinosaur bones—both real and casts, which would be a clumsy steal—the gemstones," said Diane. "Mike secures the most valuable of those in a vault. During exhibition hours he has them displayed in such a manner that they can be removed easily for safekeeping in the evening. However, we have other rare items that might be attractive to a collector."

"Was there a falling out among thieves?" asked Anne. "I'm a little unclear about the two wounded people."

"I don't have an answer for that. Neither the police nor I have much information yet. All of us are working on it."

"Well, if someone has hacked into the system, there is certainly something we can do about that," said Barclay. "Don't you have adequate firewalls or whatever you call the damn things?"

"We do," answered Kenneth. "But a determined, talented hacker can get into anything, given enough time and resources."

Barclay nodded, looking a little pensive. "Didn't we have some little hacker get into the system a while back? The one that apparently got into every system in town—except my bank, of course. Might we talk to that little beggar?"

Diane stared at Barclay for a long moment, long enough for him to actually blush and look away. Diane knew all the banks that were hacked, and Barclay's bank was certainly among them.

"I think he works for the FBI now," said Kenneth.

"Seriously?" said Barclay.

"Or the CIA. One of the two. He was quite talented," said Kenneth.

"That's all the information I have," said Diane quickly. "I'll call another meeting when we know more."

She was eager to get back to the crime lab and see what her team had come up with. She started to adjourn when Barclay looked up at her.

"I have one more item I want to talk about," he said.

He took out an envelope and tossed it in front of him.

"I got this invitation in the mail and I was surprised that you are using the museum for your own wedding. I think that is an inappropriate use of your authority. Are you using museum staff as well? Will we be reimbursed?"

Diane said nothing, merely raised an eyebrow.

Barclay smiled grimly at her.

"Thomas," said Vanessa.

Her tone was sharp and all of them gave her their attention, as if she had addressed each of them.

"Having Diane's wedding in the museum was my idea. She wanted to elope, but I wanted her to have a ceremony here, in the museum. I, with Laura, and Diane's assistant, Andie, are planning the wedding. Diane hasn't even seen the invitations."

Vanessa had caught Barclay by surprise. He stuttered a moment before he found his voice.

"I didn't realize," he said. "If you approve, then, of course . . ."

"Is there anything else?" said Diane. "No? Then we are adjourned. Good to have seen all of you." *Now go away*, she thought.

They filed out. Barclay was out the door first, muttering that he had to get back to the bank.

"Do you have time for lunch?" said Laura when she reached Diane. Vanessa was with her.

"I can make time," she said. "But I need to go to the crime lab first."

"That will be fine," said Vanessa. "There are some things I want to look at." She smiled and patted Diane's arm as they left.

As Diane turned to leave, Martin Thormond came back in, brushing lightly past the departing Madge Stewart, who tilted her head in disapproval and gazed at him suspiciously through narrowed eyes.

Martin looked very much the history professor that he was, in his brown tweed sports coat, well-trimmed beard, and spectacles. But he looked worried.

"What can I do for you, Martin?" said Diane, smiling.

He glanced behind him in the direction of the door before he spoke in a low voice.

"I got a call this morning. It was from a reporter at the *Atlanta Journal-Constitution* . . . ," he began.

"About the fire?" said Diane.

"No, funny, he did not even mention the thieves or the fire. He asked about you."

"Me?" said Diane. "What about me?"

"Now, I don't credit it. I know how reporters are. But I thought you should know."

Diane smiled. "Know what?"

She thought she would have to drag it out of him he was so hesitant to tell her.

"He asked about your involvement with drug smugglers when you were in South America," he said.

Chapter 8

The man moved in the seat of the pickup but appeared not to wake up. Maria knew he would eventually awaken, realize how long his partner had been gone, and go looking for him. She could ambush him in the dark, but she had no idea when he might wake up, and time was their enemy.

She looked down at her new little friend who insisted on being called Rosetta. She was a paradox—a little kid, yet too grown-up. She was going to get home to her mother. Maria would make sure of that.

Maria and Rosetta were hiding behind a thicket of dense foliage. Hiding had its challenges. They wanted to remain obscured from view but they didn't want to get unwanted creatures on them. The place in which they were secreted was like a curtain of flora hiding them from view of the truck driver. It was a good place to not be seen, but Maria had to do something.

"I want you to stay here, Rosetta. He must not see you. Understand?" Maria said in her raspy voice.

The little girl nodded. "You don't want him to know who helped you escape. You aren't going to kill him."

It was a statement, not judgmental.

"That's right," said Maria. "And if I fail, I don't want you captured."

"You won't fail."

Maria hoped she was worthy of the little girl's faith. She couldn't imagine Rosetta alone in the rain forest, but she had the feeling Rosetta could get along out here better than she could.

Maria put the smaller of the guns in her waistband. She picked up the club that had worked so well against Luis

Portman and eased closer to the truck. She was fairly sure that when he left the truck in search of Portman he would come down the animal trail they had followed. She selected a secluded spot by the trail to wait.

She picked up a handful of nuts and pebbles and tossed them onto the roof of the pickup. They made a rattle that was loud to her ears but apparently not to the sleeper.

She tossed more. He stirred.

She picked up a larger rock and threw it at the back window. It bounced off and landed in the bed of the truck. The man awoke. She saw him sit up straight and look around. The truck door opened and he got out. Her heart thudded against her ribs. He was a big man.

He had blond hair and sunburned skin and was dressed in the same camouflage and khakis as Portman. She was told before she visited here to wear solid colors rather than camouflage or clothes with designs. Easier to see bugs that get on you. She wondered why these men wore camouflage. It wasn't to stay hidden. His was desert camouflage. It must be some kind of macho thing.

"Luis, where the hell are you? How long does it take you to take a dump?"

He came walking down the trail, as Maria predicted.

When she was in her cage searching for a way to escape and spied the thick stick lying on the ground, she mentally practiced with it over and over—in her mind swinging it at all the pain points on the body. Swinging hard, not hesitating.

He came closer, easy strides. He wasn't worried.

Maria gripped her club tight. She listened for his footfalls coming closer to her hiding place.

One. Two. Three.

She swung hard, aiming for his knees.

He went down hard with a yelp and curses. Maria followed through with a strike to an elbow and another to the sacral plexus.

"What the fuck!" he screamed.

Maria was breathing hard and her heart thudded against her chest. She raised the club over her head and aimed at his brachial plexus when suddenly she hit the ground hard. Her club tumbled out of her hands.

The man had her by the ankle and was pulling her to

him. His face was red with rage and pain. Maria kicked at him and reached for the gun in her waistband. He found his first and pointed it at her.

"Who the fuck are you?" he asked. His hand was shaking. He was having a hard time holding on to the gun—it was the hit to his ulnar nerve.

She stopped moving and thought hard. She had to do something before the pain subsided to the point where he had better use of his hands. But then again, that might take a while. She had hit him pretty hard.

"I know who you are," he rasped. "You're that Fallon woman—Julio's prize catch."

"Why does he want me?" she whispered. She figured it might be easier to interrogate him when he had the gun. He would feel freer to talk, maybe brag.

"Money. You're worth a lot of money to some guy he knows."

"Who in the hell would I be of that kind of value to?" she asked.

"Julio won't tell us that. He trusts only that bitch he's with. But I got you now . . . and maybe I'll make the deal."

The man spoke good English. He sounded American—Midwestern.

"You don't know who to deal with," she said.

"Minor detail," he said. "I can find out. See, he's gonna be all panicked that you've escaped. He'll be calling people. Talking. Patia will be screaming and cursing. She'll let something slip. Or he will. I'll find out."

She already had her hand on the gun in her waistband behind her back. She could swing it around and shoot, if she could be sure . . . sure of her aim . . . sure she would be quicker . . . sure she could even shoot the damn thing.

His face was still screwed up with pain. She'd done a number on his knees—at least his right knee. It was hurting him.

He was having a hard time holding the gun. He needed to switch hands. He needed the gun in his good hand.

"What does May third mean?" she asked.

"What do you mean? Why you asking so many questions?" he said.

"Because, damn it, I want to know why this is happening to me. I overheard the head guy, Julio, talking with someone on the phone about May third. That's some kind of important date. That's a long way off—past the rainy season. What does May third have to do with me?"

"Julio has lots of deals going, not just you," he said.

"It has to do with me," she said. "He was talking only about me."

She had been gently pulling her leg, gradually adding pressure. *Just look away*, she willed. *Look away, damn it, just for a second.*

She waited for an opening. She knew one would come. He didn't strike her as being a patient man.

"I have friends who will ransom me," she said. "Maybe for more money than you can get from Julio's man."

"It might come to that. But, see, I get the idea this guy Julio's got is willing to pay a lot of money."

"It doesn't make sense," she said. "I'm simply not that important."

She had been pretending she was Diane Fallon. It seemed easier. It seemed like a way to get information about what they wanted without exposing her own identity to them. She wondered what Diane Fallon had done in South America that had made someone want her so badly.

"Was it Patia who pointed me out to Julio?" said Maria.

"She sometimes works for archaeologists here—a good way to get information. Julio lives off information," he said.

Then you'd think he'd have been better at gathering it, she thought. *Do they think Georgia has only one forensic anthropologist?*

His face screwed up again, apparently from a wave of pain. "My leg hurts, damn you," he said. "I might just teach you a lesson before I turn you over to the buyer."

Suddenly he made his move. She hadn't seen it coming. He acted so quickly she had no time to respond. He was on top of her with his gun pointing at her face, his good hand resting on her throat.

Chapter 9

Diane stared openmouthed at Martin Thormond.

"What?" she managed to say after several moments of being completely dumbfounded. "Drug smugglers? Someone told him I was involved with drug smugglers?"

"I told him, of course, that it was ridiculous." Martin pulled a piece of paper from his inner coat pocket. "I have his name—Brian Mathews."

Diane took the paper and stared at it for a long moment.

"I have no idea what this is about," she said, "but I'll find out." She paused. "You said he asked nothing about the events that happened here in the museum last evening?"

"He didn't. I thought that was odd," Martin said.

He stood there awkwardly, as if searching for something else to say, shifting slightly from one foot to the other. He was going through, Diane guessed, what people often go through when confronted with an accusation about someone they know. Not believing it but, at the same time, entertaining the notion that it might be true.

Hell. What some people will say.

"Thank you, Martin," she said. "I'll find out what this is about."

He nodded, gave her a lopsided self-conscious smile, and made his exit—a little quickly, thought Diane.

She turned off the lights, closed and locked the door to the boardroom. Outside the door in the hallway she smelled the familiar odor of the treacly perfume Madge Stewart wore. Diane was thinking that the scent certainly had staying power.

As she walked past the door to the storage closet adjoining the boardroom, she heard a faint noise from inside. She stopped, opened the closet door, and found herself confronting a wide-eyed and very much surprised Madge Stewart.

"Are you lost?" said Diane.

Madge smoothed her frizzy hair with a hand.

"Lost? I, uh, I guess I am." She attempted to regain her composure, smoothing her frizzy hair again. "I wasn't watching where I was going."

She fled the closet, her shoes clicking on the granite floor of the museum as she hurried down the hallway.

"This is just great," Diane whispered to herself.

In the back of the closet was a door that opened into the boardroom. Madge obviously had been listening to Diane's conversation with Thormond. That was all that was needed to make a bad situation worse. Madge would spread the rumor of Diane's involvement with drug smugglers to everyone she knew.

Diane's own heels clicked on the floor as she made her way to her osteology office. She had two offices, one for each hat she wore—museum director and crime lab director. Her museum office was decorated with Escher prints, photographs of her caving, paintings, and a desk fountain. And it had an attached lounge with a full bathroom.

Her osteology office, by contrast, was small with pale walls and comfortable no-frills furniture. There was adequate space, but no more. On the wall opposite her desk hung a watercolor of a lone wolf hunting. Perhaps that was symbolic, she thought, as she sat down at her desk and reached for the phone.

Diane called the *Atlanta Journal-Constitution* newspaper and asked for Brian Mathews.

"I have a note on my desk saying he wanted to speak with me," she said.

It was almost true. She did have a note on her desk. And no doubt, at some point he probably would want to speak with her.

"Oh, really? Let me see." The woman answering the phone sounded confused. "Well, you are a museum, right?"

"Yes," Diane confirmed. *She probably read the caller ID*.

"It must have been about Machu Picchu. That's where he is. Are you following his blog?"

Blog?

"No," Diane said. "He has a blog?"

Diane searched for his name on the *AJC* Web site using her computer while she was talking. She found quickly that Brian Mathews was a travel reporter currently on vacation, going to major archaeological sites in Mexico and Central and South America. He was recording his trip on a blog at the *AJC* Web site.

Odd, thought Diane.

"I'll wait until he contacts the museum again," she said, thanking the woman.

Machu Picchu. That's in Peru.

Diane sat for a moment, questions running through her mind about Mathews' call to Martin Thormond. Did Mathews call from Peru? Had he been talking to someone who wished her harm? Someone who thought telling a reporter lies was a way to hurt her? Was it really Mathews . . . or someone pretending to be a reporter?

Damn. As if she didn't have enough problems at the moment. She stood up and smoothed her blazer. *One problem at a time.*

Her office was adjacent to her osteology lab, which connected to the crime lab. She left her office intending to pass through her bone lab . . . stopping abruptly when she saw a box on the metal table. It was one of the crime lab boxes used to store bones and other evidence.

The bone from the backpack, she thought.

She looked in the box. It was there, lying softly but securely on brown paper over batting—the small upper arm bone of a child. It was a sad little bone. Bones of children were always sad—a life just starting . . . and ending too soon . . . often violently.

Diane put on her white lab coat and disposable gloves and picked up the bone. It was only a diaphysis—the bone shaft. The ends were gone. The epiphyses hadn't fused.

The bone was a light yellow-gray in color, the color of the soil from which it was taken. She sniffed it. It wasn't old, perhaps a few years. Not from an archaeological dig.

She measured the length of the bone and looked on a reference chart on the wall. The child was just over three feet tall. Probably between four and six years of age. Small for six.

The bone had no abnormalities, no healed breaks, no evidence of malnourishment, nor of any pathology. Murder victim? Illegally disinterred? What was it doing in the backpack with a bunch of feathers and animal parts?

Diane slipped off her gloves and dropped them in a trashcan. She walked across the room and opened the door. As she crossed the threshold, she took off her museum hat and put on her hat as director of the crime lab of the city of Rosewood, Georgia.

The first thing she saw when she entered the lab was an image of feathers projected on the large viewing screen. Elegant plumes with their parts neatly labeled.

Feathers are one of nature's many well-designed inventions. They look and feel fragile and soft, they have great beauty, yet they are great protectors, better than an overcoat.

Diane recognized the illustration as being from one of David's many databases. He was telling Izzy about feathers. They sat at the conference table looking at the screen. The new system they had recently installed for debriefing about evidence was money well spent. She pulled a chair out, sat down, and listened patiently, only because she knew when she finished with her crime scene crew, she had to go have lunch with Vanessa and Laura.

"Two main types," David said.

He clipped his phrases short, as if he were going down a bulleted list of characteristics. Probably because deep down he felt Izzy had a short attention span for details.

"Contour and down. A contour feather is the large, flat feather that covers the body of an adult bird."

"The ones Indians wear in a headdress," said Izzy. He grinned at David.

Izzy, like Jin, liked to irritate David whenever the opportunity arose. And the main way to irritate David was to act either sophomoric or not interested in his databases.

"And down is in pillows. See, I know feathers."

David rolled his eyes. "Contour feathers have a long, thick central shaft called a rachis." He pointed at examples on the projection as he talked. "The branches off the rachis are called barbs. More branches off the barbs are called barbules, and they are held together by tiny hooks called barbicels. Together these form the vane or vexillum of the feather—the main part of the feather. All this structure makes it so you can zip a feather up and down. Got that? Because I'm giving a test."

"What?" said Izzy. "Zip them?"

"In a manner of speaking," interrupted Diane. "Kind of like Velcro. It protects the bird. Now, David, will you bottom-line it for me?"

Diane was getting impatient, even though finishing meant having to go to lunch. But she knew David would expand his explanation into the variations in feathers that allowed people like him to tell what kind of bird a feather came from.

David frowned. He loved to lecture and he was usually pretty good at it. But sometimes the other members of the team were a trial and he would make it boring and long on purpose.

"I was just joshing you, David. I always thought feathers were just feathers," said Izzy.

"Everything in the universe has qualities that are unique enough that they can be differentiated apart from other like things if we just examine the characteristics closely," David said.

"And I can see you've made a fine start," said Izzy. He turned toward Diane. "Have you seen the number of data-bases he has?"

"Yes," said Diane. She grinned at David. "It's one of the things that makes us unique. So, what do we have?"

David clicked the remote and displayed the evidence from the knapsack up on the screen.

"The talons are from a harpy eagle. The mummified paws are from a woolly monkey. The beak is from a keel-billed toucan. The teeth are from a jaguar. They have holes drilled in them and were once probably part of a necklace. The holes were all made with the same tool, probably a jeweler's drill. The feathers are from macaws. The blue ones are from a Spix's macaw."

"A Spix's macaw?" said Diane. "I didn't think there were any left."

David started to answer when Neva, another of Diane's crime scene team, came out of a glassed-in cubicle where she had been working on the woven bag the evidence had been found in. They had thought it might be a medicine bag from one of the tribes. Neva slipped off her gloves and disposed of them.

"The bag is on cam two," she said, and David switched over to it. The screen blinked and came back up with a view of the embroidered bag with a woven handle. "It's not South American," said Neva. "It's Thai."

"Thai?" said David. "Really?"

Neva nodded. "It's saturated with a drug called XTR25. It's a new variant of ecstasy and pretty powerful. The DEA is going to be interested in this," said Neva.

Diane felt sick to her stomach.

Chapter 10

The museum restaurant where Diane was to meet Vanessa and Laura had an ancient medieval library look about it. The center of the restaurant was a maze of tall, vintage brick archways that created small chamberlike spaces with vaulted ceilings, each containing four or five tables of dark wood. Booths lining the walls were tucked behind similar archways.

Diane knew that Vanessa and Laura would choose a booth. They always did. More privacy. She saw them seated across the restaurant. Madge Stewart was standing in front of their booth with her back to Diane, speaking in an animated fashion.

It didn't take her long, thought Diane.

She watched Madge's gossip dance. It was like a tattletale pantomime. Vanessa said something to Madge. Madge's body language changed. She stood still, like a scolded child.

Diane sighed and threaded her way through the tables toward the booth. She was almost there when Laura noticed her, smiled and waved with a little too much animation. Diane grimaced.

Madge jumped as if Diane had goosed her.

"Oh, I have to go," she said. "Nice speaking with you, Vanessa, Laura." She smiled weakly at Diane and hurried off.

Madge was in her forties but sometimes acted like a seventh grader. And all her friends, like Laura and Vanessa, unwittingly encouraged her by coddling her. At least that's what Diane thought.

All of them were also old Rosewood several generations back. Nearly all the "old" families had strong bonds among them. But still, Diane had no idea why they excused Madge's bad behavior. She wasn't a stupid woman by any means. She was a talented artist. She also seemed to be everyone's baby sister.

"I hope you haven't been waiting long," said Diane. "But I see you've been entertained by the latest gossip."

Diane sat down opposite Laura and Vanessa. Laura had redone her blond hair in a short pixielike cut. It looked good with her small face . . . which was frowning at the moment. Vanessa's platinum white hair was in a smooth French twist. It gave her face a tranquil look, even with her piercing blue eyes.

Diane and Laura were childhood friends. When Diane was twelve years old, her father moved the family to Tennessee, but she and Laura remained friends. Diane returned to Rosewood briefly when she was in high school to take accelerated college courses from Milo Lorenzo. That's when she met Vanessa, who was a friend of Milo. It was Milo who later hired Diane as assistant director of the museum. When he was felled by a heart attack, Diane became director of the museum.

"Vanessa told Madge not to go around repeating rumors, and to remember Kendel," said Laura.

Diane fingered the menu, pretending to look at it, not wanting to look at her friends. Not because she was embarrassed by rumors, but because of a free-floating annoyance she was feeling lately toward everyone she knew.

"Kendel is still suffering fallout from the gossip Madge spread about her," said Diane.

"I told her that unlike Kendel, you would probably sue her," said Vanessa.

"I would," said Diane.

"I don't think she'll say anything to anyone else," said Laura.

Diane looked up from the menu, having decided she would order red meat when the waitstaff came. She was angry with Laura. She wasn't sure why; perhaps today she was just tired of Laura's always trying to smooth things over. Sometimes things didn't need smoothing over.

"She will gossip," said Diane. "It's in her nature as it's in the nature of the scorpion to sting."

"Now, Diane," clucked Laura.

"Did she tell you I found her in the supply closet eaves-dropping on my conversation with Martin?"

The two of them raised their eyebrows. Laura had a drink halfway to her lips. Vanessa put her head in her hand and groaned.

"What did she say to you exactly?" Diane asked them.

"I don't think that would help . . . ," began Laura.

Diane put a hand on her forearm. "It would help. This is my reputation, my career. I need to know the kind of life this rumor is taking on." She looked directly in Laura's eyes. "This can't be smoothed over. It has to be dealt with."

"She's right," said Vanessa. She lifted a hand and waved for the waitress. "But let us order first. I'm very hungry."

Laura and Vanessa both ordered the salmon. Diane ordered a filet, rare. After the waitress brought the drinks, Diane looked at Laura.

Laura sighed. "She said *48 Hours* is looking to do an exposé on your drug dealings in South America."

Diane shook her head. "That's not even the right media." She told them about Martin Thormond's call from Brian Mathews.

"Brian Mathews is a travel reporter," said Vanessa.

"Yes, he is," said Diane. "He is currently in Peru reporting."

"I don't understand," said Laura. "He called Martin from Peru? Why Martin? Why didn't he call you? Or Vanessa? Or the police, even? I mean, if he heard some rumor in Peru?"

"Why, indeed," said Diane. "Of course, there is just the caller's word that he was Brian Mathews."

"Oh," said Laura. "Yes, I see. I didn't think of that."

"Martin was rather furtive when he approached me as everyone was leaving. I know that Madge noticed him. I suspect she smelled a little gossip and hid in the closet . . . which has doors into the hallway and the boardroom. Apparently she did a little embellishing on the way to the restaurant."

"Apparently so," said Vanessa.

"Look," said Diane, "I'll take a hiatus until I figure . . ."

Vanessa shook her head. "Every couple of months you

offer to step down, whenever some drama happens. Stop it. I'll have a long talk with Madge. She'll listen to me."

Diane wasn't so sure.

"Why would someone do this?" asked Laura.

"I don't know," said Diane. "But I will find out."

Their meals came and for a short while they concentrated on their food.

"You know," said Laura after a pause, "Thomas Barclay would be easier to get along with if you would ease up on him during meetings."

"I don't know what you mean," said Diane, cutting her steak and spearing the piece with her fork.

"Yes, you do. You try to get under his skin," said Laura. "He's really not so bad."

"Perhaps. But from the board I need ideas and solutions. The first thing Thomas always wants to do is blame someone. That really doesn't help. Now, Kenneth was helpful. But for someone whose job it is to keep track of the bottom line, Thomas was far off the mark wanting to close the night classes. But in the spirit of trying to get along with him, I'll be glad to now have my wedding somewhere—"

"Nice try, dear," said Vanessa. "The invitations are out, we have your dress, everything is in play, as it were."

Diane sighed. "I hope it isn't a white dress with a veil." She had left all the wedding planning to Vanessa. "I've done the white dress thing."

"No, dear. No white dress, no veil," said Vanessa.

"I don't want one of those floppy hats either . . . or a tiara . . . though I might be persuaded by a simple gold coronet."

Vanessa smiled. "I'm sorry, dear, I get to wear the coronet. You'll have to wait to find out about the rest. We won't embarrass you."

"You've seemed unsettled lately," said Laura.

"I've been thinking a lot about Ariel. And about Frank. Frank's a good father. What he's done with Star after her family was slaughtered is fantastic. And his son, Kevin, is a great kid. Ariel would have thrived in this environment," said Diane. "I . . ."

"Feel guilty about being happy," said Laura.

Diane shrugged. "Perhaps. It's that terrible might-have-been that keeps after me." She paused and pinched the bridge of her nose to keep herself from tearing up. "But this is what is. I'll deal with it."

They ate in silence for several minutes. When they did speak it wasn't about the museum break-in. It was clear that Vanessa hadn't told Laura about Simone Brooks. That was what had Diane worried at the moment. What was that about?

It had been a long day. Diane had thin-sectioned the bone—cutting a paper-thin slice from it for examination under the microscope. The thin-section revealed that the child had normal bone growth. He or she wasn't undernourished and the bone showed no sign of disease. A healthy child before tragedy struck.

When Diane finished her examination she took a bone sample down to Deven Jin, the director of her DNA lab in the basement, for stable isotope analysis. The types, numbers, and ratios of stable isotopes absorbed from food and water the child had consumed would tell them the types of foods that were in the child's diet. If they were lucky, they would be able to identify the area from which the foods had come—maybe even pinpoint the local population in which he or she had lived. That could lead to a DNA comparison. Then, perhaps, someone would know who the child was.

It was late when Diane left the museum. Frank would probably be home already. She lived in his home. He kept telling her it would be their home, but she had resisted calling something *hers* that he had nurtured for years.

Frank's Queen Anne–style house sat several hundred feet back from the road amid huge oak trees. It was a lovely house and well maintained—like Frank—grounded in fine tradition and possessing of a sound structure.

His white Chevy Camaro was parked in the driveway. She pulled in beside it and hurried into the house, glad to be home. Frank apparently heard her drive up and was putting dinner on the table—one of his favorites and hers too—spaghetti.

Frank kissed her and took her purse and guided her in to the living room. Frank was about three inches taller than Diane's five-nine. He had salt-and-pepper hair that was still mostly pepper. And the most beautiful blue-green eyes. She never tired of looking at him or the way his eyes crinkled at the corners when he smiled.

He had been out of town for several days and this was the first she had seen of him since the events at the museum. She hugged him again.

"Miss me, did you?" He grinned. "I understand you had some excitement. Sorry I couldn't call last night."

Frank was a detective in the Metro-Atlanta Fraud & Computer Forensics Unit and he traveled periodically in connection with his cases.

"It's all right. How was your case?" she asked.

"Not good. The guy escaped from the courthouse and now the U.S. Marshals get to deal with him."

He stood a moment looking at her. She didn't know what emotion was playing around his lips. It was something between amusement and dread.

"What?" she said.

"Might as well get the bad stuff out of the way first. Then we'll eat and catch up," he said.

Diane stepped back. "What bad stuff?"

He took a breath.

"You have an enemy out there," he said. "I've received several calls telling me that you're seeing men while I'm out of town."

Chapter 11

Maria jerked her hand with the gun from behind her and fired at the hulk on her. She felt the sound of the blast ripple through her chest. It was an earthquake shaking her bones, but instinctively she knew she was not shot. She did not feel the trauma telling her that her flesh had been pierced or torn. What she saw was the shock in the eyes of the man on top of her. She shoved him and he fell onto his back, crying out as he hit the ground. A large stain of blood was spreading on his shirt. Maria knocked his gun away from him.

The gunshot had hit his shoulder. He was now incapacitated in both arms. She grabbed the kerchief from around his neck and stuffed it under his shirt and over the wound. That was the extent of mercy she was willing to give him. She began searching his pockets.

"Damn you," he groaned, and tried to head butt her.

But he was slow and Maria hit him in the side of his jaw with her fist. His head jerked back and hit the ground.

"You don't have the right to my life," she croaked at him.

All the adrenaline that had been keeping her going was fading. She ached and itched all over. She was hot, hungry, and scared—and she smelled bad. But she forced herself to continue searching him, choking back feelings of guilt. Her fingers shook as she went through his pockets aided by the light from the flashlight that she set on the ground.

She found another set of keys, more money, a Swiss Army knife, a longer knife in a scabbard on his belt, another gun, and ammunition. She took all of them.

"You cruel bitch. Don't leave me like this," he croaked at her as she gathered up all his belongings.

She ignored him. It was hard knowing she was going to leave him like she had left his partner and that they would have a slim chance of survival.

"Don't leave me like this . . . please." He was scared. It made her sick. But she ignored him.

Rosetta was already at the truck inventorying its contents. Maria shook her head with amazement. The little girl couldn't have gotten as far as she had without being a really smart and practical kid.

"They were getting supplies," said Rosetta, shaking with excitement. She had found treasure. "A lot of it is whiskey," she added, awe in her voice. "This will be good for trading."

Practical kid.

Maria looked over the contents. There was fresh food—vegetables and salted meat, most of which would not last on a long trip. But they would eat well for a while and save the jerky that Rosetta had in her backpack. There were medicinal supplies, mail, fabric, a hammer and nails, and a paperback romance.

She took the letters and threw them in the cab of the truck, hoping they contained clues as to what the hell her kidnapping was about. She grabbed one of the bottles of whiskey and one of the several knives she had acquired in the past hour and climbed in the truck. Rosetta climbed in the other side.

The seats were a brown vinyl that were worn and torn. The floorboard was bare metal—no carpets, no rubber mats. It was beat-up inside and out and smelled like mildew, but it looked good to Maria. She tried one of the keys and the engine started up immediately. It had a full tank. So far, so good.

"Let me see the map," she said.

Rosetta pulled it out of the backpack she had set between her feet and handed it to her.

Maria pointed at the map. "I'm thinking we should avoid both of these villages. They are too close by and we will be in danger from Julio's friends and enemies."

"Where will we go?"

Maria detected a little fear in Rosetta's voice. Maria didn't blame her. She was terrified herself.

"Here." She pointed to the map. "This is a railroad. It

runs along the borders of Peru and Brazil. If we can make it there, we can get a long way across the Amazon. I'm thinking about trying to get to some archaeological digs I know about, or maybe a tourist attraction, and get some help from there. We have lots of choices and they lie in this direction. The roads will not be as good, but I think it's our best bet."

"None of the roads are good," said Rosetta. "You're right about the villages. They are not good either."

Maria took the bottle of whiskey and the knife and got out of the truck. She walked to the felled man who was still groaning. She set the whiskey down beside him and stuck the knife in the ground several feet away.

"This is the best I can do for you," she said. "Keep in mind, you would have done nothing for me."

She walked away, got in the truck, and drove into the darkness, following the route she had laid out. It was a rough ride over terrain that was hardly a road. The two of them didn't speak for a long while, not until there was more than a mile between them and the men whose truck they took.

"Why didn't you tell them you are not Mama?" Rosetta asked after a while.

"If they don't know my name, they'll be searching for Diane Fallon, not me. That makes it a little less dangerous for us. And it gives Diane Fallon a little protection. From what those men have said, it sounds as if someone with a lot of money is looking for her. Their influence may have a far reach. If they think I'm Diane, perhaps they won't go looking for her in Georgia. But they're going to look for me even if they discover who I am, because I know too much—or, at least, they'll think I do. I wish I knew who it is who's looking for Diane."

"Is that where she is? In Georgia?" asked Rosetta.

"She's the director of a museum in Georgia," said Maria.

"She said she was going to work in a museum and take me there."

The little girl's voice shook. Maria thought she might cry.

"You'll be there in a few days," said Maria. She reached over and squeezed her hand.

"We need to warn Mama—in case somebody goes looking for her. I wish those men had one of those phones Julio has," Rosetta said.

"Our problems would be over," agreed Maria. "Perhaps we will acquire one along the way."

She glanced at Rosetta. She sat on the seat with her legs straight out, the backpack between her feet. She was wearing fairly new jeans with the cuffs stuffed in equally new lace-up boots that were slightly large for her.

"Nice clothes," said Maria.

"I stole them from Jopito. He's mean to me. But he has nice clothes." She paused for several moments. "I didn't steal them to get even. I stole them because I needed them."

"I'll get you home. I'll get us both home."

"That was pretty good back there—the way you used the stick on those guys," said Rosetta. "How'd you learn to do that?"

"I'm a Wii champion in sword fighting," said Maria.

Rosetta looked over at her. "What's that?"

"It's a game. You can move around pretending you are sword fighting, or playing golf, or whatever, and your movements show up in your character on a television screen. Your mother will have to get you one."

Maria glanced at Rosetta and saw the quiver of a smile, as if she dared entertain the thought that they would really get home.

Maria didn't say anything for a long while, letting Rosetta bask in the feeling of hope. Daylight was coming. She could see glimmers of light occasionally through the branches, but not a lot of it would reach through the canopy.

"How long before they wake up—Julio and the others back at the village?" asked Maria. She didn't quite believe that Rosetta drugged the lot of them and she was worried they would be followed. She couldn't imagine how a little kid could manage something like that.

"I'm not sure. I gave them a mixture of herbs I got from Uruma when I stayed with her tribe. They'll sleep for a long time, I think. If they have worms, it will get rid of them too."

Maria laughed out loud and it made her throat hurt.

"How did you get them to take the drug?" she whispered.

"I cook the food a lot of the time. I put it in the food. It was easy," she said. "I work hard and don't make many mistakes. The families I worked for put me in charge of cooking and storing supplies. That gives me power."

Maria raised an eyebrow. Rosetta was a very practical kid.

"Your English is very good," she whispered.

"Mama said I am gifted in languages. I know several languages here. I can speak for us and you can pretend you can't say anything. That'll be easy."

They rode in silence for a while. Maria concentrated on the road. Sometimes it would disappear completely and she would have to look at the compass to figure out the direction to go. Rosetta watched her closely.

"Can you find the way?" she asked after the third stop and consultation with the compass.

"Of course. I just look at the map and the direction we need to be going and make sure we are on track with the compass," she said. "Good thing they had one in the glove compartment. I thought I would have to use the stars, and that meant I would have to climb one of those kapok trees."

"I'm lucky I found you," the little girl said. "I kept looking for someone who could help me. Everywhere I worked, I would store some supplies together so that if I had to leave suddenly, it wouldn't take me long to pack. I was afraid to have a stash somewhere. If they found it, they wouldn't trust me no more."

"Is that what you did tonight? Collect your supplies from the people you worked for?" asked Maria.

Rosetta nodded. "I was about to think I would never find anybody who could help me. Then they brought you and said you were a forensic anthropologist from Georgia. I thought maybe you might be my mama. You weren't, but you could help me. Mama talked about Georgia. I thought maybe you knew her."

"We met a few times at conferences," said Maria. "I don't know her well." But everyone knew Diane Fallon's story. How she had lost her daughter to a massacre and nearly went crazy.

"If I can't find anyone I know at one of the dig sites, and we can make it to a big city, we can go to an American embassy and get help."

"No!" yelled Rosetta.

Maria jumped. "What?" she croaked.

"We can't go to an embassy, we can't!" She was almost in tears. "It was one of them that grabbed me away from Mama."

Chapter 12

Diane stared at Frank for a long moment, stunned.

"Entertaining men? Here? While you are gone? I guess you got me," she said. "I've always hired professionals to clean up the mess so you wouldn't know, but I forgot about nosy neighbors." She paused a beat, studying his face. "You weren't concerned, were you?"

They stood close together, facing each other in front of the wood-mantled fireplace in the living room. It was a cozy room with an Oriental rug, overstuffed sofas and chairs, and oak and walnut furniture.

He smiled, as if considering the prospect and finding it amusing. Then he frowned. "Only about the caller. The call was traced to a throwaway cell. That seems a little too deliberate for a run-of-the-mill prankster. And the phrase—'entertaining men'—seemed off. I thought you ought to know in case you've attracted some kind of stalker variant."

"I wonder if it's related to the phone call Martin Thormond received," she whispered, almost to herself, looking over at the fireplace screen with the bronze tree of life design.

"You've had other harassing phone calls?"

"Not harassing." Diane repeated what Martin's caller had said about her dealing drugs in South America. "I called the reporter, but he's in Peru—as in South America. Rather disturbing. I have no idea what it was about."

Frank narrowed his eyes. "It may be just someone's idea of a joke," he said, and pulled her close, holding for a moment. "But it bears watching."

It did indeed bear watching. *Rumor and gossip are potent weapons*, thought Diane. She wondered who was aiming them in her direction.

Frank gave her a kiss on the forehead. "Let's eat, and afterward you can tell me about your last couple of days. Scuttlebutt tells me that it was exciting."

It felt good to have Frank back in town. He and his partner were good at their jobs. Their success rate was so high that they consulted frequently with other computer fraud units across the country. He had been away for several days this trip. She'd missed him.

They sat across from each other at one end of the large rectangular table in the dining room, another cozy room with its own fireplace and comfortable furniture. August was too warm for a fire, but Frank's beautiful fireplace screens were almost as good.

She and Frank had made a pact not to talk about work at the dinner table unless it was about an interesting museum exhibit. The food tasted better that way. So Diane picked another topic. The rituals surrounding their upcoming wedding, though to her it was just as unnerving as talk of murder. She had wanted to go to a judge for a quiet ceremony. Dress in a nice traveling suit. Nothing fussy . . . no flowers . . . no music. Few people . . . maybe just a witness.

Vanessa, Laura, and half of Diane's staff wouldn't hear of it. Vanessa insisted that the ceremony take place in the Pleistocene Room of the museum. Diane refused to take part in planning a wedding, especially her own. "Fine," Vanessa had said. "We'll do it." And so they were.

Diane twined the spaghetti around her fork. "I had lunch with Vanessa and Laura today," she said.

"How did that go?" asked Frank.

"I'm a little nervous about what they're planning for me to wear, but at least I might get a gold coronet. I can see myself coming down the aisle with a crown."

Frank smiled. "So fitting, too," he said. "I haven't seen it, but I hear Star picked out your dress."

Diane looked horrified. "Star? The girl with the fuchsia hair?"

Frank adopted Star when her parents, his best friends, were murdered. At the time she was a troubled teen with hot-pink hair and an attitude to match.

"It hasn't been fuchsia in a long time." Frank grinned at Diane. "Besides, since you bought her the new wardrobe in Paris, her tastes in clothing have undergone a radical change for the better."

"I'm glad she decided she liked school," said Diane.

Frank put his hand over hers. "I wasn't making any headway trying to convince her to go to the university. If you hadn't made your astounding offer to buy her a Paris wardrobe if she tried school out, she'd be working flipping burgers, and not in prelaw. Thank you for that."

"I've discovered that bribery often works very well," said Diane. "Anyway, she had such strong feelings when she was wrongly accused of her parents' murders that I think she would have eventually found her way to law school or some justice-oriented program."

"I'm not so sure. Doing it right now was important for her," he said, "before bills, babies, and bad boyfriends."

"So this is how she repays me, going in with them to plan our wedding," said Diane.

Frank smiled and rubbed the top of her hand with his thumb. "Just think how much you will like it when it's over. Besides, ceremonies are important to people."

It was important to Frank. She could see it in the way he acted. He was a traditional guy. He always had been. Sometimes she didn't know what he saw in her, they were so different on many things. On the other hand, it was easy to see what she saw in him. If she had to make a list, the words *intelligent*, *kind*, *rational* would be at the top. She was doing the right thing by getting married. She believed that, she did, but she still felt edgy about it, like she had forgotten something. Except that she hadn't forgotten. It was Ariel. Ariel should be here with her, but Diane had lost her and it still hurt.

"I will make it though the ceremony," she said.

"I have no doubt. Everyone involved has good taste, so don't worry," he said, eating the last of his spaghetti. "How about coffee in the living room and you can tell me about the drama at the museum? Someone said there was a fire?"

Diane had told him little over the phone about the break-in. Only that there was one and she would fill him in later. It was now later.

Diane sat cross-legged on the sofa. She took several sips of the hot coffee he handed to her before she started.

"Are you bolstering your courage," he said, "or trying to scorch your throat so you won't have to talk about it?"

Frank was sitting on a stuffed chair opposite her. They had a coffee table between them.

"Neither," she said. "Just savoring your good coffee." She set the hot cup down on a coaster that looked like a disk of polished wood.

She started not to tell him why she was at the exhibit at that particular time. Saying that she was trying to get over her dread of the new exhibit would sound foolish. But she blurted it out—the way the look of the exhibit reminded her of the ancient ruin and how she had searched there in vain for Ariel.

"I needed to be able to feel comfortable around the exhibit. It's silly, I know."

"Not silly. You've been thinking a lot about Ariel lately, haven't you?"

"Yes. But it's not thoughts of her I want to get rid of. It's the . . ." Diane trailed off, unable to explain. She felt hot, as if the tree of life design on the fireplace were a flame. She was afraid tears would well up in her eyes.

"I know," he said.

"I was sitting looking up at the facade when I heard a groan." Diane went on to tell him the whole story of the body on the floor, the false paramedics, and the fire. "I should have been suspicious when I didn't recognize the second security guard. But we have a couple of new hires I hadn't yet seen in person."

"Don't beat yourself up over that," he said, sipping his coffee.

"This went down literally under my nose," she said. "It's my job to protect the museum. Now one of our major exhibits has been seriously damaged. I don't know if Mexico will still loan us the artifacts. All the advertisements are in place. It's a disaster."

"Do you know what it was about, what your friend was doing there? Has she talked?" asked Frank.

Diane was glad he hadn't patted her head and said, 'It's not your fault, no one will blame you, it will all work out.' He had gone straight into detective mode.

The phone rang and Diane unfolded herself and scooted down the sofa to the table that held the phone. It was Jin, the director of her DNA lab.

"Boss," he said, "sorry to call you at home, but I thought you would want to hear the preliminary report from the analyses."

"Yes, Jin, I do," she said.

"We got good samples to analyze. The blood they tried to burn away still left some traces and we have been able to piece together what might have happened. We're not finished, but a pretty good picture is beginning to come out of it," he said.

"Good. Tell me what you have." Diane gripped the receiver tight. Frank had mainly old-fashioned landlines in his house. Great for when the electricity went off.

"Looks like the guy was stabbed about where he lay. There was a struggle and some of the woman's blood was in the exhibit room too. The blood leading from the exhibit room belonged to her. Right now it looks like she may have stabbed him, tried to get away through the lab room, and collapsed. David said she has a blow to her head that she may have gotten during the fight. But that didn't take her down until later. Like I said, it's all preliminary."

"That's good, Jin. Did you do the stable isotope analysis on the bone?"

"I was getting to that. Scott did the analysis. The ratios look like the bone came from someone who was raised in the Amazon rain forest. Does that help?"

"It's another piece of the puz—"

She stopped . . . gripped the phone. . . . She couldn't breathe.

Oh God.

"Boss? You there?"

Jin's words were faint in her ears.

"She'll call you back." It was Frank talking to Jin.

She heard the sound of the phone receiver being put back on the cradle.

"What's wrong?" Frank sat down beside her. "Diane, are you ill?"

"Simone. What if Simone was bringing me . . . what if that was . . . Oh, dear God. What if it was Ariel, my little Ariel? What if that was her little bone I was cutting?"

Tears flowed from her eyes as she bent over, choking on her grief.

Chapter 13

If Frank hadn't been holding her, Diane would have fallen to the floor. All this time she had told herself, made herself believe, that Ariel had somehow gotten away during the massacre. That somehow she had hidden in the jungle she knew so well, had saved herself from the slaughter. She had wanted to believe that somewhere Ariel was alive, was well, was happy. That someday she would grow up to be old enough . . . old enough to travel, and perhaps she would make her way to America . . . to Georgia . . . back to Diane. And all that time there was also the dark fear that this moment would come.

"If it was your Ariel," Frank whispered in her ear, "and I'm not saying that it was—but if it was her, she was in the best, most loving hands."

Diane leaned against Frank for a long time. When finally she pulled away she was feeling . . . she didn't know what to feel, or believe. She balled her hands into fists so she wouldn't shake.

"Why else would Simone come to see me . . . carrying a child's bone? She found where Ivan Santos buried the dead from the mission. She found . . ." Diane's lower lip trembled and she bit it to stop the quivering. "She found Ariel's grave."

"What do the other things mean?" said Frank. "The feathers and the animal parts?"

"I don't know. Simone hasn't been able to talk," said Diane. She sat down on the sofa, suddenly tired. "I asked Garnett to find out how she is doing. I didn't think the hospital would give me the information. He said she was still unconscious with a severe concussion. They don't know if she'll recover. On the other hand, they said she might wake up at any time. You know how those injuries are."

"Does her employer know what she was working on?" asked Frank.

"I don't know. Garnett is handling everything. Since I know her, I have to at least act like I'm steering clear of the investigation."

But she wasn't going to. Except for tonight.

She and Frank spent the rest of the evening trying to talk about the wedding, about Star, music . . . anything except his work, the museum, and Ariel.

The morning brought no less pain than the evening before had. Diane was haunted by the thought that the little bone might belong to Ariel. Instead of cradling it, she had cut into it, thin-sectioned it, cut off a part and sent it downstairs to be crushed for analysis.

She knew her thoughts were irrational. Frank was right—as she did with all bones, she gave it the best of care, allowing it to tell whatever story it had to tell.

She was up earlier than Frank and she made breakfast for the two of them. It was Frank who always insisted on breakfast. Diane supposed it was a good thing. If it were only her, she'd probably sleep in and have a protein drink on the way to work. Today she and Frank had pancakes, scrambled eggs, and orange juice. A good, nourishing breakfast, but it did not sit well in her stomach.

When she drove her red SUV into the parking lot, heartache gnawed at her insides. But she had to put on a professional face. She had to do her duty.

She made up her mind that today she was going to visit the hospital. Maybe Simone would be awake. Her folks would be there. Maybe they would know something.

She was early; the museum had not yet opened for business. She walked up the steps of the huge granite edifice to the large glass doors, where the guards let her in. The first place she went was the Mayan Room to see the damage.

She smelled the soapy solution Korey was using to clean certain artifacts. She walked through the tunnel and into the exhibit room. Staff from Conservation, Exhibit Designing, and Planning were already there, busy trying to repair the damage. It was like an archaeological dig of sorts, the way her crew gently worked on the stone pedestals and display cases that looked like ancient ruins.

Korey was stooped near a soot-covered faux stone molded to resemble an intricate face surrounded by symbols. His dreadlocks were pulled back in a low ponytail and he was pointing to a dark streak.

"It's working," said the woman sitting cross-legged on the floor, soapy toothbrush in hand. "It just takes a while."

Korey caught sight of Diane, stood up and walked over to her.

"How bad is it?" she said.

"Not as bad as it could have been," said Korey. "We've been working on the soot. Trying to see if we can salvage all the faux stonework. I think we can save most of it. Some of it will have to be done over. I'm sorry."

"So am I," said Diane, looking around the room. "Damn it."

"I hear they tried to burn up the security guard. That's vicious."

"They were bad guys. The real thing," said Diane.

She walked with Korey around the room, examining the damage while Korey explained how they were dealing with it.

"How long?" asked Diane

"Let me get back to you at the end of the day on that, Dr. F. We're still working out the best cleaning formulas."

"All right. Thanks, Korey. I know this is taking you away from your conservation work."

"It's not a problem. We'll get the room back up as quickly as we can," he said.

The museum was opening its doors and the first tourists were arriving as Diane crossed the lobby to the office wing of the museum. She picked up her pace before anyone was tempted to speak with her. Later in the morning she would get David and they would visit Simone at the hospital to see how she was doing. But there was work to be done first.

Andie was already behind her desk. She stopped Diane. There was a visitor. A woman who looked vaguely familiar to Diane was sitting in the waiting area. It was a cozy area decorated by Andie in a charming way, but the woman sat stiffly, clearly uncomfortable.

Sybil Carstairs—that was her name. She and her hus-

band, Edmond, were new contributors to the museum. She
held a folded piece of paper clenched in her fist as she rose.
She didn't take the hand Diane offered. Diane let it drop
to her side.

"Mrs. Carstairs, isn't it?" said Diane.

"As if you didn't know," she whispered in a hoarse
voice.

Diane raised her eyebrows. "Please step into my office,"
she said.

As Diane passed, Andie gave her an almost impercep-
tible shrug.

Diane indicated a chair in front of her desk. She went
around behind her desk and sat down, rested her folded
hands in front of her, and looked at her visitor.

Sybil Carstairs was a tall, thin woman perhaps in her fifties, maybe sixties, Diane couldn't tell. She took good care
of herself, but didn't have the genes for looking young. She
had beautifully coiffed dark brown hair and wore an expensive slate gray silk suit. She had diamond rings on fingers of both hands. Her finger joints were just starting to
show the effects of arthritis.

"What can I do for you?" Diane said.

The woman's lips trembled.

"Slut," she whispered.

"What?" said Diane. She was beginning to think the
woman was not in her right mind and that perhaps she
should call Mr. Carstairs.

"You heard me. I don't know who you think you are, but
when I finish you won't have this job anymore to use to pa-
trol for . . ." She struggled for the right word and gave up.

"What are you talking about?" said Diane.

The woman threw the paper at Diane. It landed on her
desk and almost fell to the floor before Diane caught it.
Diane unfolded it and smoothed it out on her desk.

It was an e-mail from Diane to Edmond Carstairs asking if he wanted to meet in the afternoon for sex. Diane
could understand why Sybil might be upset, but surely she
knew that this was not from Diane.

"Mrs. Carstairs, you must know that I didn't send this
message," said Diane.

"It has your name on it," she said, as if that were defini-
tive proof.

"What in the world would I be doing sending your husband an e-mail like this?" said Diane.

Sybil waved her hand toward Diane. "Just what it says."

Diane pinched the bridge of her nose and looked back up at Sybil.

"I'm engaged to a wonderful man. I have a terrific job and great friends. If I were going to run the risk of losing my fiancé, my job, and the respect of my friends by soliciting an affair, it would be with George Clooney and not your husband. I didn't send this. Obviously, my e-mail was hijacked."

"You think this is funny? We've been married thirty-seven years. It's not funny to me."

"No, Mrs. Carstairs, I think it is anything but funny. Someone is trying to harm my reputation and I take that very seriously. Quite frankly, I'm surprised that you would take this seriously. Hijacking e-mails is not an uncommon occurrence. What does your husband say?"

"He denies that there's anything going on. And I believe him. He doesn't know why you would send him a message like that."

Her raised chin made her look defiant and a little juvenile. Clearly neither of them knew anything about the pitfalls of computer mail.

"I did not send this. I hardly know your husband. I know that the two of you are generous to the museum and we are grateful. This is a terrible thing someone did and I'll try to get to the bottom of it. But I have to tell you that it is almost impossible to trace this kind of thing."

Sybil was still angry. Diane wasn't sure if it was because she wasn't convinced, or because she was emotionally all geared up for a confrontation and found there was nothing to confront about. She stood up.

"I'll be watching you," she said. "And I'll be speaking with Vanessa Van Ross."

"Then I'm sure she'll put your mind at ease." Diane rose to see her out.

Sybil left. Walking stiffly with her head held high, she marched out of the office without glancing back.

"Boy, what was that about?" asked Andie.

She had her springy brown-red hair held away from her

face with silver hair clips that Diane thought probably came from her boyfriend. Diane explained about the e-mail.

"I'll get David to try and track it down, but I don't think there is much success in cases like this."

She made light of it, but she was worried. First the rumor about drugs, then the call to Frank about her entertaining men, and now this. She needed to get to the bottom of it.

"Another day at the museum," said Andie. "Are all museums like this?"

"You thinking of looking for another job?" Diane grinned at her.

"And miss all the drama? Nope. Just wondering."

Diane made an internal assessment of her state of mind and decided that her heart was not in administrative work right this minute. She looked at her watch.

"I'm going to visit someone in the hospital. Hold the fort. . . ."

The phone rang and Andie answered it. She held it out to Diane.

"Thomas Barclay," said Andie, wrinkling her nose.

Diane was glad they didn't have video phones.

"Thomas, what can I do for you?" said Diane.

Barclay laughed. "Funny you should ask. I just called to let you know that someone's hacked into your e-mail account. That is, unless you are soliciting an assignation."

"Oh, no. Not you, too?" said Diane. She told him about Sybil Carstairs.

"I know Edmond. I'll talk to him," he said.

That was the nicest that Barclay had ever been to her. Diane was suspicious.

"I would appreciate that very much," she said.

"This happened to my daughter. It's an aggravation, but most people know it's a hoax."

"I hope you're right," said Diane. "Thank you for your call and your help."

When she hung up, Andie was looking at her with suspicion. Diane knew it was for Barclay.

"I think he is just being helpful," said Diane. *For once.* "I'm gone. You're in charge."

Diane stopped by the museum shop and bought Simone a plush gorilla that had just arrived. Simone loved jungle animals, especially gorillas. She called David and he met her outside by his black Land Rover. They drove to the hospital.

On the critical care floor Diane asked about Simone Blake.

"Your names, please?" asked the nurse, eyeing the rather large gorilla.

"Diane Fallon and David Goldstein," she said.

"I'm sorry, the family has asked that the two of you not be allowed to see Miss Blake."

Chapter 14

Someone from an embassy had taken Rosetta. That startled Maria. She didn't say anything for a long moment. She could see Rosetta was upset. Everything considered, she was surprised the kid hadn't lost it before now. Maria couldn't imagine making a daring escape plan and executing it when she was Rosetta's age.

It was important to find out if Rosetta knew who had kidnapped her. Maria didn't know much about the massacre at the mission. She was under the impression it was the work of some rogue rebel gang. If a government or embassy personnel had a hand in it . . .

Maria gently tried to coax the little girl to explain, but gave up quickly. It was clear Rosetta didn't much want to talk about the traumatic events surrounding the attack on the mission. Maria would respect that.

She turned her full attention to the way ahead. It was still dark under the canopy, though she was beginning to see flashes of emerald, glimpses of color yet to come. Never driving above fifteen miles per hour, she frequently checked the compass and the map in the dome light.

Rosetta busied herself sewing. Maria marveled at her ability to do it in the dark.

"What are you sewing?" she asked.

"Our money into our clothes. Some of it you can put down your top, but the rest I will hide in a lot of places. If we're bushwhacked, maybe they won't get all of it."

"Bushwhacked?"

"It's a movie word. I like it. It's a holdup."

"You like the movies?"

Rosetta nodded. "Mama and I watched a lot of movies.

She got them in the mail. We watched them together, sometimes with popcorn. Do you know about Indiana Jones? He's an archaeologist like you."

"He's more of a pothunter."

"What's a pothunter?"

"He's someone who takes artifacts out of their context at a site."

Rosetta looked sideways at her. "What does that mean?"

"Archaeologists want to find out about the people who lived in ancient ruins. To do that, we have to study artifacts—the things we dig up—in the place where they are found. Pothunters want the artifacts because they are valuable or pretty. They don't care about what the things meant to the people who made them."

"I'll bet you are a lot of fun at the movies."

Maria laughed. "I like movies. I just have issues with Indiana Jones being called an archaeologist." She paused. "I did enjoy his movies, though. What else did you watch?"

Rosetta put down her sewing and counted on her fingers. "*The Little Mermaid*—that was my favorite. I liked *Cinderella* and *Snow White*. *E.T.* was a little scary, but fun. I liked *The Wizard of Oz*. We watched a lot of cowboys and Indians—they were old movies made in olden times."

"All of those are good movies."

"Mama likes science fiction. Do you?"

"Well, I like mysteries best. But I like adventures, too. I like movies about horses, and I'm a big fan of *Tarzan*."

"*Tarzan*?"

"He was this guy raised by apes in the jungle. Swung on vines, ran with the wild animals. Cool guy."

"You must be having a great time here."

Maria laughed. Rosetta dug out some jerky and a canteen of water from her backpack and shared it with Maria. It was a good, much-needed meal. When Rosetta finished, she took up her sewing again.

"Why don't you get some sleep?" Maria said after another long period of silence.

Rosetta looked up at her, needle in hand.

Maria smiled. "When you finish your project, of course. You said you have clothes for us?"

"I got you a skirt and a shirt like people here wear. You

can put them over your jeans. You need to look a little more like you live here. That's going to be hard. You're tall."

"You've made very detailed plans," Maria said.

"I've been planning a long time. Like E.T., I want to go home."

"Well, like E.T., if we can get our hands on a satellite phone, we can phone home. Maybe one of the villages we pass will have phone service of some kind. If not, the bigger towns and cities will."

"Have you got a plan? Besides the train?"

"If the train doesn't work out, I was hoping we might find some tourists. Right now, I don't know exactly where we are in terms of civilization. Just our location in terms of the map."

Rosetta made a face. "What do you mean? Are we lost?"

"No, not lost. I know the direction I want to go. I just don't know when we will get to a town that has a place we can get help. Most of the places listed on the map seem to be villages. But one of them may have a mission. We have lots of possibilities. We will get home. Don't worry."

"I'm not. Mama said if you have a good plan and carry it out good, you can get what you want. Or something like that. She wasn't talking to me when she said it and I was just a little kid. But I remember stuff. I remember her."

Maria saw her grab the hem of her shirt and hold it in her fist. Strange gesture. Then she realized that Rosetta probably had sewn something up in it. Something that reminded her of her mother, of the home she'd never been to.

Maria's main concern was getting across borders. Particularly into the United States. She had lost her passport in her effort to get away from her attackers, and Rosetta didn't even have one. If she could get to a phone and call John, her boyfriend, or Diane Fallon, they could take care of the problem from their end. At some point soon, she would have to get Rosetta to talk about the man who took her. She had to know which embassy to trust. On the other hand, that was a long time ago and the man was probably long gone.

Rosetta finally put her sewing away and made herself comfortable on the seat. "Tell me a story," she said.

Maria thought about the stories she knew. She knew

a lot of Native American mythology, but she didn't know how entertaining that would be for an eight-year-old.

"You heard of Harry Potter?" Maria asked.

"I've heard of him, but I don't know his story."

"I'll tell it to you. We'll start with *Harry Potter and the Sorcerer's Stone.*"

Maria started the story in her half-croaked, half-whispered voice, of the little boy wizard who lived at number four Privet Drive. She glanced at Rosetta occasionally and watched her as she slowly began to struggle to keep her eyes open.

"I like this story," she said. "I know what it's like to live with people who don't want you."

Maria felt a tug at her heart. She had gotten as far in the story as the letters arriving when she heard the regular breathing of sleep.

Maria drove for four hours before she had to stop for a break. Rosetta was still asleep. She hated to wake her, but if she left Rosetta and she woke up before Maria returned, it would scare her. Maria guessed they were somewhere around sixty miles by way of the road from where she had been held captive. Still too close for her comfort.

The rain forest was an emerald green and the flora was gradually getting thicker. Several times she doubted the wisdom of her decision, particularly when she had to pick her way around a fallen tree. Once she got out to scout a few feet in front of them to make sure the ground was solid. The map indicated a swampy area nearby. They had been lucky so far. The way had been easier than she dared hope.

"Rosetta," she whispered. She gently shook her.

"What? Is something wrong?"

"No, I just have to take a potty break. I didn't want you to wake up and find me gone."

"I'll go with you," she said. "I can help you find a good spot."

Maria took some cloth she had cut from the bolt of material and a gun and let Rosetta lead her to a clearing of sorts away from the trees and they both relieved themselves. On their way back to the truck they heard a muffled thump. Through the trees, Maria saw the truck rock slightly. Someone had found them. She whispered for Maria to hide and she took out her gun.

Chapter 15

Diane stared at the woman for several moments. She and David were not *allowed* to see Simone? Diane noticed that David, the professional pessimist that he was, believing that any bad thing that can happen will, did not look as surprised as she felt.

"May I ask why?" said Diane.

"How dare you! How dare you even come here." The voice was behind them and sounded vaguely like Simone's. "Leave us alone."

Diane and David both turned in the direction of the voice. The nurse also turned, but in a different direction, and busied herself in a file drawer. Standing before them was an older version of Simone. Tall, slim, blond . . . obviously her mother. Two men stood beside and slightly behind her. One was Simone's younger brother, whom Diane had met when he came to visit Simone in South America. He looked like his sister. Strong family genes at play. The other man had graying hair and a dignified air about him. Diane recognized him from a photograph. He was Simone's father. As Diane recalled, Simone didn't get along well with her mother and did not have her picture on display in her bedroom as she did her father's and brother's.

"What is this about?" asked Diane.

"Did you hear me? Leave or I'm calling security. This is your fault. And his." The woman gave David a brief glare. "This is all your fault. Every bit of it."

"Do you know why Simone came here?" said Diane.

"Chester, get the nurse to call security."

"Eileen," he said, in a resigned sort of way, but let whatever else he was going to say drop.

"Please," Pieter, Simone's brother, mouthed to Diane.

Diane was inclined to fold her arms and stay, but however strange Simone's family were acting, they were hurting. And they did have the right to bar anyone they wanted from seeing their daughter.

"Very well," said Diane. "But please understand, we have no idea what this is about."

She and David turned, walked out to David's vehicle, and got in. David didn't immediately start up the Land Rover, but sat quietly staring at the hospital.

"Last week I was a respectable member of the community," said Diane, putting on her seat belt. "Today I'm a drug-dealing whore. What the hell is going on?"

David muttered something like, "I don't know." Diane knew him well enough to know he was working through the problem. As she complained about everything that was happening she stared at the dashboard, which looked like it could have come out of an airplane. She stopped abruptly.

"David, what is all this stuff on your dash?"

"This"—he pointed to a section of buttons and knobs—"detects bugs planted in or on my Rover."

"You are kidding. Have you ever had your vehicle bugged?"

"No, but it would be too late if I waited until it became a problem," he said.

"And this other stuff?" asked Diane.

"If you are going to make fun of everything, I'm not going to tell you. However, I will tell you that some of it can access my computer."

"Really?"

"I have my little inventions I'm working on," he said. "You know how I like to marry algorithms, databases, and gadgets together." He paused for several moments. "I've been accused of dealing in drugs too. Martin Thormond got another call, this one about me. He tried to get the reporter, Brian Mathews, to be more forthcoming, but Mathews refused."

"What is this about?" Diane asked again.

"It has something to do with Simone and what she was doing here," he said.

Diane looked over at him. "Why? Because it's happening at the same time, and you don't like coincidences?"

"No, things happen to us on such a regular basis, we can't rely on simple correlation to be particularly helpful."

Diane smiled and started to disagree, but didn't say anything.

"There's an international news bit I read before we came over here. The executive director of World Accord International has gone on an extended vacation amid accusations of consorting with prostitutes."

"But the executive director is Gregory Lincoln," she said, staring at David. Gregory was their boss when they both worked at WAI, and a good friend.

"Yes. And our experience in South America connects all of us. Someone is trying to discredit and/or kill us." He glanced at the hospital again. "And the big event in all our lives is the massacre."

Diane was quiet for several moments.

"I know," she said. "The bone we found in the backpack belonged to someone from the part of South America we . . . I thought it might be . . ." Diane couldn't finish. She didn't have to. David reached over and grabbed her hand and squeezed.

"What was it Simone said?" said David. "'It was one of us.' It's been haunting me."

"Me too. Look, we know for sure it was Ivan Santos who carried out the massacre. We know why he did it—to get back at us, to stop us. So what did she mean by 'It was one of us'?" said Diane.

"We need to find out," said David. "I'm going to call Gregory. In the meantime, we need to see Garnett. He can speak with Simone's family and Simone herself if she is awake."

"We couldn't even find out how she is," said Diane.

"Garnett can," he said.

They drove to the police station and walked up to the chief of detectives' office. Diane saw people taking surreptitious glances at her, some smirking.

Christ.

Garnett's office was not as ornate as Garnett himself. Not that he actually adorned himself, but he was a sharp dresser. He liked Italian suits and shoes and wore them well. His office, by contrast, was simply utilitarian. It was furnished with faux leather and chrome chairs, a metal desk, and a long maple-wood conference table. On the sand-colored walls he had hung his diplomas, awards, and a few photographs of him shaking hands with various politicians. He also had framed a few newspaper clippings of high-profile cases he had worked on.

Izzy Wallace, one of Diane's crime scene crew, was with Garnett. They were going over a case that Izzy worked last week. They stood as Diane and David entered.

"The two of you have long faces," said Izzy.

"We just came from the hospital," said Diane.

"I hope Miss Brooks hasn't taken a turn for the worst," said Garnett, frowning.

"We don't know," said Diane.

Izzy and David pulled up a couple more chairs and they all sat down. Diane described the reception she and David had received.

"Neither of us knows what that's about," Diane said. "We were hoping you would find out."

"I will be speaking with them this afternoon," said Garnett. "That's very peculiar. They actually barred you from seeing their daughter?"

"Yes," said Diane. She paused a moment. "You may be able to get more out of speaking with Simone's father and brother—alone."

"Gotcha. It's like that, is it?" said Garnett. "I'll take Detective Warrick with me to speak with the wife and I'll talk to the men."

Diane and David went on to tell them about the calls Thormond had received, and the false e-mails about Diane, and the calls made to Frank about her partying while he was away.

"You mean it wasn't really from you?" said Izzy. "And here I thought I got lucky." He grinned at Diane.

"Not you too?" said Diane.

"Me, as well," said Garnett. "If it helps, I knew right away someone had hacked your e-mail." He turned to David. "Can you trace those?"

"Maybe," he said. "We'll see."

"Don't worry about this," Izzy said to Diane. "We'll get to the bottom of it. Most people know it's not you."

"I had a contributor come see me about soliciting her

husband. Not all people understand how e-mails can be hijacked," said Diane.

She and David reluctantly told him about the news story on Gregory Lincoln. They had debated it on the way over. Given their preferences, the two of them would rather handle the whole thing themselves. But they needed help, so they had to be forthcoming.

"Could there be any truth to it?" asked Garnett. "About the Lincoln fellow?"

Both Diane and David shook their heads. "Not Gregory," Diane said.

"You should see his wife," said David. "Look up the most beautiful woman in the world and you'll find a picture of Marguerite. She's also very nice, very intelligent, and very witty. On top of that, she can cook and ride a horse."

"You sound a little infatuated," said Garnett, grinning at David.

"To meet Marguerite is to fall in love with her, even if slightly," David said, completely deadpan.

Diane cocked an eyebrow at him.

"Gotta meet this woman," muttered Izzy. "Can she shoot a gun?"

"Marguerite is nonviolent," said David. "Unless she is in a courtroom, and then her weapons are her sharp wit and keen brain."

Diane and Izzy smiled at each other.

"We are going to contact Gregory and ask him what this is about," said Diane. "He might have some information. He keeps in touch with all of us, and he may know what Simone—"

Diane stopped when Garnett's phone rang. Garnett answered it, listened a moment, then said, "Yes, they are here. I'll tell them, Andie."

Diane realized she hadn't turned her cell phone back on after they left the hospital. Neither had David.

"That was Andie," said Garnett, leaning forward, resting his arms on the desk. "You have a visitor waiting for you. A Gregory Lincoln from London."

Chapter 16

It had been a little over three years since Diane last saw Gregory Lincoln, though she had corresponded with him by e-mail and telephone regularly. He didn't look much older than she remembered, a little grayer maybe. He was dressed casually in a sea green chambray shirt, tan chinos, and brown sports coat.

He grinned broadly and stood up when he saw her. He was being entertained by Andie. The two of them were drinking tea in the comfortable country cottage sitting area of Andie's office. Gregory gave Diane a long hug and kissed her cheek.

"Good to see you, girl," he said.

"Good to see you too, Gregory," she said. "I'm so glad you are here."

Gregory gave David a hug and a slap on the back. "You keeping all the conspirators at bay?"

"You have no idea," said David.

"This is a nice surprise," said Diane to Gregory. "You've had a long trip. I hope you haven't had lunch yet."

She didn't want to get into any unpleasant topics until after they ate. Gregory obviously needed their help.

"Oh, heavens no. Came straight here from the airport," Gregory said.

Diane turned to Andie. "Has the restaurant delivered lunch?"

"Just got here. It's in your sitting room," said Andie.

Gregory loved American cheeseburgers, and the museum's restaurant made great burgers. Diane had called ahead and ordered lunch for the three of them to be sent to her office. Andie had the waitstaff set up the meal on the coffee table between the sofa and two stuffed chairs. The food was covered with stainless-steel dome covers. A pitcher of tea sat amid the serving dishes. Diane removed the covers to a table, poured the tea, and sat down on the sofa. David and Gregory each sat in one of the chairs across from Diane.

"Very nice," said Gregory. "I hope you don't mind my coming early," he said. "And Marguerite sends her regrets. I thought I could do some sightseeing, see what kind of prostitutes you have this side of the pond. Guess you heard that story."

"Yes," said Diane. She looked at David. They were both a little puzzled.

He took a bite of his burger. "This is good. You Yanks are always first class on the burgers. You don't have to put me up. I can stay at the local inn."

"You aren't here about the rumor?" said Diane.

"What? Heavens, no. I've hired detectives to sort that out," said Gregory. "I'm here for the wedding. I realize I'm early ..."

"Actually, they haven't told me when it is," said Diane.

Gregory stopped with his burger halfway to his mouth.

"You are going to have to explain that one," he said.

It was David who did the explaining.

"Diane wants to go to a judge and have it done within five minutes. Vanessa—she's told you about Vanessa—wouldn't hear of it, nor would any of Diane's friends, and they discovered that they didn't really need her cooperation to plan her wedding. I know more about it than Diane does."

Gregory looked from one to the other. "That's not just his peculiar sense of humor, is it? He means it."

"'Fraid so," said Diane, munching on her own cheeseburger.

"So what are they going to do? When it's time, your friends will climb in your window and carry you off? Sounds rather tribal."

"Presumably they will let me know in a reasonable amount of time," she said.

"I see," said Gregory. "Well, should I spoil the surprise?"

"Please do," said Diane.

"You have less than a fortnight to set your affairs in order," he said.

Diane sighed.

"Marguerite would have liked to come. Did I tell you she is pregnant?" he said.

"No," said Diane. "You didn't have to leave her to come to my wedding!"

"Marguerite is rather odd, verging on alien in her approach to pregnancy and childbirth. She prefers to be alone. She won't have family in the delivery room—she barely allows the medical staff. On our first, I was going to be there. You know, cut the cord, bond. She looked at me the way only Marguerite can and told me that I could bond by changing nappies, teaching him cricket, and paying for public school."

"Still," said Diane.

Gregory shook his head. "She told me not to come back until things are sorted out by the detectives and she has killed all the reporters." He looked at his watch. "Tomorrow she'll be having an ultrasound. She told me not to come back at all if it's not a girl. So I may be looking around for a spot of real estate."

Diane smiled. "She doesn't think you . . . ?"

"Consort with prostitutes? Of course not. It's a mystery to me where this came from. WAI has always had its share of the political types taking aim at us, but this is taking it too far—and it appears to be only me."

"We may be able to provide a clue," said Diane. "It's been happening to David and me too."

Gregory stopped eating, put down his burger, and stared at them for a long moment. "The two of you? I didn't expect this." He shook his head. "Is it the same prostitution nonsense? Do you know who is behind the rumors?"

"Apparently I'm the prostitute—no, that's not right. It seems I don't charge. I solicit men through e-mails and we party at my fiancé's house when he's not at home. And both David and I were involved in drug trafficking while we were in South America."

"That's preposterous. Do you have any idea what this is all about?" he asked.

"David has a notion," said Diane.

The two of them told Gregory about the attack at the

museum, about finding Simone, about her parents' re-action this morning. When they finished, Gregory sat openmouthed.

"I'm glad I came early. We will have to get to the bottom of this," he said. "If the two of you were dealing in drugs, then so was I." He shook his head. "Is there anyone else from among our associates to whom this is happening?"

"None of the people I've gotten in touch with are having any problems," said David. "I haven't spoken with every-one yet."

"There is a more disturbing aspect to it," said Diane. She told him what Simone had said before she lapsed into unconsciousness.

"'It was one of us,'" whispered Gregory. "That could mean many things, none of them good."

They discussed all the possibilities that occurred to them, but when everything else was eliminated, they were left with the massacre. That was the biggest event in all their lives.

"I'm going to have to think on this," said Gregory. "For so long I've been trying to put it out of my mind."

"I've been going over the days leading up to the mas-sacre," said David, "trying to remember anything I over-heard, or saw, anything that could have a different meaning from what I placed on it at the time. But ... nothing. I'm just drawing a blank here."

"Maybe if we go over those days, something will jog our memory." Gregory looked over at Diane. "Would that be all right with you?"

Diane nodded.

Andie poked her head in. "I know you don't want to be disturbed, but I have two things. First, I contacted Frank, and it is okay for you to invite Mr. Lincoln to stay at the house." She grinned. "See what a good assistant I am? I anticipated that you would want Mr. Lincoln to stay with you, but you would need to ask Frank. Now it's all taken care of."

Diane smiled. "Indeed you are a good assistant, Andie. Thanks. What's the other thing?"

"Garnett is on the phone and would like to speak with you."

Chapter 17

Diane reached for the phone on the end table beside the sofa. Garnett and Janice Warrick had been on their way to interview the Brooks when she and David headed back to the museum to meet Gregory. She was eager to hear what Garnett had discovered. David put down his food and leaned forward, his forearms resting on his knees.

"Garnett," she said into the phone.

"We spoke with the family," he said. "Interesting. *Controlling* doesn't begin to describe the mother. She tried to stop me from having separate interviews with the father and brother. I thought for a moment Janice was going to handcuff her. Bottom line is they got a call from someone who said he was a friend of Simone at the detective agency where she works. The caller told them that Simone was working on something at your request and that it had to do with covering up things you and David were involved in during your time in South America."

"That's not true," said Diane. She felt her face flush, felt the need to defend herself when no defense should be needed. "Damn. What is this about?"

"Mrs. Brooks was adamant about blaming you for her daughter's condition," said Garnett.

"What is her condition?" asked Diane.

"She's in a coma. The doctors have no idea when or if she will come out of it."

"Poor Simone," whispered Diane.

"The brother, Pieter, said he didn't believe the caller. For one thing, his sister wouldn't go along with any kind of cover-up. His father agreed. And second, Pieter likes you and David."

"Did they have any idea what Simone was investigating?"

"Pieter told me Simone had finally opened some of her dead fiancé's effects a couple of months ago. Apparently it would have been their anniversary had he lived. He was killed in that massacre your . . ."

He didn't say *your daughter*. Most everyone still tiptoed around Diane about Ariel. She was glad they did. She only talked about her with people she was especially close to.

"Yes," said Diane, "Oliver was killed at the mission. As you can imagine, Simone was devastated. As were we all."

"Pieter said she found something among the fiancé's effects that got her all worked up. She wouldn't say what it was. But whatever it was made her *determined*—was the word he used. He said at first she seemed puzzled by what she had found, but after a while developed a sense of outrage."

"And he had no clue what it was?" said Diane. "He has such detail about her emotions throughout her discovery process. How did he know? They must have discussed something."

"I asked him just that. He said she told him she discovered some information and things she didn't understand. She wouldn't tell him what it was. He said that his sister tended to be secretive. I noticed he was embarrassed, and I pushed. His sister didn't really trust him with information that she thought their mother would dig out of him. I got the idea that Pieter is a bit of a mama's boy. Simone trusted her brother, I think, but only to a point."

"I see," said Diane. "I wonder if the things we found in the museum were from the box of Oliver's effects. If they were from Simone. I've assumed they were, but I don't know. Can we examine Oliver's effects?" asked Diane.

"I asked," said Garnett. "Pieter has no idea where they are. Apparently his sister is as good at hiding things as she is at keeping secrets. Janice told me the mother bought into the caller's story. She wanted me to arrest you and David."

"I wonder why she was so quick to believe some stranger over the phone?" said Diane.

"The father said that when Simone visited them during the holidays—when she was living in South America—all she could talk about was how she admired you and your work. Her mother was jealous of that. She wanted her daughter away from that place and job and she saw you as keeping her daughter there."

Diane sighed. "I had no idea. Thanks, Garnett. I was hoping for more answers than questions, though."

"Me too. I'll keep you in the loop. You do the same," he said.

The last sounded more like a warning. Diane thought he was probably afraid that she, David, and now Gregory would keep information to themselves. *And we would if we could*, she thought.

"I will," Diane said.

Diane hung up and turned her attention to David and Gregory, telling them what she had learned from Garnett.

"I talked with Simone a lot when we worked together," said Gregory. "Did you know she once had a sister?"

"No, I didn't," said Diane.

David shook his head. "Neither did I."

"Phoebe was her name. She was a bit older than Simone. She was a first child and all. When she was five she ran into the road and was hit by a lorry. Simone's mother had a tendency to be controlling before then, but after the accident it got so much worse. Her father, I think, used up all his energy dealing with the grief. He had none left to disagree with his wife's raising of the surviving children. At least, that was my take on him."

"That's a sad story," said Diane. "You can't blame her for wanting to hold on tightly to her other children."

"Perhaps," said Gregory. "But the ugly side of me notices that she now has complete control over Simone. Something she has never had, even when Simone was young."

Diane took Gregory home with her. Frank was bringing Thai from one of his favorite restaurants. David wanted to stay at his office and continue trying to find the people they worked with in South America and shake loose their memories. Not a pleasant activity for anyone, but Diane hoped David would find something that would help them understand.

"You Americans like your four-by-fours," said Gregory. "Does this one drive well?"

"I like it," said Diane. "Unfortunately, I've gone through several. Perps seem to like to take aim at my vehicles."

"Really? You deal with perpetrators? I would think the detectives did that."

"They do," said Diane. "I've just had a lot of bad luck."

"Obviously you are well thought of," said Gregory.

"Until I started dealing drugs and being loose around men," said Diane.

Gregory gave a short laugh. "Nice cottage," he said as he spotted Frank's Queen Anne–style house through the stand of trees. "Is this where you are going to live after you are married?"

"Yes, we are. I like it, and Frank has lived here for a long time."

Frank was already home when they entered. Diane could smell the Thai food warming. He greeted them in the entryway with glasses of wine.

"So good to meet you," said Gregory. "Diane has told me a lot about you. Must be a good chap if Diane likes you."

"And I've heard a lot about you. Your diplomatic sensibilities have had a good effect on her," said Frank.

He led them into the living room while the food warmed. They sat down and talked about the upcoming wedding that Diane knew so little about. After a while, Gregory leaned forward, taking a packet of papers out of his coat pocket.

"This is as good a time as any. I have a wedding gift for you, Diane." Gregory's voice cracked a little as he spoke. "At the time I got them, well, I couldn't give them to you. But I asked Marguerite about it and she said now it would be all right. She said it would break your heart, but you would still like to have them. Marguerite is good about these things." He handed Diane the papers.

Diane opened the enveloped as Frank looked on. She shook when she saw what it was. Frank put an arm around her shoulder.

Ariel's adoption papers.

Diane pressed them against her heart and tears flowed down her cheeks. Her lips trembled and she couldn't speak.

"They came the day of the massacre. As you know, we were out in the field. I was keeping them until that evening where I was going to surprise you and we were going to celebrate. Well, ahem." He cleared his throat. "You know what we found at the mission that evening. It seemed too cruel to give them to you then. But I thought you ought to have them. Forgive me if I overstepped."

It was several moments before Diane found her voice, and then it was a whisper.

"Marguerite was right."

Chapter 18

Maria stood just out of sight of the truck. She parted the large leaves and peeked at the vehicle. She saw no one, but the truck had a subtle erratic sway that was puzzling. She whispered for Rosetta to stay hidden and she moved closer, holding tightly to the gun.

As she watched the truck, a mottled green and black ribbon of enormous proportions undulated just above the sides of the truck bed and disappeared.

"Oh, no," she said in her pained, whiskey-sounding voice. "Not this."

She looked up and saw that she had parked under a low limb of a tree.

"Why did I do that?" she whispered to herself.

Rosetta came up beside her and she jumped.

"Sorry," Rosetta whispered. "I heard you talking. What is it?"

"A snake. A really, really big snake."

Rosetta's eyes got wide. She stood on her tiptoes and tried to get a look. "What kind?"

"My guess, from the size and color, a female anaconda," said Maria. "You know, I'm just not good with snakes."

Rosetta gave her a sideways glance. "Indiana Jones said the same thing."

Maria thought she detected a bit of smugness in Rosetta's voice.

"Stay right here." Maria took a fortifying breath and walked toward the truck, getting just close enough to see into it. A gigantic snake, bigger around than Maria's leg, perhaps bigger around than her waist, and longer than the truck, filled the bed of the pickup, coiling over and covering the cargo of food and supplies. It was olive green with markings of darker green, black, and yellow. Colors of the rainbow glinted off its scales. Its wedge-shaped head looked as big as a football. Its forked purple-black tongue licked out at least a foot into the air in front of its nose. If it weren't so horrific, it would be beautiful.

"Pick me up so I can see." Rosetta tugged on Maria's sleeve.

Maria jumped again. "I thought I told you to stay a safe distance."

"I'll be okay. I want to see."

Maria picked her up so she could see into the bed of the truck.

"Wow," Rosetta said. "That is a big one. It is called a yakumama. I have never seen one this big."

Maria put her down on the ground but held on to her hand, fearful that the little girl would run up to the bed of the truck for a closer look.

"Do you know how to get a snake out of a truck?" asked Maria.

Rosetta shrugged elaborately.

"Have you ever seen anyone with this problem?" she asked.

Rosetta shook her head. "Mostly we just leave them alone. Some people catch them, but I don't know how they do it. You don't want to make it mad."

Maria picked up Rosetta and carried her to the cab of the truck and put her inside, climbed in after her, closed the door, and rolled up the window. She sat tapping the steering wheel with her index finger.

"Maybe I can get a loop around it, tie the other end to a tree and ease forward, and she will slide out," she said, mostly to herself.

"You going to get back there and put a rope around it?" asked Rosetta, who had turned around and was watching the snake.

Maria turned and looked out the back glass.

"It's unlikely," she said.

"You could offer it something to eat," said Rosetta.

"Like what?"

"I know they like birds, and fish, and deer."

"Don't have any of those," said Maria. "Oh, well, what the heck."

She opened the door and jumped out of the cab of the truck.

"Stay here. I mean it."

She walked softly to the back of the truck, opened the tailgate, and ran back to the cab, jumped in, and slammed the door shut. She let herself have one good shiver and started the truck.

"Get down on the floor," she told Rosetta.

Rosetta slid off the seat and squatted, hugging her backpack.

"What are you going to do?" She looked at Maria, wide-eyed.

Maria didn't answer. She moved the truck forward and stopped abruptly, then did the same thing in reverse several times.

"You are going to make her sick or mad," said Rosetta.

Maria stopped and put her head down on her arms.

"I really don't like snakes," she said. "I'm going to dream about this the rest of my life."

"Mama isn't afraid of snakes," said Rosetta, climbing back onto the seat.

Maria raised her head and smiled at the little girl. "What would she do?"

Rosetta shrugged again. "I don't know. I guess she would just say, well, we have a snake."

"It appears that we do," said Maria. "I suppose it will leave sooner or later. It isn't going to want to live in the back of our truck. I hope."

Maria checked the gas gauge. They had a little over a quarter of a tank. The truck was equipped with spare tanks on the side of the bed for extra gas. A necessity when gas stations were rare. The tanks were full. *Lucky*, Maria thought, more than once. She could keep driving now, but soon she was going to have to put more gas in the main tank. And that would require working around the snake if it didn't move on.

"Isn't it funny that, just a little while ago, you were telling me about the snake in the Harry Potter story?" said Rosetta.

"Yes, very funny," said Maria as she navigated the truck along the primitive road.

"Wouldn't it be fun if we could understand her language?" Rosetta said. She had turned in the seat and was now on her knees looking at the anaconda.

"It would. Then I could politely ask her to leave," said Maria.

"Tell me some more of the story," said Rosetta, settling back into her seat.

Talking wasn't helping Maria's voice any, but it was helping Rosetta, so Maria picked up on the story where Rosetta said she last remembered. As the story unfolded, Maria kept one eye on the gas gauge and the other on the animal trail that passed for the road they were traveling on . . . with quick glances into the rearview mirror to watch for any movement of their new passenger.

When the needle on the gauge got into the red, Maria stopped the truck and looked out the back window. They still had their ride-along. Maria turned to Rosetta.

"The truck needs gas. I need to put some in the tank before it gets too dark."

"The snake won't eat you. You're too big," said Rosetta. "I don't think it will."

Small comfort.

"You could try talking to her," said Rosetta.

"I'll give it a try," said Maria.

She got out of the truck and walked over to the nearest spare gas tank. She peeked in the back of the truck. Partially under the snake, who had curled up in apparent comfort, there was a hose that Maria guessed was used to siphon the gas.

"Don't you need to be near water?" Maria said to the snake.

The snake paid no attention to her.

Maria spotted Rosetta in the rear window. Her lips were moving, but Maria couldn't hear her. She wasn't sure, but she thought the little girl was saying Hail Marys.

Maria watched the snake as she moved her hand toward a part of the hose that was clear. She grasped the hose and gently began to pull. The snake moved her head around and flicked her wet, glistening tongue toward Maria.

"Oh, shit," said Maria. "Look, snake, I just want to put gas in the truck."

Maria had read up on jungle predators before she came. Anacondas weren't the most dangerous of animals, but on the other hand, it was not a good idea to provoke one. And, though they were not poisonous, they did have a mouth full of teeth that held on to their prey better than fishhooks.

Maria freed a loop of the hose and backed off. She had an idea. She went back to the cab of the truck and got a rope that she'd discovered behind her seat. It wasn't in good condition, but she thought it would do the job.

She had to steel herself before she could go out again. All she could think about was those teeth latching on to her and that huge body coiling around her, squeezing the life out of her.

"Gotta do it," she whispered, got out and walked to the side of the truck.

Slowly and carefully she tied one end of the rope to the hose, never taking her eyes off the snake. The snake writhed slowly and silently. Maria hurried. When she had tied the rope to the hose as tightly as she could, she climbed back in the cab with the other end of the rope and began to pull the hose free from under the snake.

The anaconda's writhing became more agitated.

Damn, she thought. The only thing worse than a giant snake in the truck was a giant *mad* snake in the truck.

"Okay," she said. "We aren't completely out of gas; we can do this in stages. Give the girl a chance to calm down." At least she had the rope and hose.

Maria started the truck engine and drove, watching the needle on the gas gauge. The trail was getting narrower and the jungle thicker. She was wondering if it was a mistake to have come this way. Should they have followed one of the other roads and simply abandoned the truck near a village? Just be travelers on foot?

Still, people did use this route. The path was too wide to be only an animal path. There were ruts and old tire tracks. She kept going, but more slowly.

There was a branch hanging low over the road ahead. She wished the anaconda would take the opportunity to climb onto it.

She drove cautiously under the branch, the motion of the truck pushing it up and over the windshield . . . and came face-to-face with a man standing in the road pointing a gun at them.

Chapter 19

Sleep came easily for Diane. She drifted off without the tossing and turning of the past few nights. The adoption papers meant more to her than she could have known they would. Ariel had always been her daughter in her heart. She never thought of her in any other way. To other people, especially the authorities, the papers showed that Ariel was officially her daughter. And though what they thought didn't really matter, it somehow did. Strangely, it brought her some peace. Maybe in a few months Diane could do something she hadn't been able to do before—give Ariel a memorial service.

Diane and Frank made Gregory a breakfast of eggs, pancakes, sausage, and fresh fruit salad. After Frank left for Atlanta, Diane and Gregory headed for the museum.

"What do you think is going on?" Diane asked Gregory as they pulled out of Frank's driveway.

"I'm not sure. I think you and David are right—it hinges on Simone. That thing she said bothers me a bit."

"David and I have this awful feeling that one of our group was involved in something bad."

"You say the objects were in some sort of woven fabric handbag soaked in a drug?" asked Gregory.

Diane nodded. "XTR25. It's a new variant of ecstasy, according to Neva. I expect the DEA to interview me anytime now. This is just a nightmare for the museum."

Gregory looked over at her and smiled. "Can't be too pleasant for you personally, either," he said. "We'll sort it out. We'll follow the clues, like always. Does David still have his talent for getting into databases?"

"Of course," said Diane. "It's like a compulsion for him."

"Good. That may serve us well. We need to do a background check on all of the people on our team," he said.

Diane looked over at him, frowning.

"I know. I share your distaste for spying on them," Gregory said, "but I don't see we have a choice. We'll particularly look for movements of large amounts of money. Money itself, not simply the love of it, really is the root of all evil. Especially these days when there is so much of it to be made from doing bad things."

"I know that. Still . . . ," said Diane.

"They are our friends. I understand," said Gregory. "But something is going on and we have to find out what it is."

He took a notebook from his pocket and began writing. Diane knew he was listing the names of all the people they had worked with in South America—the interviewers, the crime scene personnel, Diane's assistants. It was not a short list. Most of them had survived the massacre because they had been in the field with Diane.

Others, like Oliver Hill, Simone's fiancé, were in the mission when it was attacked. They were support personnel who had administrative duties, handled paperwork. They were all casualties, and they'd had the least dangerous jobs.

"Do you have an office I can use?" asked Gregory.

"Yes, I'll have David set you up," said Diane. "Knowing David, he already has one set up."

"Oh, good. I'll get to be M to his Q, then," he said.

"Be careful what you wish for," said Diane.

"How is David doing?" Gregory asked.

"Good," said Diane. "Often remarkable."

"That's good to hear. I did worry about everyone," he said, almost to himself.

"None of it was your fault either," said Diane. "I think we all blamed ourselves for not seeing some warning. But in truth, there was none."

"I've turned my memories over and over looking for a sign I might have missed. There was nothing in the intelligence I was getting. I tracked Ivan Santos constantly while we were working there. He was always well away from us." Gregory shook his head. "But there was obviously something I missed—something that Simone or Oliver turned up. We will have to find it."

"Who did Simone confide in?" asked Diane.

"Unfortunately, the people she was close to—Oliver, Sister Katherine, Marta—were all killed."

"No best friends here in the United States?" asked Diane.

"Friends, yes. However, she said to me that none of them understood her choice of career. I don't believe she would have confided in them. Family either."

"How are we going to find out what she discovered?" asked Diane as she turned onto Museum Road.

"With luck, we'll ask her when she is able," said Gregory.

The huge multistoried granite structure had come into view.

"My goodness," he said. "This place never fails to impress. It's a palace compared to my not insubstantial offices."

"We're very fortunate. It suits us well and we have a lot of room to grow," said Diane as she pulled into a parking space.

Diane and Gregory climbed the steps and were let in by the security guards on duty. They took the private elevator down to the restricted part of the basement where the DNA lab was located and where David had his own private office and research space.

"You gave him a lab, did you?" said Gregory.

"I did. And he's done some interesting things," said Diane, laughing.

"Indeed, has he? I can't wait," said Gregory.

David was just coming out of the DNA lab when the elevator doors opened.

"I have you an office set up," said David.

"That was fast," said Gregory. "Did you sleep last night?"

"Enough," said David.

David led them first into his own inner sanctum, a cave-like room lined with books and computers, with a darkroom through one door. David taught photography courses, the old-fashioned way, as well as digital, for the museum on occasion. And for that, Diane had given him office space in the basement that was undergoing renovations. Like the proverbial camel, David had, inch by inch, claimed more space. And he had put it to good use.

David opened one of the other doors and stood back for Diane and Gregory.

"Good God," exclaimed Gregory upon entering.

He had come face-to-face with the enormous mandibles of a spider.

"That's Arachnid," said David.

"No kidding. What a screen saver," Gregory said.

"He means the program," said Diane. "It's one of David's pet projects, and quite secret. There are only a handful of us who know of its existence."

Gregory glanced over at David and narrowed his eyes. "Taking this secrecy thing a bit seriously, aren't you? What does it do?"

"David has combined web image search with facial recognition software," answered Diane. "At least that's what it did the last time we used it. He's been tinkering with it."

"You have to admit that it worked quite well," said David.

"Yes, it did," said Diane. "The problem is, when we find anything useful, we have to figure out what other way we could have come by the information so we can keep his secret."

Gregory shook his head. "David, I'd forgotten how much I have missed you." He chuckled. "Isn't this a bit of Big Brother? Must cause you a bit of a split in your conscience."

"I do have a lot of guilt over it," he said.

And Gregory laughed again at his seriousness.

"I have you an office here." David opened another door.

This room had two computers with printers, a couple of telephones, a fax machine, an oak desk and office chair, and a large flat-screen television. Two stuffed chairs sat in the corner with a small table between them.

"I could rule the world from here," said Gregory.

"Not yet," said David.

Just as Gregory looked at him to see if he was joking, Diane's cell rang. It was Andie.

"There's these two DEA agents for you," she said. "I have them here in my office."

"Offer them coffee. I'll be right up," she said and flipped the phone closed.

Chapter 20

Diane sat at her desk. The two DEA agents, Stewart and Bailey, sat in the stuffed leather chairs in front of her desk, looking a lot like the Men in Black. Diane expected more of an L.L.Bean kind of look—casual jacket with DEA patch and maybe Dockers.

There were subtle differences in the expressions on their faces—one countenance looking vaguely sympathetic, the other looking vaguely bad cop-ish.

So this was not a law-enforcement-professional-to-professional visit. It was to be an interview with someone they considered a person of interest—her. Diane relaxed in her chair and picked up a pencil. Gregory once gave her that bit of advice. He told her that you can sometimes acquire a psychological edge by putting a desk between you and them and trifling with a pencil. "In Western cultures," he had said, "it's subconsciously associated with authority figures such as teachers, principals, doctors, psychiatrists, and lawyers."

Diane put on her best "I'm your teacher" face and rubbed the pencil between her palms.

"How can I help you?" she said.

If they were intimidated, they didn't show it.

"Do you know why we are here?" said the slightly good agent, Bailey.

"No," said Diane.

"Really?" said the slightly bad agent, Stewart. "You have no clue?"

"Why don't you fill me in?" she said, steepling her hands in front of her with the pencil between them.

"We're here about the drugs found in the museum," said Stewart.

"There were no drugs found in the museum," said Diane. "There was a cloth bag with drug residue, which we discovered and reported. My criminalist, Neva Hurley, contacted your department about it."

"Residue," said Stewart. "Is that how you would describe it?"

"I've seen the report and, yes, that is how I would describe it," said Diane.

"Are you aware that soaking fabric in a liquid version of a drug is one way of smuggling it into the United States?" said Bailey.

"I have heard of that method, yes," said Diane.

"We understand you were involved in drugs while you were in South America," said Stewart.

"No," said Diane, "I was not."

Stewart raised his eyebrows. "That is not the information we received."

"Your information is false," said Diane easily.

"You don't seem to be curious as to where we got the information," said Bailey.

"One of my board members received a call recently from a travel reporter from the *AJC* asking about something of the sort. In addition, someone hacked my e-mail account and sent romantic assignation requests to many of the male board members, museum contributors, and members of the Rosewood Police Department. An anonymous person called my fiancé and told him I entertain men at his home when he is gone. I have no idea where this blitzkrieg of slander is coming from, nor why. However, I have people looking into it. I assume that whatever information you received came from the same malicious source."

Diane sat back in her chair, trying to maintain the impression that she was completely comfortable. She had to make an effort to keep her face blank and free of emotion when, in fact, she hated this.

"Why did you say you didn't know why we're here?" asked Stewart. "We are from the DEA. Drugs were found in the museum. You know of the accusation against you."

"No, you misstate the situation. Drug residue was found on an object some unknown person brought into the museum and was connected with the attack on the museum that is currently under investigation by the Rosewood Police Department. As to the answer to your question, if your interest had been about the fabric bag, I just assumed you would have gone to Chief Garnett, who is in charge of the investigation, or to the crime lab, but certainly not to the museum to discuss it. All the files related to the analysis are in the crime lab. The crime lab is under the purview of the City of Rosewood, not the museum."

They hesitated a moment too long and Diane continued.

"Since you began by questioning me as if you had stopped me for running a red light, I had no idea what you wanted."

"The drug found in the bag is particularly bad. It has been knocking around Asia and Europe for about four years and is just now making its way into the United States," said Bailey. "We are concerned that some found its way to you. Add that to the, ah, information we received about your time in South America. Well, you can see our interest."

"I'm sure you received no more than the barest hint of rumor about me. There is simply no information to be had unless someone made it up. I had no drug dealings in South America whatsoever, not on either side of the law."

"Weren't you trying to apprehend a man who was known to deal in the drug trade?" asked Stewart.

"No," said Diane. "We weren't trying to apprehend anyone. We knew where Ivan Santos was. We were gathering evidence of human rights violations—mass murders, in particular. We had no interest in what other criminal activity he was involved in."

The two of them looked briefly at each other and Diane could barely resist asking them if they had done this before.

"Do you have any idea why someone might be trying to ruin your reputation?" asked Bailey.

Stewart shot him an irritated glance. Diane supposed he thought that Bailey was letting her off the hook.

"None whatsoever. If you received one of these calls, I was hoping you could track it down, if only to get more information about me."

"She's in a meeting."

Andie's voice outside her door brought all their heads around. The door opened and Edmond Carstairs walked in with a bouquet of flowers. Diane dropped her pencil and put her head in her hand for a moment.

"I'm sorry, Dr. Fallon," said Andie.

"Diane, dear, I won't interrupt you long. . . ."

"Mr. Carstairs," said Diane. "I didn't send you any e-mail. Someone hijacked my account and sent those terrible e-mails to everyone, and I'm sorry about the inconvenience. Please, let Andie show you what you can do with those lovely flowers."

"But . . . ," he began.

"In fact," said Diane, "these gentlemen from Homeland Security are going to help discover who is behind this dreadful misunderstanding."

"Mr. Carstairs," said Andie, taking his arm, "please come with me. I'll explain everything."

Andie managed to steer him out and close the door. Diane sat back and rubbed her hands down her face.

"If you find the person who is fueling the drug rumor, I'm betting it will be the same person who is behind the other rumors. I can't have acquired two stalkers at the same time. I don't think it was the reporter, but he probably knows who his source is. If you find out who it is, give me some time alone with him."

Bailey managed a small smile. Stewart appeared to not know what to think.

"Gentlemen," said Diane, "I will be glad to share any information I have through Chief Garnett. The details of the evidence we process in the crime lab are not mine to share, even though the incident under investigation happened here in the museum. I'm not trying to be difficult, but rather, trying not to step on any Rosewood toes. As for any questions you have about me personally, at this point I know very little about what is going on. I know a great deal about what I did in South America. None of it involved drugs."

They glanced briefly at each other. Diane could see they weren't satisfied, but she could also see they hadn't collected enough information before they questioned her. She bet it was a last-minute decision. They had already spoken with Garnett and were going to the crime lab and got the idea they would surprise her. But they didn't have enough information to carry out a thorough interview and now they would be kicking themselves all the way back to Atlanta. Or they wouldn't go to Atlanta—they would try to interview Simone and speak with her parents. Garnett must not have filled them in on his interview with Simone's parents or they would have asked her what job Simone was doing for her. Next time they came back, they would be better prepared, maybe, but it still would be with erroneous information.

They left and Diane was about to call Andie in to see what she had done with Edmond Carstairs and his flowers when her in-house line rang. It was the groundskeepers. They had found a body.

Chapter 21

The man standing in the road pointing the gun at them was heavyset with a black beard and hair. His worn, disheveled khaki clothes drooped from his sagging shoulders and under his bulging belly and he dripped in sweat. Another man similarly dressed but with less hair and less beer belly stood off to the side. He also had a gun, but at least it was not aimed at them.

Bandits.

They would steal everything, possibly including their lives. Maria slammed on the brakes. She told Rosetta to get down on the floor. The little girl slid off the seat and snuggled up to her backpack. Maria put a hand on the gun beside her, glanced at the little face looking up at her from the floor, and stiffened her resolve.

The bandit kept the gun pointed at Maria and began walking toward the truck. The other man was edging toward the other side of the vehicle.

Was Rosetta's door locked? She must have telegraphed her concern with her eyes, for the little girl's hand snaked up and hit the lock on the door.

Maria gripped the gun and kept a frightened look on her face—which wasn't hard. Perhaps if the man saw she was afraid, he wouldn't think her a threat. He wouldn't be alert. She could beat him.

The second bandit walked around to the passenger side. Whereas the first bandit, with his squinted eyes and the rigid set of his mouth, had the look of someone focused on a task, the second one grinned as if witnessing a joke. He muttered something to his partner.

"He said, 'We got two scared birds.' And something

I didn't hear," Rosetta whispered. "I don't think it was good."

Maria could see in his face that he was someone who enjoyed scaring his victims. She switched the gun to her left hand to hide it from view between her door and her seat. The second bandit tried Rosetta's door. It was locked. He said something in Spanish again and moved away toward the rear.

The first bandit closed in on her. He held the gun up to the window and motioned for her to open the door. She tried rehearsing in her head how she was going to counter him, but she couldn't make anything work. There wasn't enough time to think.

He jerked the door. It was locked. He pointed the gun at her and yelled.

"He wants you to open the door," said Rosetta.

I'm sure he does, Maria thought. She put her hand on the door handle and hesitated. She was going to shoot as soon as the door cleared his body. She flipped the lock with her thumb.

He jerked the door open partway and then slammed it back hard against her hand, causing Maria to drop the gun. He opened the door again and grabbed at her, pulling her out. She fell to the ground and reached for the gun with her other hand. He kicked it under the truck and aimed his at her head. He was going to shoot, she saw it in his eyes.

Damn it, if she was going to die, it would be fighting. She was about to grab for his legs when a scream startled them both. The bandit turned his head toward the second man and Maria rolled under the truck and grabbed her gun. She shot the first bandit in the foot. He yelled and fell to his knees. She shot again, hitting him in the thigh. His hand with the gun appeared under the truck as she scrambled toward the front. He pulled the trigger and the sound was loud in the confined area, but she was out of the way. She moved quickly from under the truck. Dirt and plant matter scratched her face and got in her mouth. She ignored the discomfort.

The screaming coming from the second bandit continued.

The first one yelled something, but all Maria could make out was "*la niña*."

That was enough. With the driver's door open, Rosetta was exposed.

Maria hurried. Crouching, she moved around from the front to the driver's side, where the bandit was aiming his gun inside toward Rosetta.

Maria didn't hesitate. She fired the gun, hitting him in the head.

The second bandit was still yelling. She heard what he was saying now. It was something about his arm being eaten. She wished she had learned more Spanish. Any Mississippian archaeologist worth her salt should learn Spanish, she thought. Why the heck had she learned German?

She eased past the dead bandit, past the driver's door toward the rear of the truck. The problem of getting the snake out of the bed of the truck was solved. The anaconda was on the ground, wrapping its gigantic slithering body in a tightening coil around the fallen second bandit.

The strike of the anaconda is lightning fast. They aren't poisonous, but they have teeth curved back so that when they bite it is like fishhooks locking on and digging into the flesh. The snake's mouth now held the man's bare forearm in what could fairly be called a death grip. He no longer held the gun, and his hand was useless.

"*Mi brazo*," he mewled over and over again.

Maria looked at him a moment, remembering his expression as he leered at her and Rosetta.

"*Ayúdame, por favor, ayúdame*," he cried.

She closed the tailgate of the truck and walked back to the driver's side. She grabbed the first bandit's gun off the ground, but she didn't search him for items they could use. She didn't have the stomach for it. She climbed in the truck and closed the door.

"Are you all right?" she asked Rosetta, who was climbing into the seat.

Rosetta nodded her head.

"He must not have seen the snake when he jumped in the back of the truck," said Rosetta. "You already made her mad. He just made her madder."

"Evidently," said Maria. "He probably made the mistake of pointing his gun at her."

She started the truck and sped away as fast as the trail would allow. She didn't look in the rearview mirror.

"You feel bad?" said Rosetta.

"How many people have I killed? Four?" muttered Maria.

"One. Just that bad man back there. He was going to shoot me. The others were alive when we left them," said Rosetta.

Maria gave her a grim smile.

She tried to empty her mind of the events. She was doing what had to be done. She was struggling to survive. She had to get Rosetta back to her mother.

After five minutes of driving in silence, rounding a curve she came face-to-face with an abandoned truck not too different from theirs. The hood was up and the engine was steaming. Probably the bandits, she thought. Probably why they were on foot. She drove slowly through the brush around the truck, not stopping.

The trail got better and worse at the same time. The road grew wider, the jungle got thicker. Fronds grew out over the road and brushed the top of the vehicle. Maria worried that it would become too thick and the trail would peter out and disappear and they would have to walk.

She drove on.

Rosetta reached over and touched her arm.

"I did bad things. All I wanted to do was find Mama, so I sometimes did bad things."

Maria squeezed her hand. "I don't imagine you did anything too bad," she said.

"At St. Anne's when we did bad things we had to do penance. I think Mama is sometimes a Presbyterian. I don't think they do penance. I hope she's still a Presbyterian."

Maria smiled at her. "What kind of penance would you have to do? You were so young."

"Sister Alice or Father Joe made us work in the garden or help wash dishes. Sometimes Father Joe did penance with us. He said when we did bad things maybe it was his fault for not teaching us better. When Mama was there I never did penance. She just talked to me."

They had come to a narrow bridge over a creek. Maria slowed down and stopped. She got out of the truck and walked over to examine the bridge. The creek was only ten feet or so wide and it was shallow. The bridge, not large, was built of wood that was worn. It had been patched many times in haphazard ways. Maria got the feeling it had been fixed by whoever had to go over it at the time it was in disrepair.

She walked across it, stamping on the boards. They creaked but appeared strong. There was no railing. The bridge was wide enough for the truck, but just. She turned to go back. Rosetta was watching her from the front window. Maria grinned and waved at her.

"Is it strong enough?" asked Rosetta when Maria climbed in.

"I believe so." She patted the little girl on the leg. "Don't worry. Tell me more about the mission where you stayed. It sounds like it was a good place."

"It was nice. There were always kids to play with. The sisters took care of a lot of people," Rosetta said. She stretched up in the seat, looking at the bridge. "I'll wait until we are across the bridge to tell you about them."

"It won't take long," Maria said. "It's a short ride. Would you like to walk across and wait?"

Rosetta shook her head vigorously. "I'll stay with you."

Maria approached the bridge slowly. She told herself that it was at least the width of a parking space. She could make that. The bridge immediately groaned from the weight of the front wheels but she didn't stop. She listened for sounds of cracking, reminding herself they had to go only a few feet, and if it fell in, the creek was not deep. Of course, they would be without transportation.

She pressed the gas pedal and drove the rest of the way at a quicker clip, exhaling when they were on firm ground. From the rearview mirror she saw that it was still intact. Drama over nothing, she thought.

Rosetta looked relieved as she peered out the back window. "We didn't make the crocodile mad this time," she said.

Chapter 22

The body had been pulled up on the bank.

Not a good procedure for an agency with a crime scene unit on-site, thought Diane.

She saw David and two of the groundskeepers standing over the body. They turned toward her as she approached. Diane was still fifteen feet away when she recognized the body—the gray hair, charcoal skirt, and rose blouse. She stopped and put a hand over her heart. Her stomach turned over.

Dear God. It's Madge Stewart.

David said something to the groundskeepers and walked over to her.

"What happened?" she asked.

"Right now it looks like she fell into the pond. No obvious evidence of foul play. The gardeners found her. They thought she might be alive. That's why they pulled her out," he said.

"Of course. How long?" Diane asked, still staring at the body, hoping it wasn't there, that she was seeing things.

"Not long," said David. "Perhaps an hour. One of the gardeners saw her drinking a glass of tea on the restaurant patio about an hour and a half before they found her."

Diane put her hands on her face. She and Madge weren't the best of friends, but Madge was a member of her board.

"You handle this," Diane said.

"I thought I would," said David. "I'm sorry. This is a shocker."

Diane nodded her head. *Poor Madge*, thought Diane. *She loved her life*. Diane heard people approaching. She turned, half expecting gawkers from the museum, but it was the medical examiner, Lynn Webber, and the coroner, Whit Abercrombie. Diane saw Chief Garnett several feet behind them walking at a catch-up pace.

Lynn Webber was several inches shorter than Diane's five feet nine. She had shiny short black hair that always looked as if she just left the beauty shop. She wore a white lab coat over her clothes, and expensive hiking boots.

Whit Abercrombie, a taxidermist by trade, had been the coroner of Rose County for several years. He had wanted to quit several times, but people always talked him out of it. They, like Diane, appreciated Whit's apolitical, logical approach to his job. He was a striking-looking man with straight black hair, dark eyes, bright white teeth, and a neatly trimmed Vandyke beard.

The two of them eyed Diane for a moment.

"Is this someone you know?" asked Lynn, frowning.

"It's Madge Stewart," Diane said.

"Oh, no," said Lynn, laying a hand on Diane's arm. "I'm so sorry. I met her a couple of times. She loved the museum, didn't she?"

"Oh jeez," said Garnett. He and Whit shook their heads.

"What happened?" Whit asked.

"On the face of it, it looks as if she slipped in and drowned," said Diane, and David nodded. "But I don't know what happened."

"Was she hiking the nature trail?" asked Whit, with a raised eyebrow.

Diane could see he was looking at the one foot that had a shoe—a dressy, fabric kitten-heel shoe—the inch-and-a-half heel not good for walking the nature trail.

"I don't know," said Diane. "I wasn't aware she was at the museum today. We don't have a board meeting. But she takes several of the classes and, as Lynn said, she loved the museum."

Lynn looked at Whit and he nodded his okay. No one touched a body without the coroner's clearance. Lynn squeezed Diane's arm and turned toward her task.

Diane watched Lynn and David for a moment as they approached the body. She turned and looked from Whit to Garnett.

"I don't want Vanessa to hear about this from the media. What can I tell her?"

Whit wrinkled his brow. "Just what you know now. No details. Tell her not to speak with anyone beyond her household about it. I'm sure it will be in the news soon enough."

Garnett nodded in agreement.

As Diane drove to Vanessa's, she called her friend, psychiatrist Laura Hillard, and told Laura to meet her at Vanessa's. She hung up before Laura could question her. Laura was also an old friend of Vanessa and Madge Stewart.

Vanessa's estate was in the oldest section of Rosewood. The trees that lined her drive were older than the oldest member of Vanessa's family, which was saying a lot. Vanessa came from a family of centenarians and super centenarians. The large house came into view and Diane parked in the circular drive, got out, and walked to the door.

Vanessa's housekeeper, Mrs. Hartefeld—called either Hattie or Harte by Vanessa, depending on her mood— answered the door. Hattie Hartefeld preferred simply Harte and had often wondered aloud why a parent would have named an infant Hattie.

"Dr. Fallon," said Harte, "how nice to see you." She looked over Diane's shoulder and saw Laura driving up. "Well, this is a coincidence. Isn't it?" She looked quizzically at Diane.

"I called her to come, Harte. Can I speak with Vanessa?"

"Of course." She frowned as she opened the door wide and waited for Laura to approach. She let them into Vanessa's white gilded sitting room and went to fetch Vanessa.

"What's all the mystery?" Laura smiled at Diane.

She thinks it's about the wedding, thought Diane. *This is terrible*.

Vanessa came in dressed in a peach pantsuit, holding her hands out to greet Diane and Laura.

"What a nice surprise," she said.

"I'll bring some tea," said Harte, and she turned to leave.

"Harte, please stay for a moment," said Diane.

The three of them stared at her as if just now noticing the stricken look on her face.

"What is it?" said Vanessa.

"Something has happened," said Laura.

Diane nodded and asked them to sit down. Vanessa, Laura, and Harte sat on the sofa. Diane sat on one of the chairs near the fireplace where Milo Lorenzo's portrait hung. The museum was Milo's vision. He had been a professor at Bartrum University and the love of Vanessa's life. He died of a heart attack before the museum opened. Diane glanced up at him before she spoke.

"We've had a tragedy at the museum," she began.

"Oh dear," whispered Vanessa, putting a hand to her throat.

"It looks like a drowning," she said. "I'm so sorry." Diane felt tears start to sting her eyes. "It was Madge Stewart."

The three of them gasped. Harte whimpered and put a hand to her face. Diane knew Harte felt as she did. Like Diane, Harte complained about how Vanessa and Laura babied Madge, saying that she would be a much less obnoxious person if they would stop. Diane had expressed the same sentiments, sometimes in harsher words. Now she felt pangs of guilt. She imagined that Harte did too.

"What happened?" said Vanessa.

"I don't know. Her body was discovered by the grounds crew. They pulled her out of the water in hopes of saving her, but she was gone. Lynn, Garnett, and Whit are there now. I put David in charge of investigating the scene." *The scene*. It sounded so harsh and clinical—and sinister.

"Do you expect anything other than an accident?" asked Laura.

"No. But they have to investigate," said Diane.

"Oh, poor Madge," whispered Vanessa. "Poor little Madge." Harte put a hand over Vanessa's and Vanessa patted it with her other hand. "I'll handle the funeral. Madge has some cousins, but few other relatives. I can't believe this," she said.

"You'll keep us informed?" said Laura. "We need to know what happened."

"There is something about it that bothers you," said Vanessa.

Despite Vanessa's watery eyes and grieved face, she looked stern. Diane wanted to disappear into the chair.

Diane shook her head. "Please don't ask me any questions. Whit has instructed that no one outside of this room even be told of the death until he releases a statement.

I asked for special permission to come tell you so you wouldn't hear it on the news. Let's wait," she said.

"All right, dear," said Vanessa.

Diane was glad Vanessa didn't press.

Something *was* bothering her. She didn't like the way Madge was dressed. And she could tell the coroner was bothered by it too.

Chapter 23

Diane found Gregory down in the dungeon where David had left him. He was writing furiously in his notebook but looked up when Diane came into the room. He reached over and pulled up a chair for her.

"Diane, I heard about the tragedy. I'm sorry. Was the person a friend?"

"Yes," said Diane, but it felt like she was lying. The weight of all the recent events were on her shoulders as she plopped heavily onto the seat. "She was a member of the board here and a good friend to several of the other members."

Gregory eyed her. "But not a good friend to you?"

Diane slumped and confessed her guilt. "I'm trying to remember the last kind thing I said to her . . . and can't."

"It's very difficult when someone whose bad behavior we've called out dies on us and we are left wishing we had ignored their irresponsibility."

Diane gave him a weak smile. "I could have been kinder," she said.

"Knowing you, you were," he said.

"Your sentiment is appreciated," she said. "How do you like your accommodations?"

"It's rather terrific down here." He put his hands on the arms of the office chair as if to point to its astonishing comfort. "It's good to see that David has been able to turn his paranoia into such remarkable creativity."

"I think a big part of David's paranoia is an excuse to play with databases and gadgets," she said. "It wouldn't surprise me if he were digging out a new room here in the basement to house a secret supercomputer."

"He said supercomputers are above his price range," said Gregory.

"So he's talked with you about a supercomputer," said Diane. "I guess I'd better worry."

"He was going on about a friend in Oak Ridge, Tennessee, with a Cray Jaguar. I thought it was a car," said Gregory. "I thought perhaps 2.33 petaflops was you Yanks' word for horsepower."

Diane smiled and shook her head. "Perhaps I'd better check the subbasement."

"He said if he needed a large amount of computing power he could use slaves," said Gregory.

Diane sat up in her chair and looked at Gregory. "What? He's using hacked botnets?"

"He said he never used computers in the United States— or Great Britain. But he might have said that for my benefit. My guess would be China."

Diane put her head in her hands. "You are joking, aren't you?" she said.

"Actually, no," said Gregory. He paused as Diane groaned. "But David may have been. It's hard to tell sometimes, you know."

Diane looked up and smiled. Gregory grinned back. She looked down at his notebook.

"It looks like you've been hard at work," she said.

Gregory liked to work in a notebook with pen and ink. At a glance, it looked as though he was a serious doodler, but his doodles always meant something. Instead of color-coding concepts, he doodle-coded them. He had started with a list of all the people on the team in South America. He had drawn a line through the deceased members, but that didn't delete them from his analysis. He had fancy frames around others.

He was doing a network analysis—looking at how each member was connected to the others, correlating each with their World Accord job description, with their current job, with their special talents, personality traits, background, with whom they stayed in contact after the massacre. David would have gladly written an algorithm for him, but Gregory liked to use his own brain for the analysis, continually adding little things to his people map, as he called it, following strings of a web with an unknown pattern until he found the strand that led him to the spider.

The notebook was spread out so that two facing pages were showing. Diane noticed his computer screen was filled with open windows containing various reports from their work in South America. She glanced at what he had so far. His first entries were of the three of them—Diane, David, and Gregory himself—listing the rumors with the annotation "vague" beside them.

"Vague?" said Diane.

"None of the rumors about us have any detail attached to them. God knows, the journalists in London tried to find something."

"That's the way lies are," she said. "You don't need much substance to make them stick, so long as there are people out there who are convinced that where there is smoke there is fire."

"People love to believe the worst," he commented, studying his notes and tapping them with a pen.

Diane was familiar with Gregory's notation for the most part, but he frequently used a shorthand description of just one or two letters whose meaning was not obvious. Next to hers, David's, and Gregory's names he had put the letters F and A. By Simone Brooks, he had written a W. Her fiancé, Oliver Hill, had a line through his name and the letters I and M.

Gregory had listed all of the people who worked for World Accord International. He had also listed the people who ran the mission—Father Joseph and his staff—along with some of the semiregular visitors.

"What are the letters?" asked Diane. She pointed to the one by her and David's names.

"I'm labeling several variables. Neither David nor I have turned up any other member of the team who were the object of rumors. I don't know about Simone. I'm hoping your Mr. Garnett will find out something from the brother." He sighed. "I've been trying to find a difference between the three of us and the others who weren't targeted."

"And?" asked Diane.

"Nothing clear—but interesting, nonetheless. Among all the members of the team, only we three remained close friends after South America. I've called the others a couple of times a year. You know, to check up on them. But I can't say I've stayed friends with any of the team except you and David. Martine Leveque asked me not to call anymore; she wanted to forget that part of her life."

Diane winced and Gregory smiled.

"I didn't take it personally. Anyway, Martine lived outside Paris the last we spoke. David hasn't been able to get in touch with her."

"I don't imagine she wants to hear from him either," said Diane.

Martine had been an interviewer, along with Simone. They often worked together with Steven and sometimes David. She, like all of them, was traumatized by what they found at the mission that day.

"What about Steven Mays?" asked Diane.

"He lives in Washington. I helped him get on at your Diplomatic Corps. I have a call in to him. Hopefully, he'll call back soon. In the meantime, I spoke with a contact at your State Department. They know of no rumors flying around Steven."

"And Hannah?"

Diane glanced down at the notebook. Hannah Payne had been their photographer. She meticulously documented the evidence they uncovered, the mass graves, the torture rooms. She had her camera, as she always did, when they returned to the mission. She went from body to body taking photographs, dispassionately recording every atrocity. When she finished, she started over, as if crawling into the camera would insulate her from the horror. David, Gregory, Steven, and several of their excavators armed themselves and searched the mission. David climbed to the top and looked out over the area to see if the perpetrators who had committed the horror were readying for another attack. And she had gone in search of Ariel. Simone wept over her fiancé. Hannah had caught it all on her camera.

Diane shook her head to push back the memories that rose like bile in her throat.

"Hannah freelances for several news sources," said Gregory. "She's traveling at the moment. I believe she prefers not to hear from me, though she wasn't as blunt as Martine." He tapped his pen on the page. "I've been able to find many of the other team members—Maxwell, Ellis, Sharon, and several of the excavators. None have had any problems like ours. It looks as if it is just the three of us."

"What do all your initials mean?" asked Diane again.

"Oh, just observations. You and David are friends and adept—*F* and *A*. Simone is wounded, hence the *W*. Even before the death of her fiancé, she had a wounded air about her. I think that is why she was able to relate to witnesses so well. Oliver, her fiancé, was idealistic and meticulous. Hannah was armored—*AR*. She used her camera as a shield against the horrors of the world and against getting close to anyone. Steven was ambitious and sharp, that's the *AB* and the *S*. Martine was afraid and aloof. I had a lot of *A*s to contend with in my variables." He shook his head. "I don't know if any of this will help, but it reminds me of the people we knew and what they were like. I was wondering if Simone would have confided in any of them. She and Martine were good friends—at least as friendly as Martine got."

Diane started to speak when she heard the computer ping. It was one of the sounds indicating that it had found results from a search.

"David set some search parameters for our team and fed them into the computer," said Gregory. "Apparently, it found something."

He flipped to another window and they both stared at the screen for several moments, then at each other.

"Well, Diane, my dear," said Gregory, "apparently, Interpol has an alert posted for you on suspicion of murder."

Chapter 24

Darkness approached quickly in the jungle. There was still light above the canopy, but on the ground it was growing dim rapidly. Maria had been driving for hours. Her hands and arms were numb from holding on to the jerking, vibrating steering wheel as the truck climbed in and out of ruts and bounced over rock-strewn slopes and exposed roots of the giant rain-forest trees. Stinging sweat trickled down her dirt-streaked face and body. The road they were on, if it could be called a road, was overgrown with broad leaves of all shapes and shades of green that slapped the truck, reached though the open window and slapped her, and grabbed at the truck undercarriage. In other circumstances she would have loved the adventure. Now she was just plain scared.

Maria found a clearing of sorts and stopped the truck to assess their resources and clean up before light was completely gone. Standing in the back of the truck, she stripped down to bare skin to wash herself for the first time since the beginning of her captivity almost four days ago. She looked at her poor battered body covered with smudges of dirt, dark swollen bruises, scratches, and cuts.

I haven't looked this bad since that time in the cave, she thought to herself. *Of course, there was the time I was stabbed. And being buried alive was really bad.* She had made herself laugh.

She tore a piece of cloth the size of a bandanna from the bolt of fabric, soaked it in whiskey from one of the bottles in their cargo, and gave herself what had to be her most bizarre sponge bath ever. The whiskey burned like hell on her cuts and abrasions. She kept telling herself that alcohol was an antiseptic; it was killing bad things that were much worse than a little sting. Well, not such a *little* sting—actually, quite a large and painful sting.

Thinking of her raw throat and raspy voice, Maria unscrewed the cap from the bottle of whiskey, took a mouthful, swished it as hard and long as she could stand it, gargled with it, and spit it out. It was like gargling with liquid fire. Now she burned inside and out. But it should help her throat.

While Maria bathed, Rosetta took some of the fresh food from the cargo and made dinner. Maria kept an eye on her from the back of the truck as she took her whiskey bath, marveling at the little girl's skills. Maria hadn't wanted her to build a fire, but Rosetta said it was okay for a little while. Maria doubted it. They were traveling through a particularly crime-ridden section of the jungle. She feared who—and what—might be attracted by smoke from a fire. But she relented.

Rosetta had found a pot among the things in the truck, cooked a soup from the vegetables, and put out the fire with dirt. Smart girl—nutrition, no lingering smoke, no embers, no sign of a fire.

Maria put her clothes back on, wiping off as much dirt as would come off with a rag and whiskey. She smelled like a distillery, but it was better than what she had smelled like from her days in captivity. She pulled the traditional embroidered blouse that Rosetta had given her over her shirt. The skirt that Rosetta had sewn money up in, Maria folded and put in the bottom of the backpack. Life on this trip was too rough for bare legs. Dirty as her jeans were, she needed the protection and freedom they gave her. There wasn't much Maria could do with her hair. She left it in the mud-covered dreadlocks it had formed itself into, but she did tie it back with a strip of clean fabric.

For herself, Rosetta had explained that she had bathed before she put her plan into effect. Maria suspected that Rosetta disapproved of using the whiskey to wash in instead of saving it to trade, but there was still plenty of it left to trade.

Sitting in the cab of the pickup, they ate the soup Rosetta had made with bread she had brought in her backpack. The food tasted pretty good. But Maria didn't savor it. She hurried through the meal.

"Shouldn't you sleep?" said Rosetta.

The little girl looked at her with suspicion, as if she was afraid the person she had chosen to take her to her mother might not be up to the task. Maria made an effort to relax. She was frightened. How much more scared would Rosetta, a child, be? Maria smiled and squeezed her little hand.

"I'll sleep in a few hours. I want to get farther away from this area. We're doing fine. You made a good plan— an amazing plan. We've come a long way and managed to collect supplies and weapons while escaping. I'll get you home. I promise."

Rosetta nodded and put her head down, taking small bites of bread. She looked up after a moment.

"You won't leave me, will you?" she whispered.

Maria scooted next to her and put an arm around Rosetta's shoulders, pulling her close.

"No, I won't leave you. You have my promise." She paused for several moments. "Your mother didn't leave you, you know. Everyone in our profession heard the story of what happened to Diane Fallon. We all heard how she looked for you until she collapsed and had to be carried away. Everyone thought the same thing happened to you that happened to the others at the mission."

"I knew she didn't mean to leave me. They said she didn't want me anymore. But I didn't believe them."

"When people say things like that, it eats at you, doesn't it? That's why mean people talk like that—to hurt you and make you sad. No, it wasn't true. Your mother couldn't work for a whole year after she lost you. She became very ill from her sorrow … but she is doing well now," Maria said quickly, lest she give the little girl another worry. "She is going to be so happy to see you. I promise you that, too."

They ate the rest of the meal in silence. When they finished, Maria washed out the pan and soup cups with the whiskey left in the bottle and they started on their way again.

The terrain gradually changed from the half-muddy soil that had worried Maria throughout the trip to a dryer, harder soil and less vegetation. They had left the intense flora that had encroached on them from all sides. The path they followed had a slight but steady incline. She expected it. According to the map, they should be approaching a higher elevation.

She checked the map before she started out again. As the crow flies, they were on the right track. But they weren't flying. She would like to make it to a clearing so she could see the stars. She wanted to compare her compass reading with the Southern Cross star constellation to verify true south. Not that she didn't trust the compass, but she trusted the stars more. She wasn't lost, she didn't think, but she wasn't certain of her navigation—not while she was so scared.

Maria had driven about fifteen minutes when she spoke to Rosetta. "Ariel," she said, using her real name.

"Rosetta. You have to remember. If anyone hears Ariel . . ." She let the sentence trail off.

"All right. Rosetta, you hinted that we can't go to an embassy because someone from there was involved with the horrible things that happened at the mission. I know that remembering is painful for you. I haven't pressed you about that, and I wouldn't ask if I didn't think it was important to our success in getting home. But I need you to tell me what happened."

Rosetta didn't say anything. Maria let the request hang out there for the little girl to think about. Several minutes passed before Rosetta began to talk. When she spoke, her voice was so low Maria had to strain to hear it over the noise of the truck.

"Mama was gone for a long time. She was doing her work. She had left me at the mission."

Rosetta stopped talking and Maria wondered if she was going to continue. But she didn't push.

"It seemed like she was gone a long time then," she began again. "Maybe it was just two or three days. The day she left I got a bad feeling. I didn't know what was going to happen, but in my mind it seemed like the bad stuff started then, the day she left. I was just a little kid then. I don't remember everything."

Maria smiled and patted her hand. "I know, sweetheart. Take your time."

"It seemed like the grown-ups were in a bad mood. Maybe not all of them, but some were. I don't remember who exactly. But that day I heard Father Joe arguing with one of the people Mama worked with but who always stayed at the mission. I didn't understand what it was about and I don't remember what they said."

They ran over a hole and Rosetta cried out at the unexpected jarring. Maria bit the edge of her tongue.

"Sorry," said Maria, "I didn't see that." It wasn't the first hole they'd run over, but coming just as it had, it startled the two of them.

"The next day—I think—I was playing outside. I saw Father Joe in the garden. He was crying. It scared me."

"Was he hurt?" prompted Maria.

"No, he was sad. I asked him if I could bring him a drink of water. He just cried. I asked him what was wrong. He said he did an unforgivable sin. But he had told us that no sin is unforgivable if we confess and repent. I told him that."

"What did he say?" asked Maria.

"He said he'd thought that was true, but it wasn't. He said he couldn't be forgiven. When I asked him what he did, he just cried and told me to go inside. Two days later it happened. I know, because Mama gave me a calendar to mark off the days she was gone. I was scared when I saw Father Joe crying so I went to my room to see how many days before she would be back. It was three more days."

Rosetta was quiet for a long while.

It was darker than Maria meant it to be before she stopped. Just a little farther, she thought. She realized she couldn't see the road ahead more than a few feet. The headlights had become weak . . . and then dimmed to nothing. She stopped as blackness surrounded them.

Chapter 25

"What happened?" asked Rosetta.

"I'm not sure," said Maria. "For some reason we lost our headlights."

She tried turning them off and back on. They illuminated briefly and dimmed out again. Maria hadn't wanted to stop for the night under the trees. She was hoping for any kind of clearing. She reached for a flashlight, rolled down the window and let the narrow beam of the light guide her. She drove at a slow pace, looking for a place to stop for the night, shining the light to the side and back in front of them.

After a while she lost any semblance of a trail and simply drove through the brush until her light vanished into what looked like a break in the flora ahead. She drove toward it. Through a copse of trees the jungle opened up into a clearing. Maria drove the truck into it and stopped.

"Stay here. I'm going to look around," she said.

She put the truck in park, leaving it idling. She shined the light on the ground beside the door to make sure she was not stepping into something she would regret. The surface of the ground was blackened and covered in a dark stubble of twigs, stumps, and twisted remnants of vegetation.

"It looks like there's been a big fire," she said as she got out.

She shined the light into the darkness. It was a poor flashlight. The beam didn't extend far. But it did shine far enough into the burned area to show a large mound of dirt and piled-up twigs and limbs ahead of them. Maria looked for a path to drive around or over the rubble. She fixed a route in her mind and got back in the truck. Proceeding cautiously in the pitch black, she managed to get the lurching truck to a spot on the other side of the mound. Here they would be hidden from anyone coming from the direction they had come. She parked and reluctantly turned off the engine, wondering if it would restart in the morning or if the battery would be gone. She knew so little about cars. She hoped that, like her, all it needed was rest.

Maria turned off the flashlight and was shocked at how dark it was without even a glow from the dash lights.

"Okay," she said as brightly as she could, "we're camping here for the night."

"It's really dark," said Rosetta.

"It is. Are you afraid of the dark?" asked Maria.

"No . . . it's just that it's *really dark*," the little girl repeated.

"It's good to see the stars," Maria said, looking through the windshield at the star field.

Rosetta followed her gaze. "I wish they could be brighter," she said.

"Do you need to use the bathroom before we turn in?" asked Maria, grabbing the flashlight on the seat.

"I don't want to go out there in the dark," Rosetta said.

"No need to go far. We'll both go."

Maria opened her door and got out. With the motor off, the jungle sounds were loud. She hadn't really heard it so much when they stopped earlier. With the truck noise always rumbling, not much of the jungle sound had penetrated her consciousness. But now she could hear cries of night birds and the shrieks and growls of other animals she couldn't identify. Some of them sounded beautiful. Others sounded very frightening. She was glad she had found such a large clearing. She felt safer out of the forest.

She examined the ground as she walked around to the passenger side to get Rosetta. There was a lot of burned stubble, with bare soil in a few places.

"This is a fine place to camp," she said, lifting the little girl from the truck.

Maria led them only a few feet into the darkness. She'd brought torn squares of the fabric with her and handed one to Rosetta. After the two of them took care of business, Maria took Rosetta's hand and led her back toward the truck.

"Look up at the sky," Maria said. "See that pathway of stars? That's the Milky Way. That's the galaxy we are in."

"Mama told me that," said Rosetta.

Maria smiled in the darkness. "Did she tell you about the Southern Cross?" she asked.

"What's that?" said Rosetta.

"That's what I've been trying to catch a glimpse of, to make sure we're going in the right direction."

"You have a compass," said Rosetta.

"Yes, I do, but it's good to double-check your compass. Sometimes things cause a compass not to give accurate readings. The hands can be a little bent and can stick, or we could be near a place where the ground contains a mineral called magnetite that throws off the reading. In Kentucky, where I grew up, my father and grandfather taught me how to navigate using the stars. Unfortunately, I'm now in a different hemisphere and the stars are different."

"So you can't find your way with the stars here?" said Rosetta.

"Oh, I think I can. I looked at the star charts before I came on vacation here," she said. Maria turned on the light so Rosetta could see her point at the sky. "See those two bright stars there?" she said.

"Sort of," said Rosetta.

"Those are Alpha and Beta Centauri. Alpha Centauri is the brightest star in this whole part of the sky. That makes it easy to find. And Beta Centauri is the second brightest. They are called pointer stars because, if you draw a line from Alpha Centauri—the really bright one—through Beta Centauri and keep on going with the line, it points to the Southern Cross."

Maria drew a line in the sky with her finger. "Can you see that small cluster of five stars that's shaped like a long diamond?"

"I don't know," said Rosetta.

Maria took a stick and drew the stars on the ground as they appeared in the sky.

"Look again now."

"Yes, I see them. How does this help you find our way home?"

"We have to use a little geometry and a little imagination," said Maria. She shined her light on the figure on the ground. "First we draw a short line between these two points on the diamond. That forms the arm of the cross. Then we draw a line from the top of the diamond—where Alpha and Beta Centauri are pointing—to the bottom tip of the diamond. That makes the cross. If you keep going in a straight line out the bottom of the cross, it points in the direction of the South Pole.

"The really neat thing is, if we make another cross using the line between the two pointer stars as the arm of the new cross . . ." She redrew the line in the dirt. "Then draw a line perpendicular to that one. That means like this." Maria showed Rosetta with her two hands what perpendicular was. "That makes the new cross."

"Okay. I think I see," said the little girl.

"Good, smart girl. Now let's draw that line out long, the way we did before, until it meets the line coming out the bottom of the Southern Cross. The point where those two lines cross each other is the South Pole. The opposite direction is north—the way we want to go."

Maria did the geometry again in her head as she looked at the stars. She collected several sticks and arranged them on the ground so they made an arrow pointing due north.

"This way," she said, "we can still see where north is tomorrow in the daylight. I'll double-check it with the compass."

Maria was hoping the impromptu lecture on the Southern Cross would help Rosetta not be afraid of the dark if she could see that darkness could help them find their way home. As brave as she was, Rosetta must have been afraid most of the time since the tragedy that separated her from Diane Fallon. There were so many things to be afraid of. Maria wanted to make one less for Rosetta.

"Now, let's get back in the truck before the mosquitoes find us," said Maria.

Maria arranged the best bedding for the two of them she could under the circumstances. She was leaning against the back of the seat with her long legs stretched out to the passenger side propped up on the box of edible supplies they had moved to the cab. She used some of the bolt of fabric for a pillow. Rosetta curled up next to her holding the backpack like a teddy bear and with some of the fabric folded into a pillow under her head on Maria's lap.

"I'll stay awake while you sleep," said Rosetta.

"I think we'll be fine here," answered Maria.

"I'll still stay awake."

"Wake me if you hear anything you don't like. Don't go off by yourself." Maria caressed her hair.

"I won't," she said.

Rosetta was silent. Maria listened to the sounds of the jungle. She thought she heard the cry of a jaguar. She closed her eyes.

"They came in the morning," said Rosetta. Her voice was small and came with a tremor. "It was still dark and I was asleep in my room. When I heard the screaming and guns I hid in the closet. I was so scared. I kept thinking, what if Mama came back early and they got her."

Maria stroked her cheek and hair. She said nothing, but reached and held her hand.

"The bad men searched all the rooms. They found me in the closet. I thought they were going to shoot me, but they grabbed me and took me outside with the other kids. I heard someone ask if he should kill us. That was when I heard the voice. I had heard it before . . . when he came to the mission before. He said it would be a waste. He had on a big hat and I couldn't see his face, but I knew his voice. He had an accent like this." Rosetta gave Maria a pretty good imitation of a British accent.

"He asked which one was Fallon's stray cat. I didn't know what he meant—then. I thought he was looking for a cat. We didn't have one. One of the older kids pushed me toward them. The other kids began hitting on that kid for doing it and the bad men fired their guns in the air."

Rosetta stopped talking. Maria heard her uneven breathing and felt a tear as she caressed Rosetta's cheek.

"Did you know who the man was?" asked Maria.

"No. A lot of people visited the mission. But he was with an embassy man, I remember. Father Joe talked with him. So did Mama, and Uncle David and Uncle Greg—that's what I called Mama's friends. The bad man was tall, really tall, but I don't think as tall as you, and he had blond hair. That's all I remember about what he looked like. I was just a little kid. He took my shoes and my CD player. I guess he got it from my room. He said he was going to make a surprise for Mama with it. He told a man to cut my arm and put the blood on my shoes." Rosetta rubbed her arm and whimpered. "It hurt and I cried. I wanted Mama. I want her so bad now." Rosetta started crying.

Maria shifted her position and pulled Rosetta up into her arms, holding her tight.

"We'll get you home to your mama, I promise." She caressed her hair and kissed the top of her head. "You don't have to talk about this anymore."

Rosetta sniffed and Maria gave her one of the squares of fabric to blow her nose.

"I want to tell you all of it," she said after a moment. "You said you need to know."

Rosetta told Maria about the long truck ride with the other kids and how scared they all were. She told her about escaping at one of the stops. She was so small she rolled away from them into the brush when she was using the bathroom. She wasn't sure they even knew she was gone. Rosetta told Maria about finding her way to a native village, where she was taken in by an old woman who knew jungle herbs and medicine plants. The old woman hid Rosetta when the men came looking. The villagers didn't like the bad men and they didn't give her away.

During the time with the old woman, Rosetta hatched the idea of finding her mother. The men had told her that Diane Fallon didn't want her anymore, but she hadn't believed them. Not really. The old woman died the next year and Rosetta finagled a trip to a large village where she got a job working for a couple. A place to stay for her. Cheap labor for them.

That was when Ariel became Rosetta to make herself disappear. She told Maria that she went from family to family, running away when she discovered that a family couldn't help her, always looking for someone who could take her to Georgia, United States. She found that if she worked hard and always did a good job, they would give her more responsibility in the household—and that was her power. She told Maria that her idea was to find a rich family, but that never happened. It was always families like the one she worked for at the village where she met Maria. They were well off in their own little corner of the world, but actually rather poor.

The last family had her cook also for Julio and Patia,

Maria's kidnappers. That was how Rosetta came to know about the new woman prisoner. Rosetta always cooked the food for prisoners and she'd heard they had a woman named Diane Fallon. She had seen the person led in and knew she wasn't her mother, but she also heard she was a bone woman from Georgia, United States. Rosetta had found someone who could take her home. She just needed a plan.

Rosetta's voice faded so that Maria could barely hear her words, but all her hopes and fears came through clearly in her narrative.

"You are an amazing little girl," said Maria. "Your mother is going to be so very proud of you."

"We'll find her, won't we?" she said.

"Yes, we'll find her," said Maria. "I know where to find her."

"You have a plan for how to get us to her?" asked Rosetta.

"I'm forming one," she said.

"Good. You go to sleep and I'll listen for trouble."

Maria smiled and settled as comfortably as she could in the small cab of the truck. She listened to the jungle noise and thought about the things Rosetta had told her.

Julio had called himself a trip wire. He had been on the lookout for a forensic anthropologist from Georgia—apparently they thought Diane Fallon was the only one. Maria supposed that Patia figured working at an archaeological dig was a good place to keep a lookout. And it had paid off—or so they thought.

Patia and Julio were also looking out for anyone who asked about feathers and bones. Feathers and bones? What did that mean? What was it about feathers and bones? Bones she could guess—mass human burials, most likely, maybe—but feathers? Were those all the keywords that would trip the wire, or were there other things Julio and Patia were to look and listen for? And did any of this have anything to do with the massacre at the mission?

Did current events have anything to do with what Diane Fallon had been investigating? Maria had heard rumors that Fallon was collecting evidence of atrocities by a dictator she was trying to expose, and it was he who massacred the people at the mission. But then if that were the case,

Rosetta's narrative didn't quite track. There was something missing.

It sounded like Father Joe discovered something so bad that he thought it would cost him his soul. Pretty tough thought for a priest.

And what was going to happen on the third of May, *tres de mayo*? Maria was sure that was what she had heard—the third of May.

Was there really a danger of going to an embassy? Which embassy? British? People from the UK weren't the only ones who spoke with a British accent.

And speaking of accents, here they were, as nearly as she could tell, on the Brazilian side of the boarder with Peru, but everyone was speaking Spanish—no Portuguese. Was this some enclave of Spanish-speaking Brazilians? Some forgotten indigenous tribe? Or, perhaps, were they some group in exile? And who were these bad guys in make-shift uniforms? Bandits? The rag-tag remnants of a private army?

Thoughts flowed back and forth through her brain, like panning for gold, as she eventually drifted off to sleep.

The next awareness she had, it was late morning. She awoke to Rosetta patting her on the arm.

"I thought you needed sleep," said Rosetta. "I need to go. I'll stay near the truck." She hopped out.

"I'm sure you were right about the sleep," Maria called after her. "I feel better."

Maria stretched and sat up straight. She was stiff and sore but surprisingly rested—and optimistic. She had slept hardly at all after she was kidnapped and she had been ter-rified the entire time. Some of that terror had left, taken away by the sandman. She rubbed her eyes with the heels of her hands and blinked until the blur of sleep left.

"What do you say we eat something and get started?" she said, looking out the window. She decided to wait until after breakfast to try starting the truck. If she were to be disappointed, she wanted it to be on a full stomach.

Her gaze rested on the huge mound of dirt and brush they had parked behind. But that wasn't what it was.

"Stay here," she told Rosetta.

Maria walked to the mound and began climbing up the steep bank of brush and rock until she got to the top. She looked out over the huge burned-off clearing that covered, she guessed, over a hundred acres. She saw several giant earthworks, ruins of rock structures, wide lines scarring the ground, all in a pattern. Maria knew all of the major Incan ruins that had been discovered. This one wasn't on the list. Apparently it had been uncovered by the fire. It was huge, larger than any of the others that were known. And the fire hadn't even uncovered all of it. She saw ruins leading into the unburned jungle.

Here she was, an archaeologist in the middle of an un-discovered lost city, and she had no camera and no time. She didn't even have a notebook.

Chapter 26

Diane was stunned.

"Now I'm an internationally hunted murderer? How the hell did I fall to such depths?"

Gregory didn't answer. His fingers were clicking away at the keyboard, looking for more information.

They both stared at the final window he pulled up. There was her picture and her last known address. It was the wrong address, thank God—the apartment she had lived in before she moved in with Frank. There were also the names and pictures of the four men she supposedly had murdered. She stared wide-eyed at the screen.

"Well, this is just bloody ridiculous," said Gregory.

He flipped through a black notebook sitting next to the computer.

"You remember Cameron. Cameron Michaels," he said, with a quick motion of his finger toward his desktop.

Diane looked at Gregory's notes spread out on the desk. Cameron Michaels had a wiggly circle around his name and was connected to the two of them with a straight line and to Father Joseph and Oliver Hill with a dotted line. Straight line meant professional relationship, dotted meant social. If she remembered correctly, Cameron had played the Chinese game of Go with Father Joe and Oliver—a game Diane didn't really understand. Her preference was chess.

"Yes," she said. "Our UN liaison."

"He's not at the UN any longer. He works for Interpol now. I have a call in to him about the rumors, which he hasn't yet returned. I'll try again." Reading from his notebook, he entered the number on the phone, punching each key hard, as if that would transmit his determination across the airwaves. "This is just bloody ridiculous," he said again under his breath.

Diane waited. A flutter of fear threatened to invade her stomach. She looked at the dates of the murders. Yesterday. All in one day. Damn, she'd been on a homicidal rampage. In Brazil. At least she had an alibi. She felt marginally better. Still, what the hell was this about? She looked at the name of the town that the complaint originated from. Río de Sangue. She didn't recognize it. But how fitting. If she wasn't mistaken, that was Portuguese for River of Blood.

"Yes, Cameron. Thank you for answering." Gregory put the phone on speaker.

Cameron Michaels was Swiss and had worked as World Accord International's contact at the UN. Periodically he would visit them in the field and she and Gregory would update him on their progress, or in some cases, lack of progress. He was bright and was fluent in several languages. She was surprised he wasn't still at the UN advancing upward at a rapid rate. But he also had an adventurous streak. She supposed that was what accounted for Interpol. She wondered what he did there.

"Sorry I couldn't get to you sooner, but it's good to hear from you," Cameron said.

English was Cameron's second language. His first was French. He was so fluent in English he could be mistaken for a Brit when he spoke it, or a Spaniard when he spoke Spanish. A sudden flash of Ariel breezed through her mind. Ariel had a natural gift with languages. Diane switched her focus back to the phone conversation.

"So, you are Interpol's UN representative," Diane heard Gregory say. "Congratulations."

"Gives me a chance to expand my horizons," he said. "I still haven't decided what I want to be when I grow up." He laughed a happy, mirthful laugh.

"I've called you for a couple of reasons," said Gregory. "You remember Diane Fallon."

"Of course. It hasn't been that long," he said. "How is she?"

"Actually doing well, getting married, all that," said Gregory.

"Glad to hear it. That was a bad time we had," said Cameron. "I haven't played Go since. Don't have the spirit for it after Father Joe and Oliver."

"We're having some strange problems all of a sudden. Diane seems to be on Interpol's Most Wanted list, or at least their Look-Out-For list."

"What? Just a minute." They heard typing in the background, then Cameron's voice. "This can't be right." He came back on the phone. "What's the girl been up to?" He laughed slightly.

"Minding her own business." Gregory told him about the other rumors whirling around the three of them—her, David, and Gregory. "And now this. I don't mind telling you, we are getting rather cross."

"I don't blame you. How strange. Is Diane in Brazil?" he asked.

"No, she is in the United States. Rosewood, Georgia, to be exact. And she has all manner of mayors, detectives, and board members to prove it."

There was a pause.

"Someone has got it in for you. Is it happening to anyone else?" asked Cameron.

"Not that I can discover. I wanted to ask you if you are having problems."

"None that I'm aware of. Hell. I guess I need to make sure. I haven't heard anything. But what really bothers me is that someone has hacked into our secure files. That's not good."

"What degree of difficulty does that require?" asked Gregory.

"Quite a bit, I would think. It's not my bailiwick. But I'm going to find out. Thanks for the heads-up. I'll give the authorities in the town a call—Río de Sangue. Never heard of it."

"Nor have I," said Gregory. "Thank you, Cameron. It's good speaking with you again. I hope all is well."

"You too, Greg," he said. "I'll keep in touch. I have your number here."

Gregory hung up. Diane didn't talk to Cameron and it seemed to her that Gregory hadn't wanted her to. She asked him why.

"I haven't been telling anyone where I am. Just seems better to keep a low profile. I trust the people who were on our team, but not necessarily their confidants. Until we find out where this is coming from, we need to give out less information than we get. That's why I didn't tell him about Simone."

"So where are we?" asked Diane.

"Nowhere at the moment. I've gone over in my mind what this could be about, who benefits from our disgrace, who we have offended, what was going on with Simone. The only thing I've discovered is that I need more information. To that end, I'm going to try my hand at speaking with Simone's parents. Put my diplomatic skills to the test. Perhaps I can pry out of her brother where she might have put the things of Oliver's that she kept."

The two of them sat staring at each other for several moments. Gregory broke the silence first.

"We were investigators. Top-notch. Was there something going on around us that we completely missed?"

"I don't know," said Diane. "We are still assuming that Simone is connected with the rumors. We don't know that."

"No, we don't. Quite a coincidence, however," Gregory said.

"And this latest Interpol thing originated in Brazil." She got on the other computer and looked up the location on a map. "Near Peru," she said. "About six hundred miles southeast of the mission, but still in Brazil. Everything seems to point to our time there."

Gregory nodded.

"Could it be drugs?" asked Diane. "Could someone have been dealing in drugs and we not know it?"

"As hard as that is to imagine, one must consider it as a possibility," Gregory said. "We were out in the field a good deal of the time. Someone could have timed their activities to correspond to when we were gone from the mission. However, the other members of our team would have noticed something. And certainly Father Joseph or the nuns would have."

"Maybe Oliver did," said Diane. "Maybe that's what the drug-soaked bag was about. Perhaps that's what Simone was investigating."

Gregory pressed his lips together in a tight line. "She wouldn't have just taken up whatever investigation he may have been conducting, if that's what she was doing, unless she thought it had something to do with his death."

They looked at each other again for a long time. Gregory's gray eyes took on a steely appearance. "It was one of us?" he said.

"But it was ex-bloody-dictator Ivan Santos who massacred the people at the mission." Diane spoke through gritted teeth, defying Gregory to perhaps clear the man she had hated all this time.

"Yes, yes, it was Santos. But was there something else involved too? Could he have been doing a favor for someone?" said Gregory.

"That's what Simone said: 'It was one of us.' I've been pushing that to the back of my mind every time I think about it. Damn it to hell, if that's true."

Diane was silent for a long time.

"How do we find out if it's true?" she asked.

She felt helpless. As if this would be important to Ariel's memory to find the whole truth and she wasn't up to it—just as she hadn't been up to protecting Ariel. She suddenly felt like crying.

Gregory stood. "I'm going to see Simone's family. I'll come back with answers."

Diane locked the door to Gregory's office behind them. The two of them threaded their way through David's maze of equipment. She wondered what he was working on. She wondered if she should ask. On the way up to the first floor she gave Gregory the keys to her SUV. He had a lot of experience driving in the United States, so she wasn't worried that he would run into someone by driving on the wrong side of the road.

On the way to her office she met Chief of Detectives Douglas Garnett.

"Just the person I was looking for." He smiled. "Did you know there is an international warrant out for your arrest?"

Chapter 27

Diane eyed Chief Garnett. He didn't look like a man who was about to take her into custody.

"I just found out," she said. "Gregory Lincoln called a contact we have at Interpol about it." She walked across the lobby with him, threading through the visitors, heading for her museum office.

"You have an airtight alibi—I saw you here yesterday." He laughed. "Detective Warrick is trying to track down that town—Río something. It looks like they may not have telephone service. Strange that they seem to be connected to Interpol."

"I think someone picked a place on a map and hacked it into Interpol's system. I doubt the village even has a police force."

As they walked, Diane noticed a few people looking at her, then turning quickly away. She didn't think much about it until a docent did the same thing. Odd. *But people are probably hearing about Madge*, she thought.

"You and your British friend got any ideas what this is about?" Garnett said. "I hate having my people spend their time tracking down places that aren't there."

"Not a clue, so far. But Gregory is good at this," said Diane. She sighed, exhaling slowly. "What about Madge? Any news?"

"It's early," he said. "I doubt Lynn has had time to start on the autopsy."

"I know. It's just, well, so terrible, and so sad," she said.

They walked through the double doors into the administrative wing of the museum and down the hall to her office.

"The Interpol thing, is that what you came here about?" said Diane.

"Yes. Goose chase that it is, I have to follow through and do the paperwork. It's a nuisance I could do without. But at least I can say I see the woman every day; she hasn't had time to go to Brazil for a hit."

Diane entered through Andie's office. Andie was hard at work answering the telephone. All lines were ringing off the hook.

"What's going on?" asked Diane. "Are these questions about Madge?"

Andie looked up at her with wide, harassed eyes. Her reddish übercurled hair added to the hassled look.

"Dr. Fallon, this is just awful. I've asked Liam to look into it. I hope you don't mind. I know you have resources—really, really good ones—but it never hurts to have help . . . a lot of it."

Liam was Andie's detective boyfriend. Diane couldn't imagine what she had him looking into—obviously not Madge's death. Andie wouldn't have taken such a giant step as that without permission from Diane.

"Slow down, Andie, and take a breath. What's this about?" said Diane.

"The news," she said. "What everyone is calling about."

Andie clicked several keys on her computer keyboard and turned her monitor around so Diane could see it.

"This is the Atlanta news feed," said Andie.

The local reporter, an attractive woman with brown hair, wearing a raincoat and holding an umbrella, was standing in front of the Rosewood Police Station in the drizzling rain. Diane's driver's license picture, looking for all the world like a mug shot, was in the corner of the screen. Diane recognized Pris Halloran, a reporter from a small TV station in Atlanta, but judging from the logo on the screen, she was now on assignment for one of the major networks.

"Dr. Diane Fallon, director of the RiverTrail Museum of Natural History, and director of the Rosewood Crime Lab, is on Interpol's most-wanted criminals list. According to Interpol, Fallon allegedly murdered four men in Río de Sangue, Brazil. There is an uncorroborated report that the killings were in connection with a drug deal that went bad. It has been rumored for some time that Dr. Fallon was involved in drug smuggling while she was working for a human rights organization in Brazil, but that, as I said, is just a rumor at this point. In a strange note to this story, Fallon was questioned recently in regard to charges of soliciting in the city of Rosewood. So far, neither Diane Fallon nor Rosewood's chief of detectives, Douglas Garnett, have returned our calls. Odd story, Kimberly. We'll keep you informed as it unfolds."

Diane slowly sank down in the stuffed chair near her. Garnett's face was red and contorted, the veins bulging in his swollen neck.

"What the hell . . . ," he said after a moment.

Diane put her hands over her face. Disaster didn't begin to describe the situation. *This is not survivable*, she thought.

"Andie, roll the phones over to the secretary and tell her to say that there will be a statement to the press forthcoming. You get on the phone to Kendel and tell her to return from Mexico; she needs to take over as director . . ."

"No," said Andie.

"Hopefully it will be temporary, but we can't let the museum grind to a halt while I sort this out."

"But it will look like you are guilty . . . and you were here yesterday and, by the way, one day is an awfully short time for all this to happen. How long does it take to get someone on an international most-wanted list? This is just wrong in so many ways."

Diane stood up. "I already look guilty. I need the free time to clear myself. Make the call. Kendel and you will be in charge until I can sort this out. I need to call Vanessa." She put the tips of her fingers to her eyes and rubbed. "Jesus. First Madge and now this. Vanessa must be beside herself."

The phone rang again as Diane started for her office.

"*AJC*," mouthed Andie as she started to tell them that they would hear something from the museum later.

Garnett held out his hand for the phone. "Allow me to talk to the *Atlanta Journal-Constitution*," he said. "I'm sure they are trying to get me anyway."

Andie looked at Diane and she nodded. Andie handed Garnett the phone.

"Chief of Detectives Douglas Garnett here," he said.

Pause.

"No, I'm not here to arrest Dr. Fallon. I'm here investigating the most cynically vicious case of identity theft that I have ever had experience with. Dr. Fallon has had her e-mail hacked and stolen. She has been the victim of vicious rumors, and is now the victim of Interpol having their own system hacked. I don't know who is targeting Dr. Fallon, or even if she is the primary target and not the crime lab or the museum. However, I will get to the bottom of this and I am asking the Atlanta computer crimes and fraud unit for help in the investigation."

He stopped talking for several moments.

"No, she has not been to Brazil. In fact, I and a great many other people were meeting with her here in Rosewood at the times when these men were supposedly murdered. I might add, we haven't been able to verify who these men are and if they are indeed dead . . . or even exist."

When he hung up, Garnett looked at the phone with distaste. "That will help some," he said.

"Thank you," said Diane.

"We have to stop this. It's not only you and the museum at stake. Every case the crime lab has processed is in danger," he said.

"Are you really going to ask Frank's unit for help?" asked Diane.

"Yes. I'm hoping they have some international connections that I don't. It sounds like you have connections that I don't."

"Our contact at Interpol is Cameron Michaels, who worked with us in Porto Barquis. He was our liaison with the United Nations. He's now Interpol's representative to the UN. He's looking into it for me," she said.

"Andie's right," said Garnett. "This is happening too fast."

"It's obviously just rumormongering," said Diane. "They don't really care whether authorities believe the charges. They just want the rest of the world to believe it. It really messes up my life."

"That's probably the point," said Garnett.

"The first I heard of any rumor about South America was from that travel reporter, Brian Mathews," said Diane. "I'm going to try and get a phone call to him, wherever he is."

"I think he has a blog," said Andie. "He probably has his itinerary on there."

"Good thinking, Andie. Get the details for me, please. I'm going to call Vanessa, Mr. Mathews—and Colin Prehoda, and sic him on that Halloran woman."

"Good," said Andie. "You need to get a lawyer like Prehoda on that . . . that . . . *woman*. Tell him to force her to make an on-air retraction. Naked."

Diane and Garnett chuckled. "I'll do that."

Diane walked into her office and sat behind her desk. Garnett followed and pulled up a chair. She supposed he wanted to hear what Mathews had to say. She stared at the water fountain on her desk. It looked like a miniature grotto. That's where she would like to be—in a nice, quiet cave. That would be heaven.

But first she needed to call Vanessa. She wasn't looking forward to that. She also needed to postpone her wedding. She hated that idea, but with everything going on, she didn't want to walk down the aisle into the hands of U.S. Marshals, or the FBI, or whoever would come to arrest her should things get really out of hand.

Chapter 28

Maria committed the pattern of the city to memory—the mounds, the lines scarring the ground, every pile of rocks she could see. At the next overnight stop she would draw it on the back of the map. That was all she could do. Damn. Her fingers itched for some mapping equipment and a trowel. And the peace to work unmolested.

She reluctantly climbed down from the ancient vantage. At the foot of the mound the edge of a smooth-looking object caught her eye. She scraped her boot gently over its surface—an artifact. She picked up the item along with a companion piece near it. A potsherd. A fragment of pottery. A fragment of the history here. The faint markings on the scorched surface looked as if the object had been shaped by coiling a snake of clay. She flicked the edge of the piece with her thumbnail. The substance had a gray temper, perhaps slate. She took the sherds with her and slipped them in the backpack.

Rosetta had gathered up enough unburned wood and had a meal cooking. More soup.

"The vegetables will not be good tomorrow," said Rosetta. "We should eat as much as we can. I picked out the things we can save and threw the rest away."

"I can't think of anyone I'd rather be lost in the jungle with," said Maria.

Rosetta smiled.

As their breakfast cooked, Maria walked over to the arrow on the ground she had made the previous night and checked the direction it pointed against the reading of her compass. They lined up almost perfectly. Nothing wrong with her compass. She hadn't thought there would be, but it was a safety precaution to check. She took out the map and arranged it on the hood of the truck, spreading it out with her hands and weighing it down with the compass, orienting them both to the north.

She thought she knew where they were on the map. She wanted to get to a place called Benjamin Constant. But there were no marked roads from where they were to where she wanted to go. The road she could connect up with looked to be about seventy miles away. That's a long way through the jungle.

She hoped the truck would start. If not, they were in for a long walk. She put the compass and map in the truck.

"You doing okay?" she asked Rosetta. "Need help?"

"I'm fine. It's almost cooked," she said.

Food and sleep had made Maria feel better, think better. This was really a simple problem simply solved. Just get to a phone. The last few days she had been so filled with fear she couldn't think and she'd bought into Rosetta's fear of the man who worked at an embassy. Whoever he might be, he couldn't possibly have control over everyone at all embassies and consulates, or whatever official places they had here. Her plan was to call John and tell him what had happened. He would find out what she needed to do and get help for her. Easy.

As she waited for the food to get done, she took her knife and cut a couple of bandannas from the bolt of brightly designed fabric. She put one over the top of her head and tied it in back. The other one she tied around her neck as a scotch against the sweat and to afford her bare skin some protection from the bugs.

Rosetta handed her a bowl of soup. "You look colorful," she said.

"Trying to keep the bugs out of my hair. Do you want me to make you one?"

"Okay. Let's eat first," said Rosetta.

They sat in the back of the truck and ate the soup with the last of the bread. Rosetta had used a lot of vegetables, so it was more of a stew. It tasted good. She had boiled some beef jerky with it and, though it was a little chewy, it added flavor. And it was protein.

"You look happy," said Rosetta. "You like finding these ruins, don't you?"

"I do. I wish we could stay and explore. But maybe I can come back," she said.

"Would you really come back here?" asked Rosetta.

"Sure. With armed guards," Maria said, smiling at her and taking a spoonful of soup.

The sound of the jungle was loud. It was almost like music the way the birds and monkeys called to one another. She wished she had the luxury to sit and enjoy it. She hadn't expected an adventure when she got here—just look at a few sites, talk with some archaeologists, and meet up with a tour group from Atlanta. She wondered if she had been reported missing or if they just thought she'd changed her mind. Foolish not to be more definite with her plans. She wasn't a good traveler. She hadn't been careful enough.

"Good food, Rosetta. I don't know what I'd be eating if I were alone. I'd probably end up poisoning myself."

"We still have bars and the jerky I took from the Ferreras. I took a lot of stuff that wasn't mine. Jopito really liked his new clothes, especially these boots, and these protein bars were his. I'll bet he's really mad." Rosetta didn't look happy at the prospect.

"I wouldn't worry too much about it," said Maria. "Those people who kidnapped me had no right to do that. People have no right to bully you, kill you, take away your freedom, or hurt you in any way. If Jopito Ferrera lost his good clothes, it is a small price to pay. Consider it reparations for his bullying you. We did what we had to, to escape."

Rosetta nodded and took another bite of her soup. "I can cook better than this," she said.

"This is great. I'll bet you're a real chef in a kitchen with equipment and fresh food."

"I am. If you can cook, you are useful. Around here you have to be useful," she said.

"We are going to get out of this," said Maria. "I have a plan. We are going to get to a place called Benjamin Constant. I'm thinking there will be telephone service and I can call for help. We'll call your mother. She will be so glad to hear from you. I'm going to call my boyfriend and ask him to contact the embassies . . ."

Rosetta shook her head vigorously. "No, I told you, we can't. That's where the bad man is."

"Rosetta, listen to me. He can't have that much influence. Do you know which embassy he worked for?"

Rosetta shook her head.

"This is a good plan," said Maria. "We have money. We'll find an inn and wait for help. We should be safe."

Rosetta put her bowl down and started crying. She tried to climb out of the truck, but Maria pulled her back, put her own food down, and held on to her, pulling her close and kissing the top of her head.

"Tell me what's wrong, baby girl." Maria's voice was very quiet.

Rosetta cried for several minutes. Maria didn't push her. She stroked her hair and rocked her.

"I don't have any papers," said Rosetta into Maria's shirt. Her voice was muffled and so soft Maria almost didn't understand her.

"Neither do I. Mine were lost when I tried to get away from my kidnappers. They are down a river somewhere. We can get new papers," she said.

Rosetta shook her head without looking up. "No. Mama was waiting for papers. They never came before the bad stuff happened. The bad man said she was not really my mama because the papers didn't come."

The adoption hadn't gone through, thought Maria. That added a complication. There was no way she could take a child across all the borders they had to cross with no papers. Perhaps just her word that Rosetta was her child would do. But her original visa didn't list a child with her. Damn.

Maria held Rosetta so she could see her face. She put a hand under her chin.

"I've never liked paperwork. What matters is that in your heart Diane Fallon is your mother, and in her heart you are her daughter. It just means I have to adjust the plan, but I'm going to get you to her, I promise. The United States has a constant problem with illegal aliens crossing the border, so how hard could it be?" She smiled at Rosetta and hugged her. "You are going to get home to your mama. I won't leave you here."

Maria took the bandanna from around her neck and wiped Rosetta's tears. Then she wrapped Rosetta's head with it like she had her own.

"There, we both look very fashionable," she said.

"You promise?" said Rosetta.

"I do. If it looks like we will have a hard time crossing the borders, we'll just call your mama to come down here. No problem."

"She'll come, won't she?"

"She would walk over hot coals to get here. We've gotten away from the bad men. We just have to get to a place we can make a call."

Rosetta hugged Maria hard. She picked up her bowl and the two of them finished eating. Maria helped Rosetta clean the dishes and they packed everything away.

Now, for the moment she had been dreading. Would the truck start? She didn't really want to walk to Benjamin Constant. She got in the truck, pressed the gas pedal, and turned the key.

Chapter 29

Vanessa answered the phone herself.

She was probably expecting my call, thought Diane.

"Vanessa," she said, "have you seen Pris Halloran on the news?"

Of course she had. But Diane's mind was a blank about how to start the conversation. "Hello, how are you?" didn't seem to fit the situation.

"I have," said Vanessa. "I suppose this is payback for all those crime scenes you threw her out of."

"I suppose so," said Diane, wondering how Vanessa knew about that. It wasn't anything she ever had occasion to discuss with her.

"I've recalled Kendel from Mexico," continued Diane. "She and Andie will take care of the running of the museum while I find out what is going on."

"I hate the necessity," said Vanessa, "but I see your point."

Vanessa hadn't tried to talk her out of it. Diane was faintly disappointed.

"This has just been terrible," said Diane. "I . . ."

"Don't apologize, girl," said Vanessa. "Just find out who is behind all this. Do you think it has anything to do with poor Madge?"

Diane hadn't thought of that. Hadn't really thought that Madge's death was anything but an accident . . . except for the shoes.

"I don't know," said Diane. "We don't know yet exactly what happened to her. It's so sad." Then she added, "Madge was wearing tapestry-covered heels. Weren't they her favorites?"

"Yes, she loved those shoes," said Vanessa. "Why?"

"I'll tell you when I understand it better myself," said Diane. She paused for several moments. "I think, with all that's happened, I had better put off . . ."

"No," said Vanessa. "You are not postponing your wedding. There has to be a limit to how much we allow nefarious strangers to control our lives."

"Did I tell you that Gregory Lincoln arrived for the wedding?" said Diane.

"No. I received an RSVP from him. Good, I'm glad he's here. Does he have a place to stay?"

"He's staying with Frank and me," said Diane.

"I'll be delighted to meet him."

Diane bid Vanessa goodbye and hung up. She didn't think it was a good idea to continue with the wedding, but she was only the bride. Whatever . . . She didn't feel like having an argument about it. She and Frank should have just eloped and told everyone the news when they returned.

Diane called Colin Prehoda next. He had also seen the news broadcast. It was sinking in that almost everyone in the viewing area must have seen it. How many people, she wondered, believed that she was a murderer? For most people, an accusation repeated in the news media was enough to make them believe it. Accusations are powerful weapons. That's probably why whoever was behind this had chosen rumors and character assassination as their weapon—send up smoke signals and hope people would cry fire.

"You want to sue her and the station?" said Prehoda.

"Yes," she said.

"What would you consider a remedy?" he asked. Prehoda was all business when he was talking about a case. She liked that in him.

"At the moment I can't think of one strong enough. I would like to strip her and the station of everything. And I want a retraction without weasel words running all through it." Diane paused. "Make it worth your while at the same time I clear my name."

"Let me work on it and I'll get back to you."

"Thank you," said Diane.

"I'm puzzled by this," Prehoda said. "Why would they

go with a story with so many holes in it that are easily checked out?"

"I don't know. Their source must have been convincing. I've had several run-ins at crime scenes with Pris Halloran. That may have something to do with her role in it. She had been working for that small station. I don't know how she got in with a big network affiliate."

"Surely, reporters expect to be run off from crime scenes," said Prehoda.

"She didn't take it well," said Diane.

"If we can show it was payback, that's even better for us," he said.

"I'll be available if you have any questions," she said.

"I'll have many. I'm sorry about Ms. Stewart," he said.

"Thank you. Her death was so unexpected," said Diane.

Thankfully, he didn't pursue any questions about it.

"Okay," said Diane when she was off the phone with Prehoda. "Now to track down Brian Mathews."

Garnett pulled his chair closer and leaned forward in his seat. Diane turned her monitor so he could see it and Googled Brian Mathews' travel blog. True to what she had been told, he was traveling in Peru, visiting historical sites and parts of the ancient Inca trail, and posting both a written and video blog.

She looked at his itinerary. Assuming he was on schedule, he was supposed to be staying at the Cuzco Catedral hotel today. Surely she wouldn't get that lucky. She dialed the hotel number and asked for Brian Mathews. To her surprise they rang the room. She put the phone on speaker so that Garnett could also hear. A male answered. Surprise again.

"This is Dr. Diane Fallon, director of the RiverTrail Museum in Rosewood, Georgia. Is this journalist Brian Mathews?"

"Yes, Dr. Fallon. I believe we met briefly at one of your museum functions."

"Call me Diane, please," she said. It sounded good so far. He didn't sound like someone who was accusing her of drug running.

"If you will call me Brian. What can I do for you?"

Diane had given a lot of thought as to how to approach

this. She did not want to sound accusative. She didn't want him to get defensive. She wanted to keep it conversational. She had been at a loss on how to accomplish that until she heard Garnett's conversation with the *Atlanta Journal-Constitution* reporter. Might as well stay consistent.

"After several disturbing incidents, I've discovered that I've had my identity stolen," she said.

"My brother had that happen. It took him a couple of years to get the thing straightened out."

"I hope it won't take that long. It's getting more and more serious. Whoever is doing it is someone I've apparently offended grievously in some way or other. I won't go into everything that has happened, but one incident involved someone claiming to be you."

"Me? Well, damn. How so?" he said. "Just a minute, honey, I'm on the phone. Sorry. We're going out in a little while. We were supposed to attend a lecture about *Paleo-Indian Migration Through the Americas* by a professor visiting from the University of Georgia, but she was a no-show. Now the wife and I are going out on the town. So someone was pretending to be me, really?"

"That's what I assumed and am calling to verify. Someone who identified himself as you called one of our board members—Dr. Martin Thormond from Bartrum University—and asked Dr. Thormond about my involvement in drug smuggling in South America."

"What? I don't know a Martin Thormond, and I'm a travel reporter and rather enjoy it. Not interested in crime reporting. I'm more of an explorer. I don't like someone using my name. What was their purpose—just sticking their finger in your eye?" He chuckled. "That is, if you weren't drug smuggling."

"Not even close," said Diane. "I used to do human rights investigations in Porto Barquis. As I said, there have been incidences. The first instance that I'm aware of was the call, purportedly from you, to a board member."

"This is malicious, but how is it identity theft?" he asked.

"I've had my e-mail account hacked and embarrassing e-mails sent out in my name. Someone is using my name and doing some rather bad things. The call to Thormond was just the first strange thing that happened. It didn't have the ring of truth to it, so I didn't believe it was from a real reporter," she added, hoping to get in really good with him.

"I appreciate your telling me. Let me or my editor know if this kind of thing happens again," he said.

"I will," said Diane. "Thank you for speaking with me. Have you been approached by any strange people?"

"Are you kidding?" He chuckled again. "Not by anyone who didn't want to sell me something, or guide me somewhere."

Diane eyed Garnett to see if he had a question. He shook his head.

"Thanks again," said Diane. "Have a good evening on the town. I've been to Cuzco and it's a lot of fun. Around the Plaza de Armas and San Blas are many good places to go—I'm sure you've been told."

"I believe we are starting out at a disco bar just off Plaza de Armas. Thanks."

"So," said Garnett when she was off the phone, "he didn't make the call."

"No. I'm no closer to understanding what is going on than I was in the beginning."

She heard a light tap on the door that sounded like Andie's when Andie was being hesitant.

"Come in," she said.

Andie poked her head in. "I'm sorry to disturb you, Dr. Fallon. Liam is here and he has a little information, he said."

Diane raised her eyebrows. "Please, send him in."

Chapter 30

Liam Dugal was older than Andie's twenty-four years, well into his thirties. Had a handsome face, broad shoulders, soft brown eyes, and brown hair. Diane had only recently met him, but she liked him. He had helped her when she had needed help most. Recently out of the military, he was now a private detective and Diane often tossed work his way when she could.

He smiled and nodded to Diane and Garnett as he walked in. He pulled up a chair and sat down next to Garnett.

"Please say you understand what is going on," said Diane.

"I wish I could. But I do have some information. You may already have it."

"I doubt it," said Diane. "I am in total darkness. If you have even a small candle, I'll be grateful."

He pulled out a notebook, opened it, but didn't look at it.

"The, ah, murders didn't happen in Río de Sangue. That's simply the nearest large village with a telephone. The phone's in a bar on a dock on the river. The river is how they get their supplies and mail." He leaned forward with his forearms resting on his knees. The dead men listed on the warrant—Aaron Bowhay, Pico Nune, Luis Portman, and Razer Arizmendi—were local thugs in the area. Aaron Bowhay was the only outsider. He was from Indiana, a dropout military guy, soldier-for-hire type."

Liam stopped a moment and a smile tugged at the corners of his mouth. Diane saw that his eyes were almost twinkling.

"Diane apparently brutalized them," he said. "Two were shot, one was beaten with a club of some sort, another was crushed to death. Two were mauled after that." Liam grinned. "And what was it the doctor in the movie *Seven* said? 'And they still have hell to look forward to.'"

Diane stared openmouthed. "You have to be kidding. And they think I did all that?"

Garnett snorted and shook his head.

"One of the men lingered for a while. As he was dying he named you," said Liam. "Apparently you wield a mean club."

Diane was speechless. She felt the absurd need to say out loud that she was innocent, that she was here in Rosewood when the men were murdered.

"I talked to the woman who keeps the bar," said Liam. "Doroteia Pitta. She said all the men were thugs who ran with minor strong men who are hiding out in various small villages, bullying the locals to take care of them. Two of the dead men, Portman and Bowhay, currently worked for a man named Julio Corday. The other two worked for a man named Marco Calvo, who, I take it, is an enemy or competitor of Corday's."

"The woman told you a lot," commented Garnett. "All this over the phone?"

"My Spanish isn't too good," said Liam. "And she spoke mainly Portuguese. She may have misunderstood who I was."

Garnett and Diane smiled.

"She had no idea how Interpol got involved. She didn't even know what Interpol is. When I told her, she didn't understand why the international police would be interested in these guys. She said they were nobodies."

"Why me?" said Diane. "Why were they focused on me? What is this about?" She turned to Garnett. "Do you think this is related to Simone being here and what happened to her?"

"I don't know. I would say yes, just because of the South American connection, but I haven't any idea what this is about."

"It doesn't make sense to me either," said Liam. "If someone were trying to mess you up, why didn't they pick someone in Atlanta to frame you with? I mean . . . Brazil?"

"How reliable is the story of the deathbed statement?" asked Diane.

Liam shrugged. "I don't know. The whole story sounds like it's gone through a couple rounds of exaggeration. But she did know your name. She said it first, not me."

"This just makes no sense," said Diane.

Garnett focused his attention on Liam. "My people couldn't even reach Río de Sangue. I'm impressed with what you've done."

"It helps having recently been in the military and knowing people who know people who know people. The six-degrees thing works pretty well. You can get to just about anyone anyplace in the world. I found a guy who pilots one of the boats that drops off supplies and mail at Río de Sangue. He's the cousin of a guy who knows a guy I served with. I had to make a few calls in the process, however, before I located him."

"Six-degree thing?" said Garnett.

"You know, six degrees of Kevin Bacon," said Liam.

"The actor?" said Garnett. "What does he have to do with this?"

"It's kind of a game. You don't have to go more than six degrees away to connect any actor living or dead to Kevin Bacon. Usually it's less than six."

"Why Kevin Bacon?" asked Garnett.

Liam shrugged.

Garnett stuck his chin toward Liam as if making a dare. "Rudolph Valentino," said Garnett. "He died well over eighty years ago. Maybe even ninety."

"Too easy," said Liam after sitting silently for a few seconds, thinking. "Valentino was in *The Son of the Sheik* with an actor named Montagu Love. Love was in *All This, and Heaven Too* with June Lockhart—Lassie and Timmy's mom. She was in *The Big Picture* with Kevin Bacon. Three degrees."

Garnett stared at him.

"I spend a lot of time on the Internet Movie Database," Liam said.

Garnett looked like he was about to try to think of an even older or more remote actor. Liam shook his head.

"Don't even try. It's all been done." Liam grinned at him.

"It's based on the six degrees of separation idea," said

Diane. "That the world is so small and interconnected that each of us is no more than six steps by direct line of association away from every other person on earth."

"Well, that's ridiculous," said Garnett.

Liam and Diane exchanged glances, smiled, and looked at Garnett.

"If you wanted to write a letter and get it directly into the hands of the Queen of England, how would you do it?" said Diane.

Garnett shrugged. "Mail it to the palace."

"It might get into the hands of her secretary," she said. "Wouldn't guarantee the queen would get her hands on it."

Garnett shrugged again. "Then I have no idea. I have no connection to the Queen of England."

Diane smiled. "You would give it to me and I would give it to Gregory and he would give it to the queen at the next royal social event he went to. Gregory was knighted recently and his brother is a duke. He's one of those second sons you hear about. And he's been involved in charity work that the queen is also interested in. He knows her. He couldn't walk up to the palace and knock on the door and ask to see her, but he could talk to her at some social event and hand the letter over to her."

Garnett looked taken aback. "I'm two degrees of separation away from the Queen of England."

"Not so strange," said Diane. "She knows a great many people and those people know people and it increases exponentially. Nice little network analysis canon."

"Okay," said Garnett. "I get it about the famous. They know a lot of people. How about someone from a remote tribe in Africa or South America? They don't know anyone."

"Not exactly true. Even the most remote tribes have been visited by missionaries, Doctors Without Borders, or studied by anthropologists. I could probably make a connection in six or fewer steps—given enough information."

"Am I the only one who didn't know about this rule?" Garnett said.

"I believe so, yes," said Diane. She and Liam smiled with expressions of amusement.

Gregory's notebook, thought Diane. All those names and connections he'd been drawing. The name of the perpetrator was probably on that list or no more than a couple steps away—within their grasp. And she had more names he could add. If they could connect any of the names to one of the four dead men, or to these Julio Corday or Marco Calvo persons . . .

"Diane?" said Garnett.

"Just thinking about network analysis. It's one of Gregory's favorite tools."

"So," said Garnett, cocking an eyebrow at the two of them and rising to his feet, "you're thinking you can get Kevin Bacon to find the perps."

Chapter 31

The motor started in such a normal fashion that Maria found herself releasing the tension from her muscles. The beat-up truck had been through a lot the day before. Perhaps, like her, it had just needed a rest. The now-familiar noise of the engine was a relief to hear.

Rosetta let out the breath she'd been holding. Maria wished she knew some way to make the trip less stressful for the little girl. Not that Rosetta wasn't accustomed to stress, but to be so close and yet so far from finding her mother must have her in knots.

Maria continued the story of Harry Potter as she drove from the burned-off clearing into the steamy jungle again, heading toward Benjamin Constant. A place she hoped she could find help.

She had to constantly check the compass. Finding ways they could traverse with the truck that always led north was getting more difficult. They may have to get out and walk sooner than she hoped. But if she could just get a little closer to a town while they still had wheels—while they had a cab to sleep in.

The thick plants surrounding their truck seemed to grow thicker. Maria was about to suggest they would have to abandon the truck. She checked her map again against the compass. Right direction—just no road. She looked on all sides for anything to indicate the jungle might be thinning out, or that there might be a large animal trail or something. She'd go for a rabbit trail at this point. They were obviously near water. The jungle was thicker near water, and it was really thick here. *We're probably going to end up in a river,* she thought. *I can't see ten feet in front of us.* She wondered whether she should get out and scout ahead on foot.

Just as that thought passed through her mind, she saw a face between the giant leafy fronds of the plants ahead. When she blinked, the face was gone. Maria didn't doubt she'd seen a face. She had confidence that, if she saw something, it was there. She wasn't imagining things, was she?

"Rosetta, do you speak some of the local languages?" she asked.

"Some. You talking about that guy in the forest?"

"You see him? Why didn't you mention it? I thought we had a deal after the crocodile incident."

Rosetta giggled. "I told you, I didn't see the crocodile until you were already outside the truck. And I was afraid if I said anything while you were driving over the bridge it would scare you and you would drive off the bridge. You know how you hated the big snake."

Rosetta looked at her and grinned. She didn't appear to be scared. Maria supposed this was the kind of people Rosetta had stayed with when she was on her own. She looked at the child's tan little face and black hair. *The kind of people she originally came from.*

Maria hoped Rosetta's laid-back take on the situation was accurate. *I'm an anthropologist*, she thought. *If I can't deal with indigenous peoples, then I need to turn in my degree.* Of course, as an archaeologist, she only dealt with the dead.

Without warning, there was a loud thump and the truck began rocking. Maria looked in the rearview mirror. She had a passenger. At least it wasn't a snake. The new rider was an indigenous male, mostly naked except for a baseball cap and red body paint. He was going through the supplies in the back—examining the whiskey and things he probably couldn't use but perhaps thought he might trade. It looked like it was market time.

Another man jumped in the back with him, and a third jumped on the hood. This one looked in through the windshield at the two of them and grinned. He appeared to be no more than a teenager. He banged on the hood and pointed off at an angle ahead. Maria drove slowly in the direction he indicated.

"I hope this is the right thing to do," Maria whispered.

"I don't think we have a choice," said Rosetta.

"It's nice to have directions for a change," Maria said. "Think we could talk them into escorting us the whole way?"

She continued to drive at a slow rate, hoping the kid wouldn't slide off the hood. In a few minutes the jungle opened up to a small clearing with long grass huts one after the other. Many more villagers wandered near, peering at them, chatting to one another, and pointing. In the distance, on the other side of the clearing, Maria saw a man, a Westerner in his looks, cut-offs and blond hair, but native in body paint.

"Don't forget our story," whispered Rosetta.

"I won't, but we may have to alter it slightly. The guy looks vaguely familiar. If he's an anthropologist, I may have to use my real name. Full-time anthropologists are a small community and we tend to run across one another at professional meetings."

"You think you might know him?" said Rosetta.

"Possibly met him," answered Maria.

"That's good, isn't it? He'll like you," said Rosetta.

"Perhaps. Unless he's a postmodernist; then we may be in trouble. I may have had some harsh things to say about their approach to research." Maria smiled. "We'll see." She paused as she watched the man come across the compound. "I'll tell you what, I'll attach Maria to my real name, so we can at least be consistent."

"Okay, but don't tell him where we are really going," said Rosetta.

Rosetta had slipped from being a kid and into her shrewd, precocious adult mode—which she did when putting one of her plans into action was called for, and it was kind of scary. Maria went along. The kid was smart and had good survival instincts.

"Lock your door and slide over to me," said Maria.

Rosetta did as she was told. Maria placed her gun in the back waistband of her jeans. She was getting as paranoid as the little girl. She turned off the truck and pocketed the key. She opened the door slightly, pushed the lock on, put an arm around Rosetta, and pulled her out with her. Holding Rosetta on her hip, she closed the door. Rosetta put her arms around Maria's neck. Maria didn't want to get separated from her.

The man wore leather sandals, faded blue cutoffs, and had a large red stripe painted around the middle of his body. If he was an anthropologist, it looked like he may have gone native. But perhaps he was simply in the role the villagers had put him in.

The villagers were chatting among themselves and occasionally shouting to the two newcomers in their midst.

"I sort of know the language," Rosetta whispered in her ear. "A little."

"What are they saying?" Maria whispered.

"I think they are asking if we've come to look at them," said Rosetta.

Perhaps they think I'm another anthropologist come to study them, Maria thought, *Or a doctor!*

"Speak only English," whispered Maria. "I don't want him to think I'm stealing you."

"Okay," Rosetta said.

Maria scanned the compound as she waited for the man to reach them. The space consisted of three long structures with brown-gray grass roofs that looked like grassy tents thrown over a central beam. The jungle encroached almost up to the structures themselves. The largest part of the clearing was the one they were standing in at the moment. So far, the people looked friendly. Several of them were now in the back of the truck.

"We don't get too many visitors," said the man as he approached somewhat warily. He didn't seem like he was too happy with visitors now.

He was older than he had appeared at a distance. He was probably well into his forties. She had thought him a good deal younger.

"I don't imagine you do," said Maria. "Are you an anthropologist, doctor, missionary?" Her voice was still raw and it came out sounding like she'd had too many cigarettes and too much whiskey.

"Anthropologist. How did you get here?"

With great difficulty, thought Maria. He didn't give her his name, so she didn't feel the need to give hers, at least not her real name. She studied his face for a moment. She didn't recognize him, but there was something familiar about him. She must have run across him at some point, probably at a professional meeting.

"My daughter and I were attacked while we were visiting some of the archaeological sites." She pulled down her scarf to reveal her still-bruised throat. "We managed to get away, and we are trying to get to Manaus to meet up with people looking for us."

He wrinkled his brow as he looked at her throat. "Who attacked you?" he asked.

"I don't know. They looked like thugs, bandits. It was very frightening," she said.

He seemed to be considering what she said. He gazed at her through narrowed eyes. Suspicious, she thought—more so than the indigenous people here.

"These people"—he gestured, taking in the villagers— "are a branch of the Yawanawa. They don't see many outsiders."

"They were kind enough to guide us here," said Maria.

"They are very innocent," he said.

"We don't wish to disturb them, or you," said Maria. "We just want to head in the direction of Manaus."

"It will be dark soon," he said. "You can stay the night and we can guide you to a road in the morning." His smile didn't quite reach his eyes.

Maria smiled back. "We would like that. There are a few supplies in the back of the truck we can trade. I must tell you, when I got away, it was in my captors' truck. The supplies are theirs."

This time the smile reached his eyes. "It looks like Wanau has already found something he likes."

Maria looked over and saw that they had a bottle of whiskey.

"I'm Maria, and this is my daughter, Rosetta," she said.

"Hi, Rosetta," he said. "My name is Ric Johnson."

"Hi, Mr. Johnson," said Rosetta in her perfect English.

"Follow me. We'll be eating soon," he said.

Maria put Rosetta down, but held her hand. She retrieved their backpack from the truck before they followed their host. There was something about him that bothered her, but she couldn't put her finger on it. Perhaps it was his basic less-than-friendly attitude. Then again, he was probably not used to talking with anyone other than the people here. And the outsiders he did speak with wanted to cut down the jungle.

At the first hut they came to, they walked up the few rungs of the entry ladder and stepped inside. It had a wooden floor and hammocks along the sides. Baskets of fruits and tubers sat near the door.

A child ran out, laughing, being chased by another child and into the arms of a woman. Just the brief glimpse told Maria the child belonged to Ric Johnson. He had gone native. She didn't act as if she noticed, just followed him to the back end of the hut.

He pointed to a hammock. "You and your daughter can stay here tonight," he said.

"We appreciate your hospitality," said Maria.

"As I said, I don't get many visitors. It's nice to have company. You'll have to tell me about the sites you were visiting over dinner."

"I will. You wouldn't happen to have a satellite phone, would you?"

He hesitated a moment too long. "I did," he said. "I broke it. Or rather, one of the children did. They are curious about everything and tend to play with anything. The next time I hike to civilization, I was going to see about getting it fixed or replaced."

He was lying, she thought. His explanation was longer than it had to be, especially since he was so taciturn on everything else. She held tight to Rosetta's hand.

"How long have you been studying these people?" asked Maria.

"It seems like forever," he said. "We will be eating just as the light starts to fade. You can rest here if you like. This is the time I write, so I'll leave you here. Feel free to wander around. Other than being curious, they won't harm you or your daughter."

He continued his way out the back of the hut and into the next. It was when he turned away from them, his head going from full face to three-quarters to profile, that she remembered seeing him. It was from photographs in the *Chronicle of Higher Education*. He was supposed to be dead.

Chapter 32

Diane sat alone in her office. Notes of her conversation with Liam were scribbled on a piece of paper in front of her. She called Gregory's cell phone.

"Can you talk?" she asked.

"Yes. I'm waiting for Simone's brother to come down to the coffee shop to speak with me. Simone is still in a coma. I fear it doesn't look good for her."

"I'm sorry to hear that. I keep hoping for the best. I have some more names to plug into your network," she said. She briefly related Liam's research and read the list of names to him.

"I have no idea what these people have to do with me," she said, "but I was thinking maybe they could be Ivan Santos' people. Maybe currently, or maybe at one time they fought in his army."

"I'll see if I can find out," said Gregory. "I have—or rather, WAI has—a database on Santos and his activities." He paused as the hospital speaker came on with an announcement and waited for it to finish. "We are making progress," he said. "It's quite a little intelligence bureau you have in your museum there. Any number of resources at your disposal—human, machine, databases. MI-5 has nothing on you."

Diane laughed. "Yeah, and we seem to have just as many situations that need those kinds of resources. I'm going to the crime lab. Call my cell if you need me," she said. "I'll be available. I've put my assistant director in charge until I can work this out."

"Really, over this little thing?" he said.

Diane realized he probably hadn't seen the local news.

"The news media got hold of the story. I'm afraid I've

been outed as a mass murderer. It was quite an unpleasant little news report. The museum needs someone with less of a target on her back right now."

"Just think what an idiot the media will look like when this is over," he said.

"One can hope," said Diane.

"I'll come by when I finish here," he said. "Simone's mother wasn't happy to see me. She also blames me for her daughter's career choice. But there was one strange moment when I first spoke to her. Her face lit up until I said my name. I'm not quite that charming on first meeting, so I'm thinking it was the British accent. There was something about it she liked and for a moment she must have thought I was someone else."

"Interesting," she said. "Gregory, I'm so glad you are here. This would be so much more difficult without you."

"You could do it, but I'm glad I'm here too. Nice to know I'm not the only one who has slid into moral decay."

Diane smiled at the phone when they had finished. It was a comfort to have Gregory investigating this with her. His calm attitude tended to keep her calm. She sat back and gazed around her office a moment. She was struck with the surprising realization that she was actually afraid of losing her job. It wasn't that she couldn't find work somewhere else. It was this job, this museum, these people, this place she didn't want to leave. She took a deep breath and stood up. The only way to save it was to find the truth.

Outside her office, she told Andie she was going across to the other wing.

"I hope you don't mind me calling Liam," Andie said. Her face was creased into a concerned frown.

"He was very helpful," said Diane. "Thanks. And don't worry about this. Look on it as an opportunity. You're in charge of the museum until Kendel gets back."

"I would be more excited about it if it was because you were going on vacation," she said.

Diane smiled at her. "Liam did a very good job. Garnett was impressed with his work. So was Gregory."

Andie beamed. "He's really very clever."

"Hold down the fort," said Diane, as she went out the door. "Don't let anyone intimidate you. They will try. Especially the board."

The lobby elevator was just outside the large double doors leading from the office wing of the museum. She might avoid any social interactions if she rode it up to the third floor. Diane couldn't face any small talk or questions right now, or any sympathetic or curious stares. She stepped in and pushed the elevator button and the door closed before anyone else could get on.

There were no exhibits on the third floor. It was dedicated to the behind-the-scenes work of the museum—the library archives and exhibit preparations. It was where much of the work of the museum took place. It was just as busy as the other floors, but with people she knew.

The elevator came out at the overlook to the Pleistocene Room. From there she had to traverse through Exhibit Preparations to get to the other side. Her staff was hard at work. They looked up as she passed through. None looked as if they were afraid she might be there to murder them. That was good. She smiled at them and went on past offices and labs.

As she passed the staff lounge she stopped and went in for a cold drink of something. Several people were there at tables. Most did not notice her. Some nodded and smiled, looking rather embarrassed. They were some of the newer employees at the museum. The older ones were more or less accustomed to tumultuous strangeness swirling around her.

Two docents were discussing the weather, lamenting that the ten-day forecast predicted daily thunderstorms. "It probably will be fantastic weather," one said, "and I'll have canceled my plans for nothing."

Jonas Briggs, her archaeologist, and Korey Jordan, her conservator, were seated at a table in deep conversation.

"Leo Bassi said she didn't show up and didn't call. That's unusual. You know her, don't you?" said Jonas.

"Her and John too. We were at the big site together. Have you called the department?" asked Korey.

"Not yet," said Jonas. "Leo mentioned it in passing, and it just occurred to me that perhaps I should check. But I assume someone from her department is on top of it. Still, it's bothersome. It's not like her to miss a lecture without notifying someone. She's too professional for that."

Three others at another table were discussing the events in the Mayan Room and poor Madge Stewart. One was wondering if Madge was in some way involved with the Mayan disaster. "I don't think the Mexicans are going to loan the artifacts now," another said.

Diane half listened to the conversations as she looked over the drink selection, deciding what she wanted. She finally decided on a 7UP and put her money in, selected her drink, and started out the door.

Jonas looked up. "Diane," he said.

Not fast enough, she thought.

"Jonas." She walked over and he reached out a hand to her. She took it.

"You doing okay, Dr. F.?" said Korey. His dark face and his amber brown eyes were full of concern.

"I'm fine," she said.

"What the heck is going on?" asked Jonas, patting the back of her hand.

"Damn if I know," said Diane. "But I'm going to find out. Someone seems to be out to thoroughly ruin my reputation. For what reason, I haven't a clue."

"If you need anything, just ask," said Jonas.

"Yeah," said Korey, "whatever you need . . ."

"Thank you both. I'll let you know. In the meantime, Kendel is acting director. I need time to work on this."

"Oh, no, I hate that," said Jonas. "I don't mean Kendel, but . . ."

"It'll be fine. I won't be far off," she said.

"I'm sure you'll have it cleared up in time for the wedding," said Korey.

"I'm sure," said Diane. "Vanessa will insist. It seems nothing is going to interfere with the wedding."

They laughed and Diane was glad to leave them thinking she was okay with all of this. But she wasn't. She hated it. All of it. Right now she was so pissed at Pris Halloran she would like to strangle her with her own microphone cord. *But I would be the first suspect*, she thought.

Diane crossed the dinosaur overlook, headed for the west wing—the dark side—where she and her forensic team worked on dark matters, as her museum staff liked to describe the things the crime lab did behind the locked doors. Dark was how Diane felt at the moment. She punched in the code that unlocked the crime lab door and entered.

Chapter 33

The crime lab was a warren of glassed-in cubicles, a clean space for a wide range of scientific analyses. Usually there was at least one of her crew working in at least one of the cubicles processing evidence from a crime scene. Now, however, David, Neva, and Izzy were sitting around the conference table drinking coffee with Lynn Webber, the medical examiner. David and Izzy stood as Diane approached.

"Andie said you were on your way over," said David.

"She also said you put Kendel and her in charge of the museum," said Neva. Her usually smooth face was wrinkled in a scowl. Her honey brown hair was pulled back with a clip that was in danger of being pulled out, given the way she subconsciously tugged at it.

Diane was getting tired of repeating the same answer. But people would keep asking as they discovered that Diane had stepped down—even temporarily. She hoped it was temporary. She sat in the chair Izzy pulled out for her and took a long drink of her soda.

"Yes, I put Kendel in charge," she said, setting her drink down. "Someone is out to get me, to ruin my reputation, to destroy my life, apparently. I need to focus my attention on finding out who the hell it is . . . and why."

"I think that Pris Halloran is just awful," said Lynn.

Lynn Webber was out of her lab coat, slacks, and boots, and in a formfitting dress of pearl gray silk, a strand of delicate silver chain around her neck, and light gray Italian leather heels on her tiny little feet. Her hair always looked styled, but it was shinier and her makeup fresher. She looked dressed for an evening out, probably meeting someone at the museum restaurant. Their restaurant was one of Rosewood's finest places to eat.

"You're being way too kind to her," Neva told Lynn.

"You've been *here*," said Izzy to Diane, "unless you went to Brazil on your lunch break." He shook his head, looking as confused as Diane had felt these past few days. "Is there going to be some Interpol agent coming to pick you up? Can they do that here in this country?" he asked.

"They work with local law enforcement," said Diane. "Garnett has already talked with me. He's telling Interpol I've been here the whole time. And Gregory has spoken with someone in Interpol." She turned to David. "You remember Cameron Michaels."

David raised his eyebrows. "Yes. UN guy. He's at Interpol now? Really?"

"He's Interpol's UN representative," she said.

"That doesn't seem like a step up," said David. "Anything going on with his career?"

"He seemed happy with the move. I'm just glad we know someone there," said Diane.

"I'm eager to meet this Gregory I've been hearing so much about," said Lynn. She eyed Diane over the rim of her coffee cup.

Diane was glad Lynn wasn't looking at David. His usual poker face broke into an expression that said there was no way Lynn could compete with Marguerite. Neva saw him and propped her chin with her hands to stop the smile threatening her lips.

David didn't like Lynn. He didn't actively dislike her, but she was high maintenance—easy to take offense, yet easy to give it. Diane wasn't crazy about those qualities either, but Lynn had a high level of competence and tended to be very loyal to people she considered her friends. Diane didn't really mind tiptoeing around her—didn't mind too much, anyway.

"I'm glad Gregory's here," said Diane. "He's a comfort."

"So," said Lynn, "everyone's so excited about the upcoming wedding."

"It's hard to imagine how it can proceed under the circumstances," said Diane, "but Vanessa is determined."

"Personally, I think this is the way to go. Let someone

else make all the decisions, and just show up . . . and let them dress you, to boot," said Lynn.

Diane didn't want to talk about her upcoming wedding. It really did seem in the distant future. There were too many things in the way. Too many problems to solve. Right now she couldn't imagine anyone being happy at her wedding.

"Have you . . . ," Diane began. Poor Madge. Diane felt so sad. Madge had lost her life, and her death was being upstaged by other problems—including Diane's wedding. It was wrong. "Have you examined Madge Stewart?" she said simply.

Lynn nodded. "I've finished her autopsy," she said, shifting the expression on her face to suit the new topic. "I sent the report to Chief Garnett. Madge Stewart drowned. I didn't find anything inconsistent with an accident. There were no contusions, and only one light abrasion on her cheek. There was no bleeding in her lungs, no abrasions on her hands or fingers that would suggest a struggle. I found nothing to suggest homicide or suicide. She was a healthy sixty-two-year-old woman."

"Do I hear a 'but' in your voice?" said Diane.

Lynn shifted in her chair and locked her fingers together in front of her. "Yes, I suppose you do. She was dressed in expensive clothes and lovely tapestry heels. Would you go walking in the squishy ground on the bank of a lake in your good shoes—especially fabric-covered shoes? It would ruin them. What woman would do that? Those were expensive shoes."

"Yeah, but—," began Izzy.

"No *yeah, but*s," interrupted Neva. "She wouldn't. Guys might, but none of us girls sitting here at the table would."

Izzy shrugged. "I'm just saying . . . not everyone uses good judgment. She might not have known the dirt was soft."

"We've been having a lot of wet weather lately. She would have to know," said Lynn. "David showed me where she went in. The ground is pretty messed up by the men who pulled her out of the water. Can't tell much there. But there is a single chain barrier beside the trail. Beyond the chain, you have to go down a slight grade before you get to the edge."

"Yes," said Izzy, "and there is a large boulder down there

that makes a good bench." He folded his arms across his chest. "And the chain barrier is low. Anybody can step over it."

Lynn looked over at him and stood up. Izzy moved back in his chair as if he thought she was going to hit him. Lynn pulled out her chair and turned it over on its side. David and Izzy looked at each other, then stood to see what she was doing.

"Would you say the back of this chair is about the height of the chain?" she asked.

"Pretty much. It's low enough for her to step over, even with high heels," said Izzy.

Neva and Diane smiled at him. Diane saw what was coming.

"I'm about Madge's height," said Lynn.

She started to step over the chair. She was stopped by the tight straight skirt on her dress. Her foot wouldn't go over.

"If I wanted to go traipsing over the chain and down the embankment, I'd have to hike up my skirt over my thighs. Madge's skirt was straight. It did have a pleat in the back." Lynn turned to point out the pleat in the back hem of her dress. "It aids in walking, but not in climbing. Madge Stewart may have done that, but I just have a hard time seeing a woman like her hiking up her skirt. However . . . ," she said to Izzy, "she may have had a reason. This is not proof of anything. Diane asked me about the 'but' in my analysis. This is it. The shoes and the skirt bother me." Lynn remained standing and didn't pick up the chair.

"You think she saw something?" asked Neva to anyone at the table who might have an answer.

"Baby swans, maybe," said Izzy. "Lots of people are crazy about those swans. I think they are damn mean. Have you ever been bitten by one of those things?"

"Perhaps she was interested in them," said Lynn. "But she wouldn't have risked ruining her shoes over them."

"But she was at the edge of the lake in her shoes," said Izzy. "We may never know the reason."

"Perhaps not," said Lynn. "There is nothing I can point to that would require Garnett to keep the case open. Nothing. Good shoes and a tight skirt aren't enough."

Lynn looked as if she were considering something. "Did Madge use a lot of makeup?" she asked.

Diane didn't know. She thought back to the board meetings. Certainly she wore makeup, but she didn't think it was a great amount.

"Normal amount," said Diane.

"She had on what would be normal for evening wear," said Lynn. "She also had on false eyelashes, nicely done."

"What are you saying?" asked Diane.

"David, come here for a moment, please," said Lynn. Her words came out like honey.

David came around the table to Lynn and she moved closer to the chair.

"If we were together at the trail and we wanted to cross the chain, how would you handle it?"

David stepped over the back of the chair, then reached over and picked up Lynn like a bride across a threshold, and set her down on the other side. He took her hand as if to guide her down a slope.

Lynn grinned at him and slowly reclaimed her hand. "I was just thinking that she may have been with someone. A man. There are many women who would ruin a good pair of shoes for the right man. I'm not one of them, but a lot would, especially if they didn't date much and found the attentions of a man flattering. Did she date a lot or have a special friend?"

"Not that I'm aware," said Diane. "I don't think she was ever married."

"It's just a thought," said Lynn, righting the chair and pushing it under the table. "I'm meeting someone at the restaurant. Can I leave by the museum side?"

"Yes," said Diane. "Take the elevator on the Dinosaur Overlook. Thanks, Lynn."

"I'm just real sorry about this. I know she was a friend and board member. It's a tragedy."

She started for the door and turned.

"Oh, Madge had a pregnancy at least once in her lifetime," she said.

Chapter 34

Maria stared at Ric Johnson's back as he disappeared into the shadows of the next hut. She searched her mind to recall the story she had read in the *Chronicle of Higher Education*. The details tumbled out of her brain in bits and pieces. It was about an anthropology student. Kyle Manning, she thought—not Ric Johnson—from the University of Chicago. Married with children. Two of them, she thought. He was on a field trip with other students when he disappeared. The boat they were riding in capsized on the Amazon River. That was five years ago. His body was never found. Until now.

What was he doing here? Not anthropology. Where did he expect to publish his work? Under Ric Johnson? Did his Ric alias have credentials? Had he simply run away from all his responsibilities to a place where he felt he had none? Maria thought that was probably what happened. A rather mundane solution to a mystery. Better, however, than having drowned. To be fair, she had no idea what his side of the story was.

Maria looked at the hammock of knotted rope woven with grass. She knelt down to Rosetta's eye level.

"I think it would be a good idea to sleep in the truck," she said.

"Is something wrong?" The little girl looked worried.

Maria would have liked to protect her from all worry, protect her from any thoughts of danger. Have her think the trip from here on out would be easy and safe. But in their present circumstances, that was hardly realistic. She had decided earlier on to be as honest with Rosetta as she could.

"Maybe. I really don't know. But the man isn't who he says he is," she said.

"Neither are we," said Rosetta.

Maria smiled, almost laughing. "You're right. Sometimes there's a good reason to conceal who you are and sometimes there's a bad reason. I don't know what kind of reason he has."

"Who is he?" asked Rosetta.

Maria glanced at the hut he disappeared into, then looked back at Rosetta and spoke softly—easy to do with her still-sore throat.

"He was a student at a university in the United States. I saw a newspaper article telling about how he disappeared several years ago and was thought to be dead. He's changed his name. Maybe it's nothing to concern us, but I would like to sleep behind locked doors."

Rosetta nodded and grabbed Maria around the neck and hugged her.

"I don't like him either," she whispered. "He looks at us funny."

"We are an odd pair, two girls alone in the jungle in a beat-up pickup. He may be as suspicious of us as we are of him."

"Maybe," said Rosetta. "He's not happy like the people here."

Maria looked outside at the children running around playing, the adults working and talking. Rosetta was right—they were a happy group. Perhaps Ric simply had the weight of his past life on him. Perhaps he regretted not telling someone that he had not died, and now five years had passed and he probably thought it was too late.

The two of them walked outside. They watched the people, mostly naked, painted red. Maria wondered if the paint worked as a bug repellant.

Maria and Rosetta wandered over to the women preparing food. Their offer to help was met with laughter. An older woman was roasting wild boar on a skewer over a fire, another was frying grubs in a well-worn, dinted metal pan. Two young girls, Maria guessed they were about twelve, were peeling and cutting up fruit and an assortment of plants. It looked like a feast after the little food they had been eating.

Some of the younger children tried to get Rosetta to play with them, but she clung to Maria. Maria knew she was probably just pretending to be shy. Neither of them wanted to become separated. Their lives felt precarious, like they would have to flee at anytime and needed to stay prepared, stay together.

It didn't take long for the women to finish preparing the meal. The boar had already been roasting before she and Rosetta had arrived. They had only to cook the other food. The tribe was small, not more than twenty people. They all fit in the largest hut, sitting in a circle on the floor. The planks in the floor were rough-hewn and spaced an inch or more apart. They had been coated with something that made them smooth.

The food was piled on wooden platterlike planks in the middle of the circle. A couple of young women passed servings around on wooden or metal plates. The housewares were a mixture of local handmade utensils and items that came from the outside, from the modern world. A woman gave Maria food on a wooden plate for her and Rosetta. Maria watched her host, Ric/Kyle, to see when to eat. He nodded at her and took a bite of the roasted meat with his hands. Maria and Rosetta followed. It wasn't too bad. The meat was a little tough but tasted good. The grubs were crisp and the fruit succulent. The two of them ate slowly.

A bowl of hot drink was handed to them. It had a strong fruit and herb aroma. Maria saw Rosetta snake a finger into the liquid and put it in her mouth. Maria lifted the bowl to her own mouth and started to drink. Ric turned from saying something to the woman sitting by him and watched the two of them. Rosetta was holding Maria's arm and she suddenly squeezed, digging her fingernails into Maria's skin. Maria pretended to take a drink and set the bowl down. She put an arm around Rosetta, pulled her close, kissed the top of her head, and squeezed her arm gently.

Maria ate more food and periodically picked up the bowl and pretended to drink, as did Rosetta. She looked around at the members of the tribe as they ate. None had a bowl of the same drink. They laughed and talked to one another. The children tended to run around, eating from anyone's plate. The young men who had ridden in her truck were apparently telling the story. She couldn't understand the language, but the hand gestures were pretty clear. It looked like a more exciting adventure than it was.

Maria picked a time when Ric wasn't looking at the two of them and deftly and quickly poured the drink through the cracks in the floor. She finished her meal and sat watching the others. It was getting dark and they would be going to bed.

"Rosetta and I are going to sleep in the truck," said Maria to Ric. "We've had a hard time and she feels comfortable in the truck. But I appreciate the offer of the hammock."

"You must be tired of sleeping in the cramped truck. You're pretty tall," he said.

Maria grinned. "You'd be surprised how comfortable it is," she said. She put her hand to her mouth and yawned. "I think, on this great meal, we are going to turn in. Tell the cooks that their food was great and we appreciate them and you sharing with us."

Ric smiled. "I'll see you in the morning, then," he said.

Maria carried Rosetta to the truck, mainly so they could talk without being overheard.

"What was in the drink?" asked Maria.

"*Sorri*, I think she called it," said Rosetta.

The "she," Maria guessed, being the woman who taught Rosetta about plants and herbs.

"Something like that. Maybe *Saaro*. It puts you to sleep. It can kill you."

Maria took a breath and held it. So they weren't safe. Ric or the others would be expecting them to drop into a deep sleep. That's why he had wanted them in the hammock and vulnerable.

They reached the truck, climbed in, and locked the doors. Maria didn't lean against the doors or the window. Rosetta slept with her head on her lap. Maria put the gun where she could reach it in a hurry. She tried to stay awake.

Maria dreamed of *West Side Story*. She awoke to the sound of someone singing "Maria."

"Did you say something?" she asked Rosetta.

Rosetta sat wide-eyed and pointed to the driver's-side window. Ric was there with a rifle pointed at them.

Chapter 35

Diane studied her own navy leather sandals, thinking about what Lynn Webber had said about Madge Stewart and her shoes. She looked up at the group.

"What do you think?" she asked anyone who might want to answer.

Izzy was the first. He had slimmed down considerably since she first met him—not from becoming health conscious, but from losing a child. Food just hadn't been important anymore. Diane understood. Like her, he had been slowly climbing out of depression after he lost his almost grown son in a meth lab explosion. A lab that none of the more than thirty partying students from Bartram University who died there knew was in the basement. It was one of Rosewood's biggest tragedies, touching in one way or another everyone who lived there.

Izzy credited his recovery with the change from being a policeman to being a crime scene specialist, focusing on collecting the evidence that convicted criminals. Diane thought it probably had a lot to do with the friendships among the lab team. She had put together a good group and she was proud of them.

If she wasn't able to solve her problems in a timely manner, the museum directorship wouldn't be the only job she would be in danger of losing. She would also lose her job as head of the crime lab. The lab couldn't afford to have a director with damaged credibility.

"I'm having a problem with the shoes thing," said Izzy. "Dr. Webber told a good story . . . but really? The Stewart woman could have just hiked up her skirt and stepped over the chain and walked down the embankment. It wasn't steep and her heels weren't that high. Are you gals really that obsessed with shoes? Maybe Webber is. I can see that, but what about you, Neva?"

"Hey," she said, "you saying I'm not in her league?"

Izzy turned to David. "Is that what I said?"

David nodded. "Yeah."

"Well, I meant . . . look, the woman dresses up for a crime scene."

Neva smiled at him. "When I was nine I got these white shoes for Easter. Mama told me not to get them dirty. After church I went outside and completely forgot about my shoes—and my dress. I got them both filthy," said Neva. "Kids forget things like not getting their shoes dirty."

"Madge Stewart wasn't a kid," said Izzy.

"Sometimes she was," said Neva. "Look, I'm giving you ammunition for your argument."

Diane knew Neva was right. Diane's big complaint about Madge Stewart was the way her friends—like Vanessa and Laura—had babied her. Hiding in the closet eavesdropping, for heaven's sake, then running to Vanessa like she was tattling. How childish was that?

"But she was an adult," said David, "and whenever I saw her she was always well dressed."

"The woman was, well, I mean, she was on the museum board. Was she, what's the word?" said Izzy. "Was she mentally challenged? You're talking like she was."

"No, she wasn't," said Diane. "But her personality never got out of the stage where she believed everyone would always think she was cute, no matter what she did."

"She was an artist," said Neva. "We talked a few times. She liked my work."

"An artist? Really?" said Izzy. "Do I know her work?"

Diane and Neva smiled. "Maybe," said Neva. "She illustrated children's books. Her preferred style was pointillism and she used bright colors. I liked her work."

"Pointillism?" said Izzy.

"Dots of paint," said David. "Seurat."

"Not ringing a bell," said Izzy. "I'll Google it."

Diane had the feeling that none of them wanted to talk about Madge Stewart's death. She didn't either. And it wasn't up to them to solve it. It was up to Garnett. She was satisfied to leave it to him—sort of. However, Lynn's story, as Izzy called it, did leave her wondering. Why did Madge go down to the edge of the lake?

"Do you have a tox report?" Diane asked.

"Not yet," said Neva. "Lynn hasn't sent any samples over. She may send them to the GBI or another lab because of our closeness to Madge."

"How about her clothes?" said Diane.

"Same," said David. "The only thing we did was work the scene. As Lynn said, the scene was pretty well trampled. I found where her heels went into the edge of the bank before she fell in, but I haven't found any trace evidence whatsoever. I practically vacuumed the boulder. I looked for prints, but it was weathered sandstone. But that was just being thorough. It's not a surface to hold prints. I also looked at the metal posts the chain was threaded through. I didn't find anything."

"He brought the chain back here," said Izzy.

"Just being thorough," said David. "I'll check each link. There might be a partial. I'm not optimistic. The lake was deep where she went in—about seven feet. Jin dived and did a grid search of the bottom. He found her other shoe and a few beer cans."

Diane nodded. "Do you feel like it was an accident?" she asked David.

He hesitated. "As bad as I hate to say it, I'm like Lynn. Yes, I think it was an accident. But it nags at me. I don't know if it's because it was someone I knew, or because of my basic suspicion of all deaths that occur when you are under ninety and not asleep in bed."

Diane looked at the other two.

"Accident," said Izzy. "Neva said she couldn't swim."

Diane looked over at Neva.

"She said she never liked the idea of getting her hair wet or water up her nose. But she liked boating. She wasn't afraid of the water," said Neva. "She was illustrating a book about two kids learning to sail. We were talking at lunch one day outside on the patio. When she found out I was an artist, she liked talking to me."

Diane realized that she had never had a good conversation with Madge, really. Just party conversation at the museum events, or mildly unpleasant conversations at board meetings. The thought increased her feelings of guilt. She had never really tried to get to know Madge. She was a more interesting person than some of her annoying habits had led Diane to believe.

"What about you, Neva? What do you think?" asked Diane.

"Accident. Isn't the simplest explanation the most likely? For it to be homicide, the story gets too complex. And nothing whatsoever indicates she jumped into the lake to drown herself." She paused. "What about you?"

"I don't know. The shoes do bother me a little. But why would anyone do anything to Madge? She was the most unlikely person to be murdered. Unless it was some maniac wandering the nature trails behind the museum. We'll leave it to Garnett."

"He'd like us to do more of that anyway," said Izzy.

"Yeah, I know," said Diane. "I'm just a criminalist busybody."

"I didn't say that," said Izzy. He turned to David. "Did I?"

David's chuckle was interrupted by a knock at the door on the museum side of the lab.

Diane raised her eyebrows and got up and looked at the tiny built-in monitor beside the door. It was Gerda Sorenson from the mailroom. The tiny blond woman looked nervous, casting glances to her right where the crime lab guard for the museum entrance was posted. He sat in an office with a glass front and was dressed like the Rosewood policeman he was. Gerda probably thought he could come out and pull a gun on her at any minute. Many of the museum personnel were leery of the third floor west wing of the building. *If they only knew about the equipment David kept in the basement*, Diane thought as she opened the door.

Chapter 36

"Hello, Gerda," said Diane. "Can I help you?"

"I need to talk with you. I think. It's about Madge. I should have said something yesterday."

Diane thought that was an interesting thing to say. Madge wasn't dead yesterday. But Gerda saw something—she had Diane's attention.

"Please come in." Diane showed her to the seat left vacant by Lynn Webber when she departed.

Gerda Sorenson was in her forties, petite, tanned, with a slightly lined face that went along with being a sun worshipper. Her hair was pale blond and her eyes, light blue. She wore a sand-colored cotton jumper with lots of pockets, and a pastel yellow shirt.

"You know David Goldstein, Neva Hurley, and Izzy Wallace?"

Gerda nodded. The crime lab staff spent many of their breaks in the museum break room, frequently ate at the restaurant, and often visited the exhibits. Since not one of them was shy, they were well known to most of the museum staff.

Gerda sat quietly for a moment. No one said anything but simply waited for her story to unfold in its own time.

"A mailroom is like the post office," she said simply. It came out like a Zen koan.

Gerda paused and Diane half wondered if she wanted them to meditate on it. Instead, Diane nodded encouragement.

"Only I or people who work for me can put up or deliver the mail. No one can just come in and go through it," she said.

Diane cocked an eyebrow. *Ah.*

"Yesterday morning I came in and found Ms. Stewart in the mailroom going through bags of mail waiting to be put up. She had spilled part of a bag on the floor," continued Gerda.

She twisted the gold band on her ring finger as she spoke. "I was stunned. I asked her what she was doing. I used a little harsh language, I'm sorry to say. But this was serious. She said she had ordered a catalog and was looking for it. The board members have mailboxes if they want to receive mail here, and some, like her, do. I told her that she can't go rummaging through the mail, that it was against the law. She . . ." Gerda stopped a moment. "I don't like speaking ill of the dead. She's not here to defend herself."

"Nevertheless," said Diane, "we need to hear your story." Diane pitched her voice so that she hoped she was both comforting and reassuring to Gerda that she was doing the right thing.

Gerda nodded, still twisting her ring. "Ms. Stewart got all huffy. She stuck her chin out and said she was going to tell Vanessa Van Ross on me. Just like that—those words. She said she was going to tell on me. I told her it was illegal even for Mrs. Van Ross to go through the mail like that. I suggested to her that we both go speak with you. She got huffy again and said, 'Well, we'll just forget this, then.' And she stormed out of the room."

"That was all she said she was looking for?" asked Diane. "A catalog?"

"That's what she said. I couldn't imagine the . . . well, the arrogance of tossing people's mail on the floor to look for a catalog. I told her that anything that came in for her was put in her box. When she left I looked at the boxes that had been filled the previous day. I swear, it looked like she had been rummaging through them as well. Just for a catalog."

Gerda paused again. She had stopped twisting her ring and had her hands neatly folded in front of her. "I wasn't going to mention anything, even though I know I should have. She shouldn't have been going through people's mail like that. But I thought it would be better to just let it pass. Then she died. Drowned. I heard about it when I came in this morning. I didn't know if it was important, but I thought I ought to tell someone."

"You did the right thing," said Diane. "Was there anyone in the hallway or nearby who might have been with her?"

Gerda thought for a moment. "I don't recall anyone."

"How did she get in?" asked Diane.

"With a key," said Gerda. "I just assumed that all the board members have masters."

Hardly. Diane would never give masters or submasters to the board members. Only she, Vanessa, and Security had that level of keys.

"How many people in the mailroom have a key to it?" asked Diane. She knew that only Gerda and Andie were supposed to have mailroom keys.

"Just me and your assistant. And mine hasn't gone missing. I don't give it to anyone. When I'm off, Andie opens the door for my assistant."

"What was Madge wearing?" asked Diane.

"Wearing?" said Gerda, as if she didn't understand the question, or perhaps thought it to be strange.

"Was she dressed casually, or dressed up?" said Diane.

"Oh, she was fairly dressy in a casual kind of way. She wore black slacks, a rust-colored blouse, and a black shirt jacket," she said.

"What about her shoes?" asked Izzy.

Diane and Neva suppressed smiles.

"She had on a pair of Naughty Monkeys," she said.

Izzy sat very still with an expression on his face that said from now on he would leave all fashion questions to Diane and Neva.

Gerda didn't notice Izzy's blank stare and went on speaking. "I noticed because my daughter wears them and I thought they were kind of young for Ms. Stewart. They were very pretty, though. Open toed, multiple animal prints in yellow, red, and orange. Low sling heel. Perhaps I shouldn't say this, but I thought she was dressed young. She was not vulgar, mind you—she was tasteful and she looked nice—her clothes just, well, looked young."

"What about her makeup?" asked Diane.

If Gerda thought the questions odd, she didn't show it.

"Nice. Professionally done. It was really the best I've seen Ms. Stewart look. We take some of the quilting classes together at the museum and I see her regularly," she said.

"Would you say she was dressing better, dressier, younger than usual?" asked Diane.

"Yes. She was that day. But the change was fairly recent. I was in class with her last week and she looked like she usually did. That's not to say she looked bad. She was a good dresser. Just different. Not dressing to be noticed. That's what my daughter would have said about her."

Gerda paused and pressed her lips together. "They are saying it was an accident," she said. "It was, wasn't it?"

"There's no evidence at all that says it wasn't an accident. Anytime something unexpected happens to someone, we have to ask a lot of questions that may seem irrelevant. It's one of the things we do here," said Diane.

She could almost hear Izzy shouting in his head: *No, it's not! It's not supposed to be. You are supposed to let the detective ask the questions*. And he was right. She didn't look over at him.

Gerda glanced around the room as if just now realizing that this was her chance to get a look at the dark side.

"Were there any other things you noticed about yesterday?" asked Diane.

Gerda looked back at her. "No, that's all I can remember. I'll let you know if I think of anything else."

"Thank you," said Diane.

She stood and so did Gerda. Diane escorted her back to the door and let her out. Thanking her again for coming to them, and telling her that Chief Garnett might want to speak with her, but it would be all right.

"So," said Diane as she sat back down, "was Madge into something, or was this just Madge being Madge? Have any of you changed your mind about this being an accident?"

Izzy shook his head. "I still think it was an accident. This new info is suspicious, but still nothing to say the woman was murdered. Do they look like monkeys?"

Neva patted his arm. "No, but they are flashy and kind of cool." She looked at Diane. "I have to agree, but ... that 'but' is still hanging out there."

Diane looked at David, who had a very low suspicion threshold.

"It's worth some further investigation. The things we have already talked about, and her breaking into the mailroom, are suspicious, but what bothers me the most is the abrupt change in her looks, coupled with all the above. I hate to say it, but Lynn may be onto something."

"I agree that it needs looking into," said Diane. "I'll tell Garnett and he can decide." She looked over at Izzy and he grinned at her.

"Hey, little buddy." Izzy looked at Neva. "Is Mike coming back for the big wedding?"

Neva smiled. "He wouldn't miss it."

"Where is he now? Did you say in the ice again?" he asked.

Neva frowned. "Yes. He said he wasn't going ice caving again, but the company talked him into it. I'm really nervous."

"He'll be fine," said Izzy. "He's probably already finished. Isn't he due back pretty soon?"

Neva nodded. "He's supposed to call or e-mail tonight."

Diane understood Neva's nerves. The whole idea scared her too. She, Mike, Neva, and Jin were caving partners. Mike was a really good caver and expert rock climber. Always extra cautious. Mike was also her geology curator and she needed him back to discuss the new exhibit he had pitched to her before he left. She wished museum concerns were the only ones she had. She might not even be director when he got back.

So much strange unpleasantness had descended and was picking like vultures at her and her friends. Poor Madge. Whatever Diane thought about her, Madge enjoyed her life and deserved to live it. *Accident* was just not sitting well with her. And even if it was an accident, what took her to the edge of the lake?

"Do you have anything new on Simone and the Mayan exhibit?" Diane asked.

Neva shook her head. "I've given the information we have to the DEA guys. They were very interested, as you can imagine."

"They interviewed me," said Diane. "At least they didn't arrest me. They had heard the rumors."

"Oh, for heaven's sake," said Neva. "Was it unpleasant?"

"Mildly. I expect them back, just on general principles."

"David is going over the detritus from the Mayan exhibit, literally with a fine-tooth comb," said Neva.

"I'm hoping to find some transfer from the guys who attacked," said David. "I'm determined to prove the fire didn't destroy everything."

Diane nodded. "David and I are having dinner with Gregory and Frank at the museum restaurant, so I'm going back to my office to freshen up. I appreciate the work you guys are doing. I know I haven't been around much."

"Sure," said Neva. "Anything we can do, we will. You know that."

Diane left and went back to her museum office, where she had a change of clothes. She was looking forward to one evening of peace. Then again, Gregory would be back from the hospital. She was eager to hear what he had discovered. She opened the door to Andie's office.

Andie was laughing and talking to a tall man, light brown hair, medium complexion, and boyish good looks.

"Steven," said Diane in surprise.

It was Steven Mays, one of the people she had worked with in South America. Gregory and David had been trying to get him on the phone at the State Department in Washington.

"It's great to see you!" said Diane.

Chapter 37

Maria snapped fully awake as if she had been Tasered. Ric—or rather, Kyle—was staring at her through the window, backlit by the early-morning sun, his rifle aimed at her head. Behind him she saw several members of the tribe standing back, talking among themselves and watching Kyle.

"Get down on the floor," said Maria.

Rosetta slipped down and huddled under the dash with her backpack. Maria glanced at the passenger window to see if anyone was there. No one.

"Get out of the truck now, damn it!" he yelled.

Maria felt for her gun. She couldn't find it. She made a quick survey of the truck. It was on the floor under the brake. The others were in the backpack. *Shit.*

"Now! You are going to do what I say. Why doesn't anybody listen to me? Get out or I'm going to start shooting," he said. The tendons in his neck stood out as he yelled. His face was red, but not with paint.

Maria had no choice. She wouldn't be able to get the gun before he could shoot. Damn, she hadn't meant to fall asleep. She'd stayed awake for most of the night mentally going over their route to Benjamin Constant in order to keep from nodding off. She had seen some of the tribe wandering around in the dark with only a small torch to light whatever route they were taking around the compound. That had surprised her. She had been under the impression that everyone pretty much stayed inside and under some kind of mosquito netting. She had wondered if they were waiting for her to fall asleep. Deeply asleep.

Maria opened her door, pushed the lock, and quickly closed the door, locking Rosetta inside the truck, wondering if that was a good idea. Rosetta might need to run to the forest.

"What is it you're after?" she said when she faced him, hoping she looked a lot less afraid than she felt. A good thing about being almost six feet tall was that she could mimic being intimidating with a fair amount of accuracy.

"Peace," he said. "I just want some peace. Get the kid out. I mean it, or I'll shoot up the truck."

"You would do that?" she said. "Kill a child?"

"Shut up and do what I say. Do you want to take that chance?"

"Rosetta, sweetheart, unlock the door and come stand by Mommy," she yelled.

"I know who you are," he said. "You're name isn't Maria. It's Linda Chambers or something like that. I saw you at a meeting. Some big-time archaeologist everyone was afraid of."

That surprised her. "You're kidding. Afraid of me? What the hell for?"

"They said you pick at any little mistake in a paper and rip it to shreds in front of everybody."

Absurdly, she felt like arguing with him. It wasn't true, for heaven's sake. He must have been with someone whose paper she had taken exception to. But no one was afraid of her. She wasn't that intimidating in real life. Instead she said:

"The nice thing about being female is that you can change your name every time you get married. I use my maiden name professionally. When I was in graduate school, I danced competitively. I used a different name there too."

She was surprised at how easily lies came out of her mouth. Ironically, she wanted to convince him she wasn't lying to him. Confessing to a lie didn't seem to be the way to do that.

"You know who I am, I'll bet," he said.

Keep him talking. There must be some way to talk our way out of this. Find out what he wants.

"I thought you looked familiar. It took a while, but I remembered seeing a story about you in the *Chronicle*. Does your family know you aren't dead?"

"No, and I want it to stay that way for now," he said.

Rosetta had scrambled out of the truck. Maria gently shoved Rosetta behind her.

"Why? I would imagine they would love to hear that you are alive." Maria hoped she sounded sympathetic.

It was hot and sweat trickled down Kyle's face to his chest, making trails through his body paint.

"Oh, they would at first. Then I'd have to explain that I was a failure. My family expected great things from me. My wife, my in-laws expected greatness. Sylvi was always telling everyone I was going to be a professor at Harvard when I graduated. At family reunions my in-laws and my parents would say the same things to people. I wasn't going to be hired by Harvard or any of those Ivy League schools. Or they would say I would probably be a Rhodes Scholar. They just wouldn't let up. Kept setting the bar higher and higher before I had even jumped the first one."

Maria watched his rifle waver slightly. He wasn't as tall as she and he was skinny. His ribs showed and he had little muscle. Though Maria was slim, she was muscular. She rode horses, ran, worked as an archaeologist. She was strong and she was desperate—she could take him. She needed an opportunity that would make sure Rosetta would be safe.

"You were at Chicago, weren't you? That's a good school. You must have been doing well. You're here studying a rare indigenous tribe. That makes for good credentials. Not many opportunities to have a tribe like this to study."

"I have no idea what to say about these people. They sleep, they eat, they reproduce, they move from place to place. Not much else."

He doesn't have any idea how to do anthropology, she thought. She had had students like that—good in the classroom, bad in the field, no idea how to apply what they learned. She had whiners too. But Kyle was one of the biggest she had ever come across. Clearly he wanted to go home, but here he was sweating in the middle of the jungle with people he didn't understand and didn't want to understand, afraid to go home and face his family. She wanted to roll her eyes, tell him to grow up, or grow a pair. Instead she tried another tack.

"If you have a big find, you can go home a hero in the academic world. That's what your family wants. One big find and you can write your own ticket." Not true, but she could sell it.

"I told you, I don't know anything about these people. There isn't anything special about them," he said. "They are like every other damn dirty tribe out here."

"I'm not talking about anthropology. I'm talking about archaeology. On the way here I found an undiscovered Inca site. It's probably the largest ever discovered, over eighty hectares."

Kyle wrinkled his brow. But Maria was on a roll now.

"Over two hundred acres, maybe more. That's bigger than any of the known sites."

"You're lying," he said.

"No, I'm not. We camped there last night. I picked up a couple of potsherds to send to someone at the University of Brazil. They're in my bag. The pottery is Incan, I'm sure, but I'm not familiar with ceramics well enough to know the chronology."

"I'm not an archaeologist," he said.

"You don't have to be, you only have to be the discoverer. Everyone loves an explorer."

"The Brazilian government would just take it over," he said.

God, what a whiner. She was giving him a huge gift on a silver platter and here he was figuring out ways it wouldn't work.

"What do you intend to do? Kill me? Is that easier than taking credit for a huge discovery and going home?"

"I'm just going to hold you here, tie you up, and let them come get you."

"Who?" Maria felt a sick knot forming in her stomach.

"Some men I know. They come through sometimes, looking for animals and things. I told them you had escaped from somewhere south of here. I thought they would know. They are plugged in to what goes on around here."

The son of a bitch.

"Your phone works, after all, I see," she said.

Maria was going to have to take him now. There was no choice. She wasn't going to allow them to recapture her and Rosetta. She reached behind her and pushed Rosetta down, hoping she would understand and hit the ground and roll under the truck and away. She felt the little girl slide quietly to the ground, holding on to her leg too tightly. At the same time, Kyle fell to the ground with a thump.

Chapter 38

Maria stared at Kyle on the ground. His eyes were rolled back in his head, his rifle lay under him. She thought he'd had a seizure—a very fortuitous seizure—until she saw the young man in the tree with a blowgun. He climbed down with astonishing speed and agility and ran toward them.

Rosetta stood up and clung to Maria's side. A woman, the mother of the child that looked like Kyle, also came toward them, her grassy skirt swaying with her quick steps. The others, including all the children, hurried toward their houses. The young man picked up the rifle and shook it in the air above his head.

The woman began yelling at Kyle. She kicked him a couple of times with her bare feet.

"No good. No good," she said. "Stupid. Stupid."

She looked up at Maria and continued her rant. What English she used gave way to her own language. Maria looked to Rosetta.

"She says he's no good," said Rosetta. Maria had gotten that part. "She says when he came they thought he would protect them from the bad men who came and hurt the forest and stole the birds out of the trees, beat the men and women of their village. They did this for fun. He didn't protect them. He was afraid of the bad men."

The woman looked down at Kyle again. His eyes were not rolled back in his head now, but he looked dazed and was unmoving.

The woman continued her tirade, half at Kyle, half at them. Her dark eyes sparkled with her anger. Rosetta translated. Maria thought she recognized some of the words as Portuguese.

"He knows how to do nothing—he can't hunt, he can't help us build our homes, he can't even hunt for grubs. Useless. Useless." She looked at Maria. "He is useless. We try to move away and leave him, but he follows us. We go with him to trade. We need tools, plates, big handle pots for carrying—we need metal things. He gets only things for himself, for his far-talk box, he forgets to trade for things we need. He asks stupid questions—why we decorate with feathers, why we paint our bodies, what our dances mean— stupid things even our children know."

She stopped and took several breaths. Maria could see this had been building for a while.

"We hoped you came here to take him back. Then he calls the bad men—here to our homes. We have to move now. They come soon."

"How soon?" asked Maria. Rosetta translated for her.

"He called yesterday, soon after we got here," said Rosetta.

So they'd had all night to travel, thought Maria. She and Rosetta had to move fast.

"Ask her if we can have the far-talk box," said Maria.

Rosetta asked and Maria didn't need a translation to understand. The young woman used her hands as if holding the phone and beat it against the ground.

"She said it calls the bad men so they killed it," said Rosetta. The little girl sounded as disappointed as Maria felt.

Maria wondered how much time they had. All the gains they had made were wiped out by the phone call of a wimpy self-centered little bastard. Maria felt like kicking him one time for good measure herself—and she had her boots on.

"Tell her we have to go," said Maria. "Before the bad men get here."

The Yawanawan woman had apparently gotten all her frustrations out—for herself and her tribe. She nodded at the two of them and turned and left in the company of the man with the blowgun and rifle, without a backward glance at Kyle. Maria would like to have had the rifle.

She checked the gas in the last of the spare containers. Not much, just a few gallons. They would be on foot before long, but she intended to take the truck as far as it would carry them. She siphoned the gas into the truck's gas tank, got in the cab, and turned the key in the ignition. It took several scary moments for the engine to finally crank. She tried to think how far the men could have come if they had been traveling all night. She and Rosetta still had a significant head start, but whoever Kyle called may have an encampment closer than the one they escaped from. They may have better, faster vehicles. Hell, they may have a helicopter.

Maria put the truck in gear and headed out of the village. Glad to be going, hating that they hadn't gotten away clean, hating they had run across Kyle, hating that they were almost out of gas.

Maria wondered if any of her friends were looking for her. The people at the site she was visiting just before she was kidnapped wouldn't know she was even missing. The man driving her to Cuzco—the only witness to her abduction—turned out to be one of the kidnappers. He wouldn't tell. But she hadn't shown up for her lectures. The people there would be in touch with her department to find out why—wouldn't they? Surely John, her boyfriend, would be on the phone to somebody by now, since he hadn't heard from her in almost a week. Surely by now someone knew she was missing—didn't they?

But if her friends were looking for her, where would they look? Not here. Brazil is not where she disappeared. She disappeared in Peru. On the other hand, perhaps, if nothing else, they could follow the trail of dead and dying bodies she had left behind her. Surely someone besides the bad guys had noticed.

One good thing, she thought, as she left the clearing and drove into the jungle, again looking for something she could pretend was a road, was that the closer they got to Benjamin Constant, the more villages they would run across where they could perhaps find help, perhaps get gas, maybe some good directions. Maybe they would stumble upon a tourist boat on one of the rivers. Something.

"You doing okay, Rosetta?" asked Maria.

Rosetta nodded. "That was close," she said.

"Yes, it was, but we have been pretty lucky for most of our trip," said Maria.

Rosetta looked over at her. "What would you call unlucky?"

Maria smiled. "How about we eat something? Do we have any bars left, or do we need to find a fruit tree?"

"We have some bars left," said Rosetta. She dug down in her backpack and came up with a bar. "Maybe we should split what's left," she said. "Just eat a little. I have some fruit too. I took it at dinner last night."

"That's a good plan," said Maria.

Rosetta broke the bar so Maria had the larger piece.

"You take more," said Maria.

"But you're bigger," said Rosetta.

"Right now it's one for all and all for one," said Maria. "You need to eat too. You're the thinker."

Rosetta smiled and broke off another piece. They ate the bar in silence. Maria chewed slowly, savoring the taste. When the bars were gone they would be hunting and gathering for their food.

"You want to hear the rest of Harry Potter?" said Maria.

Rosetta nodded. "I wish we were magic."

"Me too." Maria resumed the story where she had left off—Harry Potter and his friends trying to get past the three-headed dog.

As she told Rosetta the story, Maria constantly watched her rearview mirror, and she watched out the side windows and as far ahead as she could see. She noticed that Rosetta did too.

They were going too slow, but they were lucky to be going at all. They were lucky they were in a place where most of the flora was in the canopy and not on the ground.

Then the jungle was thick again. Leafy branches and fronds pushed against the truck, slapping the sides. More than once she came across a fallen tree or limb that she had to drive around. She was getting tired but tried not to show it.

Abruptly, they broke through the thick growth into an open area that had been clear cut—and there was a road, a logging road. Relief. They could go faster. At least it wouldn't be such hard driving.

"Let's take a quick bathroom stop," said Maria.

They were back in the truck and moving in less than three minutes. Neither wanted to linger. Both were scared.

Maria tried to be cheerful. She put as much excitement in her voice as she could muster as she told the continuing story of Harry Potter.

"When we get you home, maybe we can rent the movie and watch it," said Maria.

Rosetta nodded. "I would like that. You think Mama has seen it?"

"A lot of people have. Does she like fantasy?" asked Maria. "You said she likes science fiction."

"I think she likes fantasy," said Rosetta.

The little girl was craning her neck, looking for danger. It squeezed Maria's heart to see her always scared.

The red dirt logging road was the widest and smoothest road they had been on, but even it was primitive—sometimes washed and rutted in places. Good thing it wasn't the rainy season yet. Maria wasn't sure she could get the truck through this road if it were wet.

"Your mama will want to see the movie with you, anyway," said Maria. "There are a lot of fun movies that she's going to want to watch with you."

Several miles passed before Maria had to make another travel decision. They came to a fork in the road. The smooth wide road went to the east. The other road, less traveled, narrower, rougher, went north—the way they wanted to go. At least it was a road. They went north.

This route seemed to have a steeper grade and the jungle closed in and got thicker again. Perhaps they were near a water source, a river perhaps. She rolled down her window and listened over the truck noise for the sounds of water. Maybe she heard something. It was hard to tell. She didn't want to stop the truck to investigate. She rolled up the window, still trying to maintain a speed that would get them to their destination in the shortest time possible. The steeper grade was getting noticeable. They weren't going over a mountain, but they were definitely experiencing a higher elevation.

Approaching a curve, she glanced in her rearview mirror. There it was, below them, down the incline of the road, the thing they had dreaded—a vehicle—gaining on them, kicking up dust, moving fast. Maybe they weren't after them. Maybe they were. Maria pressed the gas.

"I see it," said Rosetta.

They both heard the ping on their roof, then another. They were being fired on. Maria pressed the gas harder. It was to the floorboard. She looked at the needle. They were running out of gas.

"Get out the guns," she said calmly.

Chapter 39

Diane and her party sat at a round table in the rear of the restaurant. Frank came a few minutes late and took a seat next to Diane, kissing her cheek as he sat down.

Diane smiled at him. He looked good. She would like to dump everything and just go somewhere on a honeymoon. Get married later when things were resolved and calm. Instead, she sighed and introduced him to Steven Mays. They shook hands across the table.

"So you're Diane's intended," Steven said. "They said you track fraud and computer crimes. That must be pretty high-tech these days. Is it hard to stay ahead of the hackers?"

Frank agreed he had to work to stay on the cutting edge, and they had a short discussion on how enormous amounts of money can be stolen in a fraction of a second.

No one talked about anything that was at the top of their list of concerns, and none of them asked Steven why he was here. He hadn't returned Gregory's calls and when David finally got in touch with him, he seemed vague, only cursorily sympathetic and rather distant. Now here he was.

The waitress came with drinks. Diane had ordered Frank tea the way he liked it. All of them ordered steak. Diane guessed that they, like her, were hungry for red meat. Steak and potatoes were good food for when the going got tough. When the orders were taken and the waitress left, Steven put his palms on the table, fingers spread, almost like a gesture of surrender.

"This isn't easy," he said. "I know, David, Gregory, I blew you off. Honestly, I didn't want to hear from anyone from . . . from that time. The memories are still vivid, and I guess they always will be. I remember the smells, the colors, the sounds . . . the horror. I just like to keep them tucked away. I know I showed little sympathy for the predicament you're in. It's not that I wasn't sympathetic, I just didn't want to revisit that time."

He took a drink of his tea. "Nice," he said and set it down on the table. He paused for several moments. No one urged him on. They waited, sipping their own drinks.

"I was actually in Canada when I talked to you, David. I flew back to Washington in a friend's private plane. When we landed at the airport, I was met by the FBI. They and the DEA searched the plane. Said they were just following up a tip. They searched me and they searched my luggage. They didn't find anything and said everything was fine. Just routine. It was all hush-hush, didn't make the news, and everyone was polite."

He took another long drink. He seemed to be summoning his strength.

"I know that world—politics. It wasn't routine. And I know no one will mention it. My supervisors won't call me in and question me about it. They won't say anything. I also know I won't be promoted. Ever. Operationally speaking, in Washington rumors are treated as true. Can't afford the risk they might be true, so better be safe than be hit with a scandal later. If I don't find out who did this and why, my career is over."

He looked at each of them around the table. "So I came here. To help and to get help. I'm just sorry it is so self-serving."

No one said anything for a moment. Diane spoke first.

"The massacre was the most horrible thing that ever happened to any of us, and we all dealt with the tragedy in our own way. I don't judge anyone's way of dealing with it."

"That's the truth," said Gregory. "We are all a little self-serving about this secret rumor mill that's churning away somewhere. We are glad you are here. It's very nice to see you again, Steven."

Steven smiled, then grinned. "Truthfully, it's nice to be here. It wasn't that I didn't like you guys."

The salads came, then the steaks shortly after that. Steven spent the time telling Frank about himself.

"Your accent doesn't sound South Carolina," said Frank, pushing his salad away and attacking his steak.

"Something I've worked on. When I went to college, I decided my accent might hold me back." He tilted his head and smiled. "Youth can be cruel. I probably wouldn't do it now, but at the time I was desperate to change it, ignoring my parents' and grandparents' hurt feelings. I come from an old family, the kind of family that has only a handful of names it uses for their children. We have several Steven Gavins in our family." He smiled and turned to Diane. "So, Diane, a museum. Do you like being director?"

"Very much," she said.

"She also directs the crime lab here," said Gregory. "Plus, she's back to being a forensic anthropologist. Our Diane wears many hats."

Through the rest of the entrée they discussed the museum. During desserts of chocolate cake, pecan pie, and cheesecake, David and Gregory caught Steven up with their lives since South America. Steven thanked Gregory for helping him get on at the State Department, looking chagrined when he did it. Diane was sure he had thanked Gregory at the time. He probably felt it needed repeating. On the whole, it was a pleasant conversation. Nevertheless, Diane found it a little strained.

It wasn't until after-dinner coffee that they talked about what was really on their minds—who wanted to ruin them ... and why.

"Are we the only ones under attack?" asked Steven.

"The only ones we can find," said Gregory.

"Why us?" Steven said it as if he didn't expect an answer. "What do we have in common, other than being former coworkers in South America?"

"All of you discovered the massacre at the mission," said Frank. "Were there other members of your group who were with you that day—others who weren't killed at the mission?"

"Several interviewers were still out in the field when we came in that day," said Gregory. "I or David have called them. None have been having the same problems we have been having."

"By the same token," said David, "several people who were with us have not had rumors spread about them."

"How about Simone?" said Steven. "She was right there with us when we walked into the mission grounds."

They were quiet for a moment. Diane looked at David and Gregory.

"What?" said Steven.

"Simone is in a coma," said Diane. She told him about the intruders at the museum, about discovering Simone hurt, about the attack and the fire.

"My God," said Steven. "I didn't know. I'm doubly damned for being so insensitive. She's going to get well, isn't she?"

"We don't know," said Diane. "Gregory went to see her today and to speak with the family. They won't speak with me."

She briefly told him about Simon's mother, the mysterious caller, and his lie that Simone was working for Diane at the time of the attack on her.

"Wow," said Steven, "this is like getting hit by a truck. I didn't see this coming. Poor Simone. You have no idea what she was doing here, why she came to see you?"

Diane shook her head. She told Steven what they had found—the feathers, the bone, the animal parts. "We don't know what they mean, or if it was even Simone who brought them, or perhaps tried to hide them. For all we know, there could be a shaman walking around the museum wondering where he dropped his medicine bag."

Steven gave a little puff of a laugh. "Odd, however," he said, putting more sugar in his coffee.

"Did you learn anything from Simone's parents, Gregory?" David asked.

David was still waiting for chocolate to put in his own coffee. It was an odd request that the waitstaff usually forgot, despite David being a regular there. When he saw their waitress, he pointed to his cup. She nodded.

"You'd think something like chocolate in the coffee would be easy to remember," he said.

Gregory smiled at him; then his lips turned down in a frown. "I did learn a few things to add to our list of barely helpful things. I managed to get Simone's mother to talk to me, which, if I may say, tested all my diplomatic skills. The woman despises us. But I imagine, Diane, you already detected that when you spoke with her. I fear, however, that what I found out isn't much more than that which your Chief of Detectives Garnett discovered from the family. Perhaps Steven can help us make something of it."

Chapter 40

"Mrs. Brooks still insists that Simone was in the process of doing some favor for Diane," continued Gregory. "And what she was doing was somehow—unknown to Simone—illegal. The man who told Mrs. Brooks this over the phone spoke with a British accent—at least, I suspect he did, judging from her first reaction to my voice."

"I don't suppose she could distinguish what kind of a British accent?" said Steven.

Steven knew, as did Diane and the others, that there are British accents, and then there are British accents. Just as the sound of spoken American English varies greatly within the United States, varying British accents can be heard within the U.K. and around the world. Simply because the caller had a British accent didn't mean he hailed from Britain.

Even in foreign universities, students learning English as a second language must choose between American English or British English. Gifted fluent speakers of English as a second language don't speak it with a German, Spanish, French, or any other first-language accent. They speak it with an American accent or a British accent. And, of course, many people can mimic accents quite well. The man who called Simone's mother could be from anywhere.

"Did Mrs. Brooks tell you what he said exactly?" asked Diane.

"I did manage to get that out of her. Apparently she had more information than she told Chief Garnett. This mysterious coworker of Simone's told Mrs. Brooks that you had been sending bolts of material soaked in drugs out of Porto Barquis to a place in Florida where the drugs were recovered. He did not tell her what kind of drugs, nor did the woman ask. It was enough for her to hear the word *drugs*," said Gregory. "I think it is all one thing to her."

"What part did she think Simone played in this?" asked Diane. "Surely she didn't think her daughter was part of a drug smuggling ring."

"No. The chap told her that you hired Simone to track down a lost shipment of valuable South American Indian fabric for the museum, and that Simone had no idea what she was getting into or what she was carrying."

"Damn," said Diane. "She believes it still, doesn't she?"

"Yes. She won't be talked out of it. It is proof, after all, that she was right, and her daughter should have followed her advice," said Gregory.

The waitress came to refill the coffee and bring David several packets of hot chocolate to put in his. They stopped talking until she left. Diane took a long sip of the hot coffee, wishing Simone had at least written her a letter, an e-mail, or something. What was this about?

"Did Simone's brother, Pieter, have anything to say?" asked Diane. "You said you were to meet him in the coffee shop."

"He said Simone was obsessed," said Gregory. "She discovered something in Oliver's things and it made her crazy. Simone had been secretive and preoccupied ever since she looked into the boxes that Oliver mailed from the mission. She told Pieter she was finishing an investigation that Oliver had started. Pieter thinks she had collected some kind of evidence of her own, and that she was bitter and determined, but would not confide in him. She told him he was safer not knowing."

"She knew to trust Diane," said David. "Whatever she had, or whatever she discovered, it must have revealed who was involved. Otherwise, how would she know who to trust? How would she know to trust Diane? She must have discovered which one of 'us' ordered the raid on the mission—if that was what her words to you meant, Diane."

Steven went still. "What? What do you mean—one of us ordered the raid on the mission? It was Santos."

"We believe that Simone thought it was one of our team who asked him to do it," said Diane.

Steven shook his head. "No, I don't believe that. We were too close."

"Perhaps she meant someone on the periphery of your group," Frank suggested. "Someone loosely connected with the project or the mission."

No one said anything for several moments.

"No," said Diane, as if she just truly realized what Simone's warning meant. "Simone meant someone close. She said 'us.' That's who we were then—a family, an 'us.' Someone close. She meant one of our small family."

Steven shook his head. "You'll have a hard time convincing me of that."

"Perhaps, whoever it is," said David, "meant to kill Simone and stop her from revealing their identity. They caught up with her here, at the museum. These rumors were meant to distract us, to give us something to do other than investigate what they hoped was Simone's death. Destroy our credibility, cost us our jobs. It was their bad luck that she spoke to you before she lapsed into a coma."

"That doesn't explain my problem," said Steven. "I knew none of this. Why would I need to be distracted?"

"Perhaps you know something," Gregory said to Steven. "There's a reason. We just need to flush it out. It gives me some satisfaction that, if David is correct and these rumors were meant to give us a time-consuming hobby away from Simone, they had the opposite effect."

No one had anything to say. Steven looked like he had been broadsided. He kept shaking his head.

"Do you have any theories?" David asked him.

Steven was quiet for several moments. He drummed his fingers on the table.

"Okay," he said, tapping the tabletop with his middle finger. "Why now? Why did all this happen now? And why these god-awful rumors? What happened to trigger all this? You're saying Simone was investigating stuff she dug out of Oliver's belongings—belongings that she just recently felt emotionally strong enough to face going through. What if that wasn't the trigger? What if there are no boxes? Or what if that stuff was only souvenirs, after all? What if the real trigger was the announcement of your upcoming nuptials, Diane? I saw it in the *New York Times*. I imagine she did too."

Diane's eyebrows shot up. *New York Times*? Vanessa put her engagement in the *New York Times*? Why? Maybe she was garnering some publicity for the museum. But still . . . However, Diane didn't say anything to interrupt the flow of Steven's ideas.

"She admired Diane to the point that she idolized her," said Steven. "But her greatest tragedy was the death of her fiancé, Oliver—the man she should now be married to. Sometimes fierce loyalty can turn into jealousy. Simone was fragile after the massacre—even before. You know that. She was good at her job, but she was vulnerable."

David frowned. Gregory looked impassive, but Diane knew he didn't like where this was going. No more than she did. Frank simply looked interested. She wondered what his take on all of this was. He would be more objective— something Diane was having a hard time being at the moment.

If Steven sensed anything from them, he didn't show it.

"The rumor about you, Diane, may have been generated out of anger that you were getting the life she had hoped for and should have had."

"What about Gregory? You? David?" said Diane. There was a sharper edge to her voice than she meant.

"Fallout. If you were involved in drug smuggling, then chances are, we were too—close-knit group, peas in a pod sort of thing. In my case, I can see the DEA thinking they might make a high-profile arrest if it were true. What's my career compared to theirs? Politics is a dog-eat-dog world."

"My slander wasn't drugs," said Gregory. "Apparently I was too stupid to enrich myself with drug money. I was consorting with prostitutes."

Steven shrugged. "Aren't all politicians accused at one time or another of consorting with prostitutes?"

Gregory gave him a wry smile.

"What about the mystery coworker who called Simone's mother?" asked David. Diane could hear the understated edge to his voice.

"Probably was a coworker, hoping to cash in on her misfortune," said Steven. "Developing a rapport with Simone's parents. Next call, he'll say he found out Simone was involved, after all, and he'll have to tell the police. 'No?

Don't tell? Really? You'll give me money? How much?' It happens all the time."

Diane took a big swallow of hot coffee. It burned her throat all the way down to her stomach. "You really think Simone would do this to me, to us?" Diane said. "You can believe she would do that?"

"When the alternative is to believe that one of us orchestrated the slaughter of our friends and family? Damn straight, I can. And so can you," he said.

Diane pondered that for a moment. "It's not elegant," she said.

"What the heck does that mean?" said Steven.

"Too many coincidences," said Diane. "Too many things happening to all of us from different sources. It's simpler if one person is doing this to cover up something they did in South America. One person spreading the rumors, the same person controlling information to the Brooks family, the same person after Simone in the museum."

"Not everything follows the law of parsimony, Diane. Sometimes things are just complicated," said Steven.

They were all quiet for several moments. It was Steven who spoke first, spreading his fingers wide on the table in front of him.

"Look, guys, you know my strong suit is playing the devil's advocate. I'm not saying I like this explanation, or even believe it. David asked for an alternative theory. This is one—and a viable one. I believe the massacre was all Ivan Santos from beginning to end. Diane, you showed the world that he was a liar about the mass graves. He hated you for that. He hated all of us, but he particularly focused his hate on you. There may be another explanation for what's happening to us. It may not be Simone. It may be something else we don't even know about yet. She may have come here to ask your opinion about something related to her job. Didn't you say she had a human bone? Who would she take that to, but you? Maybe the fallout on us is for the same reason—distraction—but maybe it's from some completely different case she was working on. I'm just saying, it is going to take a lot to get me to believe that one of us was responsible for the slaughter in South America."

He paused. They were quiet. Diane didn't want to admit he had a point.

"You gave a fair theory," said Gregory. "And it is what we asked for. Like it or not, we must consider it. None of us like the idea of a traitor among us."

"Where are you staying, Steven?" asked David.

"Thought I might look up some charming B and B. Got any ideas?" he asked.

"You can stay at my apartment," said David. "I have a guest room."

"That would be good," he said. "Thanks. I'll take you up on it."

Diane started to make some joke about David's overly fortified apartment, but she stopped when she saw Garnett coming toward her. He looked grim.

"Diane," said Chief Garnett, "I'm sorry to disturb your dinner."

Diane gestured to a chair at a nearby empty table. Garnett grabbed it and sat down between Diane and David. Diane introduced him to Steven and briefly explained that Steven was suffering from the same problems that were plaguing the rest of them.

Then she said, "You look grim. It's not Simone, is it?"

"No. I'm not even sure it has anything to do with you. It's just troubling. There was a break-in at your old apartment. The very one you lived in. Someone trashed it, pulled out all the drawers, tore up the cushions, emptied the closets, the kitchen cabinets, the refrigerator. It's hard to say if anything is missing. Thankfully, the occupants weren't home. The destruction looks particularly thorough. Izzy is working the scene."

The first thing Diane thought of was the Interpol warrant on her. It had her old address, not where she lived now with Frank, in his house, but her old apartment, the one that was now trashed.

Diane's heart thudded against her chest. Star, Frank's daughter, was at his house . . . alone.

"Would you send a police car to Frank's?" said Diane. She rose from her seat. "They can get there before we can."

"You thinking it was meant for you?" said Garnett.

"I was remembering the warrant. It had my old apartment address, not Frank's house. But whoever is doing this may be educating themselves and may have a short learning curve."

Garnett's phone beeped. He looked at the display before he answered it. He listened a moment, his frown deepening.

"Damn it. That was dispatch," said Garnett. "They are on nine-one-one with Star; she's holed up in that panic room you built, Frank."

Chapter 41

Maria had the accelerator all the way to the floor. The tires were skidding on the small rocks and detritus in the road, which was getting narrower by the foot. There was a long drop-off on the right and a high bank to the left. They were on a precipice over a gorge. The road was nothing more than a gravelly ledge along the precipice.

Maria should have chosen the other road. She wasn't thinking. It was a good road and good roads lead to places, like villages and towns. She was in the middle of nowhere and running out of road. Damn.

Rosetta had fished out the guns from the backpack. Maria put each in a pocket with her right hand as she steered with her left. The gun she had been using was lying beside her on the seat.

"Put the map and the compass in the backpack," she said. Rosetta obeyed.

She rounded a blind curve going fast and couldn't see, until it was too late, that she was out of road. She slammed on the brakes, the truck fishtailed, and a wheel dropped over the edge on the right. The vehicle came to a grinding halt, tilted toward the passenger's side at the edge of the precipice. A wall of rocks was close up against the truck on her left. No egress. Their pursuers were closing behind them. They would be rounding the curve at any moment. Maria grabbed the club she had put under the seat, the one that was her first weapon. She started punching the windshield with all her strength, which, with all the adrenaline pumping through her body, was considerable. A spiderweb crack spread out across the windshield. She hit it again and the windshield collapsed outward. She pushed the cracked sheet of glass out and scraped the club over the bottom of the frame, trying to remove the small pieces.

"Toss those rags from behind the seat over the window frame and climb out."

Maria shoved the backpack onto the hood.

"Go, go, go. Now!" she said.

Rosetta didn't hesitate; she scrambled out of the truck onto the hood.

"Take the backpack and get as far from the truck as you can get. I'll be right behind you."

Maria climbed out, half sliding on the curved hood of the truck. Rosetta was in front of her.

Ambush was one of the best of plans. Maria, for the first time, wasn't afraid. Either the adrenaline knocked it completely out of her, or her brain understood that fear was of no use anymore. She got her gun and scrambled over the rocks blocking the road, moving to higher ground so she could see over her truck at the road behind them.

"Get farther away, Ariel," she said, using the little girl's real name. "If this doesn't work out, hide until they leave and make your way to Benjamin Constant like we planned. Use the compass and the map, the way I showed you. Find someone with a phone and call your mother at the River-Trail Museum in . . ." *Shit, where was that damn museum? Damn it.* "Rose, no, Rosewood, Georgia. If you can't find her there, call John West in Cherokee, North Carolina. Tell him what happened. Tell him you were with Lindsay, and to come and get you."

"No! You're coming with me!"

Maria heard the panic in Rosetta's voice and saw the tears in her eyes.

"I'm going to do my best. What I'm telling you is just plan B. Now, go. You can do this. You are the strongest little girl I know."

She could hear the truck now, hear them gunning the engine. If she was lucky, they would come around the curve too fast and slam into her truck before they could stop. But she wasn't going to count on luck. She had the advantage. She supported her arm on a rock and aimed. As soon as she saw the truck, she fired at the windshield on the driver's side. She didn't stop to see if she hit anything, she continued to fire as the truck careened down the narrow ledge.

She saw the automatic weapon outside the passenger side window trying to aim at her, firing over her head up the mountain, unable to aim accurately. She saw the truck swerve and skid; she saw that it was not stopping. She fired again at the passenger side of the windshield, hoping she struck the gunman. Then their vehicle hit her truck with a terrible noise. She ducked as she heard more gunfire and crawled over rocks until she found Rosetta huddled under an overhang, wide-eyed with fear, her lower lip trembling and tears running down her face. They listened at the crunch and deep squeal of metal against metal, then they heard the thunder of something big tumbling over the side into the gorge.

More bodies for someone to follow.

Don't lose it now, she told herself.

"Don't move. I don't want to shoot you by mistake, okay? I need to see if anyone survived. I don't want anyone following us."

Rosetta nodded.

"You're doing fine," said Maria.

She crawled back to look, to see if there was anyone left, if someone had jumped out at the last minute.

Her truck was hanging over the edge, caught on a tree, or something—teetering, ready to fall. She didn't see the other vehicle. She waited, watched, listened for groaning, someone walking over gravel, anything.

"Do you need help?" she called out just to see if anyone would answer.

Nothing.

"*Você precisa de ajuda?*" called Rosetta.

Maria wanted to laugh. What a kid.

She listened again. Something? Soft noise. Scraping?

"Rosetta," she called.

"Yes," she answered from the rock shelter.

Maria aimed her gun to the right and up and fired. A woman—dark hair, dark eyes, camouflage pants, and peasant top—tumbled off the top of the ledge above her and lay on her back on the talus, staring at nothing, blood spreading over her chest. Her gun clattered on the rocks at Maria's feet. She picked it up. Maria didn't recognize the woman. Another of the many strangers bent on capturing her and Rosetta. What the hell?

"Anybody else?" she said out loud.

No more sounds. Still she listened.

Maria finally walked back to Rosetta and hugged her.

"I'm sorry I broke down," said Rosetta.

"Are you kidding? You're a rock, kiddo. The best kid ever. I could never have gotten this far without you." Maria hugged Rosetta to her and squeezed hard. "Just the best."

Maria looked at the way before them. A long expanse of treetops in all directions. They were at the top of a butte that had a steep rocky slope down to the forest below. She could see the river, the one that went through the gorge, winding its way through the forest. Maria guessed that at some point it would flow into the Amazon.

It was a beautiful world. She wished she could be enjoying its interests and not its dangers.

"We have to climb down. It won't be too bad," said Maria. "There is enough of a slope that we can do it. We just have to be careful."

She took the backpack from Rosetta and started down the slope, watching the kid pick her way through the rocks and vegetation that was getting thicker. She looked over at the river again and saw a sight that made her heart flutter. A boat. A two-decker. Possibly a tourist boat.

They couldn't make it down in time, but if there was one boat, there could be another one. They could follow the river. Then she thought of crocodiles and decided perhaps that wasn't a good idea.

She was tempted to pick up the pace. But she didn't. *Don't be reckless after all this*. She got the map and compass out of the backpack and calculated how much farther they had to go. A little more than forty miles. Not far. Not far at all. She felt lighthearted all of a sudden. Maria quickened her pace when they reached flatter ground.

"It's not far," she told Rosetta.

Rosetta grabbed her hand and the two of them followed the compass toward Benjamin Constant.

Chapter 42

"I'm thankful you built the safe room," said Diane as they raced through traffic to Frank's house. She heard sirens and hoped they were heading for Star. She had her arms crossed around her middle, holding herself together.

"Me too," said Frank. His face was a tight mask. "She's in the room. She's safe. It's a good room. Strong."

The safe room was built after a violent intruder beat down the back door and broke in the house with Diane alone at home. It was on the first floor. Frank had taken a small spare bedroom with a tiny on-site bathroom and converted it to a safe room outfitted with steel doorjambs; Kevlar, steel-reinforced, fire-resistant, soundproof walls; controlled ventilation; and separate communication to the outside world. It was small, but comfortable. Frank made a few other renovations, the kind that might be made to make a home handicap accessible, to allow quick access to the room from all areas of the house. It was still a work in progress, but he had finished the main safety features first.

Diane hoped Star wasn't terrified, and was relieved she had made it to the room, scared at the reason she had to. Frank was pushing past the speed limit. Gregory was with them in the backseat. He said nothing. Diane sensed he was worried. He leaned forward, as if willing the car to go faster. He hadn't met Star, but Marguerite had when they visited Paris and London on their trip to buy Star's wardrobe— her reward for meeting Diane's challenge of sticking out her first year in college and maintaining at least a 2.7 GPA. Gregory had been out of the country at the time. Marguerite was a great help shopping in Paris. It had been fun. Star had a great time. The trip broadened her horizons, made Star see herself in a different light.

Diane had told Gregory about Star and the death of her adoptive parents, Frank's best friends, and how Frank became her guardian and formally adopted her. She still called him Uncle Frank, which brought no end of confusion to people meeting them for the first time—especially since Star tended to introduce him as "This is my dad, Uncle Frank."

Diane's mind was racing, hopping from one trivial thing to the next. Her heart thudded against her chest. She wanted to call Star in the safe room but Star was keeping the line open to the police.

They turned onto Frank's street. Not much farther to go. Diane could see the police cars in the driveway. Frank pulled in and parked in the grass, out of their way. He jumped out of the car and raced in, Diane and Gregory close behind him.

The police were in the front door. It had been smashed open with, it appeared, a battering ram. Probably took only a couple of hard hits to collapse the door. That door and all the outside doors would be next on the list to reinforce.

A policeman held a hand out before he recognized Frank.

"Duncan," he said. "We just got here. We're searching the grounds. It looks like they only made it through the front door."

Diane knew the policeman, but not well. He had been hired to replace Izzy when Izzy came over to the crime lab. He was a young man, several years younger than Izzy. He pointed to the shattered door askew on its hinges—as if it weren't noticeable.

Frank rushed past him into the house.

"Uh, we haven't cleared the house yet," the policeman said.

The safe room's outer door was a bookcase in the corner of the living room. Frank opened a small door that concealed a keypad. He punched in his code and the door opened.

Star stuck her head out. Her black hair was cut in a smooth bob with bangs. It was all one color, which Diane thought was an improvement over fuchsia and chartreuse.

She was dressed in black slacks elaborately decorated with swirls of metal studs near the bottom of the pleated leg. With it she wore an ice-blue satin blouse and jacket.

"Uncle Frank!" She came running to his arms. "The safe room works. I heard someone around the house trying to break in and I ran to the room and locked myself in and called nine-one-one. But I have to tell you, we need a PA system in there so I can fuss at the guys while they are in the house, like, 'What part of *this house is protected by a security service* don't you understand?' And I need a gun."

"Star." Diane hugged her. "You're safe, thank God." Diane had Star's face between her hands. "You did good."

"It really worked. I felt like Jodie Foster and that vampire chick in that movie."

Diane had to flip through her memories of popular culture to figure out what Star was talking about. Frank hugged Star again and kissed the top of her head.

"I'm proud of you. You're not getting a gun," he said.

The rest of the evening went by in a blur. Diane called Neva and the two of them worked the house as a crime scene. Frank and the policemen searched the house from attic to basement, assisted by Gregory, who was unable to just stand around while everyone was whirling about him. The other policemen searched the grounds.

Garnett drove up thirty minutes later. He told them that, even with all the mess, Izzy wasn't finding anything useful in Diane's old apartment. Diane and Neva weren't finding anything either. The intruders knew how to not leave much behind.

The policemen searching did find where the perps had parked their vehicle. Diane took as many measurements as she could of the ill-defined tire marks. They weren't even real tire tracks, just impressions in the leaf detritus. Still, she got a rough idea of the distance between the wheels. She might be able to narrow down the type of vehicle they used.

It was past midnight before they had the house back. Gregory helped Frank repair the door. Neva had to take Gregory's fingerprints to add to the exemplars. A terrible way to treat a guest. Gregory took it with a lot of humor, like this was just his life. Diane was dead tired. Fear about Star had drained away a lot of her energy.

Frank and Gregory were finishing up the door, Diane was wiping down the fingerprint powders left on the surfaces. She stood looking at the clock on the mantle. She had to find a way to get some answers. All of the brain power they had dedicated to crime, and they had nothing. Diane needed to talk to some of the others. Martine Leveque knew Simone Brooks and Oliver Hill best. Damn it, she was just going to have to talk to them.

Diane went into the room she had made into her private home office and sat down in front of the laptop on the desk, called up her address book, and looked for the number she had for Martine. She calculated the time difference between here and Paris—six hours. Martine would already be up, having her cup of coffee, looking out the window. That was her habit in South America. Diane dialed her number.

"*Oui*," came the answer. Diane recognized her voice.

"Martine, this is Diane Fallon. I know you prefer not to talk with me, but I really need to speak with you. Please."

There was a long pause. Diane thought she may have hung up, or simply left the phone.

"I told Gregory, I don't want to maintain our friendships. It's not personal. You understand," she said.

"I do. Simone has been attacked. She may die. I'm trying to find out why." Diane thought she heard a slight intake of breath.

"Simone?" she said.

"She's in a coma." Diane hurriedly explained what happened.

"She is saying one of us caused that terrible thing? I don't believe it," Martine said.

"Neither does Steven. He's here, suffering from the same rumormongering that I am—and that Gregory and David are," said Diane.

"My life here is very calm. I teach children to paint, I arrange flowers, I garden, I ride my horse, I surround myself with beautiful things. But I will try to help you. What do you want to know?"

"Simone was investigating something—we don't know what—that Oliver Hill had discovered before his death. Something she only recently found among his things. She decided to take it on as her own project. I think it is what got her hurt. Do you remember Oliver saying anything about an investigation he was doing? Or something bad going on at the mission? Anything he might have said, no matter how odd."

"Odd? You know—knew Oliver. He was the definition of odd. No, nothing stands out. He was always melancholy, except when he was around Simone. What a pair those two were, like two injured birds. If something was going on, you would expect David to be tuned in to it. But I guess we all have our blind spots. Even dear paranoid David." She paused.

"Birds. There was one thing Oliver said that was odd. I don't think it means anything, but . . . He was sitting out in the garden with me drinking coffee one morning, watching the birds. You remember the colorful macaws that came up. Wasn't your little Ariel always trying to get them to talk?"

"Yes, I remember," said Diane.

"Oliver asked me if I knew how the first child abuse prevention societies began. He said they were connected to cruelty to animals. That children were considered the property of their parents, which meant that parents could do anything they wanted to them. It was when someone convinced a judge that a child being abused was a little animal that the child got relief. He said that was the beginning. He thought it odd that animals and children were so often lumped together. I thought the whole conversation was strange and sad."

Diane's mind cast back to the bag that Simone hid in the museum—animal parts and the bone of a human child.

"Why would one of us betray the rest of us?" asked Martine.

"Money would be the only reason I can think of," said Diane. "A lot of it. It's almost always money."

"Perhaps you are right. How are you doing?" Martine asked abruptly.

"I'm good. I'm director of a museum here in the United States. I'm getting married in a couple of weeks," said Diane.

"Married? Oh, wonderful. Is he a good man?"

"He's rational, loving, smart, honest. Yes, he's a good man."

"All that? Are you sure he is a man?" said Martine.

Diane laughed. "Thank you for talking with me, Martine."

"I'll give you my e-mail. Let me know about Simone. I'm glad you direct a museum. That's good. Surround yourself with beauty. It's the only thing that helps." She rang off after giving Diane her e-mail address.

Diane sat in the chair thinking for a long time. She listened to the hammering in the other room. Listened to Star kibitzing.

She called up Google on the computer and typed in *parrot feathers* and *South America* and some of the other keywords describing things that were in Simone's bag. As the hits came up, Diane was rather startled by what she found.

Chapter 43

"Benjamin Constant," said Maria, looking out over the town nestled on the edge of the Amazon River.

"'Mos Eisley spaceport: You will never find a more wretched hive of scum and villainy. We must be cautious.'" Rosetta's voice was solemn. Maria laughed and Rosetta giggled.

They stood at the railing of a tourist boat taking them down the Amazon River, breathing in the wind in their face. The smells were different from the lush rain-forest smells. People made a difference to the ambient aroma, and not in the best way. But Maria wasn't going to complain.

"I take it you and your mother saw *Star Wars*," said Maria.

"A lot," said Rosetta.

Maria realized that Rosetta must constantly review her memories of her time with her mother. Her recollections of all the happy times were so clear.

They had gotten lucky on their trip through the forest toward Benjamin Constant. They had trekked as close to the river as they dared, hoping to catch sight of a tour boat. They were both tired. Maria kept Rosetta behind her, to protect her from being hit by the limbs and brush Maria was pushing out of their way. She forced her way through a thick section of growth, wishing she had a machete, and came face-to-face with a tall young blond male holding a camera and wearing Rail Riders clothing.

Maria stopped, ready to fight.

"*Você está perdido?*" he said. It sounded like Portuguese with a faint Swedish accent.

Rosetta peeked out from behind Maria.

"Sort of lost," Rosetta said. *"Você fala Inglês?"*

"Yes, I speak English," he said. "Do you need help?" His Swedish accent was more evident in English, or at least, Maria thought it was. Of course, her Portuguese was non-existent, so she couldn't really judge.

When she was over being shocked, Maria wanted to run up and hug him. She was never so glad to hear those four words. She was never so glad to see someone who not only spoke her language, but who possibly didn't want to kill her.

"Yes, we do. I'm Maria . . . Maria West," she supplied, sticking with a plan she had made of how she was going to get the two of them home across several borders. "This is my daughter, Rosetta West. Can you help us get to Benjamin Constant?"

"Ja," he said. "We're going to Benjamin Constant."

The "we" was a tourist boat like the one she'd seen at a distance on the river. This close to a large town, river and land traffic were bound to increase. She had been counting on running across someone with faster means of transport than feet. She was afraid it might be a logging truck. She was overjoyed it was a boat, not a canoe, but a large boat with many people, having a good time without guns.

She related the story that she and Rosetta had worked out as they trekked through the forest. Maria was a doctoral student in archaeology. Rosetta was her daughter. They were visiting archaeology sites, having fun, when someone tried to kidnap them. They got away but became lost in the jungle. However, they were experienced hikers and had a map, and they were on their way to Benjamin Constant.

"Of course we didn't have that far to go," she told Patrik Tillstrom and his fellow student, Hanna Vik. The two Swedish students had talked the boat pilot into stopping along the way so they could take some jungle pictures. That was why the two were in the forest. They were meeting up with friends in Benjamin Constant and taking a longer trip through the Amazon on foot. They were very excited. Maria would have been too, had she not already taken a trip through the Amazon.

Patrik and Hanna introduced them to some of the other people on the tour boat. It felt so normal. Maria felt safe for the first time in a long time. Still, she kept Rosetta close to her.

Maria told Rosetta she should speak English most of
the time, as if it were her first language. She taught her several American idioms and common popular speech inflec-
tions. "It's all in giving people an impression. You talk like
an American kid, they are less likely to think I'm stealing
you from the country." Rosetta understood, being a master
plotter herself.

"But I don't really look like you," she said, worried.

"We are in luck there," Maria told her. "John West, my
boyfriend, is an American Indian."

"Really? He's a real live Indian?" said Rosetta, wide-
eyed.

"So are you," said Maria.

"Pretend, I know, but . . . ," said Rosetta.

"Not pretend. You are a real Indian. You are a South
American Indian. You can trust me on this. I'm an anthropologist," she said, and Rosetta grinned.

They stood on the top deck of the tour boat and looked
at Benjamin Constant. It was a rough, ragged-looking
town. Maria imagined it was hard to keep things sparkling
on the edge of the rain forest. They had to wait to dock; the
pier was crowded with boats. When they disembarked, they
walked down a street that looked like a normal beach tourist strip that hadn't been kept up for about a hundred years.
The street was filled with potholes; the asphalt was worn or
nonexistent, with motor bikes and old VW buses and similar beat-up cars traveling along the streets at a slow pace.
Leaning telephone poles lined the sides of the street. Also
lining the sides were open-front shops constructed of wood
and tin, carrying T-shirts, blue jeans, magazines, sunglasses,
tobacco, toiletries, all the things you would expect from a
touristy logging community.

With much deliberation and mental hand wringing,
Maria ditched all but one of the guns in the river. The gun
she kept was the one she took from the woman. She hadn't
shot anyone with it. It seemed safer. She would ditch it
soon too, when they were safely on their way home. She
had transferred some of their acquired money from the lining of her clothes to her bra. Now it was time to shop. The
idea was to buy a few items and go to a hotel recommended
by some of the people she met on the boat.

She bought a new shirt and jeans for each of them, a

pair of sunglasses each, two baseball caps, toiletries, a towel each, socks, a magazine in English, a shoulder bag, and a doll. Maria wanted to look more like the student she said she was. Right now they both looked like they'd spent the last week crawling through the jungle. Not far from wrong.

Maria tied her hair back and each donned their caps and sunglasses. Rosetta grinned. Clearly she liked shopping.

"What do you say we go find a hotel room and a telephone?" said Maria.

Rosetta nodded vigorously. She clutched her Raggedy Ann–like doll as closely as she had the backpack all the way through the jungle. On the way, they passed an open market where they purchased bananas and another kind of fruit with a red skin that Rosetta said was good.

They started to cross one of the main streets when something on a telephone pole caught Maria's eye. Perhaps it was the new, unweathered look of the yellow piece of paper ... More likely, the drawing. She and Rosetta walked closer and looked.

"That looks like you," whispered Rosetta.

The eight-by-ten flyer had a drawing that looked very much like Maria, with her muddy dreadlocks and bandanna on her head that she had cut from the fabric. It was a copy of a drawing and suffered from being too dark, but a sharp eye would certainly be suspicious. The writing was in Portuguese. Even with her poor understanding of the language, she knew what it probably said. The word for *homicide* stuck out.

Procurado por homicídio e abdução
Diane Fallon también conocido como Linda Hall
Extremamente perigoso

There was a paragraph of smaller print near the bottom. The only good thing was that Maria didn't know who the heck Linda Hall was.

"What does it say exactly?" asked Diane.

"Can you pronounce it for me? I can read English pretty good—sort of—but I can't read Portuguese," said Rosetta.

"Sure," said Maria. She smiled inwardly at herself. She had thought of Rosetta as Superkid for so long that she was surprised there was something she couldn't do.

Maria pronounced the words as best she could. She had to do it a couple of times before Rosetta understood. Rosetta repeated the words after Maria said them.

"Wanted for murder and kidnapping, Diane Fallon, also known as Linda Hall. Extremely dangerous."

Maria read the paragraph at the end. She was a little better this time.

"It says you kidnapped a child named Rosetta Medina. I guess that's me. The Medinas were the people I was working for in the village where we met."

"Who is Linda Hall, I wonder?" asked Maria.

"Didn't that guy Kyle call you Linda?" said Rosetta.

"Yes, and he was the only one to see me in the bandanna. At least we know the little weasel didn't die. He's a pretty good artist. He should have stuck to that," Maria muttered. "But what is the Hall? What is Portuguese for hall?"

"*Sala?*" said Rosetta. "It also means room."

"Okay, which is another word for chamber. He called me Linda Chambers. Something got lost in the translation. So there is good news and bad news."

"I should have used another name besides Rosetta," said the little girl. She looked close to tears.

Maria hugged her. "Rosetta is a common name. Many girls have it. Besides, it may work in our favor if anyone asks us about it. If I kidnapped you, wouldn't I change your first name?" Maria smiled at her. "You've done great. Don't lose faith in yourself now."

"I think the person who wrote it was a Spanish speaker," said Rosetta. "It's put together like Spanish and some of the words are really Spanish."

"Okay, I'm impressed. That's useful information for us. See, you're a great kid, so keep the faith."

Rosetta smiled back, but Maria could still see the fear in her eyes. They were getting so close and Ariel wanted her mother so badly. *It will happen*. Maria would make it happen.

"Let's go check into the hotel and get cleaned up. If I can get the mud out of my hair and get rid of the dreads, I'll look less like the drawing."

They crossed the street and followed verbal directions they had been given to the hotel. The fear that had been in the pit of Maria's stomach since the ordeal began, and that had started to recede, was returning. Damn it, she was not going to accept only a few hours of peace. They needed to get comfortable and clean and she could think this through.

The thing that worried her, though, was the scope of the search for her. Yes, it was low-tech. Couldn't get much lower than paper flyers on a telephone pole. But it covered hundreds of miles, and whoever it was had access to an army of people from all over to call on. What did they want with Diane Fallon? Was Diane safe where she was?

Chapter 44

Diane stood in the doorway of the living room watching across the small slate-tiled foyer as Frank, Gregory, and Star made temporary repairs to the door so they could secure it for the night. Actually, Frank and Gregory worked on the door. Star supervised and entertained.

"So, Marguerite tells me you want to be a lawyer," Gregory said to Star as he held the door while Frank settled it on its hinges.

The door was patched with lumber Frank had in the garage. Tomorrow he would get a new door—probably have workmen come out and replace the wood doorframe with steel.

"Yes," answered Frank, before Star could say anything. "It will be a partnership. Diane and I will put them away, and Star will get them out."

The three of them laughed. Diane smiled at them having such fun repairing a door knocked down by predators. The fact that the predators were after her wasn't lost on her.

"I was lucky," said Star. "I had Uncle Frank and Diane when I was accused. A lot of people don't have anyone."

Frank looked up at Diane and smiled, as if he'd sensed her presence.

"You look like the cat who's discovered how to open the refrigerator," said Frank.

"I know what's going on. I know what Oliver was concerned about and what Simone was investigating . . . just not the *who*," said Diane.

Gregory almost dropped the door. Star moved quickly to help him catch it.

"What? How did you find out?" he said. "You discovered this since we got here?"

"I called Martine," she said.

Frank and Gregory slipped the door firmly on the hinge. Gregory and Star stepped away so Frank could check the drag. He moved the door back and forth.

"She spoke with you?" asked Gregory.

"I'll go make us some hot chocolate and we'll talk," said Diane.

As she turned, her left shoulder burned at the same time a loud report filled the room with startling noise. Diane fell back against a small table, going down with it and several of Star's porcelain figurines she had brought back from Paris.

Frank had been behind the door, adjusting the hinges. He slammed it closed at the sound. Gregory was pushing Star back from the door and to the floor, shielding her with his body.

"Star! Diane!" shouted Frank.

"I'm all right," shouted Star.

Gregory shoved her away from the front wall of the house and she crawled to an inner wall and sat with her back to it, drawing up her legs, making herself small. She had her cell phone out, punching 911.

Frank hurried in a half crouch toward Diane.

"High-powered," Gregory said. "Stay away from the front wall, everybody."

"Diane," said Frank.

"I'm okay," she said. "Just really pissed off and, shit, I burned my shoulder on something."

"Damn," said Frank. "You're shot. Don't move."

Diane put a hand on her deltoid and came away with blood on it.

"I'm all right," she said. "I may have cut myself on the glass."

Frank reached around her and helped her off with her jacket and pulled back her blouse.

"You've been creased by a bullet," he said. "Gregory, look after her. I'm getting my gun."

"I'm really all right," said Diane.

To prove it, she stood and righted the table and started picking up Star's figurines of dancing ladies in fancy dresses.

"Sit down on the rug here, near the sofa," said Gregory, leading her to the couch.

Diane heard Star on the phone with 911.

"No, I'm not in the panic room this time. Yes, I'll keep the line open. I think Diane Fallon has been shot; she's bleeding. I'm all right, just mad as hell and really tired of this. I'm putting you on my Twitter account."

Diane smiled. "Really, it's nothing," she said to Gregory. "What is Frank doing?"

"Getting armed," said Gregory. "We don't know what is going on. I'm going to move you and Star to the safe room and help Frank."

"I'm fine here," said Diane. "Get Star into the room. She's still out in the foyer. Where is Frank? I don't hear him."

"Don't worry about that now. Just put your hand over my handkerchief here and hold it firmly. I'll get Star, though she seems to have more presence of mind than the rest of us," he said.

Diane put a hand over her shoulder and held it tight on the handkerchief covering her wound. Really it wasn't that bad, she thought. The bullet just brushed past her shoulder, cutting it along the way. She doubted she even needed stitches.

She knew where Frank was. He'd taken his gun from the safe and gone outside to look for the shooter. She would go help, but he would not be expecting it and might become distracted. But she wasn't going to just sit here and worry. She stood and went to the safe and retrieved her own gun and an extra.

"Star," Diane said, when she came into the living room. "Get into the safe room and stay there."

"The police are on their way," said Star.

"I know, but I need you in the safe room. Okay?" said Diane.

Star nodded.

"I'm going into the safe room now," she said into the phone. "No, the others are staying out here. I don't know what they are going to do. They are all with law enforcement though ... I'll tell them."

"The nine-one-one lady doesn't want you to do anything rash," said Star as she went into the safe room and closed the door.

Diane gave Gregory the extra gun.

"I don't know if they plan to rush the house," she said. "We need to be prepared. And don't look at me like that. I'm fine. You wouldn't be worried if I'd simply cut myself on the shoulder. That's what it is, just a scrape. And I'm sorry about the hospitality. Here in the South, we usually do much better."

Diane went through the house turning off the lights in the front rooms. She went into one of the front bedrooms and looked out the window through the curtains without touching them. She didn't see any movement. The streetlights hadn't been shot out or extinguished in any way. That was a good sign. It seemed to her that any long-term campaign to lay siege to the house would include knocking out the lights.

Gregory had gone to another room toward the back of the house to look out the windows there. He came back, shaking his head.

"It's quiet," he whispered.

Diane listened. All she heard was the sound of the refrigerator, clocks ticking, and miscellaneous road noises. Diane felt hot and her arm started to throb. *Stop*, she willed, *it's not hurt that bad*.

She and Gregory waited in the living room. She was afraid to move, afraid to even make the floor squeak. She listened for sirens and wondered if they would come in silent. She wondered if Izzy, Neva, David, or Jin heard the call and were also on their way. She wondered what Frank was doing.

The sound of gunfire made her jump.

Chapter 45

"That was gunfire . . ." Star ran from the safe room to where Diane and Gregory were standing, stumping her toe in the dark. "Ow, damn. I heard gunfire. Uncle Frank is out there!"

"You are supposed to be in the safe room with the door closed," said Diane.

"I thought you guys might have to run in real quick and, besides, I can't hear anything from in there."

"I know that sound—it was a Glock," said Gregory, "not a rifle. What kind of weapon does Frank use?"

"Nine-millimeter Glock," said Diane.

"That means Uncle Frank is okay. Right?" asked Star.

"I'm sure he is," said Diane. She wasn't sure. She trusted Frank, but these guys were bold and vicious. She had no doubt they were the same ones who set the Mayan Room on fire just to cover their tracks. Her mind was racing to come up with a plan that wouldn't put Frank at greater risk trying to protect her if she went out to look for him.

"Let's go see," said Star.

Diane shook her head. "If we go out there, too many things can go wrong. It could put him in more danger."

"But we can't just wait," said Star. "The other guy might have a Glock too, and maybe it was his gun we heard. My dad might need help."

She was right. Diane had to do something. She could go out the back door, stay close to the house, and . . .

She was about to tell Gregory what she planned to do when the doorbell rang. Five times—two short, one long, a short, and a long.

Diane exhaled. "That's Frank," she said.

She turned on the lights and opened the door. Frank stood on the porch with a policeman in tow. The policeman—the young one who replaced Izzy—nodded. Diane noticed he had Frank's gun in his left hand, holding it upside down by the trigger guard. She told him she and Gregory were armed, so he wouldn't get jumpy when he saw all the guns inside.

"Everything's all right now, ma'am," he said. "You can put your guns away."

Diane looked at Frank. She wanted to hear from him that everything was all right. He looked grim, but gave her the slightest of smiles. She stepped aside to let them enter.

She imagined they would have to answer questions. She hugged Frank and kissed his cheek. He held her tightly around the waist, lingering. He had killed whoever it was. She could feel it in him.

The man may have deserved it, but it's not an easy thing to kill another human being. They stepped back from each other and, while Frank led the policeman to the living room, she took her and Gregory's guns and put them back in the safe.

Star embraced Frank and wouldn't let go of his waist.

"You okay?" she said. "I heard a shot. Is someone out there? Is it the guy who shot Diane? Is he dead? Did an ambulance come for Diane? If he's out there lying in the grass, can I go kick him?"

Frank looked at her and smiled. "I'm fine," he said.

Star and Frank sat down on the couch. The policeman sat opposite them. Gregory stood back in the shadows near the wall.

"The paramedics just drove up, ma'am. He said you're shot?" the policeman asked.

"It's not serious," Diane said. "The bleeding is almost stopped. I'm sure it'll just need a butterfly bandage."

The doorbell rang again, and as she went to answer it, she saw that the bullet that creased her shoulder had hit a photograph of her and Ariel.

"That damn son of a bitch," she said with such force that they all stared at her.

Frank jumped to his feet. "Diane, are you all right?"

Star and the policeman looked startled. Gregory had already noticed the photograph.

"The photograph of me and Ariel. Damn it. The bullet hit it. Damn him. Damn him."

She picked up the picture and rubbed her thumb over Ariel's face, cutting her finger on the broken glass. The bullet blew Diane out of the photograph, leaving a ragged edge beside Ariel.

Frank came over and embraced her.

"Who are those people? Why do they want me dead?" It came out sounding more teary than she had intended.

"We are going to find out," said Frank. "Let the paramedics in. I'll speak to the policeman."

Diane nodded, walked over, and opened the door. Two paramedics were standing on the porch with their cases in their hands. They were the same ones who had come several months ago, after the last intruder. They must think her a magnet for homicidal maniacs. They would be right.

"Someone has a gunshot wound?" one of them said.

"Me," said Diane. "It's not bad."

She led them to the kitchen and let them tend to the wound. She could hear the voices in the other room but not what they were saying. She wanted more to hear what Frank was saying than to have her wound looked at. But she stayed and let them clean and tend to it.

"You're right," the paramedic said. "It's not too bad. Just a deep graze. We can close it with a butterfly. Are you up-to-date on your tetanus?"

"Yes," she said. "I do a lot of caving. I stay up-to-date on things like that."

"That's good, ma'am. I thought about caving once," he said as he was treating the wound. "I'm a little bit claustrophobic. I understand that's not too good for caving."

"No, not too," she said.

They finished with her and packed up their kits.

"Let a doctor see that in a couple of days," he said. "But I don't think you'll have any trouble. Someone shot you here in your house?"

"They shot from a distance, through the open door. I was turning, or it might have been a different outcome," she said.

"Now, that's just plain wrong," said the other paramedic.

"It is. People should be safe in their homes," she said.

"You got that right. See a doctor right away if it starts to bother you." He paused. "Your finger's bleeding. Did the bullet hit you there too?"

"No, I cut it on some glass that broke. This hasn't been my night," said Diane. "It's not bad. I'll wash it off and put some Neosporin on it."

The paramedics left and Diane went back to the living room to listen. She had missed most of Frank's story. What she did hear was that Frank shot him when he turned the rifle on Frank. That frightened her. It could have been Frank that was shot. All this—Star was attacked and scared to death, Frank was almost killed, his home was damaged by a battering ram and gunfire—she had brought it all to his doorstep. She felt sick.

An arm slipped gently around her shoulders. It was Gregory. He was careful not to touch her wound.

"Are you all right?" he whispered.

"Not really," she said. "The wound is nothing. It's just . . . look what I've brought down on Frank and Star."

"I don't think it was you wielding the rifle or the battering ram," he said. "We'll figure this out. I'm eager to find out what you discovered from Martine."

Diane saw more lights shining from outside. Another car.

"Can it wait until the police leave?" she said.

"Of course," he said.

"We're probably going to have more company," she said. "Garnett will probably come by. That's likely to be him now. I expect David to show up. I need to examine the grounds in the morning."

"Why don't you let one of your people do that?" said Gregory.

Just as she started to answer, the doorbell rang again.

"I'll get it," said Gregory. "You go sit down by Frank and Star."

Diane nodded. She took a seat by Star and grabbed her hand. Star squeezed it back.

"We'll need you to come down and make a formal statement tomorrow," said the policeman.

"Sure," said Frank.

Gregory came into the room with Garnett. Garnett opened his mouth to speak, but all that any of them heard was an explosion.

Chapter 46

The hotel was a three-story rectangle, painted a mustard yellow with red trim. It was a popular building color in Benjamin Constant, Maria had noticed. Inside the lobby was a painted cement and wood decor. A few wooden chairs and tables with brightly colored tablecloths in blues, yellows, and reds lined the walls. The lobby was simple and clean. And there were lots of people, some of whom she had seen on the tour boat. It made her feel normal and safe. But, she reminded herself, it was an illusion. They were not yet safe.

She spotted the Swedish couple who had rescued them from the forest. They smiled and waved. Hanna, the young woman, came over.

"Looks like you two have been shopping," she said.

Maria nodded. "Couldn't resist some clean clothes and things from the market. Charming shops, lots of souvenirs."

"Yes, real local feel. We are eating at a lovely open-air restaurant at a pond this evening. Join us. It is not a half mile from here," Hanna said. "Easy walk."

Maria smiled and looked at Rosetta.

"What about it? Do you think I can get clean in time to go out and eat? Would you like that?"

Rosetta smiled and nodded.

"Good. Seven?" said Hanna. "We meet here. Patrik is going to find wheels. Perhaps we don't have to walk, but is good weather, yes?"

Personally, Maria would like very much to not walk, but less than half a mile wasn't far. She also wanted to skip dinner out and just stay in their room. But she thought acting normal and nonsecretive would give a better impression to anyone who might think the drawing on the flyer looked like her.

"I need to get a room," said Maria. She looked at the crowd. "I hope there is one left."

"I think they have plenty of rooms," said Hanna.

Hanna wandered off to speak with other people from the boat. Maria was glad not to have to talk anymore. She wanted to appear normal and friendly, but she didn't want to have to answer too many questions. She realized that when they got to their room, she was going to have to give Rosetta a crash course in grandparents' names, schools, and American culture. All in a few hours. She was beginning to wonder if this was a good idea.

She saw people having to show their passports at the hotel desk. Damn. She thought for a minute, watching people checking in. Not everyone showed a passport. Of course, if you lived in Brazil, you didn't have to. She thought for a moment longer. What was the name of some of the towns she saw on the map . . . a town she could say she lived in. It was her turn to check in.

Rosetta was barely tall enough to see above the counter. She put her hands on the edge and stood on her toes.

"We're up from Río de Sangue," said Maria. "Maria R. West and daughter." Maria put twice the amount of money the room cost on the counter.

The woman behind the counter took her money, counted out the price of the room, and gave the rest back.

"One night?" she said.

Maria was glad the clerk spoke English. She didn't want Rosetta to speak anything but English if they could help it. It felt as if their safety depended on illusion now. It was important to keep it up . . . to live it.

"I think one night. Maybe two. We are meeting friends who are not here yet. Should I pay for two?"

"Let us know before checkout time. You can pay then," she said.

Maria signed her name in a backward slant, unlike her own signature. She felt like someone was going to catch her at any moment. The trouble with telling lies was that they had a cascade effect—one led to another and then another. She couldn't imagine how some people could make a lifestyle of this. The woman gave her a key for a room on the third floor. Maria took Rosetta's hand and walked to the stairs, backpack and new purchases in her other hand.

They climbed the stairs and found the room at the other end of a long hall. She unlocked the door and closed it behind them once inside. The room was simply decorated— bed with no headboard, brightly colored bedspread on one Hollywood-sized bed, a table and a chair, a lamp, and a painting of a parrot and junglelike leaves over the bed. And, of all things, an air conditioner in the window. It was off. She decided not to turn it on unless the temperature started getting uncomfortably hot. There was a small bathroom with a shower and a tub.

"We've come a long way," said Maria.

"This is nice," said Rosetta. "It's a good thing we found money along the way. I thought we would be sleeping in the jungle most of the time. That's kind of hard. I have small mosquito nets stuffed in the backpack, but I didn't know how we were going to get off the ground. Hammocks are too big for me to get in the backpack."

"We did fine, didn't we? We've been lucky, all things considered," said Maria. "So, let's get clean. Do you like baths or showers?"

Rosetta took a bath first. Maria helped wash her hair and scrubbed her back, and Rosetta played in the water and laughed.

Maria combed Rosetta's wet hair straight down her back, parted on one side. She laid out fresh clothes on the bed for the two of them. Not the most stylish, but clean.

"I'm going to try to get my hair clean and untangled. When I finish, we need to talk about our story. I've got to tell you things about John and his family. Give you some names to toss around if anyone asks. Okay?"

Rosetta nodded and grinned. "We're good at making up stories."

"Yeah, we're a pair, aren't we?" said Maria.

Maria first washed her hair in Rosetta's bathwater. She figured it would take several washings to get it clean and decided not to let the water go to waste. The bathwater was a light brown when she finished. Damn, her hair was dirty.

She washed it again in the shower and covered it with conditioner she had bought, hoping it was good enough to help with the tangles. She piled her hair on her head while she washed her body. Maria scrubbed her skin until it was almost raw. She ran out of hot water but she didn't mind. All she could think of was clean. She rinsed her hair last, using her fingers to help the conditioner do its job. It took quite a while. She was expecting the hotel management to come knock on the door and ask why she was using so much water.

Finally her hair was clean and mostly untangled. Maria rubbed some of the last of the whiskey into her scalp and felt the sting. She hoped the alcohol would make her hair shine. She was tired of dull mud. And she really wanted to look different from the drawing on the Wanted poster.

She dried off and dressed in the new clothes. The underwear felt rough against her skin, but she really didn't mind. While Rosetta had been playing in the bath, Maria had washed her bra in the sink and wrung it out almost dry. It had been hanging on a chair while she showered. It was still damp, but it was clean.

She had found a sack of tube socks at the market. She brushed off both their boots. They put on the socks and boots. She put Rosetta's hair and her own in ponytails and stuck the tails through the openings in the backs of their baseball caps. Then they put on their sunglasses and looked in the mirror.

"Well, we look different. Almost respectable," said Maria.

Rosetta was about to cry. Maria knelt down and took off their glasses.

"What's the matter, sweetie?"

"Mama bought us some clothes that looked just alike." Rosetta put her arms around Maria's neck. "Can we call her? I really miss her."

"We'll go down to the desk and ask. But first, we really need to talk about what our story is. I know it looks like we are home free, but we still have to be careful. Okay?"

Rosetta nodded. She and Maria sat down on the bed and Maria began to tell her things, like John's father's name, and his sister's, his address, Maria's parents' first names. She was using her mother's maiden name as her own maiden name and she told Rosetta what that was. Rosetta was a quick study. She remembered everything Maria told her. Together they added details.

"Tonight at the restaurant will be a good time to practice our story in conversation. We may have to answer questions from authorities along the way. It needs to sound automatic. Tonight, however, don't volunteer any information. But don't sound evasive if they ask questions. People like to ask kids questions. The best way to deflect questions about us will be to ask them about themselves. People like to talk about what they are doing. It will also be good to make friends. We may need friends."

"You should do this for a living," said Rosetta, and Maria laughed.

"Okay, now, for the backpack," said Maria when she felt she had prepped Rosetta all she could. "Let's leave all but necessary things in the hotel room. I'll have to take the gun with us. I'll wrap it in our clothes. If I leave it in the room, someone might find it if they search the room."

"We need to take our money," said Rosetta.

Maria nodded. "Most of it is still sewn up in the skirt. I'll take some more out and put it down my bra. We'll carry the rest of it in the skirt with us in the backpack."

They worked until about six o'clock rearranging the backpack so they could have the things they needed with them, but at the same time, make it look touristy. Maria put Rosetta's new doll on top and buckled the flap shut. They walked down the stairs toward the lobby so they could ask about a phone. As soon as Maria looked out the window of the door leading from the stairs into the lobby she saw the man. He looked official and he was talking to someone at the check-in desk. He was holding the flyer.

Chapter 47

The sound sent Diane and everyone in the room to the floor. It rattled the windows and jarred Diane's teeth and sent a sharp pain through her ears.

"What the hell was that?" shouted the policeman.

His voice sounded muffled to Diane. She shook her head and massaged her ringing ears, trying to clear her hearing.

"Stun grenade," shouted Gregory.

"Is everyone all right?" said Frank.

"I'm fine," said Diane.

"Fine," said Garnett, though the way he was shaking his head, he didn't look fine.

"Does being scared witless, totally confused, and mad as hell count as all right?" said Star. "Do I need to Tweet nine-one-one? They haven't heard from me in at least fifteen minutes."

"I have men out there," said Garnett. "The coroner's people probably already arrived to collect the body."

"Damn," said Diane. "That's it. It's those guys. It's the same thing as the museum. They are collecting the body, and willing to use whatever severe measures necessary to do it."

Star hadn't waited to hear if they wanted her to call 911; she was on her cell phone with them again.

"The police are here, and Detective Garnett, too. There may be policemen outside hurt. We probably need backup. I think, actually, we need Delta Force."

Diane managed to get up. She stumbled to the safe and retrieved the guns.

"Hollis and I will go out there," said Garnett. He motioned to the policeman to follow him. "The rest of you stay here. That includes you, Frank."

"You need more manpower," said Frank. "If Diane is right, and I think she is, there are some vicious men out there and some of your people may need help."

Garnett hesitated only a moment, then nodded. "The rest of you stay. Star, did I hear you on the phone to dispatch?"

"Nine-one-one," said Star. "They're sending people. I hope that's all right."

"That's good. You, Diane, and Gregory Lincoln stay here," he said.

"People may be hurt," said Diane.

"It will only be the effects of the noise, right?" said Garnett.

"And eyes," said Gregory. "There would have been a very bright light when the thing went off. The idea is to overwhelm the senses. But if someone were close, they could be burned. Or the bloody bastards may have used other weapons against your people outside."

"We're wasting time," said Frank.

Frank led Garnett and Hollis, the young policeman, out the back door. Diane took a gun and followed.

"Gregory, if you would, stay with Star," she said.

Diane announced her presence as Frank started to open the back door.

"Don't argue," she said. "I'll stay close to the house and venture out only if you say it is clear. But people need help. I can be a lookout."

Frank and Garnett nodded.

Diane stepped out with them and hugged the side of the house as she made her way to the front. Frank led the others down a route with trees and bush for cover, toward a copse of trees where the dead man was supposed to be sprawled on the ground.

Diane watched them until they faded into the shadows. Frank's house was set back from the road fifty yards, give or take, which made his front yard long and wide.

In the distance, almost to the road, Diane spotted movement among the policemen who were guarding the body. Some were on their hands and knees. One looked like he might be heaving. Another managed to make it to his feet.

Her gaze scanned the ground looking for someone still down. She didn't see the guy Frank had shot, but it was hard to see.

She scanned among the trees for the bad guys in hiding, waiting for another ambush. She had a feeling they were gone, that their goal was to take the body, probably so that it wouldn't be identified. But they were so brutal she couldn't be sure they wouldn't come back for the hell of it—or for the terror of it. Their method of attack appeared to be the use of overwhelming force, even if it meant killing bystanders. What kind of people would do that?

This was all about producing so much disorientation in her and the police that their investigative efforts would be ineffective. And the bullet across her shoulder said it was also about killing her. Who had she pissed off that much?

She watched the road, listened for sirens. Where was backup? But only a couple of minutes had passed.

She could see that Frank, Garnett, and Hollis had met up with the disoriented policemen.

What were the thugs after? Something in the house or something they thought was in the house that they wanted. They were determined. And they had no conscience. Determined, no conscience.

Diane watched the road with the detailed concentration she normally put into examining a bone—which was probably why she saw the black van with the dull matte finish moving slowly down the road across the end of the driveway.

She cupped her hands to her mouth.

"Duck. Road. Van." She shouted twice before she saw them dive for cover.

She sprinted to the side of the house, out of the line of fire that she knew was coming. The night suddenly crackled and popped like fireworks.

"Dear God," she whispered.

"Not listening, lady."

An arm snaked around her waist as a gun was thrust under her chin.

"Drop the fucking gun." The voice was a raspy whisper.

Diane hesitated a second, then dropped the gun.

"Where the hell is it?" he said.

"The package?" said Diane.

"Good girl. If you had asked what package, I would have hurt you bad. I'm tired of messing around. I want the package."

"It's at the museum," said Diane.

"No, it's not." He dug his fingers in one of the pain points in her arm and covered her mouth with the forearm of his gun hand. A burning pain shot through her arm. She thought she was going to throw up.

"See how serious I am?" He rammed the gun back under her chin.

"I've been seeing all night how serious you are. I can't help it if you don't like the answer. It's at the museum."

Excruciating pain. Only his arm around her kept her from doubling over to the ground.

"We have looked in the museum. It's here."

"With all due respect—and please believe that I respect what you can and are willing to do—but you missed it in the museum because there is no way you could have gotten in the vaults."

"Vaults?"

Gotcha ... More or less.

"Five vaults in the museum, plus two in the crime lab. All of them protected by high security—way more security than this house. You're telling me you didn't know about the vaults? I would say something sarcastic about your intel, but I know you would hurt me."

"We didn't know about the vaults. That's true."

"I would never bring something of great importance here to the house," she said.

Diane was curious to know why they didn't know about the vaults, but she wasn't going to ask.

"We are going to the museum. You are going to get the package. Or we will kill everyone here, including any nosy neighbors. Do you understand?"

"Yes, I understand," said Diane.

Diane knew he intended to kill her—unless she could think of a plan. She had absolutely no idea what she was going to do to avoid her fate. She did know she was going to get these men away from Frank's house and away from Star.

When they discovered she had no idea what package they wanted, and had just made a wild guess that they were looking for something Simone had mailed to her, then they would be furious, and her death would not be pleasant.

She desperately needed a plan.

Chapter 48

"What?" asked Rosetta when Maria backed her deeper into the stairwell.

"There's a man looking for us, I think," said Maria.

Rosetta put her hands to her mouth and inhaled sharply. "Oh no. How did he find us?"

"He has one of those flyers. I imagine he's going from hotel to hotel. I don't think he knows we're here. I think he's asking questions. Let's find a back door." And ditch the gun, she thought.

They went back up to the second floor and walked down the hall to another stairway. Maria hoped it led to a different door. She walked down to the first landing again. This door didn't have a window. She eased it open and was startled when someone rushed in.

"Oh, *Olá*." A young girl rushed up the stairs, ignoring Maria and Rosetta, after saying a surprised hello.

The two of them walked out onto the street. Maria scanned the building facade looking for a broken cement block or any nook to hide a gun. She didn't linger, but examined the places as she went. She stopped abruptly at a small building beside the hotel. It was older looking and not in as good repair. One of the blocks was cracked.

"I want to check this out. Stand here so it will look like I'm tying your shoe," said Maria.

Rosetta hurried around and stood blocking the view of Maria's examination of the brick. Maria pulled on the small piece of the broken block. As she hoped, it came loose. She had to tug at it, but she managed to pull it out. There was a small space behind it, between the block and the wood wall, perhaps big enough for the gun. She pulled the gun out of her tote bag, wiped it off, and wrapped it in one of the pieces of fabric that they'd used for just about everything. The gun just fit in the space. She shoved the broken piece back and stood up. She felt a good deal of relief. If she were questioned by the authorities, she didn't want to have a gun on her. She and Rosetta walked across the street into a grassy park area and stood under some trees so they could watch the entrance to the hotel. It didn't take long for the man with the flyer to come out. They watched him hurry down the street.

Rosetta grabbed Maria around the leg and clung to her. "That's the bad man," said Rosetta, "the one with the English accent. The one who was at the mission that day."

Maria didn't ask if she was sure. She believed Rosetta. Maria watched the man as he walked down the street toward another hotel. He didn't glance in their direction, but Maria saw his profile. He wore a straw fedoralike hat, which Maria thought made him look quaint. It definitely made him stand out. He had a clean-cut profile and looked to be in his late thirties or early forties. He had light brown hair. She committed his features, what she could see of them, to memory. They didn't move from their spot, but watched him come out of the hotel and continue on across the street and get into a VW Beetle parked in front of a church. Clearly he was visiting all the hotels.

"Are we in trouble?" asked Rosetta.

"I don't think so. The clerk on duty was not the same one that checked us in. That's in our favor. I didn't put you down when I signed the book."

Maria thought for a moment where she had said she was from. She had given the name of a small town on the map she had. It wasn't far from where she had been held. That may have been a mistake.

"You said he was from an embassy?" said Maria.

"Yeah, I think," said Rosetta.

So what is he doing here? wondered Maria. Why was he looking for them, and why here? She never mentioned Benjamin Constant to Kyle or anyone. But it is a sizable port city on the Amazon. It would be logical they would flee here. After all, they did.

Maria watched the car drive away toward the docks.

They stayed in the grassy area, walking around, looking

at the plants, pretending to play. Maria had taken the doll from the backpack and given it to Rosetta to hold.

"We need to wait to make the call," said Maria. "I know you are anxious, but let's not go back to the hotel just yet."

A battered car drove up and she recognized Patrik and Hanna. He had found some wheels. Maria and Rosetta walked over and waved.

Hanna opened the passenger door and stood up, looking over the roof of what looked like a 1990s Eagle Premier with the paint worn down to the primer. "Look what Patrik found. Great, huh? We ride in style." Hanna laughed and it sounded like music. "Get in. We go eat."

The restaurant was on the banks of a pond of perhaps three acres. On one side of the pond near the main restaurant were small cabanas with grass umbrellas. Leafy plants were planted neatly between the cabanas. The main restaurant looked almost like a luxurious version of the native long huts she and Rosetta had recently escaped from. The roof was grass and the structure was of thick timbers with no walls. The kitchen area was in the center. Tables with blue and yellow tablecloths, not unlike the tables in the lobby of the hotel where they were staying, lined the room. It was crowded. Maria liked it. They wouldn't stand out in a crowd.

Patrik and Hanna led them to a table with several others from their tour group. Some of them Maria had met, some she hadn't. They sat down and looked at the menu.

Maria and Rosetta ordered *caruru*, a shrimp dish with onions, okra, and nuts seasoned with palm oil, along with *acarajé*—deep-fried black-eyed peas—and rice. Patrik ordered them drinks of something called Inca Kola.

The two of them felt like they were feasting. Maria tried to not eat too fast, but she really wanted to put down her fork and dive in with her hands.

"Your daughter doesn't look like you."

This was one of the women across from Maria. She was a botanist, as Maria recalled, from Spain—Gabina, if she remembered correctly.

Maria smiled and stroked Rosetta's ponytail sticking out the back of her cap. "No, she takes after her father," she said.

"He is from here, then?" she said.

"No, he is an American Indian," said Maria.

"Really? What tribe? They are called tribes, aren't they?" she said.

Maria suspected the woman was trying to trap her, as if she had seen the flyer and was trying to determine if Maria had kidnapped Rosetta. She was going to ask questions until she tripped Maria up.

"He's Cherokee," said Maria.

"Oh, from that place like the musical," said Hanna, "*Oklahoma*."

"No, Daddy's from the Eastern Band in North Carolina," Rosetta piped up.

She did it so fluidly Maria had to smile.

"Eastern Band?" said Gabina.

"The Cherokee were moved to Oklahoma in 1838 after gold was discovered on their land in the southeast. Many of them, including my husband John's ancestors, hid in the mountains and stayed. Their reservation is in the mountains of North Carolina. I would like to call him. Do you know where there is a phone available? I'm sure he is worried sick about us," she said.

"The hotel has a phone," said Patrik. "I used it just today."

"So tell us your story," said Gabina.

"We had fun most of the time," said Rosetta. "Didn't we, Mama?"

"Most of the time. Not in the beginning, but the rest of the time was an adventure." She smiled. "Rose is a little adventurer, more so than me, I'm afraid."

"Rose? I thought her name was Rosetta," said Gabina, smiling.

So that was it. It was the flyer, the name of the little girl— Rosetta—and the fact that Rosetta didn't look like Maria. She and Rosetta had discussed the name and come up with another story. Maria was warming up to the lies they were telling. She wondered what that said about her.

"Her name is actually Rose of Sharon. Her father is a fan of Steinbeck. Her grandfather started calling her Rosetta and it caught on in the family. You know how nicknames are."

"It doesn't sound American Indian," said Gabina.

Maria grinned. "You think we should have named her

Running Deer or Little White Dove? American Indians are pretty much like all of us. Some follow their cultural heritage to the letter and others don't, and others bring it into the modern world. John is of the latter."

"What does he do?" asked Patrik.

"He has a construction company," said Maria. "He specializes in underwater construction."

"Underwater construction?" asked one of the others. "What does he build? Underwater cities? I never heard of that."

"He built this great aquarium," said Rosetta, holding her arms wide. "It has this glass tube that you walk in and look at the fish. It's like you are the one really in a tank and the fish are visiting you. Really cool."

"It sounds like it." Gabina's smile reached her eyes for the first time. Maria hoped that meant she was won over.

"Tell me about your expedition," said Maria.

Maria's new acquaintances spent the remainder of the meal discussing their upcoming trek through the Amazon and what they hoped to accomplish. For Gabina it was collecting flora. Patrik was taking pictures. Hanna was interested in cultural anthropology, she thought—she hadn't committed to any one career yet. Midway in the tale when Rosetta finished eating, she put her head in Maria's lap. It looked so normal that Maria thought it further cemented their relationship to each other in Gabina and any other doubter's mind.

It was dark when they arrived back at the hotel. No one was at the desk, so Maria and Rosetta hurried up to the room. She stopped at their room door and listened before she opened it. Perhaps she had watched too many movies, but she had a vision of opening the door and seeing the man in the straw fedora sitting on the edge of the bed with his hands and chin resting on a silver snakehead cane.

She heard nothing, no movement, no breathing, no cane impatiently tapping on the floor. She unlocked the door and entered. No Sidney Greenstreet. No changes in the room that she could see. She searched the bathroom and under the bed. No lurking monsters. Still, she felt uneasy going to sleep. She put a chair under the doorknob, hoping that actually worked to secure the door.

"You did good," said Maria.

"You did too," said Rosetta.

"No one was at the desk. I don't know if that means they are closed for the evening and we can't use the phone, or they are just away."

"Let's go down and see," said Rosetta.

"All right. I need to call John first, because that is how we are going to get home. Is that all right?" said Maria.

Rosetta nodded, but Maria could see her lower lip tremble. Maria hugged her.

"I'm going to get you home to your mother. I promised you that, and I will. Don't worry, okay?" She rubbed Rosetta's back with her hand. "You're doing fine."

Maria wished she felt safe leaving Rosetta in the room, but she wouldn't have felt safe doing that in the United States. The man looking for them would probably recognize Rosetta. He wouldn't recognize Maria. She took Rosetta's baseball cap and pulled her hair on top of her head and put the cap over it, pulling the bill down to shade her face.

"If we see him, I'll give you the keys and you can run up to the room, okay?"

Rosetta nodded.

Maria moved the chair and opened the door.

Chapter 49

The hallway was clear. Maria expected trouble behind every door and around every corner. An uncomfortable feeling, but she supposed it did give her a survival advantage. Maria told Rosetta to walk and act normal and try not to look scared. And Maria would try to take her own advice. Of course, in a dire emergency run like hell. Rosetta giggled. They walked down the hall.

The stairway was clear until they got down to the second floor. There they encountered several people also on their way to the lobby. They were dressed like they were looking for entertainment. Maria couldn't imagine any nightlife in Benjamin Constant. But what did she know. She and Rosetta held back, letting the cluster of people proceed ahead of them.

On the ground floor, she looked through the window at the lobby. People were sitting at the tables talking, some milling around near the desk. No straw fedora. She opened the door and the two of them ventured out into the lobby.

Maria walked to the desk and asked in her broken Spanish about a phone to call out of the country. She did say *telephone* in Portuguese. Patrik and Hanna knew that Rosetta could speak Portuguese, but Maria didn't want anyone else to know, so she didn't have the little girl translate.

The clerk, a young male, pointed to a door with a window. Telephone booth. Good, a private place to call. However, it would cost them. Maria gave him money she pulled from her tote bag and went to use the phone. She felt almost sick with excitement. The two of them entered the booth. As Maria settled in front of the phone, Rosetta slid down behind her legs.

"Bad guy coming this way," said Rosetta.

Maria looked through the window. He was heading in their direction. Damn. He stood near the booth as if waiting to use it. She was wishing she had the gun. She would shoot him where he stood. *Damn it, we're just trying to get home.*

Maria ignored him and proceeded with the call. Her hands shook, not from fear, but from anticipation. The word *help* never sounded so good. Out of the corner of her eye she saw the man edge toward them. He was going to listen in. Could he hear much with the door closed? She didn't know. The conversation would have to have a lot of code. At least John was used to weird with her.

She made the call, praying he would be there. The phone was answered even before the first ring completed.

"Lindsay," he said. She heard the hope and fear in his voice.

"John," she said. "It's me, Maria Ravinel. I know you didn't want me to come on this excursion and bring our daughter, and you were right. I'm sorry. Could you come meet us here? If you could bring *Betty Boop*, Rose and I would really love it. She misses it. Her toys were lost. Everything was lost when we were attacked, everything. We are in Benjamin Constant, Brazil, right now, but we could meet you in Tabatinga."

Maria stopped for a breath. Throughout the whole conversation John hadn't said anything. She couldn't even hear him breathing, or sighing, or cringing. She wondered if he even recognized her voice, as scratchy as it was. He would recognize her middle name, Ravinel. And he would probably recognize the drama surrounding her. She couldn't seem to ever get away from it.

"Rabbit," he said, using his personal affectionate name for her. "Are you in trouble?"

His voice had its usual calm, but she could hear the edge in it, the confusion. Still, it felt so good to hear him. She wished he could reach through the phone and grab them both and pull them away from here.

"Most I've ever been in," she said. And that was saying something.

"Can the authorities help you until I get there?" he said.

"No. I'm sorry about this. Please trust me again. Rose of Sharon and I really miss you. She's afraid she is going to miss her eighth birthday party next week." Maria dropped Rosetta's age a year, hoping to further disguise her.

"Are you all right?" he asked.

"At the moment. We're at the Sao Judas Hotel. I used my real name—Maria Ravinel West. Maybe I shouldn't have."

"I'll be there as soon as I can. I've been worried. I just discovered . . . Never mind, we'll talk when I see you," he said. She heard him tapping on keys. He was in front of the computer. Probably looking up a map and distances.

"It will probably be tomorrow afternoon," he said. "I'll have to look for the Betty Boop doll. I'll be there as soon as I can get there."

"Thank you for understanding," she said.

"I believe I do. What's the number you are calling from, just in case?" he said.

She gave him the number.

"Rabbit, keep yourself safe. And Rose too," he added. "I'm sure you have an interesting story to tell. I love you."

"I love you too," she said. "Please hurry."

"I will, baby," he said.

Maria felt resentment at straw fedora man. She would be feeling total relief if it weren't for him standing outside the door, waiting. She felt sick and trapped. Damn him. She thought for a minute. She hadn't hung up the phone yet, but kept it to her ear.

Rosetta said that after the massacre she had to be pointed out to him by the other kids at the mission. That meant he didn't really know what she looked like, even though he had seen her several times before. He was probably the kind of person who thought all indigenous people looked alike. She was now a little more than three years older than last time he saw her. He probably didn't know what she looked like now, just that he was looking for either a Hispanic or indigenous kid.

She put the phone back on the hook and bent down and whispered to Rosetta. Explaining her reasoning, and what she wanted to do.

"Are you up for it?" she asked.

"I can do it. Can we call Mother first?"

"Of course." Diane started to pick up the phone, then

stopped. "Rosetta," she said next to her ear, "if he hears me say your mother's name, he will know who we are for sure. And I can't find her and talk with her without saying her name. Help is on the way, but we will have to be very careful until it gets here. This man is a danger to us."

Rosetta looked disappointed, but she nodded. She understood danger and she understood careful. They were so close to getting home. They couldn't stop being careful now.

"Okay, ready?" whispered Maria. "Showtime. Brave heart, kid."

Maria held Rosetta's hand and opened the door.

"Can I go myself?" she said.

"All right, but I'll watch you part of the way."

Maria handed her the keys to the room and Rosetta turned toward the stairs.

The man touched Maria on the shoulder.

"May I speak with you?" he said.

Rosetta pulled on her hand. "Mamaaaa," she said in a long exaggerated syllable, "come on."

"Sure." Maria smiled at the man. "Just a minute."

She turned to Rosetta, who had the bill of her cap pulled low. Maria let go of Rosetta's hand and watched her dance and skip kidlike toward the stairway door.

"Hey, *você parece uma sereia pequena*, Ariel," said the man.

Rosetta didn't pause, or hesitate, or skip a beat.

Maria followed along behind her.

The man began whistling "Hall of the Mountain King."

Still no response from Rosetta. She went along like a happy kid, not looking back, not hesitating. Maria opened the stairwell door for her.

"I'll be watching as you go up," she said.

"Okay. Don't worry," Rosetta said.

Maria watched her until she was out of sight, wondering what the man said and why he was whistling the Peer Gynt Suite.

"Now, what can I do for you?" said Maria, smiling.

The man took his straw hat off. He didn't look like some homicidal maniac. He looked quite presentable, with his blond-brown hair, light blue eyes, and fair complexion. Maria still assessed him to be in his early forties.

"Can we sit at one of the tables and talk?" he said.

Chapter 50

Diane gripped the seat of the black Ford Taurus so tightly, her hands hurt. She was desperately trying to come up with a plan. Any plan, even a bad plan. There was no way she was going to overpower this guy.

It hit her suddenly like a blast of hope—Simone had. Simone had hurt one of them bad, maybe mortally. Maybe she got lucky, maybe the guy she was fighting was the C team. Still, Simone had vanquished one and got away long enough to at least say a few words to Diane. Oddly, Diane felt encouraged.

"You try anything and the men I left back there will slaughter your friends. You understand that, don't you?"

Diane was sitting in the front seat with the man who had abducted her. He didn't consider her much of a threat—he hadn't bound her. The man looked to be in his early thirties. He was well muscled, thick necked, and had a buzz cut. He was decked out in Kevlar and weapons.

"Yes," she said, "I do understand. Tell me, just where did you search in the museum?"

"Just why do you want to know?"

"If you had searched the entire museum you would have found what you were looking for and I wouldn't be here. I'm just trying to understand my fate," she said.

She thought she saw the edges of his mouth twitch in a smile. It didn't last long.

"We had someone on the inside who was supposed to know what they were doing. Now shut up and don't ask *who*. Got that? You know I like hurting you."

Jesus, thought Diane, *Madge was looking through the mail in the mailroom. Not Madge Stewart, surely. How in the hell could she get mixed up with these creatures? Not hoping for romance. These guys would have scared poor Madge to death. But, still, what a coincidence. And they could certainly drown her and make it look like an accident.*

Diane didn't have to give him directions to the museum. He knew the way. He kept the speed limit. That was good. Gave her more time to think.

Frank probably had already discovered her missing. But he wouldn't know where they had taken her.

Plan, damn it. Don't waste time hoping for a rescue.

The problem was the others back at the house. Anything she did would be relayed back to his cronies and they would lay siege yet again to Frank's house.

The only thing she could think of was arranging it so she could lock herself in the vault and call Frank to warn him, then call for more troops. Real troops.

There were lots of weapons at the museum—hammers, nail guns . . . She could trip an alarm, or the fire alarm. And there was her security staff. They could bring down one guy, couldn't they?

Okay, she had some options. She could play it by ear and see what opportunity presented itself. Maybe she would get lucky and the ubiquitous museum snake that no one seemed to be able to catch would drop on him and it would turn out that he was deathly afraid of snakes.

As they drove to the museum, Diane wondered why the night wasn't lighter. There was a full moon. That's when she noticed the trees moving in the wind. A storm was coming, she remembered now. There was supposed to be a storm every day this coming week. Great.

He turned onto the road that led to the museum. It was a nice drive usually, but she dreaded every minute of it now. She wasn't satisfied with her plans. Mainly because they weren't plans. They were possible ideas . . . if she got a chance . . . and if everything went right.

He parked in her spot and they got out of the car, but not before he warned her again that he loved collateral damage. On the way up the steps they met Andie and Liam coming down.

"Hey," said Andie.

"What are you doing here so late?" said Diane.

"You didn't tell me being director is so time-consuming.

Kendel isn't back yet and it's just me and the support staff."
Andie seemed happy. "What are you doing back this late?"
She looked at the guy and smiled.

"I'm interviewing for a new security position," said
Diane. "We need to beef it up after what happened in the
Mayan Room."

As she spoke she made eye contact with Liam. Everyone told her she had no poker face whatsoever; perhaps
she could telegraph her peril. If she had, Liam gave no in-
dication that he understood. Then again, he was probably a
better poker player than she. He could also come up with a
plan. Liam, she suspected, was a match for this guy. *Please,
Liam, understand. Read my mind.*

"Sounds to me like a good idea," said Liam, smiling at
the guy. "You need some stronger guards, from what Andie
tells me. We're going to get some ice cream. Would you like
us to bring you some?"

"No. I won't be here long. I'm just going to talk to
Chanell about a new position," said Diane.

"See you tomorrow," said Andie.

Diane hoped that was true. She watched a moment
while Andie and Liam went to his car and got in. Damn.
She didn't think he got the message. But then, if he did, he
couldn't let her know. Still . . . Diane felt depressed. She
walked up the steps with mega guy.

"Good story," he said. "Logical. You do need better
security."

"Thank you," she said, and really did try to keep the sar-
casm out of her voice.

They entered the building. She waved to the security
staff on duty and passed them, going through the Primate
section to the bank of elevators midway between the east
and west wings.

"You didn't tell that security guard why I'm here," he
said. "I don't want them to get suspicious."

Diane stopped and looked at him. Mainly because she
wanted to have any delay she could.

"Andie is my assistant. I put her in charge until I could
straighten this mess out. I share things like that with her. I
rarely tell the staff why I come in the door, and they don't
expect me to."

He raised his eyebrows. Diane got the odd sensation that he respected that. Geez, what a relationship they had.

Okay, what vault was she going to take him to? Geology. Mike Seeger was gone on one of his extremeophile trips and the people who worked for him wouldn't be working late. She just hoped she didn't run across anyone while she was here. This guy would kill them without a thought.

"Why is it so dark in here?" he asked.

"It's the night lighting," she said. "Many of the exhibits are harmed by constant exposure to light. We give them a break at night."

At the bank of elevators she pressed the up button and waited. Diane's heart pounded against her ribs. *Think, think, think*.

"What's taking so long with the elevator?" he said.

"It's not taking long," said Diane. "This is the way they work. Please be patient. I'm eager to give you the package you want. Surely you can see that no one here is a threat to you."

Diane punched the button again. The elevator was taking longer than usual.

"Stairs," he said. "This is taking too damn long."

"This way," said Diane, and she led him through a door to the stairs located by the first-aid station.

"It's on the second floor," she said.

"The second floor? Why were we taking the fucking elevator anyway? No wonder you people are so out of shape."

They walked up the stairs to the second floor, coming out at the archaeology office. She hoped Jonas Briggs was home in bed and the custodial staff had finished with this part of the building.

"The vault is in the geology lab," she said.

"This is the place where we retrieved our guy," he said.

"Yes, the Special Exhibit Room is on this floor," she said. She looked at the hall door to Mike's office. He always put a notice up when he was gone. She was glad he wasn't there. He usually worked late, often very late. She didn't want any more people hurt by this man. She walked around through the Geology Room to the door of the lab where the vault was housed.

"Why did you put the package in the geology vault?" he said.

"It has valuable gemstones in it. It's one of our more secure vaults." Not completely the truth. They did keep a fortune in gemstones in it, but all the vaults were secure.

"What kind of gemstones?" he said.

Going to do a little larceny while he collects the package, she thought. "Diamonds, rubies, emeralds, gold, silver, platinum . . . the usual. It's the geology vault," she said.

"They are valuable?" he said.

"Yes," she answered, "very."

"I'll take them with me," he said.

"You have something to carry them in?" she said.

"Pockets," he said.

She looked at him. "Your pockets aren't that big."

"What do you mean?" he asked, as if she had just insulted a piece of his anatomy.

"We have drawers and drawers of them. How much were you planning on taking?" she said.

"Surely you have a sack around here somewhere. You can pick out the most valuable."

Diane shrugged. "I'm really not understanding why you guys didn't know about the vaults," she said. "It seems like a big oversight."

"You can believe I'm going to smack our guy around for it. Stupid pissant."

Guy, she thought. *A guy who is still alive.* Not Madge. But why was Madge in the mailroom snooping around? She wasn't looking for a catalog.

Diane's hand shook as she keyed in the lock code to the geology lab. It didn't unlock.

Well, shit, she thought. *Did Mike change it? More likely I got it wrong.*

"What's the matter? You better not be pulling something."

"Look, I just want to survive the night, okay? I'm not pulling anything. I'm just nervous, though I don't know why I should be."

She keyed in the code again. This time the lock disengaged.

"Try being more careful."

Diane had a thousand retorts, but she let them die on

her tongue. No use antagonizing any more than he was already. She looked around the lab. Scrupulously clean. Mike hated a mess. Still, his staff could have left a geology pick or two lying around. The only thing she saw was big rocks.

"What are you looking for? It had better not be a weapon."

"A sack," said Diane. "You said you want to take some of the gemstones."

"Get the package first. Is this the vault over here?" He pointed to a steel door.

"That's it," she said. She walked over to it, wondering if she had time to jump in after she opened it and close the door before he could do anything about it. Probably not. But she was going to try.

She keyed in a code.

"How do you remember all these combinations?" he asked.

Diane shrugged. "I just do. I know everything about the museum. It's my job."

"I appreciate a person who knows how to do their job," he said, as if they could be friends after all.

My job also is to protect the museum and the people in it, she thought, as the first of the locks released.

"This is a four-part process," she said. *Be patient.*

She keyed in another sequence of code, and another lock released. She repeated the process another two times and the vault clicked open.

She moved around the door to enter. He was right behind her, stuck like glue, holding the back of her neck. She tried to shrug him off.

"Will you stop that? I'm nervous enough the way it is," she said.

"Don't try anything."

"What the hell would I try?"

She flipped on the light and the vault lit up. It was a medium-sized room lined floor to ceiling with shallow drawers.

"I see what you mean," he said. "These are a lot of drawers. Are all of them filled with diamonds and emeralds?"

"Yes, there's quite a lot of precious and semiprecious stones here," she said.

She wondered if she could get him interested in them

enough to delay him. Maybe with enough time, she could think of some kind of damn plan.

She pulled out a drawer between the two of them. An array of glittering cut and uncut rubies lay on cotton batting.

"Not all of them are cut," she said. "Some, like this one, are just like they were found in the ground."

"How much are they worth?"

Diane shrugged again. She picked up a cut stone the size of a kidney bean.

"This one is valued at thirty thousand dollars."

"I'll take it." He grabbed it from her hand and put it in one of his many pockets.

"Be careful with it," she said. "The stones are hard, but they are also brittle. They will shatter."

She pulled out the drawer above that one. It was filled with vivid green emeralds. His eyes grew wide.

Diane ducked and shoved into his legs with her shoulder. He fell into the drawers, knocking the flats out of their slots, gems scattered over the floor.

She ran for the exit, pushing at the massive steel door. He grabbed her ankle and pulled her down.

"Now you've done it," he said.

Chapter 51

Diane kicked furiously at the hand that had her ankle, kicked at the man himself as he pulled her to him. He swung his arm, trying to untangle himself from the drawers on top of him. They were little more than an annoyance, but she had an opening to give one good kick to his face. The corner of her heel caught the edge of his eye. He jerked his head, but didn't back off.

"Like you said, what's the hurry?" he said. "I told you if you tried anything I would hurt you. And I was just beginning to like you. I still like you."

Diane continued to kick with all her strength. She reached with her arms, feeling the floor for any kind of weapon. But what kind of weapon would Mike have on the floor or in the ruby and emerald drawers? Her hand grasped one of the stones. She saw a flash of red in her hand. Rubies, raw, embedded in whatever rock they form in, she couldn't remember. But she did remember that a ruby was a nine on the scale of hardness, harder than a pocketknife blade. The rock was about the size of her palm.

She levered herself up when he had both hands on her legs and slashed at his forehead. The cuts weren't deep, but the forehead has lots of blood vessels and bleeds like hell when cut. Blood ran into his eyes. He lashed out with his hand and knocked the rock away.

"This is going to be so fucking bad for you," he said. He kicked at the long drawers that were now on the floor but still in his way, breaking one to splinters.

He struck at her with his fist, she dodged and he hit her shoulder. It was the same shoulder where one of them had shot her, probably him, she thought. A wave of pain arced through her, turning quickly to nausea. She was already sick with pain and he hadn't even started. She had lost her shoes with all the kicking and she didn't even have them as a weapon. Teeth, she had teeth. If he got close enough, at least she could wield a force of about a hundred and twenty pounds per square inch on some part of his anatomy. Of course, so could he.

He stood up, still holding one leg. Diane grabbed at the floor, still kicking at him. She snaked her torso around near his legs, and grabbed one of them, pulling. Nothing happened, at least nothing good, but she held on even as he was raising his hand to slap her.

The lights went out. He dropped her leg.

Hands were on her, pulling her out the door and pushing her somewhere. It happened so quick, she didn't have time to react, other than to kick, which was all she seemed able to do.

She stayed where she was in the dark, feeling around her. She felt something like a table leg. The room was quiet. Really quiet—nothing but the ambient sounds of the museum. She stayed still, barely breathing.

Suddenly after all the quiet, all hell broke loose.

The lights came. Her first sight was Liam knocking the gun from the kidnapper's hand as Liam shot him, hitting the man in the arm. The man barely flinched. He struck out at Liam, and Liam's gun flew across the room. Then they fought.

There was no fancy kicking, turning, or acrobatics; it was all arms and fists, and evasion. And it was so fast. Diane realized that she never stood a chance—not that that was a big revelation, but the realization that he had been trying not to kill her, toying with her so he could draw it out, frightened her.

She watched them fight, neither getting the upper hand, and it dawned on her that Liam was just waiting. He didn't have to win, but her kidnapper did. A noise by the door brought her attention around.

It was the police and her security. They had guns trained on the kidnapper. But he kept fighting. Liam backed off and started for his gun. Kidnapper guy followed him with his gaze. Liam stopped.

"On the ground," said a police officer.

Diane recognized Pendleton and his partner, Gracey.

Diane had had a run-in with them before. She wasn't their favorite person, but they would do their job.

Kidnapper guy stood still for a fraction of a second.

"Watch him."

Liam's warning came too late.

Diane barely tracked the kidnapper's movement. He had a knife out and threw it at Pendleton and charged Gracey, taking Gracey's gun and shooting Pendleton in the leg. The knife had bounced off Pendleton's vest, but the leg wound looked serious.

Liam had his gun now and before the kidnapper could turn, Liam fired twice, hitting him once in each leg. It had to break bone, thought Diane. The man started to put weight on one of his legs and he fell to his knees. Liam was aiming his gun at Superguy's head.

"Live to fight another day," said Liam.

The man put his hands on his head. Her security guards were also aiming their guns at the kidnapper. Gracey started to retrieve his gun.

"Leave it," said Liam. "Don't get close to him. It won't have a good end, and I don't want to have to shoot him."

Gracey looked at Liam with resentment in his eyes. Liam never took his eyes off Megaguy.

Blood was starting to cake around the kidnapper's eyes, making it look like he had on a mask, and the wounds in his arm and legs didn't seem to bother him much. Stoic guy. Diane would be on the floor in a fetal position. Not much different from where she was now, in fact. She slowly moved out from under the table.

Her security people looked over at her.

"Don't take your eyes off him," warned Liam. "You guys need to take this seriously. Diane's all right. Right now, we need to defuse this. The ambulance should be here in a moment."

"Come on," said Gracey, "the guy's not Superman."

"He doesn't have to be Superman," said Liam. "He just has to be what he is. And that's someone who just kicked your ass and took your weapon while you and your partner had your guns on him. Now pay attention, people."

Gracey glared at Liam a moment, then focused on Pendleton, putting pressure on Pendleton's leg wound.

"He looks like he's asleep," said Chanell, Diane's head of security, pointing her gun at the kidnapper.

"He's meditating," said Liam.

"He's what?" said Chanell, frowning at the kidnapper; her expression suggested she might be looking at an alien.

"Meditating. He's keeping his heart rate down to staunch the flow of blood from his body."

"Well, I'll be damned. Is he some kind of ninja?" said the other security guard.

"No, he's just a very well trained and very expensive problem solver," said Liam. "Diane apparently pissed off someone with a ton of money to spend."

"She's like that," muttered Pendleton, mostly under his breath.

"You know him?" asked Chanell.

"I know his type, recognize his moves," said Liam. "Now, less chatter and more watching. He's still armed to the teeth. The only thing stopping him is knowing that at least one of us will take a kill shot."

Gracey stood up with Pendleton's gun.

"Look, you son of a bitch, slide all your weapons . . ."

"No," said Liam. "We don't want him putting his hands on his weapons. Wait for the ambulance guys."

"What the hell are they going to do? They aren't secret ninja busters," said Gracey.

Diane was losing patience. Oddly, Liam didn't seem like he was. At this point she would be tempted to shoot Gracey. She thought she knew what Liam was waiting for—a sedative. He was treating kidnapper guy like a rogue tiger. Which, she supposed, he was.

The paramedics came through the door with a stretcher and stopped at the scene before them.

"Officer Pendleton," said Liam, without taking his eyes off superlative guy, "normally, I would say they take care of you first and leave this guy to wait. But we need to defuse this. Are you in a position to wait?"

"Sure," said Pendleton. "I'm fine. Just a flesh wound. Do whatever it is you're going to do with that asshole. I want to watch anyway."

Diane was impressed with Liam's diplomatic skills. He let Pendleton make the decision, and set it up so he would look tough for waiting.

"Okay," said Liam, "this is the tricky part."

The kidnapper looked over at him and smiled.

Chapter 52

Maria and Straw Fedora were sitting at one of the brightly adorned tables in the lobby of the hotel.

"What did you say to my daughter?" she asked.

"Nothing bad, I assure you. All these people heard it and weren't alarmed. I simply told her she was a very pretty little girl."

The man had a British accent when he spoke English. He sounded Portuguese when he called after Rosetta. Good with languages, Maria thought.

"What was with the whistling?" asked Maria.

"A bad habit," he said. "I know it annoys people, but you know how habits are."

"Who are you and what do you want with me?" she said.

"Senhor Michaels," said one of the hotel clerks. He was the one that was on duty when Maria had first seen Straw Fedora. He had two cups in his hand. "I brought you and the *senhora* coffee."

"Thank you, but none for me," said Maria. Michaels, she thought. She didn't recollect running across the name. Senhor Michaels did not look pleased. He hadn't intended to give her his real name, she realized. Given away by the clerk.

"My name is Cameron Michaels. I'm with Interpol," he said, handing her his card.

Maria arched an eyebrow. "Interpol's United Nations representative. What on earth do you want with an archaeology student?"

"I'm looking for this woman." He laid the flyer on the table.

Maria would have liked to snatch it up and throw it at him. But she turned it around and studied it. Frowning, to make it look believable—she hoped.

"You know her?" he said.

"No one I recognize. This is a drawing. Is it one of those police artist sketches?"

"It was done by someone she ran across in the jungle and tried to kill," he said.

"Really? Why do you think I would know such a person?"

He gestured to the flyer. "It could be you," he said.

She looked up at him sharply. "You think so? Really? I assure you I haven't tried to kill anyone."

She handed it back to him.

"Read it," he said. "You will find it interesting."

"You will have to read it to me. I fear my only foreign language is German, which hasn't been very useful here. I do know a couple of words in Spanish."

He read it to her. It sounded more sinister coming from him than when Rosetta read it.

"Ah, you think because my daughter sometimes goes by the name Rosetta, I am this person and I kidnapped her."

"You were lost in the jungle with a little girl you call your daughter and whose name is Rosetta. Diane Fallon, Linda Hall, or whatever her name is, was traveling through the same jungle with a little girl named Rosetta whom she called her daughter."

"My name is Maria West. And that 'same jungle,' as you call it, is huge. They don't call it the Amazon for nothing."

"You could have changed your name."

"Why didn't I change my daughter's name?"

"You may have felt that she couldn't remember a new name."

"Rose of Sharon has a good memory."

"Is that her name?"

"Yes."

"So the Rosetta that you call her is a coincidence, you are saying?"

"When she was born, she was all red and wrinkled, like babies are. My dad thought she looked like a little rose. He called her Rosetta. My mother calls her Rose and one of her aunts calls her Sharon. I call her Rosetta because I think it is pretty. Her father calls her Rosasharon—all one word. She answers to all of them."

"She is from here," he said with such authority that she wondered if he expected her to cave in and confess.

"What in the world makes you say that?"

"Look at her. She looks like some of the tribes around here."

"So would her father if he came here. He is an American Indian. A Cherokee."

For the first time, Michaels looked taken aback. He hadn't seen that coming.

"Do you have a photograph of him?"

"I did. It was lost along with my other important papers. I have to go to Rio to replace them."

"You have an answer for everything."

"Because there is a straightforward answer for all the questions you've asked me. You aren't one of those people who thinks that someone with the right answers is suspicious and a liar, are you? Because I have no tolerance for that kind of illogic. It's a pet peeve of mine and a conversation ender."

"No, of course not." He smiled for the first time. "You will have to forgive me if I lapse into interrogation techniques. I'll try to do better, Mrs. West. You put down in the register that you came from Río de Sangue. This woman"—he tapped the flyer—"was spotted near there."

An error to use that village, Maria thought. *Hell.*

"That was my last port of call, so to speak, before I got here. I was originally in Río Branco. It was several miles from there that I was attacked and lost my things. I made my way with my daughter to Río de Sangue and finally here."

"You saw no one like this woman?" said Michaels.

Maria studied the picture again. "No."

"It seems I must look elsewhere," he said.

He wasn't convinced, Maria thought. He was going to be a problem for them. She was going to have to come up with a way to get from here to Tabatinga without him.

"I need to go upstairs to Rosetta," she said, not shying away from the name. "We've both had an ordeal. I hope you don't intend to make it worse with false allegations."

"Of course not," he said. "I am just looking for justice for all the men she has killed."

"All the men she has killed? Is she some kind of black widow?" Maria said.

He shrugged.

"Good evening, Mr. Michaels, or should I call you Agent Michaels?"

"Mr. will do fine. I'm sorry to have troubled you. You see why I had to make sure."

"How did you light upon me, out of all the people here? Why do you think she is in Benjamin Constant?"

He shrugged. "Anonymous tip."

Maria rolled her eyes.

"This is a port city that leads to many other places. She was headed in this direction according to witnesses. I put up these Wanted posters and someone responded. They didn't give their name."

Maria shook her head. "Of all the crazy situations," she muttered and took her leave of him.

She walked to the stairs and didn't start bounding up them until she got to the second landing. She rushed to their room and knocked on the door.

"Rosetta, honey, it's Mommy. Open the door."

She waited.

Chapter 53

It was the same paramedics Diane had seen earlier. That was a relief. After the Mayan Room attack it would be a while before she trusted paramedics to be who they said they were. The two of them, equipment in hand, stood looking around at everyone. Their gaze stopped on Diane.

"You doing okay, ma'am?"

"Fine," she said. "As you can see, we have a situation here. Mr. William Dugal here will instruct you on how to proceed."

They looked a little confused. Diane didn't blame them.

"They just need to let me frisk him," mumbled Gracey.

He was smarting from having his gun taken and having Pendleton get shot with it. He was the policeman in charge and he'd lost control of the situation and didn't know how to get it back. Diane hoped it wouldn't make Gracey do something stupid.

"Look, we are the police here," Gracey said. "Who is this Dugal?"

"Someone who apparently knows how to fight the ninja guy," said Chanell. "It's going to take a while if I have to go over your head, and it won't look good for any of us."

"I need you to load a syringe with a strong sedative," said Liam.

"What?" said the one of the paramedics. "Who are we giving it to?"

"The guy on his knees with his hands on his head," said Liam.

"We can't just give sedatives without a doctor's instruction. He doesn't look like he needs one," said the other paramedic.

"You need him to have one," said Liam.

"Mister, we can't just do that," the paramedic said.

"You know who Hannibal Lecter is?" Liam said.

"Yes," said the first paramedic cautiously. They both looked wide-eyed at kidnapper guy. "He's like that?"

"He wouldn't do it for fun, but he can rip your face off with his teeth," said Liam.

Diane didn't know whether Liam was exaggerating, but she was glad she didn't try to bite the guy.

"Look," said Liam, "right now the main thing he wants to do is get away. And it may look to you like he doesn't have a chance with all the guns pointed at him. We, on the other hand, would like to take him alive and he knows this. Are you following?" The paramedics nodded.

"This is just stupid," said Gracey.

Liam ignored Gracey and went on as if he hadn't heard him. "His chances of getting away are very good. He's well armed. He's lost only a gun and one knife. He has a host of other weapons on him."

"He's shot," said Gracey. "Like I said, he's not Superman. He needs medical treatment."

"He can stand the pain until he gets to his buddies," said Liam. "They will have advanced medic training. They can patch him up and get him to a friendly doctor or a private clinic. They are well funded. And dangerous. These are the guys who didn't mind setting one of the museum guards on fire who was giving first aid to one of their buddies."

"You?" said Chanell. "You did that? You SOB."

"The point is," said Liam, "he'll let you get him to the ambulance where it's the two of you and maybe a guard and he'll make his escape. He won't mind killing you to do it because the chance of him getting caught again is fairly small."

"I'll get the syringe," said the second paramedic.

They loaded it with sedative and stood there holding it. Diane supposed they were wondering who was going to give it to the man. She was wondering the same thing. So was the kidnapper, judging from the smile on his face.

"Like I said, here's where it gets tricky," said Liam. "Diane, I need you to come over and hold the gun. If he moves, shoot to kill immediately."

"Okay," said Gracey, "enough is enough. This is police business."

"The faster we do this, the faster the paramedics can get to your partner," said Liam.

"This is police business." Gracey jutted out his chin and put a hand on his black slicked-down wavy hair. "We can take care of it."

But he didn't move to take care of it.

"I need someone who won't hesitate," said Liam. "Don't make this about you. You have police training, not soldier training. You don't have the skills necessary for this kind of prisoner. You hesitated a fraction of a second. That's why he got your gun. It's not your fault. It's the difference in training."

"The Fallon woman sure doesn't have the training," said Gracey. He looked at Diane with what she thought was a disgusted smirk.

Liam smiled. All the while he spoke he never took his eyes off the prisoner. Nor did he now. "How do you know?" Liam said.

"What?" said Gracey, looking from Liam to Diane.

Diane didn't know what the heck Liam was playing at, but she didn't say anything.

"See that blood all over his face and crusted in his eyes? Diane did that. She was fighting him when I got here."

They all stared at Diane in bewilderment, except Liam, and kidnapper guy—who laughed out loud.

"You don't see her with blood all over her face, do you?" Liam said. "I'm just saying, Diane is the one to do this."

Diane wondered why Liam thought that. It disturbed her.

She walked over to him and without altering the gun's aim, he replaced his hand with hers, transferring the gun to Diane. He took the syringe from the first paramedic, took a look at the bottle it came from. He walked around behind the man kneeling with his hands on his head.

"You know she will shoot," Liam said, "without—"

Quicker than Diane saw, Liam grabbed him around the throat and pumped the needle in his muscular neck. When he finished, he tossed the syringe toward the paramedics. He held the man in a headlock.

"As I was saying, she will shoot without hesitation. I think you know this. You can live to fight another day. We both know you can break out of the hospital because they aren't going to be as serious as I am about this. People just won't believe your skill level. Be nice and don't fight the drug and you won't get your head blown off by a woman."

Liam let him go. The kidnapper didn't move. Liam came back over to Diane and took the gun.

"Officer Pendleton needs attention," he said to the paramedics.

"Oh, sure," they said, rushing over to attend to Pendleton.

Gracey stared at Diane the whole time.

Great, she thought. *Now everyone's going to think I'm some kind of supersoldier.* She would be interested to know what Liam was thinking. He believed she would have killed a man without hesitation. Why did he think that of her? Was it true?

"What is he doing here?" said Chanell.

"He thinks I have a package from Simone Brooks, the woman who was injured here," Diane said.

"You mean those feathers and bones? That's what he wanted?"

"I don't think so. He seemed to want a package that was sent to me. The hell of it is, I wasn't sent a package. Or at least it hasn't gotten here. All this mayhem was a waste of energy."

The man looked over at Diane. His face was expression-less. Diane didn't know if that was the drug or his super-thug persona.

"Really," she said. "I haven't a clue what it is you are looking for. If it is the feathers, bone, and monkey parts, they have been processed and the reports sent to the detective in charge. Is it a package? Is that what you were sent to find?"

He said nothing, merely looked away.

"You know," she said, "you have this murder and may-hem down pretty good, but you are an awful detective." Diane turned to Chanell. "We have someone in the mu-seum working with this guy. We need to find out who it is."

"Here?" said Chanell. "We have one of these guys work-ing for us?"

"More likely, they paid someone to try and find the package," said Diane. "I need to call Frank. This guy left men to watch the house if he didn't return."

"I sent the police over to your home. Or at least Andie

did. I suspected he had a hostage," said Liam. "You were supposed to be at home with your family and you showed up here with this guy dressed for a mission. And it was pretty obvious you were under stress."

"I was hoping you noticed," she said.

"Hard to miss," he said. "I got out of the car down the hill, called your security, and told them what was up. The hard part was finding you. I didn't think you were in the crime lab, or you would have entered from the west wing. I had security stop the elevator and deactivate your access to the locks until we saw which door you were trying to enter."

That's why the elevator was slow and she couldn't unlock the lab the first time. Damn, Liam was thorough.

The paramedics finished hooking Pendleton up to an IV and had stabilized his wound.

"Can we carry them together?" they said.

"Gracey can take me," said Pendleton.

"You need to go with the paramedics," Liam said. "In case you start bleeding again. This guy will be fine once he's out. I'm sure the paramedics will be glad to have the two of you with them."

"When will that happen?" said Chanell. "When is this guy going to keel over?"

"Soon," said Liam. "He's pretending to be going out now, you notice. It will be real fairly soon."

"How do you know so much?" asked Pendleton. "Are you like him?"

"I hope not," said Liam. "But I've had special military training. He's not superhuman. Humans can do some pretty amazing things when they are well trained in something they have a talent for. Look at Olympians. They aren't superhuman, just very good athletes who have trained all their lives. I'm telling you this so you will respect what he can do and not decide that, since he is not Superman, you can take him. You can't."

As Liam talked to Chanell and the others, Diane went to a phone and called Frank. It took several rings. She let out a sigh when he answered.

"Are you all right?" she said.

"We're fine, are you? More police arrived and told us where you were and who you were with. They are out around the property looking for his friends now."

"I hope they are really careful," said Diane. "This guy's had some kind of elite military training."

Superlative man fell over.

"Okay," said Chanell, "is this real?"

"Real enough. Can I borrow your restraints?" Liam said.

"Are you all right?" said Frank.

"Yes. Liam noticed what was happening. Frank . . . are you and Star really okay?"

"Yes, baby, we're fine. After we discovered you were missing, all the drama stopped. Star was a little panicked over your kidnapping. She's okay now. She's staying in the safe room with that Get-Home-Safe backpack David got her for acing her chemistry finals. The house is an armed camp at the moment. Gregory seems to be having a good time. Said if he knew it was going to be this entertaining, he would have brought Marguerite and the boys. David and Steven arrived just after our second wave of reinforcements. They are shocked, as you can imagine. I'm just relieved . . . I'm relieved Liam was there for you. I was afraid . . ."

"I know. We are mopping up here. Maybe you should come stay at the museum. We have some guest rooms in the basement."

As Diane spoke to Frank, she watched as Liam took the plastic restraints from Chanell and secured the kidnapper's hands behind him, then his legs together. Diane could see that her kidnapper still had enough left in him to resist. But Liam didn't seem to be having too much trouble.

After Liam had him restrained, he took the knife that had bounced off Pendleton's Kevlar vest.

"What are you going to do?" said Chanell.

"Are you still there?" asked Frank.

"I'm sorry, I was watching Liam restrain the guy. He's been shot two or three times and Liam still had to sedate him. It's like taking care of a velociraptor."

"I think staying at the museum this evening is a good idea," said Frank. "I'm going to take a couple of days off and help you solve this."

"Frank, I've been thinking . . ."

"Don't make any decisions without me," he said. "We'll talk when I get over there."

Liam was cutting off the man's clothes when Diane hung

up. Everyone watched in fascination. Diane wasn't sure if it was because Liam was doing it or the shock of the musculature on the guy.

"The clothes will be easier to search now. I can help if you like," said Liam.

"You need to check to see if he has a weapon up his ass," said Gracey.

Diane was sure all of them had a retort for Gracey, but they all kept their mouths shut. Liam helped the paramedics tend the wounds and then truss the guy to the stretcher with the normal belts, but Liam added duct tape. The guy was out by now, snoring away.

"Officer Pendleton," said Liam. "He really needs to wake up in a prison hospital. Can you arrange that?"

"I'll give it a try. You know how bureaucrats are," he said.

"You have backup outside?" asked Liam.

"The place is surrounded by police cars," said Chanell.

"Tell them to be on the lookout for a van painted flat black. There will be several of his heavily armed buddies in it, and they will want to get him back," said Diane.

Pendleton was looking pale. Diane was glad to finally watch them go out the door to the hospital.

She turned to Liam. She really wanted to know why he thought she could kill with such precision and ease.

Chapter 54

Maria knocked again. Panic was sending electric waves of pain through her body. She felt weak and sick. *Please, no.* "Ro-Rosetta, honey, are you there?"

She heard a sound on the other side of the door. A tiptoe on wood floor. Maria was afraid to feel relief.

"Rosetta, sweetie," she said.

The door opened and Maria could see one eye surrounded by dark hair peeking at her. The door opened wide and Rosetta ran into her arms. Maria hurried inside and closed the door, locking it.

"Rosetta, baby, what's the matter?"

"That bad woman grabbed me. She tried to take me," said Rosetta, crying into Maria's chest.

Maria sat down on the bed and pulled Rosetta into her lap. She waited, letting her cry. When the tears subsided, Maria asked her what woman had tried to grab her.

"The one that asked you all those questions at the restaurant, Gabina," said Rosetta.

"Did she say why?" asked Maria.

"She wanted to talk to me without you. She said I was afraid of you. I don't know why she would say that," said Rosetta. "I told her she was a liar and pulled away, but she held my arm. I bit her and she let go and I ran and locked myself in the room and got under the bed."

Maria thought she knew what happened. Gabina believed that Maria had indeed kidnapped Rosetta. She wanted to speak with the child alone, in case Rosetta was afraid of talking in front of Maria. But Gabina had handled it all wrong.

Maria rocked back and forth with Rosetta until she hiccupped herself to sleep. She tucked the child into bed and set about securing the door. The chair seemed inadequate, but there was nothing else.

Damn that woman, she thought. She hoped her bite got infected. She went back to Rosetta and sat on the bed with her. Rosetta opened her eyes.

"The bad man knows who I am," said Rosetta. "He knows my name."

"What did he say?" said Maria.

"He said I am a pretty little mermaid. You know, *The Little Mermaid*—her name is Ariel. Then he said my name. Then he whistled my song—'Hall of the Mountain King.' I played it on my CD player that Mama got for me."

That was very cruel, thought Maria, but a man who could carry out a massacre was the essence of cruel.

"But you didn't even miss a beat," said Maria. "You were great."

"I've been pretending I couldn't understand English for years. He was nothing."

Maria smiled. "You're great."

She sat on the bed until Rosetta drifted off to sleep, listening to the rise and fall of her breathing, wondering how they were going to get to the docks tomorrow. Did Michaels believe her? She thought not. Did he have friends here? Probably.

The room was darkening and she turned on a lamp and set it on the floor as a nightlight for Rosetta.

Michaels couldn't let them leave the country. He was one of the architects of the massacre and Ariel could identify him. Was that why they had some kind of trip wire set for Diane Fallon? Maria remembered that Julio, the man who took her, was talking with someone on his satellite phone about having the forensic anthropologist from Georgia who was asking about feathers and bones. What the hell was that about?

Something clicked in her mind. What was it? What did the Yawanawa woman say to her after they tranquilized Kyle Manning? She talked about men who came and stole the birds from the trees. Damn, they were trafficking in endangered species, a multimillion dollar industry. So then, did they think Diane would come back to South America to . . . to what? Trace feathers back to their origin? Was she involved in catching animal traffickers? That didn't seem to jibe with what she knew about Diane. But she didn't really know her, other than having met her once or twice at forensic anthropology conferences—and the rumors she'd heard about her tragic time in South America.

Feathers and bones? What about the bones? Animal bones? Human bones? More endangered species, or more mass graves? She didn't know.

And then there were the children. The men who carried out the massacre clearly were taking the children and sending them off somewhere for some reason—most likely slavery of some form. Were they afraid Diane Fallon would one day discover her daughter wasn't dead and come looking for her? Ariel could identify the engineers of the crimes. They had lost track of Ariel until now. They were afraid of Ariel.

Now they had let a third party in on their secret—her. There was no way they were going to let the two of them get away. So close—just across the Amazon River—and so far. Damn it, she would swim it with Rosetta on her back if she had to.

Maria was startled by a knock at the door. Rosetta jerked awake and started to cry.

"Brave heart, Ariel," Maria whispered in her ear. "We will get to your mother, I promise you."

Rosetta grabbed her hand and squeezed.

There was another knock at the door.

"Maria?" came a loud whisper. "It is Hanna."

Maria went to the door.

"Hanna, what do you want?"

"We need to speak with you," she said.

"We?" said Maria.

"Me, Patrik, and Gabina," said Hanna.

"Gabina tried to take my daughter. She scared her to death. Rosetta cried herself to sleep after hiding under the bed for an hour."

"Gabina told us what she did," said Hanna.

Maria opened the door and slipped out into the hall. Patrik was there, and so was Gabina.

"We are really sorry. When Gabina told us what she did we were horrified and came to see if Rosetta is all right," said Hanna.

"She is not. She's been traumatized. After what we've been through, and we finally get a call through to her father, and now this." Maria eyed Gabina. If looks could sear off flesh, Gabina would be standing there wearing nothing but raw muscle.

"The paper tacked to the pole, then the man from Interpol. He was convincing," Gabina said. "I was worried about the little girl. Americans are known to kidnap children from other countries."

Maria raised her eyebrows and nailed her with another stare. She noticed the bandage around her hand and the dark spots staining up to the surface. Good for Rosetta. She drew blood.

"You don't grab a child the way you did," Maria said to her. "We were grabbed and just barely got away. And then you do it. Do you have any idea the harm you've caused?"

"I am really sorry. Hanna and Patrik said I was wrong and that the woman didn't look like you."

She unfolded the paper and gave it to Maria. Fortunately the creases across the face distorted the drawing.

"It looks like a woman of mixed race," said Patrik. "The hair is in that . . ." He looked at Hanna.

"Dreads," she said. Hanna made gestures with her fingers down the side of her head as if dreadlocks were sausage curls.

Maria was thankful they hadn't noticed her hair when they came across her in the jungle. She had tied it up under a scarf, basically trying not to look like she'd dipped her head in the mud. Her dreads were from her hair getting wet and muddy, but in the drawing it did look like that was her style.

"Rosetta is a common name," said Maria. "I explained that to Michaels when he spoke with me and, quite frankly, I found him more than a little creepy." She fished his card out of her jeans pocket. "Why the heck is Interpol's representative to the UN interested in some woman serial killer rampaging through the jungle? I think he is stalking me."

"We were afraid of that too," said Patrik.

"After dinner we visited friends. They had an Internet connection, and Gabina wanted to look up your name. That's when she told us what she did."

"And?" said Maria.

"We found your husband's company Web site. He does a lot of large projects," said Patrik.

"Yes, he does." Maria was starting to feel uncomfortable. She wasn't on John's company Web site but there might be a hyperlink to her—and her name.

"We looked for family," said Gabina.

"John doesn't believe in putting kids on the Internet, certainly not his family," said Maria. "And I agree with that."

"We did find this," said Hanna, grinning. She showed Maria a picture from a powwow.

Maria smiled. It showed John in costume in the foreground of the photograph looking very striking. The picture showed her in the background also in Cherokee costume. Only John was named, thank God.

"This is from a powwow last year—a Native American cultural festival."

"It looks like fun," said Hanna.

"It is," said Maria.

"We were thinking that when they tried to kidnap you and your daughter, it was for ransom. That is not uncommon here," said Patrik.

"My thoughts too," said Maria. "I think that Mr. UN-Interpol Michaels may be involved."

"What can we do to help?" said Hanna.

"I suspect he will be following me," said Maria, "and I need to get across the Amazon River. If I could do it tonight, I might be able to evade him. Do you know anyone with a boat?"

"They have night cruises," said Hanna. "You could take a cruise boat. That would be fun."

"Are you ready to travel?" said Patrik.

"We are always ready to travel," said Maria.

Chapter 55

Maria asked Patrik and Hanna to meet her in front of the building in five minutes, giving her time to wake up Rosetta and collect their things. She cast a final glance at Gabina before going back into her hotel room. Maria hoped the glance conveyed the sentiment that she would rip her heart out if Gabina interfered.

·"We are going to cross to Tabatinga tonight," said Maria.

The little girl looked happy and excited. "Tonight, really?"

"Yes. Hanna and Patrik are taking us to the dock and you and I are going to take a ride on a tour boat," she said.

"Do you trust them?" asked Rosetta, swinging her legs around and jumping down from the bed.

"To a point."

It had crossed Maria's mind that they had seen John's construction company and all the big projects he had built and might harbor kidnapping ideas of their own.

"We are going to meet them out front. But first we'll go out the back way and get our gun."

Rosetta nodded her approval.

"When we are on the tour boat there will be other people on it, a crowd. That will be good. We have to be alert to danger during the ride in the car to the dock. Are you up for this? We could walk to the dock. It's only a quarter of a mile."

"What about the bad guy?" asked Rosetta.

"I don't know where he is, or if he is watching the hotel. I thought it would be better if we ride in a car, but if you don't feel safe, we won't."

"Do you feel safe?" asked Rosetta.

"At the moment I don't even remember what safe feels like," she said. "I have a gun and I'll use it if anyone tries to harm us."

Maria collected their backpack and tote bag. She put money and a pocketknife in her jeans and extra money in her bra. She turned the air conditioner on so there would be noise in the room and it would sound like it was still occupied if Michaels came around. The two of them tiptoed down the stairs and out the back door.

It wasn't hard to find the place where Maria hid the gun. She hoped it was still there. Michaels could have been watching when she hid it. Or anyone could have been watching. She was wishing she'd just kept it with her.

She moved the broken piece of block and stuck her hand in the space. It was there, wrapped in cloth, heavy. She retrieved it and took it from the cloth. She wondered where people who carried a concealed weapon put it. Of course they probably had a holster. She put the gun in her tote bag and hung the bag on her shoulder. They walked around the building looking for the car.

Hanna waved to them. Maria felt guilt for thinking she might have to shoot them. What had she become? Gabina wasn't with them. She had stayed at the hotel. Maria was glad about that but was also worried whether Gabina would alert Michaels.

Patrik was driving. Maria told them Rosetta was a little sick to her stomach and she didn't want to aggravate it by riding in the back, especially since they were just about to take a boat ride. So Hanna rode in the backseat and Maria rode in front with Rosetta in her lap. She rolled down the window and Rosetta leaned her head near the breeze to add to the illusion.

The truth was, Maria was afraid to sit in the back—afraid of child locks that wouldn't release, afraid of being taken prisoner.

Hanna sat on the edge of the backseat and rested her arms on the back of the front seat so she could talk to them. She and Patrik seemed to be having fun. Maria wished she could remember what fun felt like.

They started out toward the docks, weaving between motorcycles, other cars, and pedestrians along the way. Who knew there was a nightlife in Benjamin Constant? What looked like a well-worn city in the daytime was a glittering jewel of lights at night filled with people having fun.

It wouldn't take long to arrive at the docks, even at the slow pace they had to travel. Hanna and Patrik talked non-stop. They were fascinated with powwows. Maria told them to come visit in the United States and they could go to a few. They liked the idea of dressing up in Indian costumes, of Hanna braiding her blond hair.

"Can one ride horses there?" said Patrik.

"Oh yes," said Maria. "Do you ride?"

Patrik grinned. "Yes."

"He loves it," said Hanna. "Me, not so much. You are on a huge wild animal and are supposed to be able to control it. It always feels a little dangerous to me. Do you ride?"

This time Maria grinned and she remembered fun. "Yes. I have an Arabian stallion named Mandrake."

"Stallion? You ride a stallion? Is that not dangerous?" said Patrik, though he sounded envious.

"Can be. He's a well-schooled horse that I trust. My mother bred and trained him for me. She breeds Arabians. I've ridden all my life."

"Really?" said Hanna. "We will have to come see you. Patrik would love that, wouldn't you, Patrik?" Hanna dug around in her purse and came out with a card. "Here is my e-mail address. Write when you get back. We would like to know you and Rosetta are safe."

Maria took the card, wondering what they would think about her when they discovered she was such an accomplished liar and Rosetta really wasn't her daughter and her name wasn't Maria.

Patrik parked the car in the first space he found at the waterfront and they walked the rest of the way to the docks.

The Amazon was alive at night. Tour boats glided up and down the river, twinkling like multicolored sparklers. Maria was glad to be out of the car. Every moment they were in it she worried that Hanna might pull a gun, though neither Patrik nor Hanna had done anything to suggest she would. The two of them gave Maria and Rosetta a hug at the dock where a smallish single-deck tour boat was taking on passengers for a long night ride down the Amazon toward Tabatinga.

Maria picked up Rosetta and carried her on her hip, not trusting simply holding her hand. Rosetta put her arms around Maria's neck and they boarded the boat, paying at the gangplank. Maria asked if she could get off at the airport. The steward nodded and Maria found a seat near the exit. She was less interested in sightseeing than she was in a quick getaway should the need arise, as it seemed to with regularity.

It took about thirty minutes for the boat to finally get started, each moment agonizing as Maria waited for a boarding party of thugs . . . or police. But she didn't feel relief when the boat pulled away.

The distance to the airport where she was headed was only eleven miles. But the boat was going slow. It was, after all, a tour boat. There was music and dancing on board. Maria sat with Rosetta on her lap, barely hearing the music.

She noticed several others who had not joined in the merriment. It alarmed her, thinking these might be the thugs she was waiting for, disguised as ordinary people. Until she realized they were probably workers going to some night shift somewhere in the city. It wasn't only a tour boat, but a ferry, a waterway bus line.

It took a little over an hour to arrive at Tabatinga. The vessel overshot the airport by about a quarter of a mile because that's where the dock was. They sounded a horn as they docked. Maria stood up and waited for the crew to make the gangplank ready.

She wasn't the only one getting off here. She didn't know whether that was a good thing. She would rather they be alone than among people she didn't know. On the other hand, sometimes a crowd was safer.

Most of the people getting off went down a road toward what a sign said was a power plant. The rest were going to the airport. She walked along with the crowd. Some had motorbikes stashed away and rode off in a cloud of dust. In a straight line the airport wasn't that far, but going the way of the road it was about a mile. Rosetta walked part of the way and Maria carried her part of the way.

She felt relief when they got to the terminal. It was a small, cream-colored building with rust red roof and trim. The building was landscaped with well cared for hedges and beds of flowers. It looked normal.

She and Rosetta had stayed to themselves on the walk, but several of her fellow travelers were there to catch a plane. Most had backpacks rather than suitcases. She and Rosetta fit in with their new clean T-shirts, jeans, ball caps, and backpack.

The inside was just as clean and neat as the outside. They went to the ladies' room first and freshened up. Then Maria found them a couple of seats that were out of the way and not so front and center as most of them.

Rosetta still looked scared. Maria understood. The closer she got to the prize, the more afraid she was of losing it. Maria felt the same way. Rosetta hadn't asked to call her mother. Maria wondered if it was because she was afraid the bad man would trace the call, or if she was afraid her mother might ask her not to come. Maria knew instinctively that wouldn't happen, but Rosetta was a kid who had been told lies. And as much as she tried to believe, the lies crept into her fears and made them grow.

"You doing okay?" asked Maria.

Rosetta nodded. She looked tired and Maria realized, as she saw some of the others around them settle into chairs to sleep, they were supposed to be in bed.

Maria found an out-of-the-way corner where they could sit on the floor and Rosetta could lay her head in Maria's lap and sleep. Maria wasn't able to sleep. She was tired enough but she was too wary. She dug into the backpack and pulled out some paper and a pen she had bought in the marketplace. She hadn't had a chance to draw the Inca site they had discovered. Now would be a good time. It took a few tries, but she found a way to hold the notebook so she could draw and not bother the sleeping Rosetta.

She began drawing the site from memory—the rocks, the mounds, the linear scars in the ground—changing the oblique view she had in her mind to an overhead view. She had enough experience with sites that she was good at guessing distances. She penciled estimates on the drawing. She shaded in the stones and added the jungle. Maria worked on the drawing until it was a reasonable facsimile of the site. She added her own observations, on-the-fly field notes about the settlement pattern.

Maria dug out the ceramics and drew them, front and back views. Made notes about the style, the tempering, the color. She rewrapped them and put them in an envelope she had purchased at the time with the notebook and writing materials.

All that took several hours. Periodically she would stop and survey her surroundings, looking for Michaels or anyone who seemed to take an interest in them.

Morning came and Rosetta awakened with a start.

"It's all right," said Maria. Her legs felt asleep from the pressure of Rosetta's head. And her butt definitely felt the pressure from the hard floor. Maria stood up, bringing Rosetta with her, and shook each leg.

"I think I saw some vending machines. Why don't we go find something to eat?"

Rosetta nodded.

"Are you all right?" asked Maria.

"I'm scared," she mumbled.

Maria kneeled down to her. "What are you afraid of?"

"The man," she said.

"I'm keeping an eye out for him," Maria said.

"You won't leave me if they won't let me go with you, will you?" she said.

Maria hugged her. "No, baby, I won't leave you. I'm taking you to your mother. I won't leave you."

Maria didn't know what she would do if the authorities came and forcibly took Rosetta. How would she keep her promise? She held tightly to her. "I won't leave you," she whispered.

They made another trip to the bathroom, after which Maria bought them some candy and a drink from the machines. Feeling down in her tote bag, she realized she had the gun.

Shit, the damn gun—savior and trouble.

"Let's walk outside a while and stretch our legs," she said.

"What's wrong?" said Rosetta, looking around.

"The gun," she whispered.

"Oh. Where are you going to hide it this time?" whispered Rosetta.

"Outside in one of the planters, but I have to make sure no one is watching."

They went outside and scoped the place. More people were coming in now that it was morning. The airport, which had not closed, was fully waking up. Maria and Rosetta walked around looking for all the places they could be un- observed. They played a little tag in the yard, then sat down in the garden, Rosetta with her doll, both with their candy and drinks. Maria quickly buried the gun in the loose dirt of one of the planters. The groundskeepers would eventually find it, but she hoped it wasn't until after she and Rosetta left.

They went back inside and found some quiet seats and waited. Maria taught Rosetta a few phrases in Cherokee, which delighted the child.

"Tell me about your horse. You didn't tell me you had a horse," said Rosetta. Maria told her about Mandrake, her black stallion. They were laughing when Maria saw Cam- eron Michaels walk into the airport.

Chapter 56

Diane sat with Liam in the museum lounge with a hot cup of coffee in her hands. Every part of her body ached. Bruises on her arms were already forming. Her black embroidered pantsuit was ruined. She felt defeated.

When she wouldn't go to the hospital, Liam insisted on taking a look at the cut on her arm from the gunshot. The butterfly bandage had come loose and the cut was bleeding. It turned out that Liam was a pretty good field medic.

Now she sat waiting for Frank. Dreading seeing him, only because she had decided to cancel the wedding. How could she marry him, knowing what kind of havoc would rain down upon him and Star because of her? He and Star could have been killed. She couldn't stand that.

"Thank you, Liam," she said. "That was pretty amazing stuff you did."

"You softened him up for me."

"Yeah, right. I'm sure I did," she said. "He was going to kill me and I didn't know how to stop him. What kind of people are they that they're willing to do what they do?"

"Some are sociopaths. You know that," said Liam. "Others are able to set their conscience aside for a lot of money. As I said, these guys are expensive. Who did you tick off?"

"I don't know. It's somehow connected with my time in South America. I don't know what it's about, but something happened there that has come back to bite me."

She drank more of her coffee, staring off at nothing. Liam sat drinking an orange juice and eating a Snickers bar.

"Why did you think I could kill him without hesitation?" asked Diane.

Liam was quiet a moment, chewing on a bite of candy. "I didn't know," he said. "But I'd already seen the policemen were too slow and inclined to either hesitate or to act rashly. And your museum security staff work in a museum every day." He held up a hand. "I know they are trained and they are competent, but they are still museum guards. I'm sorry. I mean no disrespect. This guy wouldn't have taken them as any kind of serious threat, and he was way faster than they are. You, on the other hand, had already shown him you were fast."

"He was toying with me," said Diane.

"Yes, he was. If he hadn't been, I wouldn't have been in time. However, I'm pretty sure he didn't mean for you to get a swipe at his forehead. Good move, by the way. Blood in the eyes, always good." He smiled. "He had pissed you off and he knew it. He knew you didn't hesitate. He believed you would shoot without any indecision. That's why I chose you. It's not because I believe you are a natural-born killer."

Diane nodded. "Thanks for that." She shook her head. "What a mess. Star must be terrified." She smiled. "She's tough, though. You'd never know she was scared."

Korey and Jonas wandered into the room, talking in low tones to each other.

"What are you two doing here?" Diane said.

They looked at her, startled. She hadn't meant to sound so sharp.

"Jonas and I just came over from a project we are working on at Bartram," said Korey. "Kind of took all night. We thought we'd stop by here."

"My God," said Jonas, "you look terrible. Did you get beat up?"

"Yes," said Diane. "We had an incident."

"Here in the museum?" said Korey.

"Yes. I'll tell you about it later," said Diane. "I'm sorry I snapped. It happened on the second floor and I was afraid . . . just afraid."

Jonas and Korey pulled up chairs. As much as she liked them, she wished they would go somewhere else.

"It must be the phase of the moon," said Jonas. "Lots of bad things happening."

Diane looked at him. He looked worried.

"We have a friend who may be in serious trouble," said Korey. "You probably know her; she's a forensic anthropologist, but mainly a professor of archaeology at the University of Georgia. She wrote me a letter of recommendation for this job."

"She's missing in the Amazon rain forest," said Jonas. "Her department is afraid she's been kidnapped for ransom, but they haven't heard anything. They didn't realize anything was wrong until she missed a couple of lectures in Cuzco. We are all deeply worried."

"Her boyfriend is a fairly coolheaded dude," said Korey. "But I talked to him yesterday and I can tell he's pretty distraught. The Peruvian authorities are looking into it."

Diane stared at them.

"What?" said Jonas.

"Forensic anthropologist from Georgia in the Amazon," she said.

"Yes," said Jonas. "You heard something?"

"Damn," said Diane. "Damn."

She stood up quickly and swayed. Liam put a hand on her arm and guided her back down to the chair.

"You think it was her?" said Liam.

"It was the one rumor that didn't make sense." Diane spoke to Liam, forgetting about Jonas and Korey.

"All the others were insubstantial, lacking detail. The thing from Interpol was just so strange and could be so easily verified," she said. "There has to be a connection."

"Well, if it is her, she's damn tough," said Liam. "If she's the one who killed those four men."

"Whoa, whoa, whoa," said Jonas. "Let's back up and act like Korey and I are still sitting here worried about our friend. What the hell is going on?" His crystal blue eyes glittered in anger.

Diane looked over at them a moment, her forehead creased in a frown. She put a hand on Jonas' arm.

"I'm sorry. I didn't mean be so insensitive. Something just clicked into place," she said. "I'm really sorry."

"She's not dead, is she?" said Korey. He and Jonas exchanged glances.

"Please don't tell us that," said Jonas. "What do you know?"

"I don't know if she's dead. I have no information about

that. But what happened to her may have something to do with me."

"What?" said Jonas.

His face was red. Diane worried about his blood pressure.

"Interpol put out a warrant on me for the murder of four men. Liam investigated and learned that the dead men worked for the criminal element in the area—people who might be kidnappers."

"Dear God," said Jonas.

"Is that all you know?" asked Korey.

"No. We know the warrant originated in Brazil. That may be where they took her. We need to alert the Brazilian authorities. We also have a short timeline of events that have occurred and some locations—and a path of where she was heading maybe. She may have escaped."

"What can we do?" said Jonas.

"I can let the authorities in Brazil know, for starters. I can call the embassy there. Gregory and I used to have contacts."

"I can start working on it," said Liam.

Diane nodded. "You were just speaking with people down there. Maybe you could speak with them again. I'll talk to Gregory and see if some of the people we knew are still working there."

"If you could do something," said Jonas, looking from Diane to Liam. "She's a great kid."

"She sounds resourceful," said Liam.

"You have no idea," said Korey. He put an arm on Jonas' shoulder. "If anyone can get out of trouble, it's Lindsay. You know that."

"But lost in the jungle with people like that . . ."

"She managed to crush a man to death in the middle of the jungle," said Liam. "The people who pass for authorities down there were trying to figure that one out when I talked with them."

Korey stared at Liam. "Crushed a man to death? You're kidding, right?"

Liam smiled. "No, dead serious. The whole thing was so peculiar I wasn't sure what to believe. This puts a new twist on it."

Jonas nodded. "I'm glad we came up here. They are looking in Peru for her."

"Why don't the two of you go home and get some sleep?" said Diane.

"Good idea," said Jonas.

Jonas was about to stand when Star, Frank, Gregory, and Chief Garnett walked into the break room.

Chapter 57

It was almost morning and Diane's head hadn't yet touched a pillow. Neither had anyone else around her been to bed.

The museum's basement meeting room was decorated like a club lounge, with stuffed chairs, dark oak tables, large viewing screen, walls lined with bookcases and sofas. It was all brand-new, part of the recent renovations. It was a room Diane liked. Now it housed refugees from attacks Diane still didn't quite understand.

There was so much to talk about with everyone there, but she needed to speak with Frank first while she still had the courage. They sat in two stuffed chairs near each other but away from everyone else.

"Are you all right?" he asked. "You've been through a rough time."

"Liam is a good field medic," she said. "He patched up my arm again."

She paused, trying to control the tears threatening her resolve.

"Look, Frank, I can't do this to you, damn it. Look at Star over there, clutching the bug-out backpack David gave her. She can't even get to sleep. Your house . . . and you . . . what you've been through. Not to mention your neighbors . . . what they must think . . . a war breaking out in the neighborhood."

"What are you saying?" he said.

Diane could see in his eyes, he knew what she was getting at.

"How can I marry you, knowing the kind of things I bring down on your head?"

"Are you going to quit your job at the museum? The

crime lab? Are you going to go live on a remote island away from everyone?" said Frank.

"Perhaps. I may lose my museum job anyway. Vanessa has lost confidence in me."

"I doubt that," he said.

Diane shrugged, trying hard not to reach for Frank.

"This is a pretty good sign I shouldn't get married. I'll never know what kinds of things in my past are going to come back and kick me and everyone around me."

"You don't believe in signs," he said.

Diane's lips turned up the smallest amount. "I should."

"Before you make a decision, wait until this is resolved. Who knows, perhaps there will come a sign that we should marry," he said.

"I can't imagine what that could be," she said.

"Don't make a decision today. And when you do, include me in it," Frank said.

"Aren't you afraid of me?" said Diane.

"I'm afraid of that vanload of supersoldiers running loose," he said. "They are the problem, they and whoever hired them. That's who I want out of my life. Not you."

Diane watched Frank for several long moments. "I couldn't bear it if anything happened to you, or Star, or your son, Kevin. Thank God he's with his mother right now."

"I know. But we also can't let the worst of humanity have that much say over how we live our lives. That is also unacceptable."

"You already had to build a panic room because of me," she said.

He smiled. "And it works pretty well. Look, Diane, I've had my share of bad guys wanting to get even. You aren't the only one who draws fire. Your enemies are just more over-the-top lately." He reached over and took Diane's hand, rubbing the top of it with his thumb. "Just wait before you make a decision."

"Wait for a sign?" she said, smiling.

"Or at least until things have calmed down," he said.

Diane didn't say anything. She was pretty sure she would not change her mind. Her own family wasn't speaking to her because of what was brought down on her mother by someone who wanted to hurt Diane. She didn't want anything to happen to Frank and his family for the same reason.

"You said I'm high maintenance. That hardly covers it, does it?" she said.

"Hardly," he said, grinning for a moment, then frowning. "We were all terrified when we discovered you were missing. Gregory and Garnett included. I knew then I didn't want to lose you . . . ever."

Diane looked over to see Gregory, David, and Steven deep in conversation. Neva had called David in for help, and he and Liam had processed Megaman's clothes, collecting an amazing array of weapons.

Garnett had contacted the GBI for help with the terrorists, as he described them. After hearing details of the wave after wave of assault on Frank's house, the GBI agreed with the classification. This put all kinds of things into play. If the guys were smart, supertrained or not, they would lie low, thought Diane.

She nodded to Frank. A rather noncommittal nod agreeing at least not to talk any more about changes in their plans until the drama ended. Frank went to see about Star. Diane walked over to Gregory and the others. She had yet to tell them about the information she had gained from Martine and from Korey and Jonas.

"My girl, you look bloody awful," said Gregory.

"I feel bloody awful," Diane said. Her head and arm throbbed. She would really rather go to her office and curl up on the couch.

"Liam told us about the ninja guy," said David. "He said you acquitted yourself quite admirably."

"I basically got my butt kicked. Had it not been for Liam, there would have been a much worse outcome," said Diane.

All of them frowned. "This is just way out of hand," said Steven. He rubbed his hand through his damp hair. Diane remembered he and David said it was raining and looking as if it would get worse. Perhaps everyone could hole up until the storm was over. Perhaps some things would solve themselves by then.

"Gregory said you discovered what is going on right before the shit really started hitting the fan," Steven said.

Garnett came over and drew up a chair.

"I thought I would join the secret detective club you guys have organized," he said.

He didn't look mad, but Diane could see he was determined. She had purposefully not included him in what they had been doing. But now she could hardly keep him out of the loop, especially if there was a connection with the death of Madge Stewart. She still couldn't wrap her brain around that one. She nodded to Garnett.

"In the beginning we just wanted to find out who was trashing us. That wasn't anything we could really worry the police with. And now, as Steven said, things have gotten way out of hand."

"So," said Gregory, "what did Martine have to say?"

Diane shifted her attention back to all of them. She didn't bother to explain who Martine was to Garnett. He would figure it out as they went along.

"Martine didn't know she had any information. I asked her if there were any odd conversations she'd had with Oliver, anything that didn't make sense at the time but might be more understandable now. She remembered this one time when they were watching the birds."

Diane told them how a pensive Oliver connected up cruelty to animals and cruelty to children.

"I don't follow," said Steven.

"Did you know that the illegal trafficking in wild animals is second only to drugs in terms of money generated? Then you have slavery—particularly child slavery. Oliver must have just discovered something when he spoke with Martine.

"The items we found in the museum—the ones we think Simone brought with her—have to do with endangered parrots and other animals that smugglers prey on. There was also the bone of a child. At first I thought . . ."

She hesitated a moment. Still trying to stop the tears from coming.

"I thought she may have found Ariel." Her voice cracked and she stopped again.

"Oh, Diane," said Gregory, putting a hand on her arm.

"I now think perhaps it has something do with the trafficking of children, either for sex or domestic slavery or both."

"But it was a bone—its owner was dead," said Steven. "That indicates something else."

"Perhaps a child died and was dumped with the animals that died. Most of the birds die before they reach the end buyer. They are stuffed into socks and hidden on the bodies of smugglers for transport. I'm sure children die from their mistreatment as well. These are people for whom life is cheap. As we've witnessed up close."

Chapter 58

Garnett's frown became deeper as he listened to Diane. She recognized he had no idea how grim this might be. He was thinking drugs because the fabric was contaminated with it. He could handle drugs. It was a problem everywhere. He wasn't thinking humans, children, the grimmest of all crimes.

"The rumors about me and David were about us being into drugs. I think that was so we would think in that direction and not in any other. I believe that whoever is head of this criminal enterprise got wind Simone found something that Oliver had discovered and was trying to tell me about it. The guys who attacked Frank's house were looking for a package that they believed Simone sent to me—something besides the feathers and other items. I haven't received a package, but I couldn't convince the guy who took me of that. However, I believe with the way they have been after it, it is something on the level of proof and we have to find it. They believe it exists so I have to believe it too. We find it, we have them."

"Okay, hold on," said Steven. "What are you saying was going on, exactly? I'm supposed to be a smart guy, but I'm having trouble connecting the dots. They seem to be spread all over the place."

"What was the one thing that was always going through the mission? Refugees, mostly women and children. A lot of us were out in the field most of the time, but Oliver wasn't. I think he got wind that some of the charitable organizations that helped relocate the refugees that Santos and other strong men created were really selling some of them into slavery. They were also, I believe, dealing in rare animals. I imagine it was a multimillion dollar operation on both fronts and Oliver was threatening to bring it to a stop, at least at the mission. That's why there was the massacre. I think the same people were threatened by Simone. They were afraid that we could put it together and the first thing they tried was to discredit us. That cost the least in terms of manpower. Rumors can be a potent weapon. But they overdid it, or we didn't react the way they thought, or they found out about the package and had to be more confrontational—something made them change strategy and now they are trying to kill us."

Diane stopped talking. Garnett stared at her. She imagined he felt out of his depth at the moment. He had been thinking of a local problem, not a global one.

"It makes sense," said Gregory.

David nodded.

"Not to me," said Steven. "We would have known if something like that was going on. Look, I hate to always be the devil's advocate here, but I'm having a hard time with this." He spread his hands out on the table. "Okay, I concede that with the arrival of Attila and his Huns, Simone being jealous of Diane is not the cause of any of this. Still, all this is so complicated. And, damn it, we were all good detectives. We would have known. If not us, then why the hell wouldn't David suspect something? There is not a more suspicious person I know."

"Martine asked that too; then she said we all have our blind spots," said Diane. "David is good at spotting anomalies. His blind spot is for things that are supposed to be there. The refugees and orphans were supposed to be there—nothing to be suspicious about. And how would we know what an organization did with the children when they placed them? We never had anything to do with that. That was the mission's work. That was Father Joseph's work. They just let us work out of their building."

"But . . ." Steven didn't finish. He just shook his head. "Do you think Father Joseph was involved? I have a really hard time with that."

David looked pensive, as if thinking about what Diane said about his blind spot. Assessing what he could do about it.

"He may or may not have known," David said after a

moment. "Father Joe may have accidentally discovered it. Hell, he may have told Oliver, or vice versa. The massacre may have been to shut them both up and cover their tracks."

"Okay, what about Santos?" said Steven. "We know he did the killings. Why in hell would he do it because someone asked him to?"

"Santos hated Diane and Gregory," said David. "He was involved in drugs. All of these enterprises are probably related in some way. Criminals tend to know each other just like people in other professions know each other. Money exchanged hands for sure."

Diane turned to Garnett. "The mercenary who took me said they had someone on the inside of the museum looking for the package. Madge Stewart was discovered in the mailroom sifting through the mail the day before her death. Now, I can't imagine these guys enlisting Madge, of all people. It is so wrong on many levels. I can't imagine her even being acquainted with guys like them, but there it is."

"They may have killed her. Is that what you are saying?" said Garnett.

"Yes. They have the means to make it look like an accident," said Diane.

"When were you going to tell me?" he said.

"The first chance I got," said Diane. "Things have been happening rather fast."

He nodded, conceding her point. "That they have. The prisoner is scheduled to be moved to the prison hospital after surgery to repair his leg and arm. However, the DA tends to think that Liam's warnings are an exaggeration and may change his mind about the move."

"They aren't an exaggeration. You know what he did to Gracey and Pendleton," said Diane.

"Yes," said Garnett. "Gracey is saying your people were in the way and interfered with his ability to stop the guy. He didn't want any collateral damage."

Diane shook her head. "That is so not what happened."

"I suspect it was somewhere in the middle," Garnett said.

"No," said Diane. "No doubt the whole episode is on the security tape. You can look at it. All of us were outclassed by this guy. Gracey is just embarrassed because the guy took his gun and shot his partner with it. I will not have him smear my people. I'll post the thing on YouTube before I let that happen."

Garnett stared at her a moment. She knew he was trapped. He had to support his people, but damn it, she was his people too and by extension, so were her security guards. And she was not going to let that little pissant Gracey blame his failures on her security personnel.

"I'll have a meeting with Gracey and Pendleton to review the situation. We'll look at the tape and discuss what to do to avoid situations like that in the future," Garnett said.

"I'll have Chanell make you a copy," said Diane. She pressed her forehead with her fingers, trying to get rid of the headache. God, she was tired.

David, Gregory, and Steven were all examining their fingernails or their shirt lapels while Diane was talking to Garnett. They looked up again when she was finished. Frank came over from his conversation with Star, who was now asleep on one of the sofas. Frank pulled up a chair and sat down with them.

"What do we do now?" he asked.

"There are small apartments down here that are very nice. We can stay here while the police and the GBI are looking for the van of maniacs. We can continue to investigate like we have been. Liam is going to talk with the authorities in Brazil to hunt for Lindsay Chamberlain."

"Lindsay Chamberlain?" they all said together.

"Who the hell is she?" said Steven.

Diane realized she hadn't told them yet.

"She's someone who I think was mistaken for me and was kidnapped in Peru and taken to Brazil," she said. "You know the Interpol warrant for me—I think she may have been escaping her kidnappers' custody and killed them in the process. If I'm right, she's in deep trouble. I'm going to do what I can to help her."

Chapter 59

Maria watched Cameron Michaels stroll into the airport. Her heart thumped in her chest. It was of mild interest to her that she wasn't surprised to see him. She had expected it. But she hadn't come this far to be defeated on the verge of rescue. She steeled herself to face whatever he was planning. He couldn't prove that Rosetta wasn't her daughter. For that he'd need a DNA test. By then she could contact Diane Fallon. Rosetta may have been wrong. Fallon may very well have adoption papers. She had certainly begun the procedure. The important thing would be to make sure that Rosetta didn't get in the hands of Michaels, and for that, Maria was willing to stay in Brazil as long as it took. She was willing to retreat to the rain forest and live there. She was willing to walk the distance to the United States.

Behind her dark glasses, she watched Michael's gaze go over the people in the waiting area. Just as his stare got to the place where she and Rosetta were seated, a group of young people walked in front of his line of sight and his search shifted to the other side of the room. It would be a short respite. She could make a run for the women's room, but he would see her for sure.

Rosetta was busy playing with her doll and hadn't noticed. Maria bent her head down and whispered in her ear, "Don't get scared, okay, but the bad man is here. It just means we are going to have to work a little harder."

She felt the little girl go stiff. Maria looked into her face and saw her large brown eyes tear up.

"It's all right, baby girl," she said. "I won't leave you. I will get you home."

Maria was wondering if she should have stayed somewhere outside while they waited for John. She just thought the terminal would be more comfortable. She could leave now and they could hide. But what if Michaels had people outside? She and Rosetta would be away from anyone who could help them.

They were trapped, but she hoped they were trapped in a relatively safe place. At least, safer than outside.

"Remember and speak only English and the Cherokee I taught you, okay?" said Maria. "He'll try to trick you, but you are smarter than he is."

Rosetta nodded. She looked determined and her tears receded.

"You're the bravest person I know," said Maria. "I have faith in you."

Rosetta looked up at her. "I have faith in you too," she said, and Maria smiled and hugged her.

Maria watched Michaels go into the office. It wouldn't be long. There would be an announcement over the PA and they would be stuck. She would have to obey the rules of the airport to have any hope of staying on the good side of the officials.

While Michaels was gone she and Maria went to the ladies' room. They waited in the small lounge connected to the room. It was a place where Michaels couldn't just come in. Maybe he wouldn't have them page her.

They waited there for over an hour. She worried about Rosetta getting panicked. She worried about herself panicking. *Calm*, she thought. *Be calm. Be who you are saying you are. Mother and daughter*. Perception went a long way to convince people. That and a truckload of self-confidence from the two of them. They had been pretty convincing so far.

"Maria West. Maria West, please come to the airport manager's office."

Rosetta looked at her, fear all over her face.

"We are mother and daughter," Maria whispered in her ear. "We've been strong throughout all this. We've weathered the jungle, anacondas, crocodiles, hordes of bad guys with guns, and one scrawny, wimpy bad guy. We can kick this bad guy's butt too. We are strong. Ready?"

Rosetta nodded. "Ready," she said.

Maria put on her *I have a right to be here* unconcerned

face and they walked out of the bathroom, hand in hand, carrying their backpack and tote bag. Maria was glad she ditched the gun.

It wasn't far to the manager's office. Maria and Rosetta threaded their way through several people on her way to the office. The airport was getting crowded. It somehow made her feel safer. Though, really, there was nothing these people could do to help her.

Another woman was on the way to the office just in front of Maria. She was young, dressed in khaki slacks and shirt, wearing turquoise jewelry. She had long black hair in a low ponytail and tanned skin. She looked Hispanic. She went into the office first and held the door open for Maria, smiling at Rosetta.

"Thanks," said Maria.

"Welcome." The woman patted Rosetta on the head. "*Papai*," she said to the man behind the desk who rose when they entered.

Maria couldn't read the sign on his desk, but she assumed he was the manager. Especially since Michaels was standing nearby in his straw fedora.

"Catia, what a surprise," he said, speaking English.

Good, he spoke English.

Behind him Maria could see the single well-maintained runway the airport had. One plane was taking off.

His office was modern, a lot of glass and shiny metal. Large photographs of the rain forest and Inca ruins decorated the walls. The woman Catia smiled at Maria's interest in the photographs.

"Did you take these?" asked Maria.

"Yes," she said.

The manager beamed. He was Rodrigo Cordeiro, according to the plaque. "My daughter is an archaeologist and a great photographer. Mr. Michaels says you say you are an archaeology student. Is that true?"

"Yes," Maria said, "I am."

"Hello." Catia's smile widened. She stuck out her hand. "I just received my degree," she said.

Maria had an idea, a way of ingratiating herself. She started to speak when Michaels beat her to it.

"As you know, I have a serious charge against this woman."

Senhor Cordeiro tapped the wrinkled paper in front of him.

Maria recognized the flyer.

"This drawing bears little resemblance to this woman," he said. "And it says her name is either Diane Fallon or Linda Hall, not Maria West."

"Nevertheless, I am making the charges," he said. "She is a murderer and a kidnapper of this native child."

Rosetta grabbed Maria around the leg. "No, she's not. My mama's not a murderer. You're a bad man."

"The child speaks good English," said Cordeiro. "Though, true, she doesn't resemble Mrs. West."

"She takes after her father," said Maria. "Before we get into this, may I speak with your daughter?"

Chapter 60

"You wish to speak with my daughter?" said Rodrigo Cordeiro. "Why, Mrs. West?"

"This is a delaying tactic," said Michaels.

"What is your hurry, Mr. Michaels?" said Cordeiro. "Sit down. There is a chair over there. Now, Mrs. West, why do you want to speak with Catia?"

"I was on vacation with my daughter when we were attacked and had our papers stolen. We escaped and had to make our way here." She left out any description of their adventure, hoping he really didn't want details anyway. "It wasn't far," she continued, placing herself far away from the village where she was held prisoner and the route where she did indeed kill the men in question.

She took a deep breath. "It wasn't a terribly long trip, but it was an interesting one. On the way we found something I need to tell an archaeologist about. I was going to send a letter to the Ministry of Culture, but your daughter is here."

"What did you find?" asked Catia, her dark eyes wide with interest.

Maria stuck her hand in her bag.

"She's going for a gun," said Michaels.

"Oh, please," said Maria. "I'm getting my notes. What have you been drinking, Mr. Michaels?"

Maria's hand landed first on Rosetta's doll, which she pulled from the knapsack and handed to Rosetta. Rosetta hugged the doll to her and whispered in the doll's ear. Senhor Cordeiro smiled at Rosetta and gave Michaels a bemused glance. Maria put her hand back in the knapsack and pulled out her notes and the envelope with the sherds.

"We came across a place where the rain forest was recently burned off. It revealed an Incan site, the biggest I've ever seen. Although the Incas aren't my specialty, I studied up on them before I came here and I am familiar with the known sites. This was not among them and it is at least eighty hectares or more. It needs to be secured against vandals and pothunters."

Catia's eyes grew even wider. She understood the significance of a find of that size. Maria was hoping that a newly minted archaeologist would jump at the information, and her father would not only feel really grateful, he would find Maria a credible person and not a killer. Appearances were everything, because that was all she had.

"There are no sites that big," whispered Catia.

Maria showed Catia her drawing and her notes. "Here is the large mound. I saw several, but this is the largest. These"—Maria pointed to some rock ruins on the drawing—"are domiciles, I suspect. Notice these lines, they are scars in the ground, possibly part of the road system. . . . These are my notes and drawings. You can see the site extends into the rain forest, so it's larger than the clearing, which is about eighty hectares, I would guess."

Catia picked up the drawings and studied them, reading Maria's notes. She nodded to her father.

"I picked up these two ceramic sherds." She handed them to Catia. "Like I said, the site needs the attention of an archaeologist. To my knowledge it would be the largest in Brazil—a national treasure."

"*Papai*," Catia said, and spoke rapidly to him in Portuguese.

"We are getting off track," said Michaels. "I'm all for your daughter's career, but we need to secure this woman. Some ancient Incan site is not going anywhere."

Cameron Michaels was frustrated. Good, Maria thought. She wanted to keep him that way.

"Where is it?" said Catia. Both she and her father ignored Michaels. "Is there any way you can tell me?"

"Do you have a map? And a ruler?" Maria did not want to show them her map. She was not sure what all it had written on it. It certainly had notations that would raise questions about her story.

Cordeiro opened a drawer and pulled out a map of Brazil and handed her a ruler.

Maria looked around the room for a flat surface. She settled on a table by a wall. Catia helped clear it of books and papers. Maria spread out the map and took her notes and looked at her figures. She was about to ask for a pen when Catia handed her one. Maria worked backward in her mind from Tabatinga to where they had been on their trek. She took the scale of the large map of Brazil and calculated some approximate distances. She quickly did some calculations and made several measurements on the map, drawing lines, and finally making a circle around an area on the map.

"I had no tools with me except a compass, but my estimate is that the site is here," she said.

Catia looked at the map and drew her finger down a river past the site and nodded. She smiled at Maria and took the map and folded it up. "This is very exciting," she said.

"Now can we get down to the business at hand?" said Michaels.

"Very well, Mr. Michaels," said Cordeiro. "We will get down to your business."

As he spoke Maria saw a plane land and begin taxiing to a gate. It had a painting of Betty Boop on its nose. She was never so glad to see a cartoon character in her life.

"Yes, thank you," said Maria. "Could I have some water for me and my daughter? Perhaps a bottle of orange juice?" She dug in her purse for some change.

"I'll get you some from the machine," said Catia. "Please, put your change back."

When Catia was out the door, Michaels turned on Maria. He closed in on her until his face was inches away from hers. He smelled like garlic.

"I've had about enough of your delaying tactics," he said.

Rosetta buried her face behind Maria and started crying. Maria picked her up and held her close.

"Mr. Michaels. Sit down," said Rodrigo Cordeiro. "You are forgetting whose office you are in. You come here with a third-rate flyer that a child could have produced and tell me you are from Interpol. Is this the kind of work they do? Sit down, I say. You will not harass people in my office or anywhere in my jurisdiction, do you understand? Until proven otherwise, this woman is a guest. And I'm still not entirely clear what your interest in this child is.

"Now, Mrs. West, do you have anything to say to his accusations?" asked Senhor Cordeiro.

"I don't know where his accusations come from. He's made this whole thing up for his own purposes. His real interest is in my daughter. After we were attacked he showed up in Benjamin Constant and stalked us, speaking to my daughter in Portuguese, which neither of us understands. He told me he was telling her how beautiful she is, and now he has followed us here. He has become obsessed with my daughter and is trying to get me out of the way. That is the only answer I have to his accusations," she said.

"Mr. Michaels?" said the airport manager.

"She is twisting my concern for the little girl into something sinister," he said.

"I believe that is a mother's job, to be vigilant to those kinds of things," said Cordeiro.

So far, Cordeiro appeared to be on her side. But soon they would come to the problematic fact that neither she nor Rosetta had passports or papers of any kind.

Catia came back with a bottle of orange juice for the two of them. She opened Rosetta's and put it in her small hands. Rosetta took a sip and wrinkled her nose.

"It's a little tart, isn't it, Rosetta?' said Catia. "It's good for you, though."

Maria opened hers and took a long swallow. It *was* a little tart.

"Are we finished with the delays?" said Michaels. "I'm here to warn you of a dangerous woman, and you don't seem to be taking it seriously."

Before Cordeiro could respond, there was a knock on the door.

"*Entrar*," said Cordeiro.

Cameron Michaels threw up his hands.

Good, keep getting more and more frustrated, thought Maria.

Chapter 61

John West walked into the office. He was wearing a dark pinstriped business suit and black cowboy boots. His white shirt had a string tie knotted with a turquoise stone. On his wrist he wore a beaded strip of leather made for him by his sister. His shiny black hair was straight and parted in the middle and hung just past his shoulders. He had a small hawk feather tied to a lock of hair in back. John liked to mix traditional Native American with modern trappings. It gave him an interesting air and clients liked it.

Rosetta took one look and ran to him.

"Daddy!" she said, jumping up into his arms. He picked her up and she hugged his neck.

She spoke to him in Cherokee, a simple phrase, but with perfect intonation. The kid was good. John responded in kind. Then he made a series of gestures with his hand—"I love you" in sign language—fully expecting Rosetta to mimic him because it's what kids do. She did a pretty fair job. Maria smiled. It was a precious moment and totally convincing.

Rodrigo Cordeiro, Catia, and Cameron Michaels looked at the two of them. Maria marveled at how the similarity of deep ancestry passed for familial likeness. Cordeiro was convinced, as was his daughter Catia. Michaels actually looked slightly confused. By this time he had probably recognized Ariel, but here was what looked and interacted like family.

Maria went up to John and he kissed her cheek.

"Are you all right?" he said.

"I am now," she said.

John's gaze shifted from one person to the other. He

zeroed in on the airport manager and held out his hand. Maria introduced all of them to John.

Rosetta pointed to Michaels. "He's the bad man they tell us about in school," she said. Maria almost laughed and wondered where she came up with that.

"I resent that," Michaels said.

"Are you going to argue with a child?" said Cordeiro. He sounded weary of the whole thing. "She knows you are trying to take her away from her parents."

There it was. Cordeiro believed her. Maria felt relief beyond words.

The airport manager turned to John. "Mr. West, Mr. Michaels has accused your wife of the murder of"—he looked down at the flyer—"of four men. He says he is from Interpol."

"Maria . . . killed four men? How?" he said.

"This piece of paper doesn't say," said Cordeiro. "He also accuses your wife of kidnapping this child from her native village."

John turned to Michaels. "Interpol doesn't make these kinds of accusations on its own in person; they work with the local authorities. Where are the local authorities?"

"Here." Michaels pointed to Rodrigo Cordeiro.

"I manage the airport, Mr. Michaels. I am not the *polícia*," he said.

"She doesn't have papers," said Michaels, playing his trump card, though Maria had already told Cordeiro she'd lost their papers during the attack. She supposed that Michaels thought Cordeiro needed reminding.

"We can get them replaced at the embassy in Rio de Janeiro," said Maria. She looked over at John. "I thought we could take a little vacation there while we wait."

He stared at her. The look in his eyes was stern. "I would have thought you'd had enough of vacations," he said. She recoiled as if stung.

Michaels clapped his hands together slowly. "Well played. I can see when I'm out of my league. Good day. I would say it's been nice."

He left the room. Maria would have preferred he stay so she would at least know where he was.

"Senhor Cordeiro," John said, paying no attention to Michaels. "My wife is not a murderer, nor a kidnapper.

She sometimes makes bad judgments about where to vacation with our daughter. But other than that, she is a good
mother. I am not familiar with your laws in this country. Is
there a provision in your law for expediting a matter like
this so I can take my family home?"

Neither Lindsay nor Ariel was at ease until the plane was
in the air for several minutes. Lindsay half believed they
would be shot down. John was up front with the pilot,
Arthur Youngblood, a cousin of his. The *Betty Boop* was
owned jointly by several corporations, of which West
Construction was one. Lindsay was grateful for it. Grateful
for John. Just grateful.

Ariel had never flown in a plane, but she didn't look nervous. She looked disbelieving. Lindsay smiled at her. She
knew she was thinking of Diane Fallon and her dream to
find her.

"We did it, kid. I guess I can call you Ariel now, huh?"
she said.

Ariel was sitting in one of the cushioned seats across
from her. She was still belted in. She unclipped her belt and
ran over to Lindsay and hugged her.

"Thank you for not leaving me," she said.

"That was never going to happen," said Lindsay, holding
her tight. "Never, never, never."

John came out of the cockpit and sat down in a seat opposite them across the narrow aisle. He smiled. "At least if I
go to jail and lose my company for smuggling a kid into the
United States, I can fall back on acting when I get out."

Lindsay suddenly realized how much he trusted her. It
was enough for him that she said bringing Ariel into the
United States without a passport was the right thing to do.
She walked over to where he was sitting and kissed him. She
put her hands in his long hair and looked him in the eyes.

"Thank you. Thank you for everything."

He put his arms around her waist and pulled her onto
his lap. "When I found out you were missing, I was . . . I
thought we wouldn't get lucky again like the time you disappeared coming back from that conference. I thought, we
won't get lucky twice. Then you called. I would do this and
more. Though you are getting a little expensive."

"I hate to ask," she said. She knew he had paid a substantial bribe to fly out of Tabatinga. "I'll pay you back," she said.

He laughed. "Archaeology doesn't pay that well," he said.

Lindsay kissed him again. For the first time she felt calm, safe. She kept forgetting they weren't home yet.

She got up out of his lap and sat down in the seat.

"Can you tell me what happened?" he said.

She and Ariel told the story, the whole story, the parts that were Lindsay's, the parts that were Ariel's, and the parts that were theirs together. It poured out of them, sometimes out of order and sometimes confused, but they didn't stop until John knew everything—Lindsay's kidnapping, the massacre at the mission, Ariel's plans to find her mother, their experiences in the jungle. The people she killed in self-defense.

"I just wanted to get back to Mama so bad," Ariel said.

John was private with his emotions most of the time, but Lindsay could see the glistening in his eyes. She was afraid to speak because she knew her voice would crack.

"We'll get you to your mama," he whispered. He looked back at Lindsay. "I'm glad you're here. It's worth any price."

"Can we call Mama?" asked Ariel.

John grinned at her. "Sure."

Lindsay wished she could bottle the look of excitement and joy on Ariel's face. John picked up the phone built into his chair and called information. Then he dialed the River-Trail Museum. He said nothing for several moments and hung up the phone.

"Can't get through right now," he said. "I'll try again in a few minutes. Don't be worried. This happens sometimes. We'll get hold of her."

Arthur Youngblood came out of the cockpit and stood at John's chair. He winked at Lindsay and Ariel.

"Who's flying the plane?" said Ariel.

"Otto," he said.

Ariel looked down the passageway into the cockpit. "Who's Otto?"

"Otto Pilot," he said. "Always take him with me."

He gave a hearty laugh. Lindsay wondered how many times he had made that joke and how many times he had laughed at it. He turned to John.

"There's a big weather system stalled over North Georgia. We won't be able to get near the place. Our best bet is to go home to Cherokee and land in our private field, especially since we kind of took that long detour from our flight plan. I could try for Atlanta, but it's bad weather there too, and they have a lot of security."

John nodded. "The bad weather is probably why I can't get through on the phone. We can drive down to Rosewood," he said.

He looked over at Ariel. She had an anxious look on her face, like maybe her dream wasn't going to come true after all.

"It's not that far," said John. "We'll get you there."

"You don't think the bad man will get there first, do you?" she said. "He knows I'll tell Mama about him and what he did to Father Joe and the others. What if he tries to hurt her?"

Chapter 62

Diane awoke from a three-hour nap and took a shower. It left her less refreshed than she would like. Star was still asleep. Frank was having coffee and doughnuts with David and Izzy. She found Gregory Lincoln sitting alone on a bench near the huge dinosaur paintings in the Pleistocene Room.

He sat with his forearms resting on his knees. He was in quiet contemplation, looking through a packet of postcards he carried with him. Each card was a small reproduction of a Vermeer painting whose subject was people doing everyday things. It's what he did when he was under stress. The cards had grown rather ragged around the edges from frequent use.

It was early, too early for visitors, so she and Gregory had the Pleistocene Room to themselves. Gregory smiled and put his arm around her shoulders when she sat down beside him.

"I love your museum. What an utterly calm environment. Even when you have all the noisy schoolchildren it is a calm place. I love the tiny unicorns in the dinosaur paintings. Quite intriguing."

The huge murals of dinosaurs, painted at a time when everyone thought dinosaurs dragged their tails on the ground behind them, were treasures uncovered during the renovation of the museum. The artist had put tiny unicorns in his artwork here and there to the delight of everyone who looked at the paintings.

"Life is good here," she said.

"I thought I might be moving here, you know, but it turns out that Marguerite and I are having a girl. So I can go home." He smiled.

Diane put a hand on his arm. "Congratulations," she said.

"After the boys, it will be quite a different experience having a girl. Marguerite is pleased. She's given up on try-ing to make the boys wear dresses on special occasions. Now I may have to install concertina wire on top of the wall around the house. I understand girls can be quite tough on parents."

"I'm sure the two of you will manage very well," said Diane.

"I heard you are canceling your wedding," Gregory said.

"I told Frank I'd wait to make a decision and we would talk. But you've seen firsthand what I bring to the marriage."

"You're telling me you invited those maniacs? That seems unlike you," he said. He went back to looking at his postcards. "I read where paintings of milkmaids in their day were considered sexual. I have to say, I see a serene woman pouring milk. I'm afraid I would make a terrible art critic. I don't seem to have the knack for all the underlying symbolism that other people see."

"I might as well have invited them," said Diane. "They were after me."

"Seems as though you will have to quit working here too," he said. "Wouldn't do to expose the museum visitors to deadly criminals."

"Frank went through all that—Am I going to move to a deserted island to live out my days, etcetera," she said.

"He has a point," Gregory said, looking at *The Girl with a Wine Glass*. "Now, she looks like she is about to make some poor decisions. You could, of course, join your CIA or some such group where your ability to draw out bad guys would be welcome."

Diane smiled. "That's a thought. The problem is, I love my life here. I love Frank. I just don't want to see him or Star hurt."

"None of us like to see the people we love hurt." He put the postcards back in his jacket pocket. "What is so odd about this is it shouldn't be happening. You should be safe here in your museum—safe even in your crime lab, with its connection to criminals and their doings. I haven't been able to get a handle on this. I realize now that there was some criminal activity going on at the mission in Brazil that I missed utterly and completely. I've accepted that. I believe you are right, that it had to do with smuggling endangered animals and their various parts and selling humans into slavery. But I have no idea who was behind it. I'm completely stumped. Simone must have found more damning evidence than the bag of feathers and bones to have generated this kind of extreme response. I've made calls to some environmental policing groups, trying to get a handle on who's who in that world. No luck so far. Just a lot of information about things we already know, such as how lucrative it is. They gave me a few names, but I didn't know any of them. David asked for the names so I gave them to him."

"I'm going to contact my post office and see if perhaps they lost a package that was supposed to come to me." Diane shrugged. "David suggested that perhaps Simone set up several post office boxes and has the package being forwarded from post office to post office—letting the U.S. Postal Service keep it in their custody for a while. That's the kind of thing he might do."

"That could be it. She also could have left it with a lawyer to be forwarded to you or to the authorities in the event of her death. Unfortunately, she appears not to have made provisions for a coma," said Gregory.

"I don't suppose Simone's family received anything," said Diane. "Would any of them have told you?"

"The brother or father, perhaps," Gregory said. "But I don't think Simone would really trust any of them with something like that. Crime is an alien thing to her family. They are perplexed and out of their ken over this."

"Whoever is behind it believes the package exists. I have to believe they are right," said Diane. "It's somewhere, and we need to find it—first. If it is making its rounds in the postal system, perhaps that will come to an end soon and it will be delivered to me. Perhaps Charlotte will find something soon. I'm sure that's why David wanted the names of known animal traffickers."

"Charlotte? I don't believe I've met her," Gregory said.

Diane looked over at him. "David is probably going to introduce you today. He said he's going to tell you about her. But it is a secret. Only a few of us know about her and her brother. So you must keep it a secret. He'll make you swear in blood."

Gregory gave a little laugh. "I'll keep mum. Tell me, who is this Charlotte and her brother?"

"Charlotte and Arachnid are two of David's programs that rely heavily on databases and complex algorithms," said Diane.

"Now, I could have guessed that," said Gregory.

"Arachnid is a program that's like a search engine and facial recognition software combined. We used it to find information about a black widow murderer a while back. Worked quite well. You'll love Charlotte. She's like the network analysis you do, only with the power of a computer behind it. It not only places people in a social network, it locates degrees of separation. Like, if I know Vanessa and she has a son, and you know your father-in-law and he has a cousin, it might find if Vanessa's son and the cousin have ever crossed paths in whatever location we are investigating. The power of it is in access to databases. David even takes it down to the level of hobbies and habits of the people in the network. You know David, if something is complex, it can always be made more complex. That's probably why he covets a supercomputer. Can you imagine a world with David and a supercomputer?"

"For someone who is afraid of Big Brother, he certainly likes to invent Big Brother programs," said Gregory.

"The irony isn't lost on him. That's why he keeps it all a secret. He doesn't want anyone else to get their hands on it," said Diane.

"So if the names of these animal and human traffickers I gave David have crossed paths with any of us, this Charlotte will find it? That will be helpful. That actually makes me feel better."

"Remember, David likes to keep his programs secret," said Diane.

Gregory smiled and shook his head. "I wonder if he has thought of tapping into some of the social networking sites. He would get a wealth of information there. Seems like Charlotte and her brother could be put to effective use," said Gregory. "I can see it now. Jane and Jack Smith on a family vacation just happen to take a picture with Notorious Joe in the background and post it with their vacation photos on their Web site, where Arachnid finds it and discovers that Joe was in the Bahamas when he said he was in Alaska. Cool."

Diane laughed. "I'm sure David has thought about that very thing. Sometimes I don't inquire into too much detail about his computer activities."

Neva, one of Diane's crime scene team members, walked into the Pleistocene Room, smiling. She wore jeans and a purple museum T-shirt with GEOLOGY ROCKS printed across the front along with a glittering picture of amethysts.

"You look happy," said Diane.

Neva sat on the bench with them. She brushed her honey brown bangs back with a hand.

"How are you, Neva?" said Gregory. "You do look happy."

"I'm good. I heard from Mike. He'll be coming home soon. Has some great stuff for the museum." She grinned.

"I hear 'more to the story' in there," said Diane.

"His company told him they were going to an ice cave. That was just a cover because they wanted to keep the real destination a secret—you're going to hate it," said Neva.

"What?" said Diane.

"He went to the Big Deep," she said. "They collected truckloads of extremophiles. He said it's loaded with them."

"What?" said Diane, glaring at Neva.

Neva grinned. "He said you'd look like that."

"He didn't insist that he would go only if he could bring his museum boss and caving partner?" said Diane.

"Mike said you'd say that," Neva said.

"What's this Big Deep?" said Gregory.

"The deepest cave in the world," said Diane. "It's about eight thousand feet deep."

"Good heavens," said Gregory. "It sounds treacherous. And you would find that relaxing?"

"It is and I do," said Diane. "Wow. Wow. He got pictures, I hope. The rat," she added.

"Loads of pictures," said Neva. "All the cavers had really great cameras on their helmets and, of course, they had their official photographer. Mike has all these ideas for an exhibit."

"I can't wait." A wave of regret washed over Diane. What if she weren't working at the museum then? What if she were banished to some deserted island? God, she loved her job.

"So tell me, Neva," said Gregory. "You cave too. Do you find it relaxing?"

Neva shook her head. "Diane goes for the calm of it. I go for the excitement. My heart beats too fast in a cave for it to be relaxing."

"You and Mike are an item, is that right?" asked Gregory.

Neva nodded. "I suppose. I'd marry him in a minute if he would ask."

"Don't girls ask these days?" said Gregory.

"I'd be too afraid of a 'no,'" said Neva. She sighed. "Mike is way more educated than I am."

"Really?" said Gregory. "Talking to you, you sound very educated."

"Working where I do, I can't help but pick up all kinds of knowledge about a lot of things, but . . ." She shrugged.

"It appears to me that you are selling yourself quite short," said Gregory. "Education is more than a piece of paper with special letters on it. It's the content of your mind and your awareness of it. You have all that."

"You are such a nice man," said Neva. "No wonder your wife is crazy about you."

"Is she really? I'm glad to hear it. It's hard to tell with Marguerite sometimes." Gregory smiled at Neva.

Diane was staring at the bones of the wooly mammoth as Neva and Gregory spoke, remembering Milo Lorenzo, the man whose dream was behind the museum, the love of Vanessa Van Ross's life, and the man who hired Diane as assistant director. It was here he had a heart attack and died. He was much younger than Vanessa and it was a shock and a tragedy.

"Neva, you are an artist," Diane said, still staring at the mammoth.

"Yes," she said.

"Do you ever do drawings of Mike?" she asked.

"Are you kidding? All the time. I'm working on a series from the cave photographs we have. You know that one where we just came out of that cave and we were so tired, he'd taken his shirt off and was taking a drink of water? I'm doing a painting of it. I think it's going to be one of my best."

Neva took her cell phone off the loop of her belt and called up her photos. "Here is a head study I did of him."

Neva handed it to Diane and she and Gregory looked at the pencil drawing of Mike's face. She had caught him well, the planes and angles of his handsome face, the intense expression he often had, but with a spark of humor that you could see mostly in his eyes.

"My dear, you are quite good. Do you do commissions?" Gregory said.

"Whenever I can get them," said Neva.

"I have this favorite photograph of Marguerite that I'd love for you to do."

Neva nodded and grinned. "Sure."

"Neva," said Diane, "would Madge draw someone she was in love with, even if it was unrequited?"

Neva's eyebrows shot up. "Yes, she would, she sure would. I would. I do. Damn, I didn't think of that. She should have lots of drawings of him, if there is a him. If you like to draw, and she did, you just can't help yourself."

"Could you recognize drawings of someone that the artist was in love with as opposed to, say, a commission she may have been doing?" asked Diane.

"That's a good question. Hmmm. At my house it would be the sheer quantity of drawings of Mike. Except that I also have lots of Jin, David, you, Andie. I like to draw. And that's an element too. You fall in love with whatever you're working on at the moment. But can you tell if it is someone you're in love with? I don't know. What did you see in that photograph of the drawing I did of Mike?"

"I saw Mike," said Diane. "Him and his personality. I saw who he is. Maybe that's it." Diane shrugged and looked at Gregory.

"I was reminded of this photograph I love of my wife. Not that she looks like this bloke, Mike, but I suppose I must have seen the love. Interesting. I'll have to go back and look at my Vermeers with that in mind. It puts art in a whole new perspective."

"Neva, if I call Vanessa and the two of you can get access to Madge's home and her workspace," said Diane, "can you go through her drawings and paintings and see if there is someone who was special to her? It may be a person of interest we need to talk to."

Chapter 63

Andie caught Diane midstride as she was leaving the Pleistocene Room heading for the basement.

"There's a storm coming," said Andie.

"Looks like it," said Diane. "The wind is really whipping the trees back and forth out there."

For the middle of the day, it was looking dark.

"You look a little anxious," said Diane. "Is everything all right?"

"I just wanted to run some things by you," said Andie.

"All right," said Diane. She led Andie to one of the benches and they sat down.

"We've been having some cancellations because of the weather forecast—a lot of them," said Andie. "Some are rescheduling for later, like next month, but some aren't."

"Cancellations in bad weather are expected. We've had them before," said Diane.

Andie nodded. "I know. It's just . . . cancellations on my watch are a little scary. And some of the staff—not many, but a few—wanted to know if they could bring their families and sleeping bags and sleep in the basement tonight if the weather turns really bad. It's a little unusual, I know, but I told them they could. I was thinking they can set up in that big room that's finished but not decorated. The bathrooms nearby are finished, and that seems like a good camping place." Andie stopped and took a breath. "Is that all right? I mean, in an emergency? But then I got to thinking about insurance, and now I'm not so sure. But then, I can't turn people away."

"I think, for a few people who have nowhere else to go, that's fine. You're right. We can't turn our staff and their families away in an emergency. Is the weather supposed to get that bad? I haven't been listening to the news."

"You know how weather reports are. They like drama. But all week we are supposed to have lots of rain, lightning, tree-uprooting wind, and possible tornados," said Andie. "Then again, maybe it's just drama."

Diane raised her brow. "I didn't know. By all means, they need a place to come. The basement is a good idea. We'll need to try to control the level of kid activity."

"I sent Ami to the museum store for some games and toys. I thought it would be a good idea to have something to do. We can lock all the exhibit rooms, of course," said Andie.

"Sounds like you have things under control," said Diane. "You are in charge, remember."

"Yeah, of the museum, but you are still the primate curator," she said.

Diane frowned. "Is there an issue with the primate exhibit?"

"Sort of . . . ," she said.

"Is Kendel back yet?" asked Diane.

"That's the thing. Kendel is still in Mexico. She thinks she can get them to go ahead and loan us the Mayan exhibit. But the price is, they want a loan of our"—Andie made a face—"our primate exhibit—the new resin figures in their habitats. Kendel said she wouldn't normally think of it, but it would go a long way toward fixing the little PR blip we suffered. And it will look really good in their advertising to see 'Mexico Special Primate Exhibit On Loan From River-Trail.' Lots of coverage. Their museum is way bigger than ours and has more visitors from all over the world."

Diane nodded. "It's a good point. All right. We need to have something to replace it with that's a little different. I'll work on an idea and we'll get the planners on it." She smiled at Andie. "How do you like being director?"

"How do you know if you're making the right decisions?" said Andie.

"Sometimes you don't," said Diane. "You make the best decision with what you know, keeping the goals of the museum in mind. And always keeping in mind the possible consequences of your decisions." Diane smiled. "Sometimes you just call it like you see it."

"It's those consequences that are the little devils," said Andie.

"You're doing fine," Diane said.

"Are you all right?" asked Andie. "A lot's happened to you."

"Pretty good, considering," Diane said. "Liam was terrific."

Andie grinned. "I was scared to death when he told me to get to the police station and tell them to go check on Frank's house and he was going back to help you out. I had no idea how in the world he got all that information out of that short interaction on the steps. I just thought you were stressed out about the Mayan exhibit and the rumors and stuff, and I thought some big hefty-looking security guards were a good thing."

"Obviously Liam is very experienced and a good detective. I was in serious trouble. I'm very appreciative of his help, and yours," said Diane. "You are doing a great job, Andie. Hopefully this mess I fell into will be resolved soon. And if you would like to stay in the museum tonight, you know the couch in my office makes into a bed."

"Thanks. What about you?" said Andie.

"I've got one of the new mini bedrooms in the basement near the media-meeting room," she said. "It's all very nice."

Andie stood. "Thanks. I've been terrified I'll screw up the museum," she said.

"That would really be hard to do, so don't worry," she said.

Andie went back to the office and Diane started for the stairs to go down to the basement with the others. She looked up and saw Lynn Webber, the medical examiner, walking through the front doors dragging a huge canvas case behind her, her patent-leather heels clicking on the granite floors.

"Lynn?" said Diane.

"I hope you don't mind. You've seen my little apartment, all that glass, and high up near lots of trees. Can I stay here until the storms pass?" she asked.

"We have some mini bedrooms in the basement . . . ," began Diane.

"Got it covered," said Lynn. "This is my get-the-hell-out-of-Dodge bag. My family think I'm nuts to have gotten something like this, especially when I told them how much it cost. Every time I talk with my brother or my dad, they say, 'Well, have you used that get-outta-town white elephant yet?' Well, this is my chance. We are in for some seriously bad weather and I can't stay in my apartment. I'll pitch my tent in your basement, if that's all right."

"Tent? Right. I forgot, it comes with a tent and a sleeping bag," said Diane.

"You have one?" said Lynn. Her face erupted into a wide grin.

"No, but David is a real fan. He gave Star a Get Home backpack to keep in her car," said Diane.

"I have one of those too. I just love stuff like that. Well, I've got everything I need, including my e-book. I'm set. All I need is to borrow some trees from one of your displays . . ."

Diane looked at her in horror.

Lynn laughed and laid a hand on her arm. "I'm joking. If you could see your face."

Diane smiled. "We have a large room in the basement that is finished but empty. There are restrooms nearby. But be forewarned, some of the staff will be joining you with their sleeping bags . . ."

"Then I'd better go pick me out some prime real estate," said Lynn.

Somehow Diane couldn't imagine Lynn roughing it in any way, even if the tent was on a polished granite floor with a bathroom ten feet away.

Diane smiled again. "I'm on my way down to the basement. I'll show you where the room is."

They got on the elevator with the giant canvas bag that was at least four feet long.

"How are you going to pitch the tent?" asked Diane.

"I don't need a tie down and it has its own support structure. I think it will do just fine," Lynn said.

And I thought David was strange, thought Diane.

"I had an idea about Madge Stewart," said Diane. She explained her thinking about Madge's art—that she might have made drawings of a man she was interested in.

"What a brilliant idea," Lynn said. "I'm sure she did just that. Let me know."

Diane knew Lynn wanted to be right about the romantic angle and Madge's death—she had a feeling she was.

"I'll let you know. Neva is checking it out now," said Diane.

"How about your other problems, those terrible rumors?" said Lynn.

Diane looked over at her and realized she didn't know about last night's drama. She related as briefly as one could about Frank's house being under siege and her being kidnapped by the Terminator and taken to the museum to be rescued by her assistant's boyfriend.

Lynn stood gaping at her.

"You think that's something. I had an argument with my new neighbor over his cat," Lynn said finally.

The elevator doors opened and Lynn stepped out. Diane led the way to the huge room.

"We are making progress with the rumor mill," said Diane, "but we've got a lot of gaps to fill in."

Diane opened the doors to what looked like a ballroom. They hadn't decided what exactly to do with it. A ballroom was one option. It would be great for fundraiser functions. It also would be a good area for a series of storage vaults, an idea that Diane liked. That was the thing about having such a large building—lots of options for what to do with the space. Right now it was a big empty room with very hard floors.

"If you change your mind, we have these really cute bedrooms," said Diane. "Each has a soft bed, a chair and desk, and nightstands."

"This will be fine," said Lynn.

Diane left Lynn to set up camp and walked back to the meeting room where she had left Frank and the others. He and David stood when she entered. Frank smiled at her and it actually made her heart ache. She smiled back and fought off tears.

Stop it, Diane, she thought. *Break down when this is over.*

"Izzy and Garnett went over to Colin Prehoda's," said David. "Someone ransacked his office and his home in the same manner your old apartment was tossed."

"Looking for that package," said Diane.

"Presumably," said David. "On an optimistic note . . ." He

handed her several photographs. "Supersoldier's clothes yielded a lot of trace fibers. You're looking at copper nano-fibers from his socks. They're pretty diagnostic, so if we can find a match at any of the crime scenes, we're good."

Diane examined the microscopic image that looked like tangled string.

"They aren't that unusual," she said. "I have several pair I use when I'm caving."

"Ah, but yours are of a different color. These are from a batch made especially for the military," said David. "They have their own palette of colors—Desert Dune, Combat Black, among other nifty names."

"Military? Stolen, you think?" said Diane.

"It's what I'm thinking. I've got a call in. The next photographs are the most interesting."

Diane studied the next set of photographs of microscope images of what looked like honeycomb structures. She cocked an eyebrow at David.

"What am I looking at? I'm not familiar with this kind of fiber."

"Cutting-edge stuff," said David. "These boys have been shopping at high-tech places. These"—he pointed at the photographs—"are nanofibers that have been produced through the combination of polyurethane and high voltage. The result is a fabric that can trap toxic chemicals. Cool, huh? The company uses the fabric to make suits that protect from hazardous materials. Or at least, that is what they intend. It's still in the experimental and testing stage. And I haven't even begun to tell you about the lightweight Kevlar body armor he had on. These guys somehow got access to some high-powered military closet. It wouldn't surprise me if some Men in Black arrived at the museum and demanded all the evidence."

"How top secret is it, if you know what it is?" said Diane.

David looked at her as if she had insulted him.

"Actually, some of the stuff isn't all that secret, but it is experimental and restricted in its use," David said.

"This is good, David. Can we find out if the GBI found any of this trace on Madge Stewart's clothing?" said Diane.

He shook his head. "They haven't," he said. "Just normal fibers, they said. But what is normal, really?" He grinned.

"I've often wondered that myself," she said. "How is Charlotte coming?"

"Still humming away. You know, if—"

"No, there is no way we can afford a supercomputer. And if we could, what the hell do you need with that much computing power? Sometimes you scare me, David." She gave him a lopsided smile.

David and Frank grinned.

"But he can get you smiling," Frank said.

"Charlotte has connected Ivan Santos with specific drug dealers and smugglers of endangered animals. But we already suspected he probably knew those kinds of people. She is still working on other levels of connections," said David. "The weather is kind of interfering with her progress."

Diane looked up as Gregory came strolling into the room.

"I got an e-mail just now," Gregory said. "Apparently your phones are a little touch and go at the moment. It seems we have some good news. You are no longer an internationally wanted woman, and Cameron Michaels is coming to visit us."

Chapter 64

Rain spattered against the huge double doors of the museum. The parking lot outside was covered by a thin sheet of water, creating a gray, watery appearance, like a lake on a cloudy day. Diane had closed the museum to the public. The only people coming in were staff looking for a shelter in the storm.

Frank put an arm around her shoulders and pulled her to him.

"I've always liked rainy days," he said.

"Me too," said Diane. "But, I don't know, it feels strange today, foreboding somehow."

"You think it might have something to do with what's been going on?" he said.

"I'm sure it does. I just can't seem to shake the depression that's settled over me." Diane laid her head against his shoulder. "I'm glad you're here," she said.

"Me too."

"You know I love you," she said.

"I know," he said. "I'm counting on it."

Diane laughed.

"How is Star doing?" she asked.

"She's helping Andie wrangle kids in that cavern you call a ballroom," he said. "She's having fun."

A large dark SUV pulled up and parked near the door. Diane squinted to see through the gray film of rain. A figure got out of the driver's side and made a dash for the door. Diane held it open. The man doffed his hat and hit it on his pant leg, knocking off the rain.

"Damn, what weather," he said.

"Cameron," said Diane, "it's been a long time."

"Diane. Good to see you," he said, attempting a smile. "This is like the rainy season in the Amazon."

Diane introduced him to Frank.

"I wasn't sure you got the message I was coming," he said. "I went to your home, but the police were there. What was that about?"

Diane explained the happenings of the last few hours. She tried to make the story briefer with each telling of it. Cameron listened with a serious, pensive expression.

"And these mercenaries are after some kind of package?" he said.

"Apparently. And I haven't a clue as to what or where. I don't even know if I'm looking for something as small as a ring box or as big as a refrigerator. But you need to get warm and dry. Let me take you downstairs," she said.

As she turned away from the doors, out of the corner of her eye she thought she caught movement deep in the gray mist where the tree line started. It was subtle. She wasn't sure she saw anything. She turned her head and smiled at the guard on duty in the lobby. Chanell had told them to be vigilant. She didn't repeat the warning.

Diane took Cameron downstairs to the lounge where Gregory and Steven were talking and basking in the heat radiating from the fake electric fireplace. Fake or not, it looked cozy.

The two of them rose from their chairs and greeted Cameron, shaking his hand.

"Good of you to come," said Gregory.

"Nice to see you again," said Steven.

Cameron nodded. "I realized I needed to be a little more supportive. I've been kind of distant from all of you," he said.

"We appreciate your coming," said Diane. "Let me get you some coffee. Are you hungry?"

"Not hungry, but a cup of hot coffee, black, would be nice," he said.

Cameron took off his raincoat and gloves and his straw fedora. Diane thought he looked weary. There were dark circles under his eyes and his hands looked shaky as he handed her his coat. His eyes met hers and for a moment she thought he was looking for something in the depths of hers.

Diane took his wet outer garments from him and laid the coat across the back of a chair and the hat and gloves on the glass table next to it. She poured him a cup of coffee from the pot in the corner, walked back over to where he had taken a seat by Gregory and Steven, and handed it to him. He warmed his hands on the hot mug.

"How is Simone?" he said. "Gregory told me she was critical." He took a sip of coffee. "I'd forgotten how good your coffee is, Diane," he said.

"Still in a coma," said Diane. "We hope she is healing."

"I was sorry to hear about her. I confess, I don't quite grasp what is going on," he said.

"Neither do we," said Gregory, "but I'll tell you what we know."

Gregory laid out everything to Michaels in his meticulous fashion, the rumors, the attack on Simone, and the attack on Diane.

Diane didn't really want to listen to the whole thing again. But she listened, hoping to hear something that would spark an idea, a memory. She glanced at Cameron's shoes as Gregory spoke. They had gotten soaked in the rain as he ran for the door. It was a shame. If she wasn't mistaken, the blucher-style crocodile-skin shoes cost eighteen hundred dollars. She wondered if he was still married. Married men in bureaucratic jobs didn't spend that much money on shoes.

Frank caught her looking at the shoes. She smiled at him.

Cameron's clothes were nice too. Expensive. Diane decided he must have gotten a divorce.

David came through the door just as Gregory finished bringing Cameron up to current events. He shook Cameron's hand and pulled up a chair.

"I just heard from Hannah Payne. Remember her, our photographer in South America? I just got an e-mail from her," said David. He sounded excited.

Diane was suddenly alert. News. Something. Maybe a piece of information they didn't have.

"Do you remember how she took photograph after photograph of the massacre that day?"

Gregory, Diane, and Steven nodded. Cameron hadn't been there. It was not his week to visit. He had come later, after the bodies were removed.

"What did she say?" asked Diane.

"Simone had asked her for all the photographs from the massacre she took that day. She said she mailed Simone a CD of them five months ago. She hasn't heard from her since."

"You think that is the package?" said Cameron. "A CD?" He glanced at his watch. "It's quite a storm out there," he said. "I had to land in some place called Vidalia and drive up here. Traffic at the Atlanta airport was shut down. Does Rosewood have an airport?"

Diane looked at him, wondering about the non sequitur. "No," she said.

"Hannah hadn't really looked at the photographs she took," said David, who also looked at Cameron a bit puzzled. "She just put them on a CD and stored them."

"Why weren't they part of the investigative record?" asked Diane.

"That's a good question," said Gregory. "Surely they were part of the record, though I never saw them. The group from the UN did a thorough job. They interviewed all of us for hours," he said.

"David, do you think that's what's in the package?" said Diane.

"I don't know. There's something kind of wrong about it. There are more copies available. Why would this particular copy be so important? It's not a one-of-a-kind set of photographs. That may be part of it, but I'm thinking there is more. Simone got them five months ago. Why didn't she send them then? It wouldn't have taken her this long to go through them."

Diane stood and paced a moment. She turned around. "I wonder why Simone requested the photographs. For whatever reason, perhaps it was something she saw in the photographs that made her want to open Oliver's boxes, and that started this whole round of investigation," said Diane.

"Perhaps there was something she thought she remembered," offered David, "but wasn't sure. With Hannah's photographs, she could check her memory."

"Unfortunately we don't have Hannah's photographs here," said Cameron.

"We will soon," said David. "Hannah is e-mailing—"

A loud crack of thunder reverberated through the building and the lights went out.

"Damn," said Gregory.

"There goes the computing power," said David. "They'll shut down automatically and won't come back up until the main electricity comes back on. They don't take from the generators." He shook his head and stroked the dark fringe of hair that was a horseshoe circle around his balding head. "I was really hoping we all could brainstorm over the photographs. I know that was going to be painful," he said, "but we need to figure out if Simone is right."

Diane felt very relieved that David's computers had shut down. She couldn't face those photographs right now. She wasn't sure she ever could. From the look on the others' faces, they couldn't either.

"The generators will kick in in a moment," said Diane.

Just as she spoke the lights flickered and came up again. "We have a lot of experiments and other things going on in the building that require constant electricity," said Diane. "David keeps his computers out of the loop to save on electricity."

"How long will your generators hold out?" said Cameron.

He appeared to Diane to be uncomfortable, disconcerted.

"Several hours," she said.

"You look like you're not too good with severe weather," Frank said to Cameron.

"No, I'm afraid I'm somewhat of a baby in that regard," he said.

"We appreciate your braving the weather to come here," said Diane.

"Had I known you were in for such inclement weather, I'd have had second thoughts," he said. "But I wanted you to know we have discovered that it was not you who killed the men in South America." He grinned at Diane. "It was some archaeologist named Lindsay Chamberlain. She must have been the one into drugs also."

"I am familiar with her," said Diane. "Her specialty is archaeology of the southeastern United States. This was her first trip to South America. We believe she was kidnapped and escaped. She has a sterling reputation. I don't think there is any real possibility she is a murderer or a drug smuggler."

"Really? Well, my informants must have been wrong," he said. "This is very strange. But the important thing is, you are not on our wanted list." He smiled again.

"I appreciate that," said Diane. "One less thing to worry about." She rubbed her shoulders as if they suddenly felt the extra weight lifted from them.

The door swung open and Korey Jordan entered, heading toward Diane.

"Hey, Dr. F.," he said. "I'm sorry to bother you. I know you have guests."

"This is Korey Jordon. He's our head conservator," said Diane. "He keeps all our collections in good condition."

"Yeah, well, we have some problems there," he said. "The storm, the electricity, the computers." He threw up his hands. "The worst has happened—the dermestids are loose in my lab and in several exhibits, including the primate exhibit. I'm thinking they may like resin. This really shit—" He looked at Diane's guests. "Sorry for the language, but dermestids are a disaster for the museum."

Diane's eyes grew wide. "They're all over the museum?"

"Are they dangerous?" said Cameron.

"Are they mine?" said David.

"Dermestid beetles are what I and the animal curator use to strip the flesh from bones," said Diane. "The colonies are sequestered. David keeps mine in the crime lab; the mammal curator keeps hers in her lab. They aren't dangerous to humans unless you happen to be allergic to them. However, they eat museum exhibits. God, this is a disaster." She closed her eyes and put her fingertips on her eyelids. "Shit is right. We have to contain this." She dropped her hands and stood up.

"Is there anything we can do?" asked Gregory.

"If you see a bug, step on it," said Korey. "You know, I hate those things."

"I'm sorry. I have to attend to this." She turned to Cameron. "You look exhausted. We have some bedrooms here that are very nice if you would like to refresh yourself."

"I may do that. I would kind of like to be alone. I hadn't expected this would be so painful after all this time," he said. "And I am tired."

Diane nodded and put a hand on his shoulder.

"I'll point him in the right direction," said Gregory to Diane. "You and David go attend to your bug problem."

"Want some moral support?" said Frank.

"I may need your superior problem-solving skills," she said.

The three of them left the room with Korey. Diane felt sick. She felt like she was destroying the museum. How had this happened? The beetles weren't secured by electric locks.

"I don't get it," said David. "I'm sure our dermestids are secure."

"We need to go to the conservation lab first," Korey said.

Chapter 65

Diane rushed up the steps to the second floor, toward where the conservation lab was located. Frank and David were close behind.

"Slow down, Dr. F.," said Korey. "The beetles are fine."

She stopped and swung around to him. "What? Korey? What is this?"

"This is practically everyone I know being paranoid."

Korey looked pointedly at David. David shrugged at Diane.

"I was supposed to get you up here, but not to trust anyone I didn't know personally. So I made up a story."

"I don't understand," said Diane.

Korey smiled. She thought she saw tears in his eyes, of all things.

"The environmentals need checking," he said, rubbing his eyes. "We're getting too many particulates in the air. Just come to my lab. It will be clear."

Diane exchanged bewildered glances with Frank and David, then followed Korey to the lab. Korey shut the door behind him and locked it.

The first person Diane saw was Jonas Briggs. He was standing by a tall woman and man. The man was American Indian. The woman, if she wasn't mistaken, was Dr. Lindsay Chamberlain. Diane smiled. Chamberlain was safe. Why the secrecy? Was she afraid the people were still after her?

"Mama. Mama."

Diane stopped still. She couldn't move. A flashback. She was having an auditory hallucination. Diane took a deep breath, trying to calm herself.

"Mama."

Diane saw her. Between Lindsay and the Indian. Apple green overalls, pink and green striped shirt, and bright sparkling red shoes. She ran to Diane and stopped in front of her.

"Mama. I've tried so hard to get back. You still want me, don't you?"

It was when David fell to his knees sobbing that Diane realized she wasn't the only one who saw her.

Diane kneeled to meet the little girl's eyes.

"Ariel?" Diane's voice cracked. She could barely get sounds to come out of her throat.

"Dear God, Ariel?" Diane grabbed her and held her. Felt her beating heart against her own. "My baby," she whispered.

Diane looked into her face, her bronze skin, dark eyes, perfect little nose and lips, her long black hair that someone had braided for her, wrapping the plaits in light green ribbon. Diane caressed the downy hair at her hairline, rubbed the back of her hand on the little cheek, touched her perfect little ears, examined her small little-girl hands. Diane hugged her close and cried, long, shaking sobs.

"How is this possible?" she said finally.

Diane looked over at Frank, who stood quietly with tears streaming down his face. She stood, still holding on to Ariel, holding her close. How small she was. How light.

Diane walked over to Lindsay Chamberlain, carrying Ariel on her hip, holding her around the waist, feeling the little arms snake around her neck. Lindsay's eyes, like everyone else's in the room, brimmed with tears.

"How?" Diane said.

"She saved my life," Lindsay said. "Some very bad and dangerous people thought I was you and kidnapped me. Ariel saved me. She told me who she was and we traveled across the Amazon searching for a way home. She is a remarkable kid. She has been looking for someone who could take her to you ever since she became separated from you. Her story is extraordinary. But there are evil people out there and we feared they had made their way here."

"You need to tell her the whole story, the way you told it to me," said the Indian.

Diane looked at the stern face and Korey introduced John West.

"He's the man who built the cofferdam at that galleon site I worked on," said Korey.

That experience was the main reason Korey got the job at RiverTrail.

"Were you in the Amazon with them?" Diane asked John.

"Briefly, at the end, to extract them from Tabatinga," John said.

They sat down at one of Korey's worktables, Ariel in Diane's lap. She didn't see how she could ever let the little girl go again.

Ariel peeked around Diane. "Hi, Uncle David," she said.

David broke down again. "Hi, Ariel, baby. I can't think of when I've ever had a more wonderful day," he said. "I may become an optimist after this."

Frank sat next to Diane and she introduced Ariel to him.

"We are getting married," said Diane, smiling at Frank.

If there was ever a sign, this had to be it. She decided to tell her up front because she knew others would.

Ariel looked a little uncertain. Frank smiled at her and put out his hand.

"I've heard so much about you, Ariel, that I feel like I know you. You are your mother's heart and I am so happy to meet you."

Ariel grinned and snuggled close to Diane. Diane kissed the top of her head. Her hair smelled like shampoo.

"Someone fixed your hair pretty," said Diane.

"That was John's sister. She opened her store for us and we got some clothes. That was a good thing because ours didn't smell so good."

Diane laughed. "What about those glittering red shoes?"

Ariel pointed at John. "He said to get home I needed ruby slippers."

"Looks like they worked," said Diane.

"We flew into the Cherokee Indian Reservation," said Lindsay. "The weather was bad here and we wanted a private airport. We tried to call but were unable to get through because of the weather. We drove down here and finally were able to get hold of Korey at his home. He and Jonas helped smuggle us into the museum."

Before they started their story, Korey brought cold

drinks from the small refrigerator in his office. He gave Ariel an orange juice. She sipped it and smiled.

"This is better than the orange juice at the airport," she said to Lindsay.

Lindsay and Ariel, as they had with John, took turns telling the account of what had happened to them. It was a long narrative but they were not interrupted.

Diane listened. Horror and guilt filled her alongside the joy. She held Ariel tighter, stroked her hair, listening to each of them. Lindsay was right. Ariel was extraordinary. The thought of her going from family to family trying to find a way to her was breaking her heart. Why hadn't she kept looking? Why had she left Ariel in the jungle?

Lindsay stopped talking, reached across the table, and grabbed Diane's forearm, squeezing so tightly Diane almost cried out. Lindsay frowned. She was looking sternly into Diane's eyes.

"Ariel was taken far away very quickly with the other children. For whatever reason, the engineers of this atrocity wanted you to believe she had died in the massacre. She went to amazing lengths to get back to you. She deserves your unadulterated joy."

Diane cocked an eyebrow at her.

"Your face is easy to read," said Lindsay. "And I am very straightforward. I owe Ariel. Without her intervention they would have killed me when they found out I wasn't you. Whatever I can do in my life to make Ariel's life better, I will. That includes being frank with you."

Ariel looked at Diane. "She got a lot stronger after dealing with the snake in the truck," Ariel said. "By the time we got to the mountain pass, Lindsay set up a good bushwhack."

Diane laughed. So did the others. Lindsay smiled and shook her head.

Ariel and Lindsay finished their stories. Diane wasn't keeping track of time and she didn't know how long it took, but it was a long time. She looked forward to telling Gregory.

"You think you were followed here? Do you know the name of the man who is behind this?" asked Diane.

Lindsay nodded. "He's the man who tried to take Ariel from me in Benjamin Constant and Tabatinga. His name is Cameron Michaels," she said.

Chapter 66

The weather was in full force outside the building. The wind buffeted the huge museum windows, rattling the glass so much that Diane thought they might break.

She sat with Frank, David, and the others in the conservation lab, discussing what they were going to do.

"Those mercenaries of his are outside around the museum," said Diane. "I thought I saw some movement when we let Cameron in the front door. I wasn't sure then, but I am now. So, any ideas?"

Korey and Jonas had none.

"You have children in the basement?" said John.

"We have lots of potential hostages," said Diane.

"Get Cameron," said Frank. "He's the one in charge. He's the one cutting their checks. Cameron is in here with us. It should be easy."

"The mercenaries can easily get in here with us too," said Diane. "They are so rabid, the possibilities frighten me."

She hated speaking like this in Ariel's hearing, but the little girl absolutely refused to be away from Diane. She had tried to get her to take a nap on the couch in Korey's office, but she refused, shaking her head vigorously. Diane understood. She could hardly bear to let her go for a fraction of a second.

"Frank's right," said David. "We have to get Cameron before he makes his move."

"What does he want, exactly?" said Lindsay. "The package that seems to obviously be some kind of evidence against him? To stop me from telling you of his involvement?"

It hit everyone at the same time: Of all of them sitting in the room, Ariel was the only one who could put him at the scene of the massacre.

Diane hugged Ariel tighter.

"You're right. We've got to get to Cameron," said Diane. "First I need to alert security that there is a problem."

"It would be good to get in touch with Liam. He is very handy in these situations," said David. "Is he on the premises with Andie?"

"I don't know," said Diane.

She went to Korey's phone and called Andie's office. Fortunately the in-house lines were working. But no one picked up. They were probably in the basement helping with the kids.

Diane knelt by Ariel. "Baby, I need to get the bad man out of our lives. I want you to stay here with Jonas and Korey. I know you are brave. After what you went through, you are the bravest person in the world. Will you stay here with them and let me take care of this?"

Diane thought of asking Lindsay to stay, but she could tell Lindsay wanted a piece of Cameron and she had proved to be tough in the face of bad guys. Diane guessed her boyfriend, John, was pretty tough too. And frankly, until she could get a handle on things, she needed as many tough people with her as she could find.

Ariel nodded and hugged Diane. "I love you, Mama," she said.

"Oh, Ariel, I love you so much," she said. "This is the happiest day of my life. You remember Gregory?"

Ariel nodded.

"When he came to visit this time, he brought your adoption papers. They came through just before the bad things happened. He was going to surprise us with them. I have them now. It's official. Not only are you my little girl in my heart, you are my little girl to the whole world."

Ariel hugged her neck.

A knock on the door brought all their heads up. Korey went to the door.

"Yes?" he said.

"Hey, Korey, is that it? It's Steven. Is Diane there?"

Korey looked at Diane and she nodded. He opened the door and Steven hobbled in.

"What happened?" said Diane.

"Oh, I tripped and fell. One of those teeth-rattling thunder episodes . . ." His eyes grew wide.

"She looks like Ariel," he said, staring from Ariel to Diane.

"It is Ariel," said Diane. "She's alive and home with me."

Steven put a hand over his mouth. "Oh my God. Ariel. My God. How in the world?" he mumbled.

"Very long story," said Diane. "It was Cameron. He's the person Simone was trying to tell us instigated the massacre."

"Cam? No," said Steven, rubbing his ankle. "Are you sure?"

"Yes, and he has men stationed outside the museum," said Diane. "I'm going to confront him."

"I should have guessed something when I saw those shoes of his. I'll go with you." He stood and winced.

"You stay here with Korey, Jonas, and Ariel," she said. "I'll be back when the museum is secured."

"But," he said.

"Protect Ariel and the others," said Diane. "I'm counting on you."

"Good luck," he said.

Diane, David, Frank, Lindsay, and John left the conservation lab and took the stairs down to the first floor. The security guard was not on duty.

"Damn," said Diane.

She looked on the floor of the kiosk where the guard had been sitting. Gone. Diane checked the front doors. Locked. Maybe she went to the bathroom, she thought.

Diane went though the double doors to the east wing where the security office was, expecting the worst. What she found was the security guard. Chanell, Diane's head of security, came out of her office.

"The wind was whipping the glass so, I was worried it was going to come crashing in," Chanell said. "We're watching the monitors. Liam has been helping us with surveillance."

Diane nodded. "It just worried me when I didn't see the guard. I think those soldiers are out in the woods around the museum, so get ready. Do you know where Liam is?"

Chanell shook her head. "He's supposed to call in in fifteen minutes," she said.

"Can we call for help?" said Diane. "Are the phones working?"

"Still dead," said Chanell. "We're on our own."

"Okay, Chanell, we have a lot of people in the museum that need protecting."

"Don't I know it," she said. "We are on top of it, Dr. Fallon."

Diane nodded. "We're going to the basement to confront Cameron," said Diane.

"You're sure you can trust that Steven guy?" said Lindsay. Diane nodded.

"He's been a friend for a long time," said David. "He worked with us bringing mass killers to justice, or at least trying to. Steven Gavin Mays the third is a good guy, if a little stuffy."

They went out into the lobby, heading for the stairs. Lindsay stopped suddenly.

"Shit," Lindsay said. "I thought something was happening on May third. *Tres de mayo* was what Julio said, I thought. People who are somebody the third are often nicknamed Trey. He wasn't saying the third of May, he was saying Trey Mays. Damn it. Steven Mays is the guy who had me kidnapped."

Diane's heart dropped to the floor. She turned and ran to the stairs and up to the second floor to the conservation lab.

Too late. Jonas was on the floor, blood running down his face. He groaned and tried to rise.

"He has her, hit me, shot Korey," Jonas said.

Frank found Korey on the floor, blood pooling under him. "It's not that bad," Korey said. "The son of a bitch took Ariel. Jonas and I are fine. Go find her."

Diane shot out the door and back down to security.

"Steven Mays is out there with my daughter," she said.

That brought her a bewildered look from Chanell.

"This guy kidnapped a little girl and has her somewhere near here," said Frank. "Jonas and Korey are in the conservation lab hurt and need help. Do you have a gun?"

Frank had his gun. Diane armed herself with one from the security office. To her surprise, both Lindsay and John were armed.

How could I have been so stupid? Diane thought, as she headed out the door. She stopped. He could have already taken her in a car to who knew where.

"Have you seen any cars leave?" Diane asked Chanell.

"No, we've been watching pretty close," she said.

Diane thought a minute. "The back road behind the museum," she said. "They have a car there." She raced for the back door. Damn it, she was going to get Ariel back. Her little girl didn't come all this way to be lost to her.

Chapter 67

Diane asked Lindsay and John to find Cameron and get out of him by any means necessary where Steven might have taken Ariel. She, Frank, and David were on their way to search the grounds. Chanell caught up with them before they got out of the building.

"A couple of the back cameras have been disabled, just a few minutes ago," said Chanell. "That'll be where they went out. Do you want security to go with you?"

"I need you to protect the people in the museum," said Diane.

Chanell nodded. "We'll do that," she said.

"We need to split up," said Diane, to Frank and David. "The backyard of the museum is too big."

"No," said Frank.

"I know it's not safe," said Diane, "but we need to cover as much ground as possible. Please."

Frank studied her face a fraction of a second and nodded. "Be careful," he said.

All three were familiar with the grounds. They all jogged the nature trail on a regular schedule. Diane could search it with her eyes closed. Good thing because, with the storm cloud cover, it was pitch-black dark. They had elected not to take flashlights because that would make them targets.

Diane hurried, scanning every time lightning lit up the sky. She was sick with fear. This couldn't happen again. She couldn't survive it again. What kind of mother was she to let this happen to Ariel another time? Diane ignored the pelting rain as she searched. The wind almost knocked her down.

Lightning flashed and she saw the sparkle of a red shoe. Ariel. Diane ran to it.

It was the aftermath of the massacre all over again—
finding Ariel's bloody shoes. Diane felt sick. "Damn it," she
said through her teeth. Only this time it wasn't bloody.

She hurried on. She had never before seen a rainstorm
like this one. The rain was coming down in sheets and the
wind was blowing it straight sideways with such ferocity
that the drops were stabbing her skin like hundreds of tiny
knives. The limb of a tree broke with a loud pop overhead
and came crashing down beside her. She pushed on against
it. Her eyes grew accustomed to the dark; she became used
to the shadowy landscape. She watched for movement that
wasn't wind and rain.

She thought she heard something.

"Ariel."

A male voice calling Ariel. Had she gotten away? Diane's
heart leaped with hope. She listened through the howling
wind. She breathed in the rain. It felt as though she were
going to drown in it. She could hardly see. She coughed.
The lightning flashed again and there was a figure—a black
silhouette strobed by lightning flashes. She ran toward it. It
wasn't Frank or David, she knew their silhouettes. She saw
the sports coat flap in the wind at the next strobe of light.
Steven.

Then she heard him.

"Ariel, damn it, you little brat. Where are you? God, you
are a lot of trouble."

Diane took aim and fired.

If her aim was good, she blew out his right knee.

She saw him go down. She ran to him and watched him
writhing on the ground.

"Where is she?" yelled Diane. Blood was washing from
his hand. She thought she saw a little half-moon of teeth
marks. Good for Ariel.

Steven rolled over and tried to raise his gun. Diane fired
into his shoulder. He grunted and passed out.

"Damn it," she said out loud.

She picked up his gun and put it in her waistband. She
looked for a hiding place.

"Ariel," she shouted.

Why would the little girl ever trust her again? Twice she
had let her down. Diane wanted to cry. Instead, she waited
for the next lightning and searched.

Nothing. She moved forward down the hiking trail, more slowly this time, looking for hiding places.

"Ariel, honey," she said, but it came out as a croak.

The next flash of lightning, she saw another shoe. She ran to it.

"Ariel," she shouted as loud as she could.

"Mama?"

The voice was so soft Diane wasn't sure she heard it.

"Ariel," she shouted again, "it's Mama. Where are you, baby?"

"Mama."

It was louder this time. Coming from a thicket beside the ditch up ahead. Diane raced to it. Lightning flashed and Ariel came running to her. Diane held her.

"Baby, I'm so sorry."

"I bit him, Mama. He won't try to hurt me again."

"No, baby, he won't."

"Well, ain't this cute?"

Diane pushed Ariel behind her and turned to the voice.

Another supersoldier. He had caught them out in the open.

"You're the bitch that chewed up James." His laugh sounded like some weird sound effect coming through the deluge of wind and rain. "He's really pissed. He'll like it that I found you. You still got no notion where that package is? I'll bet if we put a gun to that runt's head, you'll come up with it right quick. Now drop your gun. You don't have a chance to raise it before I pop you one."

Diane stood looking at him, thinking.

"Drop it, bitch, or I'll drop you."

Diane dropped the gun. It splashed and disappeared in the puddle of water beside her.

"Now, come over here," he said.

Frank was right. They shouldn't have split up. But if they hadn't, they may never have found Ariel.

"Come. Over. Here. Now," he barked, trying to yell above the howl of the storm.

The lightning flashed a dozen, two dozen times, until it was a giant, continuous, arcing electrical spark lighting the sky, and Diane heard the sound of a freight train, saw the giant shadow, saw the supersoldier turn.

"What the hell?" he said.

Diane reached behind her and pulled Steven's gun from her waistband. Before the man could turn back toward them, she aimed the weapon with firm hands and fired at his head and neck until there were no more bullets. She knew from the jerks of his body he was hit multiple times.

Diane saw him snatched up by the storm just as she jumped for the ditch beside the trail, holding Ariel to her.

They didn't move, hardly breathed, until the roaring noise subsided.

"What was that?" whispered Ariel.

"That was our friend the tornado," said Diane. She squeezed Ariel to her. "Love your heart, baby girl," she said.

"Where did the tornado take him?" asked Ariel.

"I hope a long way from here. Kansas maybe," said Diane.

Diane was afraid to leave the bushes and the ditch, afraid of finding another soldier and not having any more bullets, or encountering another tornado. She settled into as comfortable a spot as she could find and pulled Ariel on top of her, trying to cushion her from the hard wet ground.

"Are you all right, baby?" Diane asked her.

"I'm fine. Lindsay and I had to do stuff like this all the time," said Ariel.

"You like her, don't you?" said Diane, smiling into the darkness. Sticks poked at her back and she was wet and tired, but she was never more comfortable.

She felt Ariel nodding. "I was afraid she might leave me if everything got too hard, but she didn't."

"Ariel, baby, I'm so sorry . . ."

Ariel put a hand on Diane's mouth. "You didn't leave me," she said. "The bad man took me away. I love you, Mama."

"And I love you, baby," Diane said.

The rain began to let up and the wind died down to a hard breeze, but it was still dark.

"Ariel. Diane."

Another voice in the darkness. This one belonged to Frank.

"Here," she said.

She got up and ran to Frank, carrying Ariel. He embraced them both. He had the ruby slippers in his hand.

"We need to get back to the museum," said Frank. "I found Liam in the woods—or rather, he found me. He's been tracking the mercenaries. He has them all taken out but one."

"Our friend the tornado took him to Kansas," said Ariel.

Frank stared at her a moment. Then he looked at Diane.

"That's what happened," she said.

"You're kidding me, aren't you?" he said.

"Nope. It was a sight to see," said Diane.

"I see you found Steven," said Frank.

"Ariel bit him and got away. I shot him," said Diane. She was starting to feel giddy if not homicidal.

Frank put an arm around her and they started back. They found David bending over the form of Steven, who was groaning.

"What I don't understand," said David, "is, with all that time spent in the jungle, why you didn't learn."

"Learn what?" rasped Steven.

"Who's the most feared in the jungle?" said David.

They left Steven to be picked up by the paramedics whenever they got out there, and they walked back to the museum. Diane took them through a side door that led into the Pleistocene Room. They hurried to the security office. Chanell was gone. The guards told them that Chanell went to give first aid to Cameron Michaels.

"They said that woman went to town on him," one of the guards added.

Good, thought Diane.

They found Michaels lying on the couch in the meeting room. Lindsay had a baseball bat in her hand.

"Confiscated from the basement encampment," said Gregory. He stared at Ariel.

"My God in heaven, it's true. I was afraid to believe it." Gregory knelt in front of her. "Do you remember me?" he asked.

Ariel nodded.

"As soon as you get phone service, I must call Marguerite," he said. "She will be overjoyed. Ariel." Gregory hugged her. "This is the best," he said.

"How is Cameron?" said Diane.

"He'll live, unfortunately," said Gregory. "He has a lot of

broken bones. But he's not saying much, just that we can't prove anything. I don't know what he thinks we can't prove after this night."

"Something terrible," said Diane.

She thought of Simone running from the supersoldier, trying to hide her proof, shoving the bag of feathers, animal parts, and the bone under the display case. Diane ran it through her head as if she were Simone, and she knew where the package was.

Chapter 68

Across from the Mayan display was the back entrance to Mike's office with the sign on the door saying when he would return. Simone saw a safe place for her package—under the door to an office that wouldn't be used for three weeks.

Diane opened the door and there it was on the floor. A bulky envelope that just fit in the space under the door, addressed to Diane Fallon from Simone Brooks.

Diane took the envelope downstairs and opened it at a table with Gregory, David, and Frank. Ariel had stayed with Lindsay and John while Diane searched for the package. She sat in Lindsay's lap watching her mother open the package.

Simone had laid it all out in typewritten notes. Photographic and testimonial evidence filled in by some guesses on her and Oliver's part. Diane laid the photographs on the table. She felt sick.

David and Diane both were right. Simone had remembered seeing Cameron's briefcase at the massacre site. It hadn't registered with her for a long time. And one day, out of the blue, she remembered it. She asked Hannah to send the photographs she took so she could check and make sure her memory was accurate. It was.

Diane thought of all of them. Family for a time. They had known one another so well back then; at least Diane had thought so. They had known Simone to the point that she and David could put themselves in her shoes. They hadn't known Cameron and Steven at all. How could they have missed seeing what they were? Steven had been good at his job. He had seemed compassionate. What happened?

Diane looked at Hannah's photograph of the briefcase with Cameron's initials sitting by Father Joseph's desk. When Simone saw the picture she knew that her memory was correct. She saw the briefcase, saw that Cameron was actually there the day of the massacre instead of afterward. That inspired Simone to open the boxes that Oliver had sent to his and Simone's apartment in the United States for safekeeping. It had been shocking to Simone, as it was to Diane and the others who stared at the photograph now.

According to what Ariel witnessed, thought Diane, Oliver must have confronted a shocked Father Joe with it and it broke his heart to discover he was sending children into slavery.

The crimes had started with selling endangered parrots to collectors. It went from there to selling people—the people who came through the mission displaced by war and disaster, people who came for help.

Then Ariel came into Diane's life. Because of Ariel, Diane was spending more time at the mission, so they had to be more careful in order not to be discovered. They hated Diane for that. That was a guess on Simone's and Oliver's part, but Diane thought they were probably right.

One day several months before the massacre, Cameron was about to be discovered with a truckload of women and children whom he could not deliver because the buyer had just been arrested. There was nothing to do with the human cargo on the spur of the moment, so Cameron shot them. Oliver acquired a photograph taken by a partner in crime that showed Cameron, gun in hand, shooting a child in the head. He also acquired the man's testimony.

Diane sat down and put her head in her hands. Ariel started to come over to her, but Lindsay whispered in her ear and Ariel waited.

"You are disgusting," said Gregory to Cameron. "In the name of heaven, how can you live with yourself?"

Cameron lay on the couch in pain from the broken bones Lindsay had given him, one forearm over his forehead as if shading his eyes.

"You pompous bastard," said Cameron. "It's all about the money. A fucking lot of it. Life is cheap. You and Diane proved that every time you opened a mass grave. People come and go. That's the way it is."

Gregory shook his head, like Diane, unable to fathom Cameron's and Steven's thought processes.

The paramedics arrived and took the two of them away. Diane was glad to be rid of them. She put her face in her hands. She felt so tired. Ariel jumped out of Lindsay's lap and ran over to Diane and hugged her.

"He was a bad man," said Ariel.

"Yes, he was," said Diane.

Lindsay stood up. "I think we will be going," she said. "I'd like to go to sleep for about a week or two. And I'd like to stop and see Korey and Jonas in the hospital before we leave town."

Diane walked over to her. "Thank you. I wish I had the words to express how grateful I am for what you did for Ariel—and for me."

"Ariel saved my life," said Lindsay. "I am grateful for that. I'm grateful to know her. She is just the neatest kid."

Lindsay squatted to Ariel's level and hugged her. "You are a great kid," she said, tears threatening to spill over the rims of her eyes.

Diane noticed that Ariel was about to cry too. She stooped down with them.

"What are all these tears?" she said. "Lindsay lives just down the road, only two hours away," said Diane. "We can visit next week if you like."

"Really?" said Ariel.

"Really. If it's okay with Lindsay," said Diane.

"You are welcome anytime," she said. She hugged Ariel again.

John West spoke to her in Cherokee. Ariel repeated it and gave him a hug.

"We need a ride to our car," said Lindsay. "Korey brought us to the museum in one of your vehicles. We're parked at the motel down the road."

"I can take them," said David. "I need to get out for a while."

Diane was about to go to her tiny bedroom and lie down for a nap. She was sure Ariel must be exhausted too. Just as she rose from the sofa where she was sitting with Frank and Ariel, Neva walked in carrying a notebook. She looked grim. *Not any more grim*, thought Diane. *Not today. I've had enough.*

Neva smiled. "Congratulations. Little Ariel. I can't believe it. What you must be feeling," she said.

"Can hardly put it into words," said Diane.

Neva sighed and frowned again. "You were right," she said. "Lots of drawings. Vanessa and your friend Laura brought all Madge's artwork to Vanessa's house for safekeeping. Vanessa is the executor of Madge's will. I didn't have to drive to Atlanta to find it. I just had to go to Vanessa's. Anyway, Madge wrote a romance comic book about the two of them. You know, the kind they used to do in the fifties. It's pretty good, or would be if it weren't so poignant."

"Anyone we know?" said Diane.

"Surprise, surprise," said Neva. "He'll be here any minute. I've asked him to come by. He doesn't know he's meeting Chief Garnett. The storm did some damage to the police station, blew half the roof off. So Garnett has, in effect, deputized the museum."

Diane took the notebook, which was actually an artist's drawing book, and opened it, looking at the pictures of a love story with Madge as the focus. It made sense now.

Diane walked up to her office where Neva had arranged for him to come. She met Garnett on the way. Vanessa was with him.

"Diane, is it true? Is Ariel alive? Is she here? Harte and I have been beside ourselves since we heard the news."

Garnett looked at Diane, surprised. "Your Ariel? Your daughter, Ariel?" he said.

Diane grinned. "Yes, my daughter, Ariel. That's part of what all this was about, the rumors, everything. I'll tell you all about it later. It's a remarkable story."

"Can we meet her?" said Vanessa.

"Yes. She's with Frank. They're playing with the kids in the basement. Apparently Andie and Star did such a good job of entertaining them all, they don't want to go home."

"Why don't you go meet her now, Mrs. Van Ross?" said Garnett.

"Oh?" she said.

"Please, let me, Neva, and Diane do this. You know, police business," he said.

"You're right, of course. I'd rather meet little Ariel anyway." Vanessa smiled and went off to find Frank.

Diane, Neva, and Garnett proceeded through Diane's office into her private lounge area.

Martin Thormond stood up and greeted them, wearing his usual tweed sports coat with the patches on the elbows, looking like the history professor he was.

"It was certainly a stormy night last night," he said, stroking his short beard.

"It was indeed," said Diane.

"Martin, there is no way to ease into this," said Diane. "We know you were helping the men who were harassing me. What I don't know is why."

Martin sat slowly down on the sofa. The others pulled up chairs and sat across from him.

"They came to me and told me that I would help them or they would kill me—after they cut my hands and feet off. I believed them. You don't know what they were like."

"Oh, I think I do," said Diane. "I got to know them up close and personal."

"Then you know what vicious thugs they were. They were looking for some kind of package sent to you at the museum and wanted me to find it. They also wanted me to spread these rumors about you and say they were from a reporter. It was go along or die. Like I said. I believed them. I'm sorry. It wasn't something I wanted to do. Or even enjoyed doing."

"What about the money?" said Garnett.

Diane knew he was guessing. To Martin he must have sounded totally convincing. His shoulders slumped even farther.

"I know this sounds crazy, but they made me take the money. They grinned, saying they paid well. And, yes, it was a lot of money and I like money, but they forced me to do what they asked and then forced me to take money for it."

"Did they force you to kill Madge Stewart?" said Diane.

Martin blanched. Diane thought he was going to disappear into the couch, he was sinking so low.

"I didn't kill her. It was an accident," he said. "She slipped and fell into the water trying to act like a young girl. I didn't do anything to her," he said.

"You didn't help her," said Diane.

Martin sneered and for the first time looked like he might rise from sinking into the sofa. "She hated you, you know," he said. "She loved the idea of smearing you."

"Liking me isn't a prerequisite for a person's right to live," said Diane. "I'm hardly that arrogant. How did Madge get involved?"

"That was so stupid. She overheard me talking with one of the men and was just all giddy with the notion of helping me, like we were spies or something. It was embarrassing. It got to where I hated coming to board meetings. I couldn't seem to get rid of her."

"But you did," said Neva.

"I didn't kill her," he said.

"Why didn't you get help?" said Garnett.

"I didn't kill her," Martin repeated.

"You just watched her drown," said Garnett.

Martin stood up. "If I'm not under arrest, and I assume I'm not, since I'm in the museum, I'm leaving," he said. He got up and walked out, his back ramrod straight and chin high. No one tried to stop him.

"Is he going to get away with it?" said Neva.

"Unless you can prove she was murdered," said Garnett.

"Well, damn it," said Neva. "How about the guys who attacked Diane? Are they going to get away with everything they did?"

"No, they aren't," said Garnett. "We've got Diane's testimony, we've got Liam's testimony, we've got Frank's, Star's and that English guy's testimony. We've got a lot of fiber evidence from the crime scenes that, according to David, is pretty diagnostic. And we've got the guys that hired them that we can flip. So, no they aren't getting away with it."

"Do we still have them in custody?" said Diane.

"The GBI picked them up, most of them. One is missing, I understand."

Diane left her office and found Frank and Ariel in the ballroom. She watched Ariel playing with the other kids, watched her laugh, watched her turn her head and look at Diane, grin and wave. Diane waved back. Frank came over and put an arm around her waist.

"It turned out to be a good day after all," he said.

"The best," said Diane. *The best.*